Praise for *The Artist and the Innkeeper*

Italian painter Bernardino Luini created gorgeous and serene religious works in the early 1500's, but he is unjustly overlooked today. For anyone who finds the art of the Italian Renaissance magical and appealing, yet wonders about what might have gone through the minds of its makers, *The Artist and the Innkeeper* offers an imaginative window to that world. This is appealing historical fiction, the story of a painter trying to balance his faith and human emotions.

Frederick Ilchman, Chair, Art of Europe,
and Mrs. Russell W. Baker Curator of Paintings, Museum of
Fine Arts, Boston

I am delighted to encounter a work such as *The Artist and the Innkeeper* where Bernardino Luini's magical ability to conjure the Christian narratives of his time is brought to the fore. Ioffredo's novel charmingly captures the spiritual and evocative nature of early Italian Renaissance paintings and builds our appreciation for the lives, communities, and landscapes that inspired such gorgeous art.

Deborah Hartry Stein, PhD, Independent Art Historian

Imaginative, romantic and suspenseful, *The Artist and the Innkeeper* is a compelling tale replete with the sights, smells and sounds of Renaissance Italy. Bernardino and his muses prove worthy characters in this captivating tale of art, poetry, conflict and love.

Emily Nagle Green, Author and Executive Adviser

THE ARTIST
AND THE
INNKEEPER

ALAN IOFFREDO

Publisher: BookBaby

7905 N. Crescent Blvd

Pennsauken, NJ 08110

Copies are available on the author's website:

alanioffredo.com

Printed in the United States of America

First Printing, 2020

Print ISBN: 978-1-54399-609-8

eBook ISBN: 978-1-54399-610-4

Cover Design   Anya Ioffredo

Cover Photograph   Katie Jameson

Map Illustration   Nora L'Heureux

Editing Services   knliterary arts

For my two Catherine's

Art is the work of the whole spirit of man...
That which is born of evil begets evil; and that which is born of valour
and honour teaches valour and honour.
All art is either infection or education.
It must be one or other of these.

Ruskin, *The Queen of the Air*, 1898

Lago di Maggiore

Lago di Lugano

Lago di Como

Luino

Como

Seromo

Monza

Milan

Lombardia
Duchy of Milan

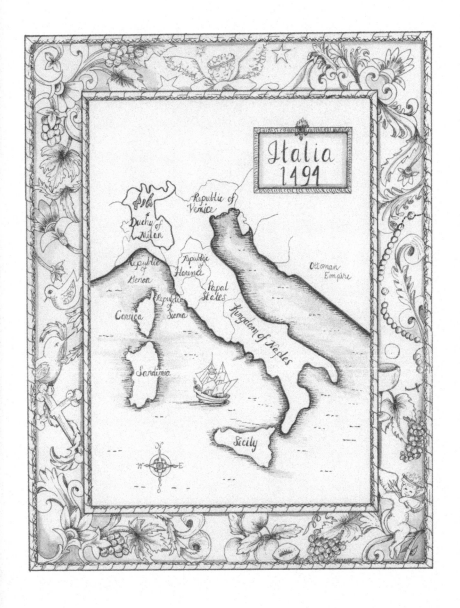

PREFACE

Renaissance painter Bernardino Luini came to my attention as part of the successful marketing campaign for the liqueur Amaretto di Saronno. Branded the *potion of love,* the centuries old beverage was introduced to the Americas by my immigrant father, Carlo Ioffredo, more than fifty years ago.

Engaged by the church, Bernardino Luini travelled to what was then Serono in 1525. Local legend speaks of the artist lodging along Via Varesina with a beautiful innkeeper. Bernardino invited the nameless woman to sit as the Blessed Mother for Serono's cathedral frescos intended to honor Mary. So grateful was the innkeeper for this role that she prepared as a gift the amber-colored, spirited and sweet liqueur today branded simply as DiSaronno.

The commercial success of Amaretto di Saronno altered the trajectory of my family's life. Fascinated that events five centuries before could do so, I sought to learn more about the artisan who inspired the beverage's formulation. I turned to one of Bernardino's contemporaries for insight— the renowned biographer, architect and artist, Giorgio Vasari. What I discovered surprised me. Vasari's nearly total omission of Bernardino, one of the period's most prolific fresco painters, was for art historians a mystery. It remains so today.

Of all the deficiencies we have reported in Vasari's book, "Lives of the Most Eminent Painters, Sculptors, and Architects", this is the most unforgiveable and incomprehensible.

Reau speaking of Vasari's omission of Bernardino Luini in his
Iconographie de l'Art Chretien

It is this significant silence on the part of the old gossip [Vasari] that renders the task of delineating the life of [Bernardino Luini] one almost of impossibility...There must be some reason for this curious circumstance, and many writers of modern time have endeavored to fathom the mystery without success.

George Charles Williamson, *Bernardino Luini*

I poured through available research. I visited museums and observed Bernardino's paintings. I enjoyed hours in the Swiss and Italian churches fortunate to host the artist's well-preserved frescos. I was moved by Bernardino's depictions of saints and sinners – much of it created within dark and imperfect environments.

The mystery remained but there were clues. Jealousy and disdain may have caused Vasari to brand Bernardino as *del Lupino* or *little wolf* while ignoring his peer's outsized contributions to Renaissance art. Such contempt may have extended to others afraid for their reputations and made them reluctant to credit the artist's brilliant frescos and poetry. None of his poetry survives.

I wondered at the artist's secrets and ultimate disappearance and listened for the voice of the innkeeper five centuries ago who inspired him as no other might have. This is their story.

THE ARTIST
AND THE
INNKEEPER

ALAN IOFFREDO

PART I

Bino

Luino, Italy ~ 1496

It was a late fall evening and there was just enough chill in the air to make him want to finish his chores and get inside. He'd been gathering kindling for his mother and their neighbors—work which neither posed a challenge nor offered much fun. His older brother was assigned those tasks.

Bino didn't complain and delighted in making the most of a boring job. He took to arranging the dry wood in ways that would make his mother and their neighbors smile. Advent was nearing so on this day he fashioned small mangers complete with human and barn animal stick figures and ripe figs where the Christ child would lay. Sometimes he would hide and spy on the cottage owners to witness their reaction. His reward came if they noticed, smiled and called others' attention to his creations.

The sun was setting over the great lake and Bino stilled for a moment and looked west. He wasn't disappointed. There, in impossible splendor, was a half sun on the horizon. The water reflected the sky and both were bathed in pink, white and blue light. The long, lean clouds had rough edges and seemed to shuffle the blue and pink bands as if they were game cards.

A breeze stirred and Bino pinched his coat about his neck. He sat on his wood pile and watched the light play. The wind over the lake moved the sky into new and changing shades. The clouds resisted but within seconds there were red, violet and green and they each fought for the sun's notice only to be disappointed as it drifted further away. Since able to remember,

Bino couldn't recall witnessing anything so beautiful in Luino—his village on the shore of the great lake. Surely this was what Mamma meant when she spoke of God—the God of all things. And a prideful thought occurred to him; could he ever hold and inspire an audience the way this sunset did?

When the colors and light were no more, Bino rose and walked the short distance to his family's cottage and entered. On a fire sat a pot that filled the room with steam and appetite.

"You're late, Bernardino!"

He knew she only used his proper name when upset and he responded, "I'm sorry, Mamma."

After an uncomfortable pause, Bino added, "I wish you could have seen what I saw."

Antonina looked at her son with sympathy and concern. Bino was *her* boy—one who had little in common with his father and brother. They did nothing that wasn't purposeful or on time and teased Bino for his lack of discipline and perspiration. They also couldn't fathom his kindness. Bino sought no compensation for his labors. Gratitude and a meal were worth more, he argued, than the meager coins their neighbors would have to scrape together to make his father happy. He knew better than to argue with their ribbing. Bino was at home with his imagination and didn't want or need the approval of others.

"There is fresh water in the basin so bathe your hands and neck and join me. Papa and Ambroglio grew tired of waiting for you and left for the village."

He responded by scrubbing his hands and face before repeating, "I'm sorry, Mamma. I collected the wood before seeing you were right."

She turned towards him and asked, "What are you talking about?"

Antonina pulled a footstool over to where her son was drying himself, sat and looked up into his eyes. He was almost as tall as her now and she missed his chubby face and running her fingers through generous brown curls of hair. Where once stood a child now stood a lean young man with expanding shoulders and dark eyes. He resembled her long-gone father but what distinguished Bino from others were his large smooth hands and strong forearms.

Bino took his mother's calloused hands in his before beginning, "I sat and watched the sun set over the lake and the sky became rich with many colors."

She embraced his enthusiasm and asked, "What does this have to do with me?"

"The colors depended upon the sun, the light was rich because of the lake, and the movement of the clouds was hastened by the wind before the moon rushed the wind away. Someone had to orchestrate all that. It must be the God you speak of."

Antonina smiled, stood and with her thumb made a cross upon her son's forehead. Whatever reason she had for being angry with him was forgotten. She hugged him knowing he wouldn't object to the gesture and motioned him to the table. He sat and she served him broth with fish and vegetables.

She sat with him after serving herself a smaller portion. Bino waited before joining her in a blessing.

"We thank you, Lord, for all that sustains us from within and without, Amen."

They ate their meal in silence.

Afterward, he helped her ready the kitchen for the next day. He swept the floor as his mother hummed melodies learned in church. Wishing to avoid his father's questions, Bino retired to the bed he shared with his brother Ambroglio. He carried a candle to their corner of the room, sat upon his straw mattress and was near to blowing it out when his mother approached.

"Bino, next week the Church remembers Saint Catherine. Will you come with me?"

He smiled and asked, "Will it mean a day without chores?"

With a grin that betrayed no surprise, Antonina replied, "Yes, I suppose it will."

"Then I'll go, Mamma. Won't Papa be angry with me though?"

"Not as much as he will be with me; better to leave Papa to me."

"Mamma?"

"Yes, Bino."

"Why do they make such a fuss about Saint Catherine?"

"I suppose it's because she proved herself worthy."

"Can you tell me about her?"

Antonina wasn't sure whether Bino had forgotten her past descriptions of Saint Catherine or simply wanted the company of her voice. She was sympathetic enough to set aside her intended sewing, sit upon the foot of Bino's bed and relay the tale the parish priest had long ago shared with her.

She cleared her throat and began, "Catherine was the bright and beautiful daughter born to the king and queen of Alexandria. Her mother and father were pagans who did not believe in our God. When she was little older than you, Bino, Christ's mother Mary appeared to Catherine in a vision."

Bino's curiosity stirred him and his eyes opened wider.

"What did Mary tell her?"

"It's not so much what Mary said to Catherine, Bino, as what she did. Mary offered the Christ child to Catherine in a kind of spiritual marriage."

"I don't understand."

"Mary wanted Catherine to know that devotion to her Son would be enough to sustain her throughout her life—that she wouldn't need another unless he was the most worthy of men."

"What did Catherine do?"

"She became a Christian and vowed never to marry anyone unequal to her in faith and fidelity to God."

"Did such a man exist?"

"Yes."

"Who?"

"The one promised her by Mary—Jesus. She accepted no other."

"Were her parents angry with her?"

"Yes, though not nearly as much as those who called upon Catherine as suitors."

"Was she okay, Mamma?"

"You wouldn't say so but we can be sure that Catherine enjoys the company of our Father in heaven."

"Why wouldn't I say so?"

"Catherine's sacrifice moved many to convert to Christianity. The king's subjects witnessed her willingness to forego wealth and a favorable marriage; she could have married a prince. Instead she satisfied herself with prayer and generosity to the poor."

"Why was that bad?"

"Her unusual behavior drew attention to her father. If a king couldn't govern his own daughter, how, they asked, could he lead and protect his people? Those who thought themselves superior challenged Catherine and the king."

"What happened?"

"It's late, Bino; I'll finish the story another time."

"No, Mamma, it's okay; I want to know."

With some reservation, Antonina began again, "The throne was stolen by the king's rivals but they were unable to capture the hearts and minds of the people the way Catherine did. Wishing to put an end to her influence, they murdered many of the converted and sentenced Catherine to death."

Bino was silent and his eyes shifted from his mother to the flickering candle.

"Why was the new king so angry, Mamma?"

"Catherine was willing to speak the words of Jesus; the Word is truth and truth is power. The new king was threatened by the power Catherine had over his people."

"Why didn't God do something?"

"Who said He didn't?"

"How, what do you mean?"

"The rival king intended to make an example of Catherine and execute her publicly on a spiked wheel. When his soldiers tried to do so, angels of the Lord broke the wheel in two, sparing Catherine's life."

"Was she set free?"

"No, Bino; she was martyred by the sword but it was too late. She had already won the admiration and loyalty of the people."

"Was it worth it, Mamma? Was Catherine wise to deny the king?"

"I'll leave that for you to answer. But consider this, amidst all the difficulty we live with today, amidst our vengeful wars and unjust plagues, about whom do we still speak and pray?"

"Saint Catherine?"

"Our Lord and Saint Catherine."

Bino smiled, "Good night, Mamma."

Antonina made a sign of the cross and whispered softly, "May Saint Catherine's spirit look upon and protect you always, amen."

When his mother left, Bino blew out the candle and closed his eyes. Within a moment an unusual chill stirred him and she was present. Vivid and clear, Saint Catherine appeared to him.

With a mix of excitement and fear, Bino wanted his mother to see what he saw. He sat up and screamed, "Mamma!" but his throat produced only a whisper.

Am I dreaming? There, atop the great lake, amid the billowy clouds reflecting brilliant pink and blue, stood Saint Catherine. She smiled at him in a manner that eased his anxiety. Her spell was cast.

Bino grew quiet inside and his breath slowed. His limbs and loins settled into the mattress and he felt a *pace del corpo*—a body peace, and it made the vision of Catherine more real. He memorized her features, the color and texture of her robe and veil and the delicate nature of her hands. He thought her beautiful.

Catherine unfolded her arms as if to welcome him but he could step no closer. As quickly as she appeared, she faded from view leaving only an empty sky. He waited a moment hoping for her return and his disappointment grew. Bino slept; in the morning he recalled nothing of the vision.

Before retiring, Antonina looked in upon her son's bed. She knew Bino was prone to talking in his sleep and so smiled a mother's smile when she heard him say, "I'll draw you tomorrow."

Padre Castani

Luino Parish Church, 18 months later

Padre Castani stopped into the chapel for his afternoon prayer and was greeted by a familiar sight. There on the fourth rung of his hand-carved ladder was Antonina's son, Bernardino. "How are you today, *Leonardo?*" the priest teased while smiling upward at the boy of fourteen.

Bino was dressed in a loose-fitting shirt and pants which fell below a stained apron. He looked over his shoulder and saw the priest smiling. Padre Castani had little hair, was thick in the middle and clad only in a simple brown robe tied at the waist with cord.

"I am well, Padre. I only hope our Mother looks as well."

The priest studied the fresco which had fallen into disrepair—one of few decorating his chapel walls. This one was most in need of restoration and he was pleased and not a little surprised at the marked improvement. Where before the Holy Family had been indistinguishable, Bino had returned its members to form.

"Our Blessed Mother hasn't looked this well since Bethlehem, Bino!"

"I thought priests were obliged to tell the truth, Padre."

"My conscience is clear, son. Did you stop for lunch?"

"No, Padre. I'm not hungry."

"You must eat boy, Saint Joseph wouldn't want you to starve."

"I promise to once the plaster dries."

Jesu Cristo, whispered the priest. Only months before the boy's father had begged him to take his son on. "Why?" he had asked. Bino looked strong and healthy enough for any ambitious man to put to good use.

Bino's father responded, "He's no use to me in the orchards. I need help harvesting olives and chestnuts. It is enough that I have Ambroglio. This one would rather sketch pictures of our trees, pray to your God or write poems making little sense to anyone but his mother."

Padre Castani had been inclined to refuse the father's request and was about to do so when approached by Antonina. She was among his most faithful parishioners and gave the little she could extract from her husband's purse to his offertory.

She explained, "Bino is special, Padre, rich in faith and at home in your church. He has good hands and can read and write well. You may even make a priest of him though he's too young to take the vow."

"We'll give it a try," relented the priest.

Guided only by the father's criticism of his own son, Padre Castani expected a lack of initiative and diligence. Still, he imagined the boy could prove useful in copying the texts the bishop forwarded en route to the larger Milanese churches. Bino was accepted as an apprentice.

During his first two weeks with the priest, Bino did his chores and ran simple errands. He'd wake early, milk the goat and fetch water enough for their daily needs. In the evening he would light the hearth and assist with the preparation of their meals. After dinner, Bino read assigned scripture aloud and demonstrated fluency with the language of the church. He asked questions, listened thoughtfully to the priest's replies and appeared to understand the Word.

Padre Castani was puzzled that Bino spent his free time in the chapel. It seemed to the priest not to be prayer that occupied the boy but something separate. It was as if he was searching for something and unable to find it. The priest invited a conversation—one he hoped would lead to an understanding of how the young man could better put his gifts to use.

And so it was that they met in chapel one morning. Padre Castani began by outlining the liturgical essays he wanted Bino to transcribe when he noticed the boy fidgeting and looking about.

"Is something wrong, Bino?"

"I'm sorry, Padre, no. Well, yes."

"What is it?"

"The chapel walls, Padre."

The priest looked around but could see no obvious problem. The church enjoyed good natural light and the candles would not be lit for some hours. The beamed ceiling and plaster exhibited settling cracks but were otherwise clean and sturdy.

"What troubles you, son?"

Bino was worried about giving offense so remained silent, preferring instead to return his gaze to the chancel walls bordering the altar.

Placing his hand on the young man's shoulder, Padre Castani began anew, "We have much to discuss, Bino, so please tell me what distracts you so."

"The chancel walls, Padre."

"Yes son, what about them?"

"They're no longer beautiful."

"I don't understand."

"Forgive me. I'm sure they were once beautiful, but they aren't anymore. See how the images have faded and fallen into disrepair. They no longer…"

It was obvious to the priest the boy was unaccustomed to candor, perhaps out of fear of fatherly rebuke; he urged him on.

"It's all right, Bino, please continue. No longer what?"

Bino moved his eyes from the walls to the priest. He held them there and they regarded one another for a moment before Bino found the courage to speak his truth, "They no longer honor the Holy Family or inspire those who come each week to take communion. Your voice, Padre, may be enough for their ears, your words may be enough for their minds but these walls do little for their eyes and hearts."

Padre Castani sat in stunned silence. This farmer's son, who was not yet fifteen, was telling him how to better inspire God's flock.

Bino's focus didn't falter and the priest was the first to look away.

"I don't know what to say, son. You may be right but even if I agree, we have no funds to retain an artist to restore our chancel to her former glory."

"That's not a problem, Padre."

"It isn't? You've discovered some gold, have you?"

Bino smiled and replied, "Gold I lack. I believe I can help or would like to try."

"You?"

"Yes, Padre. Before I came here, I did a little painting under the tutelage of Signor Pastore in the village. It wasn't difficult and he thought me a good student."

The priest sat with his thoughts for a moment before responding. "If I said yes, would you be willing to commit equal time to your writing assignments?"

With great enthusiasm and a broad smile Bino responded, "Yes, Padre, with pleasure. *Grazie, mille grazie.*"

Padre Castani wasn't sure why he had said yes to Bino a year earlier. Was it that he appreciated what the boy had to say or the candor with which he said it? It no longer mattered. Bino had been right and all who visited the church credited the priest with the vision to make their chapel come alive. Antonina's loss had been the church's gain. And better yet, the only cost to the priest had been the food upon the boy's table. Even Bino's materials were donated by those who attended Sunday service and remembered the apprentice who once took the time to arrange their firewood in creative ways.

Where once had been tired frescos of the saints there were now colorful and expressive renderings of the same. Signor Pastore had joined him those first months and taught him well. Bino's mentor revealed the chemistry behind the lime plaster mix and the water-borne colors crucial to the frescos' original application. As one, their work was uncomplicated, fresh and improving week-by-week. It was obvious to Signor Pastore and Padre Castani that Bino was a quick student and it wasn't long before the pupil, with unusual humility, surpassed his mentor in skill and dexterity.

"Signor Pastore would be proud of what you accomplished here, Bino, in such a short time. Our heavenly Father smiles upon you."

"You're kind to say so, Padre. But it is I who should be thanking you."

"What's this you say now?"

Bino stepped down the ladder, placed his brush in a cloudy bucket of water and wiped his stained hands on the cloth tied about his waist.

"Padre, I came here a year ago a great disappointment to my father and a worry to my mother. All I had were words and visions and no knowledge of how to use them to anyone's advantage."

Padre Castani interrupted, "I still don't see why…"

"Please Padre, let me finish. You see, you opened your door to me and let me see inside. Not like others see inside each Sunday. No, you let me stay here and imagine what was possible with faith and my hands."

Tears welled in the priest's eyes and he reached for the kerchief stuffed deep within the pocket of his robe.

"I see, Bino. I see. Let's give the credit to God. Finish up here and join me for an early dinner."

The priest left him and moved to his private prayer space behind the altar. He knelt, offered a blessing and dwelled on the selfishness that had kept Bino's gifts a local secret for too long. He knew what he should do; he knew what he must do.

Piero

He sat there and understood. There wouldn't be more situations like this for him—father in service to the son. Piero knew his comfort and station had everything to do with his prodigious son and nothing to do with his meager skill with numbers. He pondered the curious path his life had taken and the debts left unpaid. The financial ones were settled; the human ones were his aim.

Dare I ask? Piero wondered whether Leonardo would bother to answer and remained still. His son, himself indebted, had come to this rectory as a favor to his broken-hearted patron, Ludovico Sforza—the Duke of Milan—when the Duke's beloved wife died.

"Beatrice and I will rest here," Sforza said to Leonardo, "and she would have wanted her favorite scene—the Lord's final supper—imagined on this great wall."

Leonardo argued against the project and lost. So amid gossip and rumblings of displeasure, the much-acclaimed artist and inventor from Vinci interrupted other activity to come to this room adjacent to the church of Santa Maria delle Grazie. Piero heard his son's complaints and saw through them. Leonardo enjoyed the attention while creating a mural worthy of the mother church in Rome.

The son had invited the father to sit this week as one of the twelve at the table. The stillness caused Piero's neck and a shoulder to ache and he couldn't be silent any longer.

"Where does Beatrice rest now?"

No response came. Leonardo glanced over his outstretched arm and focused on the source of the unnecessary question. Piero remained seated at the table and appeared to glow under his yellow tunic and long white beard. His eyes were focused elsewhere while the palms of his hands, as requested, were held up and outward. The gesture would suggest to anyone present Piero's wish to keep the artist at a distance.

Leonardo studied his father's hands and focused on the curled arthritic fingers. He twisted the image in his mind and applied several brushstrokes to the mural—a larger-than-life depiction of the disciples' reaction to Christ's claim that one present would betray Him.

Piero continued, "I fear for the Duke, Leonardo. While he's distracted by sadness and local rivals, French royals plot his demise. Doesn't he see that? I understand your fealty to him but with this extravagance any debt owed is surely resolved."

When no reply came, Piero changed subjects. "What news have you from home?"

Leonardo woke from his reverie. "I beg you be silent, Piero; I have no interest in gossip or speculation. The Prior complains my work is beyond due and I don't wish to feed his ignorant and impatient mouth."

Long ago the son had stopped referring to Piero as "Father." Over his forty-and-five-year life, they'd experienced good and bad times, forging a unique bond. But since his own birth owed more to accident than intention, the son behaved with little deference to the father.

It was his father's evolution in character Leonardo wondered at. At one time selfish, Piero enjoyed more benefits than deserved from his son's acclaim and lofty connections. Nearer to death, Piero was seeking a more constructive relationship—one that might do some good beyond their immediate circle.

Piero again interrupted, "I'm cold and uncomfortable. Not even Saint Andrew could have borne this trial fifteen centuries ago!"

"Bravo, Piero. If you're able to look as uncomfortable as you claim to be, I'll beg a second helping of wine for you at noon. And Saint Andrew was sure to have been as uncomprehending upon hearing the unthinkable from Christ."

"Did Andrew have to endure an arrogant son?"

"Much worse, Piero, much worse."

Leonardo dabbed his brush to the wall. Twenty-four months had come and gone since he had begun this commission. Working from right to left, all but the final quarter of his ten-meter-wide-by-half-again-as-high tribute to the Sforza family was complete.

The Duke was satisfied. With one mural he would call attention to Leonardo's genius, affirm his allegiance to the church and safeguard the souls of his family. What neither the Duke nor the artist could have known at the project's inception was how soon their much-loved wife and friend, Beatrice, would call this mausoleum home.

Leonardo missed Beatrice's company and forgiveness; she had overlooked his unconventional passions while not smothering him with unearned compliments. Still, the artist wished to put her memory behind him and be done with Christ's *last meal* so he might determine where to earn his next. Only Saints Bartholomew, James and Andrew remained and for reasons he could no longer recall, Leonardo had invited his father to sit as the latter.

Che pensavo io?—What was I thinking?

Piero apologized, "Forgive me, Leonardo. I am old and have lesser fears while you are sure to be preoccupied by the Duke's heartache and political jeopardy."

Not sure he'd heard correctly, Leonardo returned his brush to the workbench, descended from atop the scaffold and focused his attention on the wrinkled figure seated at table. Something his father had said stirred him.

"Relax a moment, Piero. What did you just say?"

Startled at his son's sudden proximity and feeling threatened, the old man searched for spoken words.

"I said my age gives me less to fear while you worry after your friend and the consequences of a fall from power."

Leonardo stared at his father, whose face was expressionless and difficult to read.

"You are right, Piero; you don't know how right you are. I'm impatient with you because I'm jealous."

"Jealous, you? The one whose name is spoken in the streets? Artist to the court and man of science, jealous of what?"

"Don't misunderstand me. I'm jealous of your lack of ambition and the peace such complacency brings. How can you have anything to fear when nothing you have can be lost?"

Piero lifted his hands from his lap and rubbed them together seeking warmth. In a moment he looked up. "I'm not sure I understand."

"I don't expect you would."

"But you, everyone invites your help. I have no right to be proud and yet I am."

"Don't be, Piero. Neither one of us deserves credit for gifts we cannot claim as our own."

"Be that true, surely you've made much of your talent; even God would acknowledge that."

"Was it so, Piero, was it so. I'm afraid my conscience isn't clear."

"Now you speak like that honest priest. What was his name?"

"It matters not; I'm aware of my sins. I have the ear of royals. Women with a history and men with a future beg my attention. They pay me handsomely in coin and company for that which is second nature."

"What are you saying, Leonardo?"

"I'm saying all of that should have proved enough, Piero, but I want something more."

Piero rose from his seat and spoke, "Go on."

"My ambition extends beyond the beauty created here to what is revered in this day and place—position, recognition and power."

"You're not so different than those hailed in Florence and Venice."

"Am I not? I've invested much time here. If the French remove the Duke, there is no guarantee they'll retain me and if they do…"

"What is it?"

"Won't compliance with the French betray the loyalty shown me by the Sforzas?"

"Better not to worry about that just yet."

"Perhaps you are right, Piero. T'would be better we distract ourselves with the recent news from Spain."

"True enough. Had they listened to you, our allies would have sailed and discovered the *new world* before the Spaniards."

"Let's credit Signor Colombo and his Queen. I didn't press the idea hard enough and hold no grudge. My penance is certain; long after they've forgotten me, the name Cristoforo Colombo will be spoken."

"You may be right, you may be wrong. Why should we care? We'll be dead."

"Mother of God, I do care! Can't you see that?"

"See what? Turn around and look at what you'll soon finish here. It's unparalleled and alive!"

Leonardo shook his head. "I don't know, Piero. Christ was betrayed for thirty pieces of silver. Am I no more clever than Judas?

"What are you saying—that you should work for nothing?"

"Maybe. Or maybe I'm simply saying there is someone out there who would."

"You speak nonsense. Are we done today, Leonardo?"

"Yes, you may leave."

"I think I will. May I ask a favor first?"

"Would it matter if I said no?"

"True enough. Is there room for another student at your workshop?"

"And you ask because?"

"The Prior relayed a letter from the pastor in Luino. He speaks glowingly of a young artist worthy of your tutelage and generous of nature. Can we extend an invitation?"

"While it's never safe to accept as truth any priest's appraisal of talent, my own circumstances guide against such an invitation."

"Granted. How would you have me respond?"

Leonardo thought for a moment before speaking, "Since you intend to remain in Milan, offer to greet the boy and introduce him to our friend Gian Stefano."

"Gian Stefano Scotto?"

"The same."

"And why would you have me greet him?"

"Who better than you to measure the lad and alert him to the wolves and thieves?"

"I accept the compliment."

"As you should Piero, as you should." He bowed and gestured towards his father. "Until tomorrow morning, Saint Andrew."

Bino

Village of Luino, six months later

Bino could be excused for flinching. He would never get used to his older brother's blows and this was another such occasion. Ambroglio laughed as his younger brother covered his face with both hands.

"Rise swine! I'm going into town with you and Mamma."

"Why would you go? I don't want you there."

"They may like your fancy brushwork at church but don't think the place belongs to you."

"I never said that. Leave me be."

Ambroglio grinned and stepped away. "How did you grow so useless?"

Bino couldn't understand Ambroglio's hatred. He knew his brother assigned little value to artistic gifts so stayed out of his way and remained silent when his father praised Ambroglio at his younger son's expense. Bino couldn't help but wonder if it was his own indifference to his father's neglect that made his brother resent him so.

Ambroglio stood tall, dropped his bed clothes and dressed with greater attention than was normal. He carried himself as one satisfied with his place in the family. His father depended entirely upon him and assured him of his superiority in all things that mattered.

Their mother argued the opposite point of view but the spoils of her husband's orchards weren't hers to share. When he eventually died,

Antonina would content herself with prayer while Ambroglio would organize the work and distribute any profit from the orchard. Ambroglio needed only a single piece to fall into place—the hand of a village girl by the name of Mina.

Bino put all thoughts of his brother aside and wondered at the reception he and Padre Castani would receive at this morning's unveiling. The priest was honest in all things but lately closed-mouthed. It was as if he was harboring some great secret—one he couldn't wait to share. The artist wished the mystery would end soon.

Villagers gathered outside the Luino chapel. Noon approached and the sun was high in a cloudless sky. Padre Castani greeted everyone and invited all to come in and be seated. Benches were arranged about the chancel. A step higher, in front of the altar, was a crude stand upon which leaned a large, cloth-covered object. Curious newcomers had little to do but estimate its one-by-two-meter dimensions. The priest alone understood it would be the first of a pair of surprises.

Mina and her father had the shortest distance to walk and were early enough to sit adjacent to the altar. Ambroglio, Antonina and Bino were among those arriving last when few seats remained. Padre Castani saw them come in and retreated to the chapel entrance to greet them.

"Such a special day, *signora*. Bino, what's taken you so long? Bring your mother and brother forward."

Before Bino could speak, Ambroglio declined the invitation. "I'll remain here, Padre."

Antonina cast a disappointed glance in his direction but didn't bother to argue. "Is there room enough for us forward, Padre Castani?"

"*Si', si' signora*, I'm sure Bino told you about our little surprise, no?"

Smiling at her younger son, Antonina responded candidly, "He told us nothing, Padre."

The priest brought Antonina and Bino forward and asked Mina to make space for Antonina. Mina was pleased to do so and greeted the older woman warmly. Antonina returned the kindness by reaching for and holding Mina's hand.

The priest's chair had been removed from its usual spot and relocated to the side of the altar; here Padre Castani invited Bino to sit. Doing so made him uncomfortable and caused many in attendance to wonder at the unusual gesture.

When all were settled, the priest stood before the covered object and thanked everyone for their presence.

Beginning with the accompanying gesture he spoke the words, "In the name of our Father, His Son and the Holy Spirit, Amen. I know the Lord bestows a special blessing upon all of you this day. Time away from your farms and God's creatures does not go unnoticed and grace will be your reward."

Padre Castani cleared his throat and started anew, "We gather to pray each week, yes, but at times it's appropriate to celebrate the gifts shared by one of our own."

The priest gestured to the artist and continued, "Our friend Antonina's son, Bernardino, whom we know as Bino, joined me eighteen months ago. I don't believe it's an exaggeration to say removing him from the family farm was a gift to both him and his father."

Most in attendance laughed at the polite slight—none harder than Ambroglio who delighted in his brother's embarrassment. The priest raised his hands.

"Let me continue, please. Bino has been a faithful servant to our church. And if we today enjoy a more beautiful chapel, one we all draw inspiration from, we have this young man and Signor Pastore to thank."

While most present focused on Padre Castani, Mina instead cast her attention to the young artist. She'd seen him before and wondered at his age. She observed his discomfort and empathized.

Mina noticed and studied Bino's arms which as crossed escaped from their sleeves. She appreciated their length and strength and imagined how they might feel about her. Color came to her cheeks and she unconsciously squeezed Antonina's hand tighter.

When the priest's words were spoken, Bino lifted his eyes from the chapel floor to Padre Castani and his mother. *How curious*, he thought. Antonina's eyes were wet with tears and she appeared to be comforted by the very young woman from whom his brother sought favor.

Padre Castani interrupted his thinking. "Bino, please join me."

The artist, startled by the invitation, rose and moved slowly over the short distance separating them.

"It's time to reveal what Bino's finished since completing our chapel frescos some weeks ago."

The priest's attention and flattery towards Bino annoyed his brother and he was poised to exit before noticing Mina and her father sitting shoulder-to-shoulder with his mother. He couldn't leave and miss the opportunity to re-introduce himself. He would stay and speak with her father.

Concluding his introduction, Padre Castani reached for the hidden object's cover and tugged it up and away. All but the oldest persons present leaped to their feet to catch a glimpse of what had been revealed.

First there was silence, then curious whispers and mumbling. Bino and the priest were confused by the audience's reaction and looked to each other for understanding.

Unveiled was a full-figure portrait of Saint Catherine imagined as Christ's joyful bride. Hands raised to heaven, Catherine wore a radiant smile, gold halo and blue and white gown. Her feet were bare and supported atop a cloud. It was executed beautifully on a discarded wooden door. The material's imperfections added to the painting's substance, grounded the saint's story and rendered Catherine approachable.

From his position in the rear of the chapel, Ambroglio couldn't see well and assumed the silence spelled trouble for his brother. With a smile that portended his brother's comeuppance, he excused his way forward before stopping a body length away from Bino's painting.

Ambroglio couldn't believe what he saw. His eyes travelled from Saint Catherine's feet to her open arms before settling on her eyes. Her eyes held his and spoke of forgiveness; he was unable to look away.

With Bino at his side, Padre Castani remained silent while observing his people. The priest was moments away from offering an apology and dismissal when the most unexpected thing happened. The parishioners close to Ambroglio fell to their knees and prayed.

Ambroglio, hearing the commotion around him, witnessed the unusual spectacle. Mina and his mother were on their knees as were villagers, widows and harvest workers who normally looked upon him with more fear than gratitude. *My brother? How is this possible?*

Bino observed the parishioners with like wonder, his eyes settling on his brother's. Why was he just standing there? When Ambroglio turned from the crowd to again focus on Catherine, Bino saw an unexpected expression on his face; it looked something like remorse.

Ambroglio, hypnotized by the Saint's expressive eyes, bowed his head. Could he explain this to his father? Could he explain it to anyone? How could someone he thought as useless as his brother accomplish this? How could Bino bring people to their knees and make them feel as he was feeling?

Ambroglio shook his head from side to side, whispering to no one, "Enough, enough." He stepped towards Bino and the priest.

"Excuse me, Padre. May I have a word with my brother?" Padre Castani shuffled aside but remained close enough to hear.

"Bino, you painted this?"

"Yes, and..."

"Stop! Listen for a moment." He paused before continuing, "The woman in the painting, the saint, she makes me think."

Bino doubted his brother's sincerity for a moment before confirming otherwise. "Does she make you think better of me?"

"No, that's not it. She, the woman, she makes me think less of me."

Bino wasn't sure how to respond and said only, "I'm glad you came, Ambroglio; you needn't stay."

Satisfied, Padre Castani walked towards the congregation and invited all to rise and return to their benches.

"Please everyone. I have something else to share."

The priest smiled at Bino before continuing.

"Some weeks ago, I wrote of Bino's ability to the church in Milan. I had little hope of a reply but am pleased to report an encouraging response."

He paused for dramatic effect and shifted his attention to Antonina before continuing, "Gian Stefano Scotto, a peer of Master Leonardo, welcomes our son to his workshop in Milan. With the proper mentoring, Bino can develop his talent and use it for God's greater glory. Perhaps one day soon a portrait as lovely as this one will adorn a proper church in Milan."

All sat a little taller and expressed support for the idea with the exception of the young artist himself. Wonder and a thousand questions filled his thoughts. *Could I do such a thing?* The invitation and praise were inconsequential.

After dismissing well-wishers, Padre Castani found himself alone with Antonina, her sons, Mina and her father. Bino's mother interrupted an awkward silence.

"You were kind to share your seat with me, Mina. I knew your mother and she would be proud of the young woman you've become."

Mina blushed and wasn't sure how to respond before her father did so for her. "It is thoughtful of you to say so, *signora*. If you don't mind me asking, how is your husband? I'm certain there is much he could teach me about farming."

"He is well and too often occupied, *signor*; the orchard is more wife to my husband than I am. Let us repay your kindness though. She turned and winked knowingly at her first born.

"Ambroglio, accompany Mina and her father home. Be good and answer our neighbor's questions. God's abundance knows no bounds."

Ambroglio and Mina shared a polite glance while her father accepted the invitation. "Your offer is too appealing to ignore, *signora, grazie*."

Pleased with his mother's instincts, Ambroglio held an arm open towards the chapel entrance. Mina nodded but first stepped in the direction of Bino and Padre Castani.

"Thank you for including us, Padre," she said, and then looked shyly towards Bino. "You are very good. I've wondered many times what Saint Catherine looks like; I needn't wonder anymore. She is lovelier than I could have imagined."

Bino accepted the compliment and offered a lone word of gratitude. He paid less attention to Mina's words than her relaxed body language. He appreciated the way her cheeks and ears moved with each smile and the gentle lean of her blemish-free neck. He committed the combination to memory.

His mother raised her voice, interrupting his appreciative stare. "Your manners, Bino?"

"*Mi dispiace, signorina*—forgive me. I'm pleased you came and liked my painting. I am grateful for your kindness."

Ambroglio escorted Mina and her father away so only Padre Castani remained in Antonina and Bino's company. The proud mother began, "This is unexpected news, Padre; how can we repay you?"

"I ask only for your prayers, *signora*, as I must now find a capable replacement."

Bino spoke up, "That isn't necessary, Padre; I don't wish to go to Milan."

"Bino!" reacted his mother. "You don't know what you're saying. Is this how you show gratitude?"

The priest reassured Antonina, "Please, *signora*, let's hear what the boy has to say."

"The lake, this village, they are my home, Padre. I'm happy here. What reason would I have to go to Milan where princes and master artists claim their fortunes?"

"I see, Bino. Anything else?"

"Where would you and Mamma be without me? I can't leave."

"Can't or won't?"

"What difference does it make?"

"It makes all the difference to God, Bino. What would He want for you? Remember the servant who buried the gifts of his master, what was his fate? What instead was the fate of the one who employed and multiplied his gifts?"

Bino recalled the passage. It was one he pained over since he rarely wanted more for himself than that which was freely offered.

"I don't wish to seem ungrateful, Padre, it's just that…"

"Pray on this, son. Our Father will lead you to the right conclusion. And know you would go to Milan with three guardian angels: your mother, this humble church and Saint Catherine." And then looking towards Bino's painting, Padre Castani continued, "See her expression? Christ's *bride* invites your courage and an open mind."

That evening Bino wanted nothing of the fanfare thrust upon him by his family and neighbors. He excused himself, trekked the short distance to the lake and sat quietly while nature's curtain closed on his peculiar day.

A sliver of the moon shown in the sky and there was light enough to return home. The hour was late and no one remained awake. Bino stirred the hearth, added kindling and sparked a blaze. He warmed his hands by the fire.

When comfortable, the young artist retreated to the dining table and took a seat facing the hearth. A short while passed before Bino rose and selected a sheet of parchment from his father's modest supply. He found a quill, its accompanying ink and sat again.

His mind was a collage of rapidly changing images—parishioners kneeling, his mother's tears, Mina's face and neck, the sun setting over the lake, Ambroglio's remorse and Master Leonardo.

And then there were Mina's words: *You are very good.*

Bino shifted on the bench, rolled his shoulders, clenched and unclenched his fingers before staring at his hands. He felt restless, unquenched, aroused, fearful and yet resigned to accept others' ambition for him. He committed his prayer to paper.

> *If you're listening, should I go?*
> *And was I to leave, what would you have me know?*
> *I am to seek knowledge but could any teacher be as*
> *   wise as you?*
> *And if found, might my heart be salvaged too?*
> *I hunger for more, Lord, than I fear you can forgive.*
> *Your spirit is my craft, not the desire with which*
> *   I live.*
> *I want to paint, write poetry and make love; my con-*
> *   fession is my song.*
> *If tenderness be my guide, how could my brushwork*
> *   be wrong?*
> *Should I go? Is there a home there for me?*
> *Faith demands I trust all mystery.*

The decision is yours, Father, and yours alone.
Lead, I'll follow you.
I pray you one day carry me home.

When complete, Bino re-read his words. He closed his eyes and whispered a second prayer—a favored one from Saint Anselm his mother had shared with him.

Let me seek You in my desire. Let me desire You in my seeking.

Satisfied, Bino stood and restored pen and ink to their proper places. The poet returned to table and retrieved his written prayer. He carried it to the hearth and held the page's edge over the flame. His words became fire, smoke and ash. The rising vapor mixed with itself and multiplied in strength. Outside the cottage, a gale-like wind relieved the stone chimney of its contents. Bino's prayer, once confined to heart and fiber, drifted towards the stars.

Caterina

The little one heard voices. They came from beyond the curtain separating the bed she shared with her youthful aunt from that of her parents. Caterina was alone and for a while content to listen in on the conversation between Isabella and her mother and father. She didn't catch every word but didn't have to; she appreciated the excitement signaled by their voices. "Tomorrow," her mother said, "all will change for the better."

Caterina had but six years and was an only child. Her father, a stonemason and gilder, had brought the family to Serono when word reached him of the church that would be built there. Her mother's parents died after a brief illness and her father invited his sixteen-year-old sister-in-law, Isabella, to join them. "You're my daughter now and a fit companion for Caterina," he argued. And he was right.

Her father won a commission to help with the construction and beautification of the new pilgrim church. The work would take years and yield steady wages—something new to their family and reason enough to believe in miracles.

Nearly forty years had passed since the first of Serono's miracles. A long-ill boy by the name of Pedretto had been greeted bedside by a special visitor. The boy recounted the Virgin's appearance, healing presence and cure. Mary requested he build a church on the spot to recall Her Son and compassion for those in need. The cornerstone of a new and grander pilgrim church, the Sanctuary of the Blessed Virgin of Miracles, would be laid the morrow.

Caterina listened a while longer before restlessness caused her to rise and walk to the room's only window. She stood on a stool and struggled to push open the wooden shutters concealing the moonlight from her corner of the room. She threw her weight against them for a moment before the shutters gave way, tripping her backward and allowing a cool breeze to invade the space.

The commotion and billowing bed curtain brought her father to her feet.

"*Carina, cosa fai?* What's going on?"

"I couldn't sleep Papa. I got up to see the moon and the wind made me fall."

"It's late, *Carina*, but as long as you're up, why don't we take a peek."

"Can we, Papa?"

Eduardo lifted her into the air and sat her upon his strong shoulders. He rotated his body toward the window so the little girl would have a better view. She sensed something unusual in the air. "What's that smell, Papa?"

"I don't notice anything. What do you smell?"

"I don't know. Is someone burning something?"

"That could be. The wind is strong and can move an odor farther and faster than a day on horseback."

"Is that a long way?"

"Yes, it is."

"The stars, Papa, they seem brighter tonight."

"Tomorrow's a special day and God wants few clouds in the sky."

"Will Pedretto be there?"

"No, Carina. The Blessed Mother brought Pedretto to heaven some years ago."

"Isabella says his soul will be there."

"She's a smart girl."

"Will you make it a beautiful church, Papa?"

"Of course; I promise she will be a proud and beautiful church. Talented artists will come and visitors are sure to follow. All will want to see Mary—the author of Pedretto's miracle."

"Can I pray for a miracle too, Papa?"

"Sure, what would you like?"

Caterina thought a moment before responding confidently, "I want you and Mamma to be like this always."

Eduardo lowered his little girl to his chest and focused on her eyes. "How do you mean—*like this*?"

"Happy, Papa—happy so you will only say kind things to each other."

Eduardo was silent for a moment—a little part of him waking somewhere deep inside. He pulled his daughter into his chest before whispering, "That's a good prayer, *Carina*. Pray for me that I might keep my job and honor Mary and your mother with my hands."

"I will, Papa. Can I pray for someone else too?"

"Who did you have in mind?"

"I don't know—someone who isn't as happy as we are."

"There are plenty of those people, *Carina*, and Mother Mary is sure to hear your prayers."

"I'm sleepy, Papa."

Eduardo kissed her head and cheek and laid her atop her blanket. "Rest well, *Carina*."

Bino

"Drop what you're doing and follow me."

Gaudenzio and Bino first looked at each other with expressions of surprise and doubt before Gaudenzio spoke. "Do you mean us, now?"

"Of course, you, and of course, now," replied Scotto.

Without delaying a moment longer Bino and Gaudenzio moved quickly to the barrel in the center of the room and thrust their muddy hands into the cool cloudy water. Quickness was a familiar and necessary component of their daily labors so only seconds passed before their hands emerged clean from the make-shift tub. They shook them and what moisture remained found its way onto stained waist aprons.

They followed Gian Stefano into a room they had been forbidden to enter before. The space was irregularly shaped and the perimeter was bounded by tall walls capped by a beam-and-plaster ceiling. An uneven and peculiar light settled about them. Bino, squinting as he looked towards the ceiling, soon understood why. The walls had been treated with experimental colors and textures, some of which captured and held the light, others that reflected it away.

Gian Stefano stared at the young men and wondered. He had reluctantly accepted the pair—Gaudenzio Ferrari and Bernardino—at the urging of Leonardo, or so claimed his father, Piero da Vinci. He had done so to win favor with Leonardo, thinking it was perhaps a commission his mentor had been too bored or proud to accept, only to learn Leonardo had fled the city. *What good to me is an absent genius?*

Scotto was stuck with the novices. They showed promise but so did many others and he thought it might be too late to invigorate their creativity. He dismissed the thought and without humor raised his voice.

"You're here because *someone* thought you the better of our disappointing class of painters. And it wouldn't surprise me to learn you consider yourselves capable of high art. Let's put your doubts to rest. You know less about fresco painting than the flies my goat sweeps off its ass."

Laughter echoed from a dark corner of the room, causing Bino and Gaudenzio to shift their attention. Having believed themselves to be alone with their master, they were surprised to see an elderly man amidst the shadows, seated on a stool. His eyes were not discernible but below his nose and chin was a long white beard. It hung parallel to a walking stick he held steady with a single hand.

"It is true, you can draw, you can paint *a secco* but you're not worth piss to this workshop until you master the composition and application of plaster and pigment on these walls. Not much has changed. You will learn as the ancients learned. You will become students of chemistry, temperature, and humidity and learn that fresco is less an individual effort than one of careful coordination of group action. Am I clear?"

"Yes," they replied in unison.

To his thinking, Bino was eager to be doing something, indeed anything, other than the repetitive tasks and finish work that was the occupation of each new apprentice under Scotto's employ. The challenge was welcome. The instruction began. And the silent guest watched.

Beyond, in the shadows, Piero da Vinci—the quiet father of the bold son, the *accidental* father to the city's most talked-about genius, remained attentive and expressionless. He was there at Gian Stefano's invitation—his reward for having discovered Bino and pointing Padre Castani to Scotto's workshop. He had neither the need nor inclination to credit Leonardo with the idea. His son had fled Milan to wait and see where the city's political future would lie.

The young men returned their attention to Gian Stefano. What the master artist lacked in grace was more than made up for with skill and experience. They saw their mentor's work in the city's magnificent cathedral—a building so grand it took their breath away. To see it was to want a life outside the workshop, away from its tedium. Eighteen months was enough!

This was more than just a fanciful wish; the Vatican welcomed more church construction and it was happening across Lombardia and beyond. How better to combat the heretical, anti-Catholic ideas crossing the Alps from the north? The build-out would mean opportunity for masons, stone cutters, carpenters and the better fresco artists of the day. Most sought treasure while others sought notoriety. Men like Leonardo and Gian Stefano wanted and achieved both. Bino wanted only to be relieved of boredom, to create inspiring spaces and to one day return home.

Aware that his friend was daydreaming, Gaudenzio pinched Bino in the ribs.

And then from his teacher, "Would you like to return to your father's farm, Bino?"

"I'm sorry, Master Scotto. No."

"Then raise your sleeves and listen to what I have to say to you."

Gian Stefano paused to think for a moment before continuing. "Ours is wet work in dry places. The integrity of each fresco relies upon one set of conditions today and opposing conditions tomorrow. Conceive your child well and she'll be appreciated five hundred years from now; ignore the elements, and she'll fade from view within twenty springtimes."

Scotto's conception metaphor reminded Bino of his inexperience. Gaudenzio and the other apprentices passed time with drink and lies about female conquest. Bino would listen and laugh and, when challenged, keep his virginity a secret.

Each and every day over the succeeding twelve weeks, Gian Stefano introduced a critical stage of the fresco process. He introduced, tested, rehearsed and repeated concepts until the methods and behaviors were routine.

They devoted the first month to the study of wall preparation, brushing and moistening experimental areas before applying the first of two plaster layers. The first layer, the *arriccio*, was coarser and resulted from one part slaked lime to two parts filler.

"For filler we must use river sand or ground marble. Sand from the sea is no use to us since it carries salt. And the grains should not be too smooth, lest they bond poorly with the lime."

Early in their tutelage Gian Stefano prepared a mixture and invited them nearer.

"Thrust your hands in and squeeze it as you would a woman's behind. If it doesn't feel right, don't marry it; you'll have an unproductive day. But if it feels as this does, you'll go all day and won't want to quit until the firelight dies."

Bino pushed his arms elbow-deep into the gray mud and held them there a moment before clenching his fists, allowing the cool granular material to escape between his fingers. The smell wasn't harsh, somewhat familiar in fact, and the twin sensations aroused him.

"She feels fine?" asked Scotto.

"Yes, very good," responded Bino.

"As it should be. A sculptor must have a feel for his clay, no?"

Gian Stefano continued, "Once applied to the walls, the *arriccio* will dry and can remain indefinitely before the process continues."

"The second plaster layer—the *intonaco*, is the one we color. We dampen the *arriccio* and apply only the amount of *intonaco* that can be painted before it dries."

Before Bino could ask the question, Gaudenzio spoke up, "What distinguishes the *intonaco* plaster from the first mix?"

"Ah, you ask the right question."

Gian Stefano looked skyward as if searching for a delicate description from the gods. Finding it, he grinned from ear to ear.

"If the *arriccio* can be compared to a mature woman, the *intonaco* has more the feel of a baby's flesh. Instead of coarse sand, we employ fine sand or, better still, *pozzolana*—volcanic stone. It is ground and carried to us by those hedonists from Naples."

Bino enjoyed the way Master Scotto spoke and his meaning was understood.

"Feel it wet, lads. It is useless to us dry. Apply only what you can color that day, no?"

The instruction continued with each calendar turn. Meanwhile, "L'Anziano," the name given to the old man by Bino and Gaudenzio, remained anonymous. He appeared on fewer occasions but remained an engaged visitor to their experimentation chamber. Scotto never addressed him or wondered at his absence.

"Do you think him mute, Bino?" asked Gaudenzio one afternoon as they felt his stare.

"I can't say but I'm not bothered by him. He seems to be quite interested in us and our progress."

"You're wrong about that, friend."

"Why do you say so?"

"It isn't us that he's interested in. Each time I look his way, he's focused on you."

Bino couldn't argue or explain the point. He was sure of one thing. He did not need to speak with the old man to communicate. They did so with a nod, a smile or a simple, empathetic stare. It was as if the old man knew exactly what he was thinking as he was thinking it. And then one day, without a word, he stopped coming.

The next month proved the most challenging. Master Scotto demonstrated how to transfer each section of a *cartoon*—the outline of each intended fresco—to the *intonaco*.

"First, we mark our boundaries on the damp plaster by pressing cord into the surface like this."

Bino and Gaudenzio grew wide-eyed as they observed Gian Stefano's strength and dexterity. Balanced often on a single foot, Master Scotto's arm and calf muscles tensed as he forcefully pressed the thick string into the wet surface of the intonaco. Where necessary, he used a straight edge but more than not his eye proved enough to render horizontal and vertical lines true.

"Madonna! How does he do that?" they whispered to one another.

"Bring me the *cartoon*. Be quick!"

They carried a portion of a larger drawing to him while Gian Stefano wet the *intonaco* with a brush.

"*Guarda, guarda,*" he bellowed. "Watch me now."

With their help he centered the *cartoon* over the damp plaster and together they pressed it forward.

"We attach one piece of the drawing to the wall at a time and begin pouncing."

The students watched with a combination of respect and amusement as Master Scotto used a dull-edged tool to quickly trace the outlines of the drawing onto the intonaco.

"You and the idiots assisting must have a sense of urgency or you're doomed. *Capite*—understand?"

Month three arrived and the formulation and application of various pigments to the *intonaco* remained for them to learn and practice.

"You will make due with less of the rainbow—you, especially, Gaudenzio. I know how color arouses you."

Bino was amused. Gaudenzio was a slave to color and the limited color palette available to a fresco artist would pose a challenge for him.

"We create jars of *mestiche* by grinding our pigments and dissolving the powder in water. We make enough of each color to support a full project. To do otherwise creates an avoidable problem since no two batches of the same pigment produce identical color."

Gaudenzio looked nervously into the prepared color bowls and saw several flavors of black, two of red and cinnabar. Mixing the latter with white yielded a fleshy pink. There were various yellows, earth green and burnt sienna. These would have to do until imagination or experimentation allowed otherwise.

"Listen well. The ideal time to apply the colors to the *intonaco* is within several hours of the plaster application to the wall. Plan ahead, start early and get this right. Begin too soon and the colors will run. Wait too long and the plaster cannot absorb the pigment."

Gian Stefano excused himself and the apprenticed pair set about experimenting with the colors on dry and damp walls.

Gaudenzio interrupted his own labor to observe his friend. Bino both inspired and annoyed him. His friend never questioned the point of any exercise, wasn't easily distracted and needed little praise or purse to be satisfied.

"How do you do it?"

"What?"

"How do you remain so focused? How do you go about your business without wanting more?"

"Why would you think that?"

"Well, don't you?"

Bino thought only a moment before responding.

"I would prefer to be doing this somewhere else. But otherwise, no."

"You amaze, friend."

Bino returned his brush to a bucket and turned towards Gaudenzio.

"Brother, were it not for an interested priest and Master Scotto, I'd be in a hot, dusty orchard or carrying barrels of chestnuts to market in Luino. Instead we're here with our arms in *honey* with talent enough to put a roof over our heads and food in our bellies. Do you believe that happens by accident?

"It's just our fate, Bino."

"God, fate, call it what you want, but ought we not be grateful?"

"Maybe so, we should have our cards read. You might not be so grateful when you learn the ugly destiny awaiting us. What if this is all there is? What if you produce nothing worthy of attention or fail to enjoy the love of a beautiful woman? What if your gift goes unnoticed for the next hundred years?"

"That would be a sad fate. But those aren't the circumstances I ask for."

"Ask for?"

"Pray for."

"I don't know, Bino."

"You can't *know*, friend. You can only experience. How can you paint what you don't believe?"

"More than a few of us do."

"For that I'm sorry."

Gaudenzio shook his head, dropped his brush and asked, "Why do you believe, friend?"

Bino thought a moment before responding, "Faith is an odd thing, brother. I believe so I might see."

The artist from Luino had accepted his teacher's invitation and found him alone in his study. The room was cluttered with columns of books lining the walls and half-painted canvases leaning against a dusty dining table.

"Welcome, Bino, clear the mess and find a place to sit."

"Grazie, are you well, Master Scotto?"

"Yes, yes, and how is your work coming?"

"It goes well. We should be done soon if Gaudenzio limits his embellishments."

Unsettled by the invitation and never before having stepped into Gian Stefano's apartment, Bino surveyed the untidy room while searching for a place to sit. Discarded drawings, pencils and manuscripts littered the chairs and judging from the odor, Scotto's chamber pot had gone too-long full.

Noticing his student's paralysis, Gian Stefano rid two opposing chairs of debris and invited Bino to sit.

Once settled, Scotto stroked his beard, looked into Bino's eyes and inquired, "How long have you been with us now?"

"Nearly three years, Master Scotto."

"Is that right? It doesn't seem that long. You've made good progress."

"It is kind of you to say so."

"I'm rarely kind, Bino. What do you think of your progress?"

Bino wasn't expecting the question and was unsure of how to respond.

"I like fresco work; it suits me. I don't mind the precision and the time alone. It serves as a kind of prayer. I do believe there is more I can learn."

"Yes, I see." Scotto paused before beginning anew, "What if I told you there is nothing more I can teach you?"

Bino sat and wondered at that for a moment before responding. "Intending no disrespect Master Scotto, I would say you are wrong."

"Two things are true, Bino. I am old and I am right."

"Are you dismissing me then, Master Scotto? Am I free to go home?"

"Free? You have always been free, Bino. Do you believe yourself a prisoner here?"

"No, forgive me, I didn't mean it like that. It's just I was sent here to grow as an artist and I wasn't expecting you to tell me there was nothing left for me to learn."

"Ah, you misunderstand me, Bino. I said there was nothing left for *me* to teach you. I'm afraid there is much you must learn."

Bino rubbed his face with the palms of his hands and rose from his seat. "Master Scotto, I beg you to speak plainly."

"Sit, sit, Bino. *Ascoltami*—listen to me. You are my finest student. Your technical proficiency puts you head and shoulders above your peers— Gaudenzio included. Not since I sat in Leonardo's company have I seen a hand as keen as yours. You've even proven shrewd enough to borrow a trick or two from the arrogant *one*. Compare your work to his. Yours is clean, solid and responds entirely to what we ask of you. And still…"

Gian Stefano's pause filled the room and became too painful for Bino to let go.

"You are not pleased, Master Scotto?"

"I would be pleased if I thought your work reflected more than simple piety. Artists are best when they agitate, Bino. We cannot agitate by simply regurgitating the beliefs of others. We cannot inspire the population with dull interpretations of a cleric's wish list on a cathedral wall. You must have something to say."

Bino slumped against the wall. He couldn't deny the truth of Master Scotto's criticism; he felt it himself. There was little of his soul in his work. It was simple. It was easy. It was passionless.

Gian Stefano looked at him sympathetically. "Perhaps we've kept you too long within our walls. Why not leave us for a little while, taste Milan and let her fill your senses. To paint saints and sinners you must know what it is to be both. Pray yes, but also drink, eat with gusto, be with the poor, make love and observe the hypocrisy of the rich. Return to us after having laughed and cried a little—when you have something to confess, no?

A curious smile crossed Bino's lips.

"Our parish priest never spoke those words to me, Master Scotto. Such a change won't be easy for me. Where shall I go?"

Stefano thought only a moment before responding, "I know a man who keeps a lively studio some distance from here; I'll write a letter of introduction. Make a temporary home there while he puts your talent to practical use."

"And my mother, what should I tell her?"

"The truth. Tell her you must unwrap the gift you've been given before it can be shared with the world."

Argento

It was evening and Bino sat alone. He had chosen to write a bit before either his candle or creativity expired. He sat at a small desk adjacent to his bed—the latter nothing more than blankets heaped upon a stack of canvas-covered wooden frames. He slept in the loft space above the studio kept by Master Scotto's childhood friend, Signor Argento.

Argento was among the fortunate few—an artist supporting himself outside the patronage of the church or Milanese royals. For those who could pay, Argento created landscapes and object art. For those who could pay more there were flattering portraits of wives, children, dogs and mistresses.

Signor Argento was a burly man whose appetites knew few bounds. He had no wife, many girlfriends and possessed sufficient wit to charm even the most dour patrons. He kept his customers' secrets and had the uncanny knack of knowing when and how to leverage these to his economic advantage.

Argento was amused by Bino's youthfulness and naïveté. He couldn't recall ever being as green and wasn't sure what to do with the uncorrupted boy from the shores of the great lake. He knew even less about how to react to Bino's habits which included morning prayer, blessings before meals and passing references to Saints Catherine and Anselm. Assured it was only for a while, he had said yes to Gian Stefano's protégé;

Scotto was an able judge of talent and knew too many people who could help or hurt him.

The morning he met Bino, Signor Argento had him sketch a scene and portrait and the matter was settled. What Bino lacked in energy and street smarts he made up for in execution and speed. Argento did the math and his mind readied its invitation.

"What wage are you seeking, son?" he asked Bino that decisive morning.

Ignorant of his worth and unaccustomed to financial negotiations, Bino responded, "Fifteen *soldi* per day, plus bed and board if you please."

Signor Argento feigned disappointment and replied, "You ask for much, friend, and it would seem your hand at portraiture lacks refinement. You may take the loft above the studio; as for the rest, you will have to learn it before you earn it."

"I am an eager student, sir."

Unaware that Signor Argento was prepared to pay him three times the amount requested, Bino was pleased for the diversion. The time away from the physical demands of fresco work was welcome. He used found time to craft poetry, people-watch in the marketplace and listen in on the *private* conversations downstairs between Signor Argento and his patrons. He reasoned the intelligence he gleaned might one day please Master Scotto.

Words on paper—Bino shared his reflections and experiences with his mother, Gaudenzio and Master Scotto. He would have shared news with Piero, his curious chaperone from Gian Stefano's studio, but knew neither his name nor address. Instead he practiced writing verses and by candlelight, reread the poem he had last begun.

Do I alone notice, do I alone see?
Is all as you would have it be?
You lift a sunrise and drop rain enough to wet the
    farmer's earth.
Harvest follows and abundance so plentiful we can't
    ignore your worth.
You gift us one another and talents we together
    may share,
And for most, a special someone, who above the
    rest, cares.
And when that self-same sun finishes its arc across
    the sky,
A moon you raise to bid our day-long compan-
    ion goodbye.
A miracle all; it seems to me.
Yet without a lover to share such bounty, is all as you
    would have it be?

The poet set his verse aside, extinguished his candle and slept for what seemed only a short while. He woke to Argento's bellow.

"*Rise*, Bino. I make you a special gift today."

Bino studied the face of Signor Argento, searching for clues. "What have I done?"

"It's not what you've done that rouses you; it's what you will do." Then, noticing the inked poem near Bino's bed, Signor Argento lifted it and read.

"What goat shit is this? Where do you find such nonsense?"

Bino grabbed the paper from his landlord's hands before he could read farther. "It may make no sense to you but it was worth my penny on the street. I like to read what others have to say no matter the import."

Pointing to a bowl in the corner, Signor Argento continued. "I brought you some fresh water. Throw it on your face, pull a bone through your hair and climb below to meet our studies. They will arrive any minute."

"Studies? What do you mean studies?"

"You will see soon enough and won't be disappointed." And then, thinking a moment longer, Signor Argento continued, "You have seen the ladies undressed before, no?"

It took several seconds for the question to register. "Undressed?" And then lying, "Of course, why do you ask?"

"We've been granted a unique commission—let's just say a project removed from the tedium that is our lots."

"What are you talking about?"

"It's our good fortune, Bino. We are to create a bath scene—women at bath!"

"Who would want such a thing?"

"It matters not, Bino. We'll be paid handsomely if the ladies are rendered, shall we say, accurately."

"I'll leave this to your capable hand, Signor Argento—surely this is the better project for you."

"Why did you come here, Bino? Did you come just to sit quietly in your room, pray and paint more of your angels and halos? Or did you come as I did as a younger man to reach your hand into the *fruit bowl*? To learn what you might grab, sniff and taste?"

Bino sat stunned. With few words Signor Argento reminded him why Master Scotto had bid him to leave.

With a rare display of empathy, Signor Argento leaned over Bino's frame. He delicately clenched a handful of the younger man's curls and twisted Bino's face towards his own. "A wise man once told me that nothing can come from an artist's brush that hasn't first passed through his eyes, heart and loins. Understand?"

"Yes, I think so. Who are these studies you speak of?"

"Ahh, now you ask the right question. You must see, appreciate and understand the female form before rendering her for our client."

"Yes, go on."

"I have hired a few maids from the bar. You may select one and she will remain, pose and be a *friend* to you as long as you wish."

"And she won't be offended by this crude request?"

"The fairer sex understands something you don't yet comprehend, Bino—money makes any offense easier to bear."

Bino grimaced and exhaled the words, "Give me a few moments; I shall come downstairs."

When Signor Argento left him, Bino stood, walked to his chamber pot and relieved himself. He washed his face and hands, teased his hair from across his eyes and forehead and selected the cleaner of two shirts and trousers from the hooks behind his door. Once dressed, he noticed his feet were soiled and sat again to clean these with the cloudy water remaining in his bowl. Satisfied, he placed his feet in sandals before descending the ladder to the workshop below.

"Ladies, our artist has arrived," welcomed Signor Argento as Bino sheepishly stepped into the room.

He felt the intrusion of their eyes and would have given anything at that moment for the gift of invisibility. Absent it, something shifted, turning his vision from all that was inside to out. His awareness grew and his senses were enlivened by the presence of four young women. Bino bowed to them as if they were ladies and he was their servant.

Unaccustomed to such deference, the women stared at Bino and whispered to one another. Argento spoke to silence them.

"Ladies they aren't, Bino. Their names, tastes and comfort are of no consequence to you. Look them over and select one so I may dismiss the others."

Bino thought him rude and found it impossible to hide his embarrassment with his mentor and the task at hand. He took a deep breath and surveyed the room. The four girls were of like stature and were draped in un-dyed robes that did little to distract from what lay beneath. Cloth belts were knotted about their waists. Their hair, pinned high above their ears, gave the impression they were taller and more sophisticated than was the truth.

Bino was too uncomfortable to make eye contact. Instead he felt an urgent need to hold something to hide the tremors radiating from his knees through his gut to his hands. He found and lifted a rag with his left hand, a brush with his right and the props masked his nervousness. Armed and curious-looking, he stepped forward and circled the foursome.

Bino projected his eyes to the ceiling and watched himself walking slowly about the girls. He witnessed his shy separation and realized the space and its furnishings made it impossible for him to hide.

His perspective returned from above and the artist examined his audience over his left shoulder. He was fascinated by the girls' bare ankles and the manner in which their hands gripped their slack robes about their waists. He appreciated their ears and hair and noted the gentle beauty with which God crafted woman—the strands of dark hair framing the ear, the unblemished lobe hanging as a miniature banner from the fleshy staff that was each girl's neck. He'd never been invited to look so closely and he wouldn't waste the opportunity.

As he circled, the women turned to face him. He focused on one's throat and the soft valley at its base. Here was much to admire and Bino reasoned it the delicate passageway for each breath, nourishment, and words that could alternately arouse or hurt.

Before this moment, he had reveled in sunrises, sunsets, the beauty of nature and the bold craft borne at the hands of masters—all evidence of the Father's gifts. And yet this day, as a consequence of Argento's vulgar mission, he identified God as more sculptor than orchestrator of the human experience.

Eager to be selected, the girls posed and postured. His wondering at what each hid under her robes whet his appetite. Bino's blood rushed, his chest thumped and he could taste the iron in his mouth. His senses expanded further, enough so he could smell Argento's sweat and the room's supply of oils and pigments.

The young artist moistened his lips with his tongue and inhaled deeply. *They must think me a fool. Each is surely more experienced in these matters.* Each, he was sure, delighted in his embarrassment at having to choose. Silly questions entered his mind. What would Padre Castani say? Would his physical arousal be noticeable? He could imagine them laughing even while the room was as silent as a sunset.

Time slowed and Bino examined their figures. The women, reading his shyness and discomfort, relaxed their hold on their respective robes and allowed the artist generous views of their shoulders and the tops of their breasts. One of them turned, smiled and quickly fanned her robe in such a way as to reveal the fullness of her chest and areole. With the distraction, Bino stumbled and coughed.

Impatient and no longer entertained, Signor Argento shouted, "Enough!" With a swift swing of his arm he selected the girl who had made the bold gesture—pointing to her and dismissing the others.

Bino felt relief at not having to choose—a decision he felt was sure to bring pride to one girl and injury to the others.

The three left quickly with Signor Argento—a coin enriching each of their palms. Bino was left alone with the other.

The girl smiled at his awkwardness and broke the silence. "Where would you like me?"

Had he been his brother Ambroglio, Bino would have teased, *In my lap*. Instead, he lifted his head and motioned towards an upholstered chair in the light.

The woman paused before sitting and asked, "All the way off or like this?" She released the material clutched about her neck and gathered her robe below her breasts.

With surprise at her casual gesture, Bino stuttered, "N-no, that is enough... I mean that will be fine for now."

Without direction the model twisted her figure so it paralleled the room's only window; she lowered her chin while tilting her face towards Bino. This had the effect she desired—illuminating the space between her collar and the roundness of her belly. Bino's intoxication grew.

"Am I poorly positioned, sir?" she asked before covering her breasts with her hands.

He wasted no time interrupting, "Stop, I'm sorry, your position was as it should be."

She grinned knowingly and dropped her hands.

Bino stared and stuttered, "A...another thing—you may call me Bino."

She smiled and replied, "All right then, Bino it shall be."

"What may I call you?"

"Any name you like."

"Oh, of course. Perhaps you could suggest something."

She thought a moment before continuing, "When I was a little girl, before I lost my mother, she would tell me a story I fancied. It mustn't have been true but I liked it all the same. It was about a hopeful peasant girl from Monaco."

She looked towards the window before continuing, "She was poor though pretty and virtuous—imagine that—and all the kingdom's ambitious men overlooked her station to invite her hand in marriage. "I'd like to honor that girl; Monica, I'll be."

Bino reflected a moment. "The story is a fine one, *signorina*. And since I delight in your company as Bino why don't I cast you as Nica. Would that be all right?"

"Nica? I like that. Bino and Nica we'll be."

The two exchanged an appreciative look and Bino, finding himself in an unplanned fantasy with a willing muse, felt gratitude and inspiration. *Thank you, Signor Argento.*

With the artist seemingly under her spell and making no movement towards his tools, Nica asked, "Am I to be drawn or do you intend something else?"

And then blushing, Bino responded, "No, I mean, yes, forgive me; I must find my easel and pencils."

"It's okay, you know. I don't mind."

"I'm sorry?"

"It's all right if you just wish to look for a while."

"No, I..."

"Truly, I don't mind. You seem different from those who come to the tavern."

"What do you mean?"

"I'd rather not talk about them; would that be all right?"

"Yes."

Bino pulled a bench from across the room to a spot closer to Nica. He sat upon it for a brief while with his sketch pad before abandoning it in favor of the floor. The artist enjoyed this perspective more with the visual benefit of being at nose level with Nica's delicate knees. His pencil moved across the page quickly.

His eyes moved to her feet. They were bare and tilted down so that only her toes kissed the floor; the top of one foot faced him while the other revealed its arch and the delicate turn of an ankle. From here, he followed the line extending from the top of her toes to where her robe rested above closed knees.

His pencil demanded his attention but his eyes were drawn to Nica's flesh. And so back and forth his focus shifted—to a facing shin, to the paper, to her delicate calf muscles, to the paper, to the hint of thigh above one knee.

Nica shifted her focus from a spot across the room to the artist at her feet. She studied him and asked questions to which she knew the answers.

"You must have a girlfriend. Has she posed for you?"

"No, I mean, there is no such person."

She observed his hands—one supported a thin board upon which rested his drawing pad while the other was busy moving across it. His pencil work was quick and confident and the forearm of his drawing hand appeared to pulse with each stroke.

"You have done this a long time?" she asked.

He raised his eyes to hers, not understanding, "I didn't realize you had to leave so soon."

"No, you misunderstand. For someone so young, you draw well."

"You are kind to say so. When I was half this age, it was the only way to avoid the real work of my father's farm."

"You can tell me to be quiet. Tis a bad habit I have."

Bino said nothing. *How can I object to your voice when you provide such treasure for my eyes?*

Before long she asked, "Why do you prefer it down there?"

"We've been commissioned to paint a bath scene; it helps to become the pool."

"A bath scene?" She laughed and teased—parting her knees and lifting one before crossing it over the other.

Bino swallowed hard and looked away. He deflected his embarrassment by standing and stretching his arms above his head. Doing so had the unintended consequence of making visible his arousal. Realizing so, he spun about, sat upon his bench and covered himself with his sketch board.

"Forgive me, Nica, I mean no disrespect."

She adjusted her position and laughed. "You'd hardly be a man if these didn't have an effect on you."

Nica had leaned forward in the chair, lowering her chin and elevating her hands into her tangled mass of black hair. The new position freed her breasts from her robe and made them appear as ripe fruit to the farmer's son.

Bino sat transfixed. She looked as a goddess might—sitting on the edge of a pool, confident that whatever she might ask for would surely be granted. He pulled forward a new sheet of paper and his pencil worked anew as his eyes again moved from flesh to paper and back again.

Bino used his pencil deftly to shade the contrast of Nica's hair and areole against her pale breasts. He was intrigued by their unequal size and marveled at the delicate beauty of her nipples which leaned upward as if *girasole*, sunflowers in search of light.

Bino felt the pull of Nica's eyes and his attention was drawn to her comment and question. "You've never seen a woman without cover before, have you, artist?"

He thought to lie but saw no advantage in it. "Not without a child suckling there."

"Do you like what you see?"

"Very much."

Nica smiled. "My arms are tired. Would it be all right if I moved?"

"Yes. I'm sorry."

And with that Nica brought her hands back to her robe, lifted it over her shoulders and stood. "May I see what you've drawn?"

Bino's first reaction was to pull his pad to his chest but he did not deny her. Without standing he turned his pad up and outward for her to see.

Nica brought a hand to her mouth and hid a smile. "You make me look like a mischievous princess. And my hair!"

"Forgive me, you did encourage my fantasy. And yes, I drew your hair badly; I haven't quite figured out hair just yet."

"We'll have to keep trying, won't we, Bino?"

"Will you return, Nica?"

"Better to ask Signor Argento; he may have other ideas. He knows where to find me. Tell him to bring my coin there?"

"Must you leave?"

"Si'. Though if not soon, you'll have these drawings to keep you company, no?"

He blushed and withdrew the drawings from her sight.

An awkward moment followed before Nica covered herself and stepped forward. She reached for his right forearm with both hands and held it firmly. "So strong," she said. She kissed him on the cheek before whispering, "Practice," in his ear.

They separated and regarded one another for a moment before Bino bowed and pledged, "I hope you found me worthy, princess of Monaco."

With a grin and nod Nica stepped away, placed her feet into sandals and raised her cape about her robed shoulders. She left the studio without speaking another word.

When Signor Argento returned, he heard humming and observed Bino's enthusiasm. The artist was smiling, light on his feet and owned the posture of a more confident man.

"Well?"

"What?"

"How did your morning go?"

"Since you ask, it went well. Nica, I mean the woman, cooperated and made my work much easier."

"I'm sure of that. Let me see your drawings."

"Let me finish first. We worked on two positions and…"

"Positions? I underestimated you, Bino! Better the experienced hen invites the young cock to play, no?"

"No, no, it is not what you think. Anyway, you must make it possible for her to come again; there are other poses you would wish for a bath scene."

"I see. The first pose is, shall we say, *a casa*—the rest you pay for. Understood?"

"That is fine. If you tell me where to bring her pay, I'll explain the arrangement."

"Leave the wench to me. The more beautiful you render her, the richer I become."

After their meal and the setting of the sun, Bino retired to his room. He lit a candle, reclined on his straw bed and relived the events of the day. Nica occupied his every thought, her flesh his imagining. He positioned Nica's drawings opposite his candle and studied both one last time before extinguishing his candle. He recalled the comfort between them and regretted the words he lacked the courage to speak.

There was no prayer that evening, only his intention to yield to Nica's request. The saints would still be there tomorrow. *Practice* he would this night.

Bino rose refreshed the next morning, fed on a little bread and asked Signor Argento for a canvas and supplies with which to lay out his bath scene.

Pointing to a curtain-draped closet opposite them, Signor Argento responded, "We aren't rich with oil like Master Scotto so use what I purchased yesterday with care."

Bino found a corner of the studio near where Nica had sat the day before. He carried and placed his sketches there before setting his large easel adjacent to the chair. He lifted and positioned his canvas upon the easel before staring at the blank surface.

He closed his eyes and imagined Nica in various stages of undress. Her scent seemed to linger and her tangled mass of black hair, dark eyes and blemish-free shoulders aroused him, distracting from the task at hand. Bino opened his eyes and held his pencil sideways against the canvas. He turned it end-over-end, measuring the distance across. Satisfied, he began to sketch their patron's fantasy.

Five nymphs would occupy this scene and he imagined one semi-immersed in the center, two on one side entering the water and two on the other beginning to disrobe. The girls on the right he drew in profile—one delicately leaning over, touching the surface as if to measure the water's comfort, and the other placing her tunic upon the shore. Those on the left reclined at pool's edge—a stone outcropping beyond which he sketched hills and trees.

Nica's likeness filled the center position well—the other four figures played subordinate roles. Once begun, Bino was lost in its execution. After applying color to his illustration, the canvas became a collage of flesh and water set before a garden landscape. Hours passed and the artist felt neither hunger, thirst nor guilt at his unusual commission.

Bino was distracted only by an insect making its way up his shin towards a knee. He looked upon it with curiosity before lifting it delicately with his free hand and moving it out of harm's way. He returned to his stool and regarded the painting.

What he saw was his departure; this was not an interpretation of the Holy Trinity. It was not a pious view of Saint Catherine. Nica was its subject—an unabashed goddess whose naked beauty demanded God be reasoned as equal parts sculptor and savior.

Bino wanted Nica's company again and soon. One visit wasn't enough. Her physical appeal was undeniable but he had glimpsed something else. It was quiet and beautiful - surely more than could be mined in one sitting. Nica had been patient with him, kind even, and her eyes betrayed a secret she wasn't yet ready to share. Before him, on canvas, his *muse from Monaco* was delivered from poverty by her true nature. *Could the same be achieved in her world?* Bino pondered his intention and thought it possible.

Bino was stirred the following morning when Signor Argento's nameless patron arrived. He had come to sample the artist's progress. Bino threw clothes on, washed his face with day-old water and rushed down the ladder to the studio below. There he observed Signor Argento hand his illustrations to their guest.

The man was just beyond middle-age and well-appointed with a salt-and-pepper beard, cap and a dark military cloak about his shoulders. His complexion was scarred and ruddy and his expression joyless.

Bino approached the man and extended a hand in good will, "Good morning, Signor, I'm Bernardino or Bino if you prefer."

The man did not reach for Bino's hand. Instead he inspected Bino from head to toe and returned his attention to the drawings. "Where are you from?"

"Excuse me?" replied the artist.

"I asked where you are from."

"Forgive me. I'm from the village on the eastern shore of the great lake—Luino. Have you been there?"

Without pausing the patron responded, "Not unless there was reason to be."

Bino lowered his hand, feeling the sting of discourtesy.

"Is this all you have?" the patron asked.

Argento spoke up, "We've only begun this week, Signor—there will be more."

Bino retrieved his covered painting from across the room. "There is also this."

Bino delicately removed a dust cloth before handing the painted canvas to Argento. His mentor studied it, recognized the girl at its center and understood at once the quality and effort behind it. Argento remained silent, knowing better than to presume its appeal to a customer. He handed the piece to their guest.

The visitor studied it as Signor Argento, looking over his shoulder, marveled at Bino's execution, colors and the innocence of the bathing scene's subjects.

"I have no want for this. I'll take the drawings."

Bino reacted with surprise and silence while his employer delicately remonstrated, "Signor, surely you'll want the painting—look at the color, the brushwork."

The visitor insisted, "The drawings and nothing more."

"But why, what would you prefer? We wish to please."

"I ask for a bath scene and instead you give me a *baptism*. Your boy reveals nothing—an arm, a leg, a breast. What are these to my cause?"

Signor Argento understood what Bino did not. "I see. I beg you return next week, Signor. We'll have what you're looking for."

The man regarded Signor Argento for a moment, extended his hand with two coins in exchange for Bino's drawings and spoke, "I won't have you waste my time; be prepared for my next visit or it is sure to be my last."

Their patron fled and Bino, pleased not to have forfeited his fondest reminder of Nica, returned his painting to its position across the room. Signor Argento approached him and spoke.

"Bino, do you understand what happened here?"

The artist responded, "No, though I'm pleased we don't require clients of his kind."

"Bino, you don't understand. Our guest, men like him, don't see women as you do. You see beauty and tenderness. He and those with whom he keeps company see a distraction from all the ugliness they carry inside. You see the prospect of life-long affection; he wants your painting for no other purpose than to arouse his imagination and forget all which haunts him."

The truth of Argento's words was undeniable and Bino listened with care as Argento continued.

"I'm neither like you nor this client. I have seen your drawings, admired your paintings and have even read the poetry you're too embarrassed to admit is your own. I'm a mule while you're more a priest than the pretenders in Rome. But I have been poor and hungry, Bino, and disliked both enough to know I shant let pride make either likely again."

Bino turned to face him. "What are you asking for?"

"You have an extraordinary gift. Use it to give our patron what he wants."

"What he wants? What purpose is served satisfying his twisted lust? Aren't we just encouraging him to be less than human?"

"I ask you to overlook his peculiar tastes because he *is* human and something far more important—he will *pay* us handsomely."

"Pay, pay! All I've heard since arriving in Milan is *pay*. I ask only for enough to fill my bowl and decorate my canvas. But I grant I know little of your world, Argento." Bino shook his head from side to side, resigned to serve while disagreeing about the reward for doing so. "I hope it's as you say, Signor. Money doesn't make all offenses easier to bear."

"You'll come to my way of thinking, son, and enjoy doing so."

"What would you have me do?" responded Bino.

"Invite the girl back, strip her bare and reveal everything with your brush."

The crudeness of Argento's request troubled Bino. "And what if she objects?"

"Women like these never object to feeding the hunger of men. They reason it better to have the coin of fools than the respect their chastity once deserved."

"I'll do what you ask but I won't like it and I won't put my name to it."

"Fair enough Bino. 'Tis better the secret remains ours."

Bino

Bino felt anxious the afternoon Nica returned to the studio. He understood and accepted Argento's defense but remained ill at ease with a project he thought vulgar. When he woke that morning, he relieved some of his guilt by writing to his mother. He spoke of Milan, valuable experiences won but nothing of the compromises he felt compelled to make. He imagined her reassurance and felt better for it. Antonia was the source, he reasoned, of the grace and patience that sustained him.

Expecting Nica, Bino freshened up. He went so far as to borrow a superior blade from Signor Argento to rid himself of the shadow darkening his complexion. The tavern maid was due within the hour and he wasn't sure he had the words to describe his dilemma. *Wouldn't it be better to tell her the truth about my project and let her decide whether she wished to be used in such a manner?*

It was still early and Bino heard the studio door open and close; he didn't bother to glance downstairs since Argento was also expected. When no footsteps followed, Bino grew suspicious and descended the loft ladder. At its base he spun about and saw Nica leaning there, her back supported by the door. Her eyes bore into him and hinted at comfort and confidence.

Bino approached and sensed something different about her. Her hair was no longer pinned above her head but hung delicately around sun-colored cheeks and nearly bare shoulders. A loose-fitting dress fell below her knees while her arms and hands were drawn up behind her back.

His eyes widened. *What man wouldn't trade places with me at this moment?*

She understood his appreciation and wasn't above teasing him. With a seductive look and a deliberate whisper, Nica inquired, "Was I missed, *ar-tee-sta*?"

Following her lead, Bino smiled and replied, "You never left me, poor and virtuous princess of Monaco."

Nica giggled and put her host at ease. "Unfair! I call you what you are; you call me what I pretend to be."

"How would I know who you are? You wouldn't even share the name your mother gave you."

"Better that way, Bino. Argento spotted me on Strada Mercato and said you wouldn't mind if I arrived early. Are you pleased to see me?"

"I am. My recollection of you is a poor substitute for the real thing."

"You're kind to say so but Argento knows many willing to sit for you."

"No other would do."

Bino was being honest. He had thought of little else since Nica had left and Argento's invitation to have her return and strip bare fueled his own fantasies. He could no longer deny his loneliness and need for intimacy. Nica elevated and excited his senses enough to make him wonder. He worried the effect she had on him would make it impossible to ever return to Scotto's dull studio. Or worse, could he become someone easily manipulated by Argento for unholy gain?

Nica pushed herself away from the door and stepped towards the place she had occupied the first morning. "What shall we try today?"

Bino's cheeks warmed as he pondered the question. *Would she notice?* "I don't know. Is there something you'd like to try?"

Nica turned and studied him. "You have a secret desire, don't you, Bino?"

Marveling at her perception, the apprentice protested. "I have no secret. I was just wondering how a poor and less virtuous girl from Monaco might appear while waiting for her prince."

"You surprise me, artist."

"I'm sorry. Forget…"

"No, I'm not offended. Your imagination is safe with me."

Nica stepped towards him and looked through his eyes. "I like your idea. If we were outdoors and were to dine in the woods, where might my prince lay his picnic cloth?"

Bino glanced about the room, hoping for a comfortable reply. He moved towards Argento's straw mattress in the corner and with newfound courage, repositioned it so it benefited from the light. He threw a clean sheet down and rested three lilac stems remaining from a still-life engagement upon it.

"May we pretend you reclined here?"

Nica wore a curious smile and stepped towards the flowers. She bent at the waist to retrieve one and lifted it to her nose. "The aroma grows one's appetite."

When she leaned into the light, Bino was treated to Nica's semi-transparent figure. There was the roundness of her bottom, the space between her thighs and the tapering of her calves to delicate ankles. His eyes relished the unexpected gift—one the artist wished he could freeze and enjoy a little longer.

Nica pinched a part of the lilac blossom between her thumb and forefinger and moved the moist residue to the back of each ear. "This will do," she said.

The tavern maid shifted her eyes from the blossom to Bino. She observed his casual posture, arms crossed over his chest and forearms displayed to their best advantage. "What is it?" he asked.

"Your arms; they are strong and yet delicate enough to draw and paint."

Bino was unaccustomed to compliments and said only, "My father would have preferred otherwise."

Nica returned the flower to its place below before bidding him, "Turn away and I'll tell you when I'm ready."

Bino did as he was told. He heard little other than the shifting of her feet and the delicate sound of the straw mattress yielding to her weight. Two minutes seemed ten as the occasional poet grew impatient for the visual treat awaiting him.

Nica finally gave voice to the three words he longed to hear, "I am yours."

He turned slowly, preferring to sip rather than gulp the vintage offered him; Bino was not disappointed. He found her reclining on her left side without her dress and underclothes. Her body faced him and her right leg crossed the left in a manner that hid her sex. Her right hand held a single lilac to her nose while the other stems were positioned at her center. She looked alone as if waiting for her lover and there was a hint of sadness in her expression. Bino could only stare.

Impatient for a reaction, Nica asked, "Are you quiet because I disappoint you?"

The artist blinked and spoke, "No." He paused and thought. "I am quiet because I'm not sure I can render in a drawing how lovely you are. Your prince is sure to have his loyalties tested by one as alluring as you."

Bino reached for and lifted a pencil towards the ceiling while teasing, "My kingdom I surrender for this Queen!"

Nica laughed and held her pose, "Draw, Bino, while I imagine the prince's surprise upon discovering me under-occupied."

She didn't speak as a tavern maid would and Bino was given to wonder about her background and education. He would someday ask her but not this day. Instead, he began to draw.

As was true the first time, he delighted in each patient look, the texture of her skin and the slow rotation of her form from one pose to another. If this were work, he thought to himself, *why ever would I play?*

The artist drew and drew. He thought his muse masterful at revealing everything and nothing. She shifted expressions as deftly as a character actress with each page the artist let fly to the floor. What began as seduction evolved into looks of a more nuanced kind—melancholy, doubt, and resignation. She was, he believed, revealing what they shared; she looked very much alone.

Nica's circumstances and service to other men quieted her in the artist's company. Yet all her lips couldn't speak, her soul *screamed* to the only other person in the room—someone, she sensed, capable of empathy. Armed with her expression, posture and appetite, Nica revealed what she believed all vulnerable women sought, security and tenderness. *Will Bino notice? Could any man?*

The light began to fade and with it the warmth of the studio. Nica felt the chill and alternately rubbed the tops of her thighs and crossed her arms over her breasts.

Bino stopped drawing and paid closer attention. With his pencil at rest, all that was instinct and fire claimed him. He envied her hands as they roamed her figure, bringing warmth wherever chilled flesh demanded. To remain apart was torture.

Bino stood and moved with purpose to the door. He secured it with a hinged crossbeam before arriving at Nica's feet. She turned her eyes and attention to him and he proved no match for his other nature. He didn't speak. Instead he unlaced his shirt and lifted it above his head. He opened it, knelt and wrapped her chest and arms with it. She welcomed its warmth and aroma as the artist's focus shifted to her bare feet. He lifted, kissed and rubbed each in succession with oversized hands. No one had ever done such a thing for her and it felt indescribably good.

Bino kneaded the chill from her toes before ascending to her calves and the delicate flesh behind each knee. He was patient and waited until her sighs and expression invited him into her arms. Their eyes connected and Bino caressed her cheek with his left hand.

Nica marveled at his selfless attention and control. *Don't you realize I want you?*

She didn't finish the thought. With one swift swing of his hips Bino straddled her. He held his shirt tight across her arms and chest and told her, "I'm going to kiss you now."

She smiled at his newfound confidence and teased, "Better to ask me, artist."

He smiled and whispered, "May I kiss…"

Nica leapt upward, almost toppling Bino when their lips met with a ferocity exceeded only by her gratitude and his need. She used her right hand to rip free the shirt separating them and the union of their flesh warmed and comforted them.

The artist's hands sculpted the small of her back and shoulders while she held the rear of his head fast. His appetite drew him to her neck, ears and lobes before releasing her to the blanket below.

Tears welled in her eyes and she whispered, "Why did you keep me waiting?"

Bino regretted his lack of courage to act sooner and said the first thing that came to mind, "Doesn't the most satisfying meal follow the the lightest appetizer?"

"You're the first to ask permission for a kiss."

"How can that be, princess?"

"Enough words. Kiss me again."

Bino moved his lips to hers before shifting his attention again to her ears, neck and breasts. His eyes delighted in their perfection and he used his hands to guide the maid's nipples to his mouth and tongue.

Nica yielded to the artist's exploration and her soft cries assured him of her pleasure. With each breathy sigh, the artist's hunger grew and the throbbing at his core intensified. His mouth and hands painted her shoulders, arms and chest until she could take no more and seized upon him with a single word, "Please!"

Bino relented and kissed closed eyes.

"Are we safe here, Bino?"

He assured her they were and she responded with eyes open, "Then let me be your first."

He paused before asking, "How did you know?"

"The day you had to choose—we all knew. You looked so uncomfortable and believed yourself unworthy."

He might have defended himself but was rendered silent when Nica reached below him to release his sex from his loose-fitting trousers. She stroked him with a clenched hand before welcoming him within. His discomfort proved no match for her experience and she guided them to a satisfying rhythm.

Bino misread Nica's moans for discomfort and believed she must want their coupling to end. He sought his release and dipped his hips in rapid succession. Nica understood his response and restrained him with her legs and whispered words.

"Stay with me, Bino. Don't rush. Go slow and the reward will be better than you imagine."

"I cannot..."

Nica held him fast and placed a finger across his lips. "No words. Look into my eyes and do only what they ask."

The tavern maid released the pressure levered against Bino's hips and he was free to again move against her with a steady, less urgent rhythm. When his breathing and movement accelerated, she repeated her resistance and forced him to slow and penetrate deeper.

"Yes, like that, Bino, *va bene cosi'*."

The pace was maddening to Bino but with each instance she restrained him, his pleasure intensified. Nica frustrated his attempts to command the rhythm of their lovemaking and her strength proved equal to her resolve. When her breathing quickened, Bino felt her lift their hips off the mattress and press her fingers into the flesh of his shoulders. He was ready and stole control by placing a hand beneath her hips and holding her fast.

Their pace quickened and Nica was surprised by what for her was a rare and welcome sensation. "*Si', adesso Bino, si'!*"

Bino was lost in his own need and delayed no longer. He thrust Nica's arms above her head, pinning them to the straw, and mirrored her urgency. She abandoned all restraint and accepted him heart, body and soul.

The rush came and they grew dizzy with pleasure. He collapsed atop her and cradled his brow against her beating heart. When his breath stilled, Bino whispered, "You are an unexpected gift, Nica and I am yours."

Nica closed her eyes and embraced him. Gone for a little while were her mother's screams, the indifference of those who once cared for her at the orphanage and the fear which normally accompanied the sale of her body for another's pleasure. She knew the disappointment of her kind—the disappointment in believing *any man could rescue me from harm.*

She cautioned him, "Don't offer what you cannot give, artist. Pleasure isn't love and love isn't pleasure."

Bino accepted her doubt and kissed her lips before falling to her side. He was too tired to interpret the string of emotions cascading through his mind: satisfaction, gratitude and something less welcome, guilt.

Nica turned to face him and studied the curious look in his eyes. As if to console she whispered, "We own a little of each other now."

"I don't understand, Nica."

"You will; it's a small gift only patient lovers share."

"I'm grateful you share this gift with me."

Bino rose and lit several candles. He returned to bed, reached for her hand and stared at the shadows dancing across the ceiling. He had more to say and their lovemaking made only the truth possible.

He began, "I want you to know something, Nica."

"Be quiet, Bino. Nothing need be said."

"Forgive me. I must." He paused before continuing, "Our patron, the man who pays Argento for my drawings."

"Yes, what about him?"

"He doesn't seek beauty. He wants only images of vulnerable women with which to quench his lust."

"Go on…"

"What right has he to see you or any woman that way? The money is of no consequence to me."

Nica marveled at his innocence. "Few of us have the luxury you enjoy, Bino. If adherence to God's laws filled the stomachs of bar maids, there would be no need for my sisters to lay with the lonely and miserable."

The truth of her words stung him. "I'm sorry. What would you have me do?"

"If he willingly opens his purse, let him have his guilty pleasure. One day we may all be forgiven."

"You don't speak like a barmaid and he may not be who he pretends to be."

"What is he to us?"

"To us he is nothing, but what is art that does not inspire?"

"You impress, Bino. First an artist, then a lover and philosopher. Be silent and kiss me again before a girl changes her mind."

It was several days later when Bino woke to the sound of Signor Argento humming. He rubbed the sleepiness out of his eyes, noticed the light pouring through the loft window and thought immediately of Nica. He wanted to visit her but she wasn't yet willing to share her address. He wondered if her circumstances were even worse than he imagined. Uncertain of Nica's arrangement with his less generous host, he had dropped spare coins into the waist pocket of her dress.

Bino rose and relieved himself in the corner waste bucket. The latter was attracting flies so he brought it downstairs intending to empty its contents in the rear alley. He despised the exercise since their neighbors were careless and the foul brew raised an awful stench under the summer sun.

Argento spotted him. "Ah, Bino. Be a lad and bring my *stew* out with yours."

"Will doing so grow my wage?"

"A rare joke from a serious student—you're learning a thing or two. It must be the woman, no?"

Bino held his breath and executed the foul task before returning to the studio.

"I've not heard you humming before, *signor*. Why the good humor?"

"Your *favorite* patron appreciates your work. He requests more pieces."

"Curious."

"Why so?"

"What twisted purpose could he have for such a collection?'

"That isn't for us to answer, son. His money is no worse and surely more plentiful than ours. Besides, I don't hear you complaining about time spent with the tavern girl. May I assume she's refined your *brush stroke*?"

Bino leapt to Nica's defense. "She is more than she appears."

"How can she be? What honorable woman would shed her dress for such a pittance and purpose?"

"Can't we do better by her?"

"What are you saying?"

Bino responded, "She gives the retired soldier what he wants. I am but the messenger."

"You're a fool. The girl would lift her skirt for a penny if the opportunity presented itself. Why would we pay her more?"

Bino fought the urge to scream and remained silent. *A mercenary couldn't be relied upon to understand.* He knew he could do as he wished with his own money and needed little of it. If help is what Nica required, it would come from him.

Padre Castani

Days of walking beneath the summer sun from Luino to Serono were not as isolating as Padre Castani feared. While he hadn't succeeded in convincing anyone to join his pilgrimage from home, the priest happened upon others curious about Pedretto's healing and all manner of miracles attributed to the Blessed Mother.

As they journeyed and crossed paths with those leaving Serono for cities as distant as Rome and Naples, the priest welcomed their stories.

We witnessed a soldier visiting Mary's shrine with an infected wound. After falling upon his knees, he rose and removed the wrapping about his leg; below remained only a scar as evidence of his injury.

My cousin traveled to Serono and made her appeal to Mary. She was afflicted with plague symptoms and was invited by a voice to leave her windows un-shuttered during the night. Who would ever consider such a dangerous thing, Padre? Within days her symptoms left her.

Padre Castani accepted the tales with patience and good humor. Even if they weren't true, he hoped to find in Serono a little of Mary's grace. He sought to rekindle the feeling that had invited him years earlier to a celibate and prayerful life. *Mother, let me honor my commitment to all your Son was and remains.*

Two days passed with the recounting of conjured miracles before the real miracle of Serono appeared before the priest and his fellow pilgrims.

The travelers stepped from the dirt path and studied the horizon where the outline of the grand church first appeared.

The day was hot and dry and no breeze blew to make easier their journey. Their comfort mattered little now. The church commanded attention and stood like a stone vault safeguarding a holy secret. It rose dramatically from the flat earth and dwarfed the only objects available for perspective—the original shrine commemorating Mary's visitations and a lone tree. Scaffolding, cloth and pulleys obstructed a portion of the structure but the cathedral's stones and style were true and a provided inspiration for those nearing the end of their journey.

Upon arriving Padre Castani likened himself to the stray shepherd who happened upon the manger in Bethlehem. Guided by a different star, he led his adopted sheep to Serono. His cloak was modest and his skin was moist with dust and perspiration. He had no gift to present to the Blessed Mother so he instead took a knee, lowered his head and led the group in prayer. The faithful set aside their hunger and thirst in imitation of him.

They found themselves in a heavily trafficked plaza fronting the church. A construction foreman noticed them and wondered how he would relay words sure to disappoint. With the day's quota of intrusions exceeded, access to the church would be denied. Still, he was a sympathetic man and Padre Castani's reverence wasn't unnoticed.

The pilgrims followed the priest when he approached the foreman and asked, "*Signor*, may we enter our Lady's church at this hour?"

The man smiled, crossed his arms and replied, "Until we give Our Lady the keys, Padre, it would be more correct to say *my* church."

The priest saw no benefit in arguing the point. "I see. May we enter your church? We've come a long distance and pledge to stay out of your way."

The burly foreman looked beyond the priest and thought a moment before responding. "Too many follow, Padre, and our work is much delayed. You alone may enter; the others must return tomorrow."

Those behind him protested loudly and the priest turned to them, raised his hands and urged calm. "Don't be angry with this man; like all God's children he has a job to do. Let's rest our weary legs in the shade of the church and pray our journey may serve as atonement for our sins."

As the priest led his flock away, the foreman called out to him, "Padre, you reject my invitation then?"

Padre Castani turned and offered, "Forgive me. I don't wish to appear ungrateful. Your invitation is kind but I cannot go where my brothers and sisters are unwelcome."

An old man pushed his way forward to reach Padre Castani. He carried nothing, leaned awkwardly to one side and had a tattered cloak thrown over his shoulders. He shifted his focus from the ground to the priest's eyes and spoke, "Padre, we've come all this way. Will you at least say mass for us under the tree?"

Padre Castani considered his own fatigue while noticing the pain present in the man's eyes. "If it's possible brother, I shall do it." And then not wishing to embarrass the man with an invitation intended mostly for him, the priest stepped aside and raised his voice, "Before offering a mass for Our Lady in this sacred place, I invite you to clear your conscience through confession. Sit now and rest in the shade of Mary's church. In turn visit with me so you might find the forgiveness afforded those with contrite hearts."

The words no sooner escaped Padre Castani's lips before a stiff and cool breeze swept over them. Some interpreted it as evidence of the Holy Spirit.

The priest and pilgrims captured the attention of two girls calling Serono home—young Caterina and her sister Isabella. Pointing to Padre

Castani, Caterina turned to her companion and asked, "Isabella, what's he saying?"

"The priest? He's making the best of a difficult situation. They won't allow the group in the church so he's calming them with an offer of confession and communion."

"Can we join them?"

"Us? What would an innocent like you have to confess?"

"I'm not perfect, you know."

"Well if you're not, I don't know who is."

"It might make me…. I mean it might make us feel better."

"Feel better?" Isabella looked at her curiously. "What are you going to do, Caterina, make up sins?"

Their attention was diverted by the priest. Padre Castani directed everyone towards the shade of the tree and church before establishing himself thirty paces away. He shifted his focus to the old man and those behind him, inviting, "Recall the words of Jesus, 'Be not afraid,' for our Lord is good, patient and, above all, merciful."

When no one came forward, Padre Castani sat in silence beneath the tree. The earth below its canopy was less dry and a small amount of clover cushioned his backside. He closed his eyes in prayerful meditation. A while later he opened them, expecting a string of those prepared to make a confession. Instead, not a single soul stood ready to speak.

The priest pushed himself to his feet, swept off his robe, cleared his throat and spoke. "Who among you has the courage to unburden your heart before entering our Lady's church tomorrow? Come and reassure yourselves of God's mercy."

Nervous glances and pokes were exchanged among his audience but no one came forward.

"I see," said Padre Castani before hearing some laughter from the crowd. *Are they laughing at me?*

He didn't see her there but at his side, in the shadow of the great tree, was a young girl.

Padre Castani lowered his eyes from the light and needed a moment before appreciating Caterina's size and seriousness. Her skin was bronzed by the sun and she wore a gray dress. Both stood in contrast to uncombed blond hair and blue eyes.

Before the priest could speak, Isabella rushed forward, grabbed the girl's hand and spoke, "Forgive us, Padre, my sister doesn't mean to waste your time. *Andiamo*, Caterina."

"Wait, please," urged the priest. "All are welcome. Caterina, is it? Please join me."

Caterina looked to Isabella before reclaiming her hand. Her decision sure, she accepted Padre Castani's invitation.

The girl's company stilled the priest's nervousness. He'd been anxious for the group at being denied access to the church and his inability to move them towards the sacrament of reconciliation. He knew Caterina, as one of Mary's innocents, could change all that.

Holding one of the girl's hands between his pair the priest began, "I am Padre Castani. Have you come with your sister to make a confession?"

"I'm not sure, Padre."

"Let's sit here a moment and you can tell me how I can help. Would that be okay?"

"I think so."

"How old are you, Caterina?"

"I have nearly twelve years and Isabella has twenty-one."

"Does Isabella look after you?"

"A little. Papa and Mamma are very busy so Isabella is teaching me to read."

Revealing his surprise, Padre Castani continued, "She reads, does she?"

"Yes, she does, and I'm getting better."

"That's wonderful. Would you like to talk about your favorite story?"

Caterina paused while thinking. "Maybe sometime. When I heard you speak of forgiveness the way you did, I thought you could help."

"I see. Do you think you've done something to hurt others?"

"I don't know." Caterina paused for a moment and looked down at the earth before returning her eyes to the priest's. "What if you see something wrong and don't tell anyone because it might hurt them?"

The priest observed the change in her eyes. "That could be the best question a child has ever asked me. If your conscience makes such a secret too heavy to hold, it's better to share it with Christ."

Caterina appeared undecided for a moment before beginning, "My Papa is a good man. In fact he came here to make Mary's church beautiful."

She paused again and looked away, unsure of her course. The priest allowed the silence to fill the space between them until a butterfly distracted them. They followed it with their eyes until it rested on a nearby root. It remained there, drawing attention to its winking, orange and blue-tipped wings.

The moment fed Caterina's resolve. "One day I wanted to surprise Papa with a meal. It was a day Mamma and Isabella were out and he was to come home for lunch. He called my name and because I wanted to surprise him, didn't answer."

The priest witnessed as tears pooled in the corners of her eyes. "I was wrong not to answer, Padre. I should have answered."

Padre Castani reached for her hand. The move startled the butterfly and it took flight. "Continue, child."

"I was hiding. When Papa didn't see me, he invited Signora Giovanna in. She is a widow my mother befriended when she lost her husband."

The priest felt Caterina's shoulders shudder and said nothing until a tear fell upon the top of his wrist. He understood what was coming. He didn't need to hear more but knew Caterina must give voice to her pain in order to heal.

"They said things—awful things I didn't understand. They did things, things I couldn't help but hear and see. I was there. I was there and said nothing. If I only had spoken, *I'm home Papa, Papa, I'm home,* none of it would have happened."

Padre Castani was humbled by the girl's confession. *What words can salve a wound like this?*

The priest used his free hand to gently lift Caterina's chin. Her swollen eyes were reluctant to unite with his.

"Child, listen to me. This burden is no longer yours to bear. By Mary's grace and her Son's mercy, I release you from what isn't your sin but the selfish choices of others."

Caterina looked hopeful but not clear on the priest's meaning. "Padre, I've said nothing of this to anyone. Was that wrong?"

"No, child. It was kind and brave."

"Mamma would be so hurt, Padre."

"Yes, and we would not wish the *penance* for this sadness borne by her."

"Is that punishment?"

"Some would say so. I prefer to think of it as medicine when our souls need healing."

"What should I do now, Padre?"

"Better to ask what we should do, Caterina. What I ask isn't easy. Can you continue to be brave?"

"I think so. What should I do?"

"You must first forgive yourself. You are not responsible for what happened."

The priest let the weight of his words sink in before continuing.

"We must then forgive and pray for your father and Giovanna."

Caterina thought and responded, "I'm not sure I can pray for Giovanna."

"And yet that is what our Father calls us to do, child. Can you do those things for Him?"

"I will try, Padre."

The priest released Caterina's hand, whispered a brief prayer and drew a crucifix with his thumb upon her forehead. "Holy Spirit, rest upon Caterina and her family this day and always, in the name of the Father, His Son and the Holy Spirit. Through God's grace, I release you from this burden. You may go now, child."

The priest looked up, expecting to see Isabella. What instead greeted him, in the shadow of the afternoon sun, was a line a dozen persons long. The oldest pilgrim led the way.

"Look, Caterina," the priest said. "Look at the small miracle your courage inspired."

The girl smiled as Isabella approached.

"Padre Castani?"

"*Si'*, Caterina?"

"Would you like to see the church later?"

"You can make such a thing possible for me and those who've remained?" he asked, gesturing to the smaller crowd.

"I can't, Padre, but Papa can."

"Be it so, bring him to me when he's finished with his work." And then looking again at the line. "And I'm finished with God's."

Caterina

Caterina knew the cathedral's nooks and secrets better than the foreman himself. Her father welcomed her company and it wasn't long before her patient interest led her to make ready the correct tool to carve lumber or score stone. His daughter never appeared to tire and he didn't fully appreciate the delight she experienced watching him reveal the beauty hidden within wood and stone.

The stonemason was unaware of Caterina's discovery of his tryst and so had no explanation for her more frequent visits to the church. Few could be ignorant of her arrival. Each day since that fateful day, Caterina lifted her voice to the cupola above and bellowed, "I'm HERE, Papa! Papa, I'm HERE!"

Caterina resolved to protect her father. Whenever Giovanna brought a snack or meal to the church for him, she would intercept her, express gratitude and gift the food to anyone but him. *Forgive me, Mary; I mean only to make things right.*

On the day of her introduction to Padre Castani and first confession, Caterina winked at the construction foreman, skipped past the sentry at the side entrance of the church and sought out her father. It was midafternoon and she found him resting with his crew; they were seated upon a column lying diagonally across the floor. The men shifted their posture and tongues when the innocent girl approached.

Her father noticed the curious bounce in her step and the broad smile across her lips. *You grow more beautiful each day.* When the attention of his men fell upon her, his mood changed to one of concern. "*Carina*, what news do you bring from outside?"

"*Ciao*, Papa! A new group of pilgrims arrived after lunch. There are a few dozen people and the foreman said they couldn't come inside."

"He must do his job, Caterina, as we do ours."

"I know, Papa, it's just that a kind priest kept them from giving the foreman trouble and he won't abandon them to come inside. Instead, he's hearing confessions and saying mass."

Wise to her intention, the stonemason interrupted, "I can't let them in, Caterina."

She twisted her blonde hair with her right hand and replied, "I know, Papa; there is too much to be done here."

He noticed *that peculiar smile* and knew she wasn't finished. "Let me guess, Caterina, you have an idea."

"It's really your idea, Papa; you've always said there is no point in picking up a tool when shadows fall upon the wood and stone."

"True, I have."

She pointed. "Aren't those shadows there, where you've all been working?"

The men's eyes moved in unison to where the delicate girl pointed. Seeing the potential for an early dismissal, one of the crew spoke up, "She isn't wrong, *capo*."

The stonemason smiled and shook his head. Knowing his daughter's persistent nature and the chance of getting anything more from his men in the diminishing light, he stood and declared to his crew, "The afternoon is my gift to you. Use it well, soothe your weary muscles and return to me before the cock crows. Am I clear?"

They cheered in unison, "*Si', capo, si' e grazie!*"

The crew bowed towards Caterina and departed. She then directed her attention to her father and wondered at his patience with her.

Known to family and friends as Eduardo, the mason bent over to retrieve something from the floor. As he did so, Caterina marveled at the breadth of his back and the strength of his shoulders. Years of reaching for, lifting and manipulating stone and lumber added muscle to his frame. His image as a strong leader was softened by the generous curls upon his head and a nose wide enough to smell humor in challenging situations. His words were chosen carefully and rarely harsh and it was this truth his daughter most admired.

Eduardo lifted something from the floor into the light.

"What is it, Papa?"

"It's a nice-sized feather, *Carina.*"

"Was there a bird in the church?"

"Other than you?" he teased.

Caterina smiled and approached. "May I see it?"

"Yes, consider it my first gift to you. It looks to be from a dove."

"Truly? Mamma will say it's a sign."

A man of limited faith, Eduardo wasn't inclined to his wife's point of view. Still, never had he seen a bird within the church, certainly not a dove large enough to shed such an impressive feather.

Caterina twisted it in the light. "What's my second gift, Papa?"

"Second gift?"

"Yes, you said this was my first gift. What's to be my second?"

Eduardo leaned over and kissed the top of his daughter's head. He lifted her chin with his left hand and spoke, "Time is short little one; let's go meet your priest."

While he waited by the door, Caterina rushed outside to retrieve Padre Castani. She found him with a smaller group enjoying the water and fruit villagers had offered them. Some of the pilgrims left seeking shelter—the rest sought food beyond the priest's consecrated bread. Their souls were satisfied but their stomachs needed filling.

When he spotted Caterina, Padre Castani rose and embraced her.

"Child of Mary, tell me where you've been."

"I've been to see Papa and I bring good news. He invites you to come!"

"That is good news, Caterina, but I cannot come without those who would follow me."

"They are welcome too, Padre."

"You are a prayer answered, little one. I won't ask by what magic you make this possible nor will we tempt fate and delay." And then turning to his diminished flock, he said, "All of you, Mary provides. Be silent and follow me."

Caterina, Padre Castani and a dozen pilgrims strode past the church's main entrance and the puzzled stare of the construction foreman. The priest smiled and offered a cross in the air with his hand; he did not stop to explain. At the side entrance the group found a sentry, Caterina's father and a third man.

Caterina ran to her father's waist, looked up and pointed to the priest, "Papa, Papa, this is Padre Castani."

Eduardo shared a generous smile, introduced himself and welcomed the visitors. Extending his hand, the priest spoke, "Bless you; we are grateful for your daughter's kindness and your invitation. We will do our best to avoid distracting you."

"You needn't worry, Padre. There is light enough for your people to see but not enough for our labors."

And then to the pilgrims, Eduardo declared, "Your journey ends here; welcome to Serono's Virgin of Miracles church."

The group threw up a cheer and Eduardo continued, "Better you share your gratitude with Mary since She makes this possible—she and our late local hero, Pedretto."

Caterina and the twelve followed their guide inside while Eduardo paused before steering Padre Castani with a gentle hand. The interior of the church was silent save for the footfalls of those ahead of them. The priest inhaled deeply while his eyes adjusted to the diminished light. He could feel the chill of the surrounding stone and smell an aromatic mixture of lumber, candle wax and the perspiration of those who labored there.

Eduardo misinterpreted the priest's curious look and said, "We are years from finishing, Padre; I hope you're not too disappointed."

Padre Castani reassured Eduardo of his gratitude and began a ceiling-to-floor review.

The stone carver continued, "Once the foundation was complete and her walls grew from harvested stone, I was engaged to bring our Lady's church to life."

The priest looked at Eduardo and reassured him, "Your labors are not in vain. Progress may be slow but all that is worthwhile takes time. With God's grace you'll be present when her majesty is revealed to the Bishop of Rome."

Eduardo smiled; he couldn't imagine what such a visit would mean to the village of Serono.

He thanked the priest and asked, "Where are you from, Padre?"

"I have a small parish on the great lake at Luino. The journey might have taken three days but my feet objected and arrived in four."

Eduardo invited him to return when the church was nearer to completion. "You could be Caterina's special guest."

"It would be wonderful. And your daughter speaks so well of her mother and you that I may have no choice but to accept your invitation."

The priest's words pushed gently against Eduardo's conscience. His infidelity hung like a veil over his heart and he wasn't sure how to relieve the pain.

"Perhaps when our work is done, Padre, we'll have occasion to visit you in Luino."

"Our community would welcome you. Be warned though. We have nothing as grand as this to capture your attention. Our lake, though, is a gift—one that reveals God's majesty with each sunrise."

"And have you need of an engraver in your church?"

Padre Castani chuckled at the idea and thought immediately of the boy—the one he'd sent away. He thought of Bino often and wondered. More than a few years had passed and he recalled, as if yesterday, the morning the quiet young man had spoken with conviction about the empty church. "Your voice, Padre, may be enough for their ears, your words may be enough for their minds but these walls don't do anything for their hearts and spirit." *And those walls he brought to life.*

"Our church is a modest one, Eduardo. You could fit a dozen of her within these walls. But someone young once told me my interpretation of the gospel wasn't enough to inspire the faithful. He argued that a place of worship should delight the entirety of our senses."

"Few would agree more and yet I know many priests who would challenge such a notion."

"True enough. This young man proved his point, though, not with his tongue but his brush; he enriched our church with character and color. We were witnesses to his gift."

And then observing the tall blank walls and ceiling surrounding them, Padre Castani spoke again, "He would encourage your progress, Eduardo. I can only imagine what his hands might render on canvasses as grand as these."

Bino

It was Bino's twentieth birthday and no one knew it. *How could they?*
He had nearly overlooked the occasion himself and would have if a letter
hadn't reached him from his mother. She relayed news from home, wondered at his long silence and reminded him of the special anniversary of his
namesake—Saint Bernardino.

Antonina wrote that this was the centennial anniversary of the
Saint's ordination. Buried only sixty years before, Saint Bernardino was
still remembered by the faithful for his tireless care of Sienna's plague vic-
tims. Now the artist *heard* his mother's voice from a more-privileged woman's rooftop overlooking the cityscape before him. "Bino," she reminded,
"many of us owe our faith to your patron saint."

The artist found himself in a familiar place—close to his studio and
far from anything resembling home. He counted the four years since he
had left Luino and marveled at how little he thought about his family's
home. Questions paraded through his mind. Why didn't he write to his
mother more often? Why hadn't Padre Castani made his promised visit to
Milan? Would his father or brother ever care to see him again? He could
only answer the first. He would write to his mother when he was no longer
embarrassed by his work. There was honor in his feelings for Nica, but his
conscience resembled the view before him, a busy city obscured by the
smoke of a thousand stoves.

Through the haze he settled his focus on Milan's cathedral. It interrupted the landscape like a stone goliath towering above an army of humble Davids. He would not have designed a tribute to God in the same manner and his imagination went to work rearranging the church's proportions, lines and attitude.

It was time to return to his labors. He'd been excused during nap time—the hour during which the daughters of the house rested between portrait sittings. *I feel for them. It must be awful to sit still while their mother gossips on and on about little of consequence.*

Bino supported himself, palms forward, against a half-wall and focused again on the church in the distance. Guilt washed over him as he pondered his teacher and his friend—Master Scotto and Gaudenzio. At least they occupied themselves creating something more worthy of God's approval. *Instead I'm having my talent exploited by Signor Argento to affluent gossips and lonely soldiers. I must do something.*

Complicating his emotions was Nica. Since joining Argento nearly two years before, she alone was the salve for his tortured conscience. He saw little fairness in that and the truth scared him. His coins and affection seemed a poor return on her investment. *Saint Bernardino, indeed.*

She must be tiring of me. Three weeks had come and gone without a single visit. It wasn't like Nica and he was annoyed with Argento's excuses. "The girl is aware of your commission in the city. Why would she intrude when there is no coin to be earned?"

Argento's lies were bad enough but nothing troubled the artist more than his landlord's insinuation that Nica's legs were open to all. "You're acting like a jealous boyfriend. Would you deny others the pleasure of her attention?"

Are you with other men? Though afraid of the answer, Bino had put the question to her during their last visit.

Nica embraced his face with both hands, met his curious eyes and responded, "Because of your generosity, it's no longer necessary." Her response had comforted him while making her absence all the more confusing.

Bino returned downstairs and completed the twins' portrait to their mother's satisfaction. He made a quick retreat from the family's lavish home and, as was common, failed to collect the commission he was due. It was delivered by a sprinting servant bearing a leather purse. Once in his possession, Bino thought to use it as leverage and force Argento into sharing the truth about Nica's whereabouts.

Restless, lonely and hungry for Nica's embrace, Bino arrived at the studio and opened the outer door. He was relieved to find her there facing away from him.

I've missed you. The sight of her figure in the dim light comforted him. Her hair was arranged differently but what captivated Bino was the exposed flesh on the backs of her legs. Her robe was much shorter than the one he'd known and proved a welcome diversion for weary eyes. He was silent in his appreciation until she sensed his presence and spun around. The woman saw the disappointment written across his face and spoke. "You must be Bino."

The artist inhaled deeply and rubbed his eyes with calloused hands. "I am who you say I am. Who are you?"

The woman smiled at Bino and relaxed her hold on the robe gathered about her neck. She stepped to a nearby bench, sat on profile and revealed a leg and breast before responding. "Your mate invited me to sit for you. He claims you be as masterful as Leonardo." She looked at him suggestively and asked, "Was he exaggeratin'?"

Her words made no sense to him. He gave voice to the only thing that mattered. "Where's Nica?"

"Who?"

"Nica—the tavern maid. You know her by a different name but her coloring is like yours and she speaks incessantly of wanting a better life, better than her mother could hope for."

"I don't know. We all say those things."

Bino measured her and was given no reason to believe she was lying. He released from a different quiver.

"Argento, where can I find him? I want you to take me to him."

"I cannot."

He read something in her eyes that stole his sense of calm. Intuition took over and the artist narrowed the distance between them. She sensed the change of spirit and gripped her robe back about her neck.

With confusion and concern the maid stood and asked, "Must I give the money back?"

"You may keep the money as long as you take me to where Argento found you."

Assured of her reward, the girl found her boots, threw a coat about her shoulders and allowed the artist to follow. She led him across foot bridges, through alleys and away from the heart of the city. With each unfamiliar step and turn Bino felt farther from home and closer to what must be done. *She knows something and isn't telling me.*

They arrived at the tavern—one tucked away within the poorest quarter of the city. Bino could only observe the blighted atmosphere and marvel at any girl's survival.

She saw the artist shake his head in disbelief and countered, "It isn't so bad when you get used to it. Tis wer yer'mate comes for a good time, found me and the others; we help each other out y'know."

"Will I find Nica here?"

The girl looked at him sympathetically and responded, "I don't know which girl yer claimin be yours."

Bino looked about them. He'd never seen poverty like this and he needed to keep his breath shallow to avoid the choking odor of human and animal waste. The artist reached into the purse he had carried across the city and extracted a coin. He placed it in the woman's palm and said he intended no harm.

"I believe yer," she said, sincerely, before turning away.

Bino stepped into the tavern and allowed himself a generous breath. The odor shifted from waste to stale port and perspiration. *How does anyone get use to this?*

The room grew silent. Bino stepped forward and a plank underfoot shifted and drew further attention to his arrival.

"I'm looking for a girl," Bino said loudly.

No one responded.

"I say I'm looking for a young woman, dark of hair and eyes and generous with her smile. She may have mentioned a man named Argento or sitting as a model in my studio."

"Leave will ya!" a woman's voice rang out from the shadows.

Bino searched for the voice and not finding it, asked again, "Do you know her? I'd like to give her something."

"I bet yer would, like that last bastard."

A stout and wrinkled woman pushed her way into the light. She was short and round and carried an expression that left no doubt to her meaning. "Be gone! Boys with soft hands don't belong here."

"Has someone hurt the girl then?"

"Let the girl be, damn yer; she may one day be well enough to care for her child."

Well enough! Child? The words fell like bricks upon Bino's heart. *Who would do such a thing?*

Bino was afraid for Nica and began to protest when several male patrons rose from their benches and stood with the woman.

"Yer best leave," she repeated.

With no visible support for his cause, the artist exited.

Helplessness dampened his senses. Bino could neither hear nor see well; all around him felt and looked gray. Even the stench that so bothered him before was barely noticeable.

"You!"

Bino was woken from his stupor by a small, red-bearded man pushing against his left arm. His eyes were bloodshot and his breath revealed drunkenness.

"What is it?"

"What have ya in yer purse?"

"Leave me be."

"Would ya share it w'me if I took yer ter da girl?"

"Don't fool with me, old man."

"I'd rather drink w'yer den fool w'yer."

There was something believable in the man's voice and Bino assigned little value to Argento's coins save their utility in finding Nica.

The artist opened his purse, extracted two coins and put them into the soiled outstretched hand of the little man. "Two more will be yours if you take me to the right girl."

"Don't tease me, boy, I've got plenty a punch left n'me."

"Take me to the girl. The money matters nothing to me."

The man grabbed Bino's sleeve and pulled him in the direction of the alley. The artist followed—unintimidated by corridors as foul as they were unfamiliar. They were not ten minutes from the tavern when a steady rain began to fall. Not long after, the small man stopped, coughed and spun around.

"Dis be where she lives."

"How do I know you're telling the truth?"

"I ner lie wid my next drink or meal at risk. Y'll find er here, lad."

Bino made a sign of the cross and dropped two more coins into the open palm of his guide.

The worn man noticed Bino's gesture and hesitated only a moment before closing his hand about the coins and saying, "Was me t'know yer wer a Christian, I might'a done yer fer nothin'."

Before his conscience interfered with his luck, the tavern dweller shuffled away. Bino turned and stared at a thick and bruised wooden door. He rapped upon it gently before letting himself in from the rain.

Amidst the darkness he heard a familiar voice inquire, "Who's there?"

"Io sono l'artista, Bino. I come to find my friend, Nica."

There was no response and Bino continued, "Nica, is that you?"

"Go away, Bino; you shouldn't have come. I can't visit you anymore."

"Why? What's happened? Has someone hurt you?"

There was more silence, through which Bino thought he heard a muffled cry. He stepped forward and turned past the entryway into a candle-lit, windowless space. Nica was on the floor facing the wall. She was curled under a blanket atop a frameless straw mattress.

Bino approached and knelt next to her bed. Without raising a hand to soothe her, he whispered, "Nica, what's happened?"

She produced a desperate sigh and whispered haltingly through tears, "They came and wouldn't leave. I begged and begged but they had no souls to reason with."

"Who came? Who hurt you?"

She continued, "You were right, Bino. The sick soldier came with another. He said he paid handsomely for me and intent on making a man of his son.

The words made little sense to Bino. *Sick soldier...son?*

"I don't understand; let me help you."

"No, Bino, I don't want you to see me like this."

Nica stopped talking and held her blanket fast about her.

Bino persisted, "Please, tell me what I can do for you."

"You can do nothing for me. After it happened, after they stole everything from me, I begged my neighbor to take my child. I didn't want my son to see me this way."

"You never spoke of him. What's his name?"

"He's a bastard. He has no name."

"He can have my name."

"You know nothing of the world, artist."

Her words stung and Bino chose the moment to reach out and touch her shoulder.

She screamed in protest while turning to face him, elevating her head and torso into the glow of the candlelight. The blanket fell away revealing her once-lovely form. The gruesome sight startled him and he fell backward.

"Do you see? See what those animals did to me?"

Bino found it hard to look at her. Nica's right eye and the cheek below it were swollen and purple. There were teeth marks upon her neck and one of her breasts. Bruises marked her arms where blows had fallen.

"Why did they come, Bino? Why did they have to come?"

The artist was repulsed and dumbstruck. When he could look no more, he pushed himself off the dirt floor and turned away. His mind raced—at once filled with guilt and anger.

"You. Your son. What have I invited upon you? I'm so sorry, so very sorry."

Nica wept into her blanket and looked away. "Leave me, Bino. You won't ever be able to look at me again without shame."

He spun around and argued, "No, it's not true. I'll come back, Nica. I'll come back and take you and your son away from this awful place. We'll find the men who did this to you and have justice."

"You don't understand, artist. Your place could never be with me. Women like me don't escape. Our fate is to be used and used again. I have nothing left to offer you."

"Nica, please, don't send me away. In time…"

"I have no time for hope; I have only to care for my son."

Bino turned in the direction of the entryway, his face a mix of confusion and disgust. He thought of saying something more but could find no words beyond, "Why God?"

He fled the darkness in favor of the rain.

Nica

A week earlier

Nica kissed her drowsy son on the cheek before lifting a wool blanket over his bed clothes. They shared two rooms and this evening she found his space lit well enough by the moon to avoid lighting candles. A candle spared was another two pennies in her purse.

The tavern maid hummed Luca's favorite melody and he drifted off to sleep. She kissed his forehead and knelt next to his bed. Buoyed by her son's affection and Bino's friendship, she felt sufficient gratitude to offer a prayer to whichever nameless god might be responsible.

Nica looked out her son's small window wistfully. *How long it's been since anyone proved he cared as much for me as Bino.* The money she earned at the tavern and through the artist's generosity gave her a sense of independence and elevated her spirits. Nica smiled and tingled below at the thought of his passion before continuing her thought. *Bless his simple heart, strong arms and gifted hands.*

She redirected her attention to Luca and made a decision. *I will visit Bino tomorrow and tell him about you. He is sure to understand. I know this now.*

Nica moved from Luca's narrow room to the larger adjacent one off the entryway. It was lit only by a small hearth fire four steps from her bed. Opposite the hearth were a table and twin carved stools upon which she and Luca enjoyed their daily meal.

She intended a bath this evening and filled a half barrel with fresh water. This was accomplished through six trips to the cistern located at the end of the alleyway. She would warm her bath with water heated over the hearth flames. The effort was a concession to her comfort and the chill of the season.

Bino's muse was near to transferring the boiling water to her bath when she heard voices outside. Chatter in the alley was common but these voices were unfamiliar. She grew suspicious and the flesh on her skin rose with a rap upon the door. A loud voice followed, "Are you there, girl?"

Nica didn't respond. She looked in the direction of the voice and realized her door wasn't yet barred for the evening.

Again came words she wished weren't hers to hear. "I say, are you there, girl?"

Nica took a deep breath and spoke up. "Who do you look for, sir?"

"We are patrons of Signor Argento and eager to make your acquaintance."

Signor Argento? "The hour is late, sir, and I'm not receiving anyone. You may visit me at his studio the morrow."

There was an exchange of voices outside before silence and the hope that they departed. She moved to bar the door when it exploded open against the shoulder of an intruder. A second man followed. Nica screamed and backpedaled. Two body lengths away, the unwelcome pair was hunched over and squinting—doing their best to identify her against the glare of the firelight.

The young mother didn't have time to leap into her son's room. She backed against the nearest wall and grabbed what she thought might deter them should they come closer; she lifted a stool and held it as a shield.

The younger intruder was drunk and disheveled and shifted his apprehensive eyes between Nica and his companion. The older and larger of the two was kneading the pain from his shoulder. Soon he lifted his eyes to hers and Nica felt the weight of his stare.

She didn't recognize him from the tavern. She would have recalled the ugliness of his pockmarked face and the contrast it offered against a neatly groomed beard. Both men wore expensive military-issue coats.

"It is her, son. The artist's work is true. Now we need only learn why she's been so inhospitable."

The bewildered son lifted his eyes to Nica and said, "My father isn't one to compromise; would be better for you to listen to him." Then to his father he bellowed, "Go ahead. Tell her, sir. Tell her why you wage war against your own blood."

"Silence," volleyed the old soldier. "The whore needn't know anything of your peculiar tastes. I mean to cure you of those this very night."

Nica glanced quickly towards Luca's room and then, feigning confidence, rested the stool on the floor before responding. "I'm afraid you're better acquainted with me than I with you. Why do you come at this hour?"

The older man took two small steps forward. "You ask the right question, girl. You see, I've so-far failed to diminish my son's unnatural appetites. I've tempted him with your flesh as revealed by Argento's boy but his illustrations aren't enough. No, I believe the only thing able to cure this half-man t'would be for him to experience the very thing. Don't you agree?"

The soldier didn't wait for Nica to answer. He turned to his son and asked, "Doesn't she please you, Rotto? Doesn't she favor her drawings?"

"Let's be gone, sir. This is madness…"

"Silence, Rotto! I swear I'll beat you in front of the whore."

Nica studied the young man. He looked desperate, hungry and embarrassed. His father wouldn't relent and demanded an answer.

"How can I answer, sir, when in the drawings she has no dress to hide her sex."

"True enough, son."

There was no mistaking the father's purpose and Nica raised her voice in protest. "You must leave; my neighbor arrives any moment and will do battle with you."

Undeterred, the old soldier took two more steps forward and looked through her. He grinned and gave voice to his intention. "Do battle? You don't understand, girl. I've paid handsomely for your charms. My son will taste the flesh I gift him."

Nica would have raised her voice but feared the fate which might befall Luca if he woke and was discovered. Instead, she implored them, "Please, I'll do what you ask, another place, another time."

Aroused by her fear, the old soldier decided. "This time and place will do. And if you're to be the boy's first, better this bed than the flea-ridden one you earn your meals in."

"No, please!" Nica argued. "Your son is sure to be more comfortable above the tavern—Argento will tell you."

"Quiet, whore! Rotto will prove himself here, away from those who might restrict access to your many treasures."

Nica shifted her feet, lifted and readied the carved stool above her head.

The old soldier laughed at her defensive display. "Notice her fear, Rotto. I'll help you tame this one."

The soldier grabbed his son and pushed him towards Nica. "Now, boy. Take her dress, now!"

The awful command sealed her fate. Nica would know the full force of Rotto's misplaced rage. With a volley of blows to her face and shoulder, she abandoned the stool and consciousness. What remained of her senses soon knew the taste of evil.

Bino

Winter rain fell as Bino rushed from Nica's home. The artist looked to the sky, hoping to wake from his nightmare, but the moisture failed to rinse the pain from his heart and conscience. He ached inside and felt the whole of his anger and sadness behind his eyes.

The artist howled like a lone wolf into the night sky before launching himself towards the end of the alleyway. He wanted to punch something. Instead he lifted two abandoned basins adjacent to the cistern and heaved them into the darkness. Each slammed against stone and brought screams of disgust from Nica's neighbors.

"Be gone, animal!"

"Animal am I," volleyed Bino into the night before sprinting out of the narrow passageway.

Unsure of where he was, Bino began to walk through Milan's damp and lifeless streets. There was no moon to light the way. He hadn't eaten or slept for hours and whatever remained in his stomach wanted to come up. He fell to his knees and relieved his gut—the aftertaste as bitter as his mood. Dio, *where were you? Why did you abandon her?*

Doubtful of his faith, Bino stood and moved again. He passed several homeless drunks and eyed each suspiciously. He screamed at them and anyone who might hear, "Why did you hurt her?"

He climbed a hill hoping to find a way to escape the labyrinth of alleys surrounding him but the rain grew in strength and limited Bino's visibility. Nothing looked familiar. *Where is the cathedral?*

The artist's mind and body occupied the same dark place and he couldn't fathom whom to blame. In an instant the answer was clear.

Argento! For a coin he must have given up Nica's whereabouts and brought the wolves to her door. He will admit to it.

A gust of wind nearly knocked him off his feet. Bino spotted steps and the prospect of shelter below. He moved underneath, forcing a rat to abandon its meal. His desire for vengeance yielded to a need for cover and he collapsed there.

Hours later the rising sun chased away the wind and rain and Signor Argento found himself alone in the studio. From below he called upon the artist he presumed to be asleep above and no response came. *Where is the dreamer this morning?*

Argento picked up a broom and began sweeping a puddle of rain-water back below the door. This done, he mounted the ladder to the loft. His apprentice wasn't present nor were any drawings of the new model Argento paid to visit Bino the afternoon before. *Was he displeased with her or so smitten they left together for an evening of entertainment?* Argento discounted the last possibility. He didn't know what to make of the poet's unusual chastity.

More troubling than Bino's absence to Signor Argento was the absence of the last patron's payment. The fee he'd negotiated was generous enough to make even a mercenary blush. *I'll share something extra with the boy.*

Argento was counting anticipated profits when he heard the studio door open below.

Bino stumbled through the entryway. He was cold, wet and numb from his night of exposure. He lifted his eyes from the floor and looked about the room; it appeared no different than it had the afternoon before. *Where is he?*

He lifted his voice. "Argento!"

From above came his response. "Be quiet, fool. Where have you been?"

Argento descended and looked at the young man standing motionless by the door. Something was different about him. The typically fastidious artist had wet hair, stained clothing and glassy eyes.

They regarded one another in silence before discomfort caused the elder to inquire, "By the devil, did you spend the night on the street?"

Bino didn't answer. Instead he stepped around Argento and retrieved a blanket from the same straw mattress where only a year earlier he had first tasted bliss. He threw the blanket around his shoulders obscuring the fire raging inside.

Argento followed him. *If he doesn't wish to explain himself, so be it. Let's talk business.*

"Did our patroness pay you yesterday?"

Bino paused before responding. With a voice softer than Argento could hear, he said, "I went to find Nica."

"Who?"

He repeated, "I went to find Nica!"

Argento didn't expect the news and wasn't sure what it meant anyway. "How did you find her?"

Bino lifted his eyes to meet his mentor's—the man Master Scotto had believed better suited to introduce him to a life fully lived.

"You ask how I found her? I found her helpless; I found her beaten and violated; I found her robbed of hope and the son you told me nothing about."

The news shocked and discomforted Argento and he looked away. "What you say troubles me; you shouldn't have gone." And then, as if to relieve his conscience, "I knew nothing of a child."

"All you can say is I shouldn't have gone?"

Bino ran his right hand through his wet hair, moving the tangled strands from his face. Patience abandoned him and he stepped with purpose towards Argento. He gripped his host's shoulders and begged, "Was it you who told them where she lived? I won't be lied to. Was it you?"

Argento attempted to back away but his intention was no match for Bino's will. "I, I…"

"I curse you! What price did she command? Was the profit from my regrettable drawings not enough?"

Argento defended himself. "The soldier, he mentioned nothing of his purpose. He only said he wished to meet the girl who inspired your work—a treat, he said, for his son."

"You Judas! You sold Nica as a treat? What did you imagine he would do with such a treat?"

Bino shook him vigorously before thrusting him backward across the room. "These twisted sods imagined the girl in my drawings was theirs to play with and they destroyed her."

Argento fell upon the tile floor and recoiled in fear. "She will heal, Bino; she isn't the first whore to accept unwelcome cocks in her bed."

Those words. Better nothing was said than those words. The artist's visual acuity dwarfed his other senses by a factor of ten and he imagined Nica's tormentors and Argento's undeserved label staining her beautiful nature.

Bino was overcome with rage. He threw off the blanket and reached for the hearth poker. He rushed with it towards his helpless landlord and swept it across his legs. Argento was unprepared for the blow and felt its full force.

The artist was mad with anger and drew the rod upward to inflict a second blow when a plea intruded upon his conscience from across the room.

"Enough!"

The artist spun about to face the voice; Bino was more than willing and twice as able to do its speaker harm. That all changed. The person the artist saw there was familiar and yet so unexpected, he was rendered still. The room was quiet save for Bino's breath and the thin wail escaping Argento's lips.

The visitor spoke again, "You've been here too long, Bino. It's time to go."

He was right. It was the truth. The artist stared with disbelief at his makeshift weapon before throwing it towards the fire. It rattled the embers there before settling on the stone floor. Bino's eyes returned to the intruder.

"We never knew you had a voice. All that time in Master Scotto's workshop, I, Gaudenzio, we thought you mute."

The visitor leaned upon his cane with his left hand while combing his mature beard with the right. "I was watching, listening and measuring you. I see the breadth of you now and know a little of the sadness you find yourself in."

"I don't even know you, *signor*, and yet I believe it fair to ask if you can help?"

"Help I can. If you agree, get your things and leave with me."

Bino turned towards Argento and said, "I wish to be rid of this place and you. I seek only restitution for the victim of this selfish man's neglect."

Argento said nothing, leaving it instead for the older man to offer, "We shall do right by the girl and her son, Bino."

With genuine surprise the artist turned to the visitor and asked, "How can you know this girl and make such a pledge?"

"It isn't the first pledge I've made where you're concerned. Come with me."

Carrying only his coat, comb and sketchpad, Bino abandoned Argento's studio. Few words were spoken between Bino and the aged man as they walked along the cold and damp streets of Milan. The odd-looking pair drew frequent stares from other pedestrians, shopkeepers and those leading coaches away from foul-smelling alleyways. To those hailing his guide by name, "Signor Piero," Bino observed a humble nod and raised cane.

The artist's heavy heart was muted by his companion's steadying hand and the fatigue borne of a fitful night. When Bino thought he could walk no further, they arrived at an outcrop of buildings adjacent to a grand church, known to the artist as Santa Maria delle Grazie. Master Scotto had often spoken of it during his apprenticeship.

"I've not ever visited this church," volunteered Bino.

"Yes, I know. There will be time for that. Today you wash and rest; tomorrow we talk. Agreed?"

"Yes, but please tell me who..."

"We agree then."

Piero stilled Bino's curiosity and entered the nearest of the stone buildings. Within it there was a great room with a hearth, stove, long table and countless chairs—all superior in quality to those the artist had been accustomed to since arriving in Milan five years before. Upon the walls hung tapestries with commercial themes associated with city-states near and far—Florentine gold, Venetian shipping, Roman architecture. Below on easels and smaller tables were maps and technical drawings and more than a few paintings by what seemed a familiar hand.

"This is my home," whispered Piero. He pointed with his cane. "You can bathe there within the large basin." He continued, "Follow me. You'll find your bed here."

Piero shuffled through a doorway to a dark space with Bino a step behind. The artist could see nothing inside until Piero forced a shutter open with his cane. Light filled the small room, illuminating a narrow mattress lifted above the floor by two thick boards and four blocks. It reminded the artist of Padre Castani's bed within the Luino rectory. To the right, below the open window, was a desk and chair. To the left was a chest—its lid sealed.

"I leave you alone now to rest and repair; there will be time enough to talk tomorrow. You'll find some clothes in the chest. Take what you like; they remain from men who exchanged their garments for priests' robes."

His host turned and stepped through the door when Bino appealed, "You haven't told me who you are. Before today, I've only ever seen you in the company of Master Scotto. I know of no reason you should know my whereabouts and invite me here."

The older man stopped and looked over his shoulder, considering the question, "Who I am is less relevant than what and whom I know. Today I am Piero; you may prefer another name for me."

Bino was left to wonder at his meaning while acknowledging any home was better than the one he'd left behind.

The artist returned to the main room and stripped off his clothing. He measured the temperature of the basin water before thrusting his head into its coolness. It felt to him like a second baptism—a reawakening of self and purpose.

Bino held his breath under the water, recalling his mother's favorite prayer from Saint Anselm: *Let me seek you in my desire. Let me desire you in my seeking.*

He lifted his head from the basin and filled his lungs with fresh air. With a wet cloth he scrubbed the dust and sweat from his neck, shoulders, arms and legs. When clean, he used a second cloth to dry his scalp, face and chest. The chill on his damp back grew uncomfortable so he walked to the hearth, dropped his cloth and turned. He couldn't recall feeling as welcome as he once felt in the company of Padre Castani.

Bino re-entered his bedroom, opened the chest adjacent to his bed and found clothes enough to warm his weary frame. Before putting them on, he lifted each piece to his nose, the scent from a dozen donors reminding him how far he was from Luino.

He sampled several shirts until settling on two layers—the first felt smooth across his muscular frame, the other coarse and heavy. As night clothes he chose a pauper's pant. What it offered in comfort it lacked in length, falling short of his ankles. Satisfied, Bino returned to the chest and discovered several stray objects things. There were two books with unfamiliar titles, a small quantity of paper, a drafting instrument and an ink jar. He withdrew these and placed them on the desk.

He was too fitful to sleep so instead sat at the desk. He focused attention on the ink container and shook it before pulling free its ceramic plug. He dipped the dry pen into the jar before uniting its moistened tip with the center of an empty page. He wrote two words there, *La Prima,* before expressing in verse his gratitude for the girl he'd left behind.

> *La Prima*
> *I came without expectation and you were there—face,*
> *   smile, flesh, hair.*
> *A treat you were to homesick eyes, beauty real—a*
> *   moon rise.*
> *Your name I never knew, your son the same. Your*
> *   heart ever true, my passion flamed.*
> *You were patient; I was weak. There was little of my*
> *   soul you didn't reach.*
> *Poverty and virtue you wore with care, asking little,*
> *   affection dared.*
> *So grateful am I. Could you ever know? I was a dark*
> *   canvas; you were the snow.*
> *Others may follow to quench my flesh-full thirst.*
> *They may be my salve, but dear Nica, you alone are*
> *   the first.*

Piero

The poet woke a little more than thirty-six hours later and couldn't fathom where he was. Gone was the street and studio noise to which he'd grown accustomed. In its place he heard monastic chanting—melodic and mesmerizing. He closed his eyes and listened to the chorus, unconcerned by the hour, the duration of his rest or the unique situation in which he found himself.

When the voices stopped, a rooster cried in protest and Bino rose. He pushed his shutters open, adjusted his eyes to the light and took notice of the odd clothes he'd worn through the night. *On whose back have you travelled and what say you of the journey?*

He felt the morning chill and moved to the adjacent room hoping to find a fire there. He was a few steps into the space when the old man noticed him and reacted.

"You live."

Startled, the artist looked towards the voice and found Piero at a table. A large volume was sitting open on a stand a full arm's length away.

"Forgive me. I don't wish to disturb you."

"Fear not, books I have aplenty. 'Tis good company I lack."

"But the stand, it's so far away."

"A concession to old eyes, Bino. Your sleep, it was good?"

"Oh yes, yes." He paused a moment before continuing, "When we arrived yesterday, I demonstrated poor manners. Forgive me."

"Confessions aren't necessary, though it was in fact two days ago you settled here."

"*Madre* Maria, can that be true?"

"It can be and is. It would seem not only your heart needed rest."

What could he know of my heart? "Yes, well…you seem to know more of me than I understand."

The old man retrieved his cane from the tabletop and used it to lift himself from his seat. He took a tentative step toward his guest before several more confident ones brought him closer. He looked intently into Bino's eyes before speaking.

"It will all be yours to understand, Bernardino da Luino. You might have heard of my son, with whom you have something in common. He escaped this place and left his mark even where none was invited."

"How would I know him? I am of no consequence in Milan to anyone but Master Scotto and a young woman who surely wishes she'd never heard my name."

"My son is Leonardo. Together we came from Vinci."

The claim was too preposterous to be a lie so Bino merely repeated, "You say you are the father to *the* Leonardo?"

"The very one."

Though Master Scotto and fellow apprentices were well acquainted with Leonardo, Bino had yet to cross paths with the son—the eccentric genius from Vinci. As the artist pondered the truth of Piero's claim, he couldn't help but imagine an altogether different father—surely one less mortal than the frail man before him. *Wasn't Leonardo born to gods— surely not a silent and vulnerable mystic?*

"You don't believe me," whispered Piero.

"In fact, I do," responded the artist before continuing. "Forgive me, Master Scotto spoke of Leonardo as lively, tall, with auburn hair and fair of skin—a lover of animals and music. I imagined your son's gifts to be a product of someone or something otherworldly. I mean no disrespect but you appear to be the father of one hundred other men rather than the one Lombardia knows as Leonardo."

Piero smiled. He couldn't count the occasions the same point had been made or intended.

"If it be a sin to be unremarkable, I am guilty!" he exclaimed.

"I don't mean to..."

No offense taken, Bino. I know a little of how Joseph felt in shepherding Jesus as I am no more responsible for Leonardo's hands than was Nazareth's humble carpenter."

It was Bino's chance to smile. "You give yourself too little credit, I'm certain."

"I'm likely to change your mind, Bino."

"Very well, Piero. By what good fortune do I find you interested in my escape from Signor Argento's workshop?"

Piero studied Bino thoughtfully, deciding what version of events was better suited to inspire.

"Sit, Bino. I wish to share my story with you."

Bino selected a chair across the table from the one the old man earlier occupied. They both sat. The room was quiet save for the growls of Bino's empty stomach and the gas escaping his bowels.

"Forgive me; I am as hungry as I am anxious to hear your tale."

The old man waved a hand and pushed a plate full of dry bread and ripe fruit towards his guest. When he was sure Bino was comfortable and beyond several swallows, he began.

"I am old now, but fifty years ago my wife and I occupied a cottage in the fruited hills not too distant from Florence. I made coin enough measuring the expenses and revenues of local farmers and lenders and an even better living when an important handshake was required. Our circumstances were adequate though unexceptional; the same could be said of our children."

Bino interrupted, "Surely your son exhibited…"

"Be patient. Like other comfortable men, I grew restless with my life and work and began to drink. There was a tavern nearby and I escaped there often. The hours away from my wife and children grew and too few kindnesses were shared with those who had a right to expect better."

The artist thought he saw tears well in Piero's eyes and for a moment nothing was said.

Piero took a deep breath and continued, "I attracted the attention of a tavern maid, Caterina; she was one of a pair employed there. As with many of her kind, she was attractive and uneducated. There was something special about her, though; she possessed a genuine curiosity about my circumstances and work. Never before had I been peppered with as many thoughtful questions by one of her age and gender."

Piero coughed and invited Bino to pour each of them a cup of wine. The elder sipped before continuing.

"I had no right, but I shared her bed, Bino. Not long after, Caterina grew with child and gave birth to a son. To her credit, she gave no voice to my responsibility. My purse was helpful but not her aim. Those early years Caterina sought only the boundaries and tutelage I could afford our child."

The old man raised his voice. "Our bastard son became the genius the citizens of Florence and Milan know today as Leonardo. The maid's attentiveness to his questions fueled his ambition and scholarship. She alone is worthy of our praise."

Bino was surprised and full of wonder. "And your wife, your other children?"

"Though I did my best to support them, they were casualties of the tavern girl's gifted child. When it became obvious Leonardo's genius warranted mentoring and a broader audience, I claimed him as my own and brought him to Florence; he was only fifteen at the time."

Silence filled the space between them and Bino let it linger. When no explanation for his rescue followed, he spoke.

"A remarkable tale to be sure, Piero. How am I a part of it?"

"Your humility blinds you even now, Bino. When you were but fifteen, a letter came to us from your parish priest. He spoke of you as proudly as the barmaid spoke of our son. He described someone with uncommon gifts, which, if honed, might one day rival Leonardo's."

The old man rested his cane against the table and rubbed an ache from his knee. He then raised his eyes to Bino's and said, "We never accept such claims, especially from those whom might have other motives. As a test, we had Master Scotto invite you to serve as apprentice. I came each day; I sat and watched your instruction."

"You said nothing. You offered nothing."

"True, but I left convinced of your potential."

"So little time, how so?"

"Throughout Leonardo's tutelage he arrogantly professed, *poor is the pupil who doesn't surpass his master*. It was that way with you. There was nothing left for Scotto to teach you."

"You give me too much credit, sir."

"And with those words you distinguish yourself from my son. You see, Bino, Leonardo never heard a compliment he thought equal to his genius."

The artist stood and responded, "You're not suggesting your son is unworthy of the accolades rained upon him?"

"Not at all. But it is one thing to earn accolades; it is another to insist upon them."

Piero's meaning was clear to the artist and he responded diplomatically.

"Can't your son be forgiven for letting the attention whet his appetite for more?"

Piero focused above and pulled at his beard.

"I don't need to forgive my son, Bino. I'm more responsible for his inflated sense of self than his mother or any patron."

"How so?"

"Just as the baker takes pride in his bread, I basked in the attribution of Leonardo's gifts to me."

"I am fortunate. My mother convinced me all talent was owed to God."

"A shame your mother wasn't there to convince me of the truth all those years ago."

Bino read the regret in the old man's eyes and recalled his mother's piety before changing the subject.

"Why did you come for me, Piero?"

"Why indeed? My time is short, Bino, and I have some fear for my soul. So while my son comes to terms with his legacy, I'm attempting to remedy mine."

"I don't understand."

"You wouldn't, would you? When I look at you, Bino, I see a man uninfluenced by the magnitude of his talent and the treasure it might yield."

"I don't share your son's genius, Piero."

"It would be more correct to say yours is of a different flavor, absent the greed."

"What would you have me do? I took Master Scotto's counsel and am poorer for it. Better I return to my mother and the parish of Luino."

"Rid yourself the thought. 'Tis one thing to forego the trappings of success while another to deny the people, the church, indeed the Duke and God, your creative heart and hands. Leave Milan if you wish; in fact I'll introduce you to the right people should you want to go to Rome or Venice, but don't return home. Don't bury your imagination and faith in the God of our fathers."

Bino circled the room. Visions filled his thinking before his intention settled on the one causing him the most pain. He walked towards Piero, took a knee before him and spoke simply.

"You once cared for a tavern girl. I cannot go forward and do what's best for me when my own tavern maid lays ruined. I beg you to understand. Though her son wasn't mine, I must atone for her exploitation."

"I know your pain, Bino. I might have saved Leonardo's mother but was too concerned with my own reputation. I asked her to remain in Vinci and it was there the cruel plague stole her. She died alone."

"I'm sorry, Piero. And I don't want that for Nica; she's done nothing wrong."

"Few can claim that and be truthful. We shall reach out to her in the days to come. She will recognize your kindness because nothing will be asked in return."

"I am unable to pay you for such generosity; I have only the clothes that arrived with me."

"Fear not, Bino. My purse is as heavy as my conscience. We'll endeavor to make both lighter."

"*Ti ringrazio.* My mother and priest would also wish to thank you."

Piero stood, pulled the artist to his feet and kissed both cheeks.

"Remain with me a while, son. There are things you must see and more than enough opportunities to explore."

Piero begged his guest's pardon to rest. The artist returned to his room and considered his host's remarkable story. He wondered at the small miracle—Padre Castani's letter falling into the hands of Leonardo's father. *Was it a prayer answered? Was it by God's hand or Saint Catherine's?*

After their midday meal, Piero invited Bino to follow him to the convent's refectory—the dining hall adjacent to the great church for its seminarians and women religious. The structure was generous enough in size to make Bino curious. Piero explained the building was intended to be the final resting place of the Duke, his wife and extended family. The Duke's recent arrest at the hands of the French allowed for its present, more practical use.

They stepped into an entry corridor and Piero waved to a young priest. While Bino's company invited stares, the old man's presence appeared familiar and raised no suspicion. They walked fifteen paces more before entering the dining room. Their transition from the midday sun to the hall's comparative darkness made it difficult to see.

Piero grabbed Bino's elbow with his free hand and steered the artist in the direction to which his cane pointed. Arriving at the center of the room, Piero stopped, turned towards the artist and invited him to focus his attention on the rear wall above his own shoulder.

"My friend, what is it you see?"

Bino could make out little. His eyes strained to adjust to the peculiar gray light seeping into the space from small windows on opposite sides of the room. And then, with subtle majesty, what appeared there begged his attention. The artist escaped so quickly from Piero's grasp, he caused his unsteady host to thrust his cane forward.

The artist was too distracted to offer an apology and stopped only when he could appreciate the scale of the mural before him. *What is this? Who was able to execute a thing so bold?* Bino paced to his left, back to his right, forward and back again—all the while straining to see details. He appreciated the genius of it and was at a loss to understand why the room was empty of admirers.

The mural stood as tall as three men and twice as wide. The artist hadn't seen its equal before—a painting unlimited in dimension and influence. Piero's intention was clear. Here, a mortal had been able to capture in two dimensions what Christ and his twelve apostles had experienced so passionately in three.

Piero was amused by Bino's reaction. "It is something, no?"

"It's remarkable; is this by your son's hand?"

"Do you ask because you think him capable of such a thing or because you identify me as Saint Andrew?"

Bino shifted his focus. There, seated at Christ's right hand, between James and Judas, was Piero's likeness.

He smiled at the old man and said, "You fill Andrew's sandals well."

During his apprenticeship, Bino had seen more than a few versions of Christ's last meal; none compared with this one and he couldn't pull his eyes away. He likened the mural to a painting with prose. Each of the twelve apostle's eyes, hands and postures provided a glimpse inside his soul. Here were ordinary men seated at table reacting to the impossible news one of them would betray a friend.

"Tell me what you see, Bino."

Piero expected the young man to answer while still facing the wall. He was surprised when Bino turned to him and spoke from memory.

"I see the darkness of Judas, his head below all others, reclining away from Christ. I see the soldier Peter leaning above him offering to defend his friend Jesus from a fate he cannot comprehend. I see the power of the Trinity—the twelve huddled in groups of three below three panes and adjacent to three doors."

"Good, very good. What more?"

"There is much more. Your son pulls our attention to the Lord whose feet lay as they did on the cross and whose hands reach for the bread and blood he soon sheds for all."

Bino paused and looked towards the stone floor and up again as if a thing just occurred to him. "And there you are, Saint Andrew, revealing your innocence with the emptiness of both palms—hands free of the stain of blood and treasure."

Piero smiled and said, "The former perhaps, the latter I'm not so sure."

Turning again towards the mural, Bino repeated the words he had oft heard Padre Castani say: "Mercy is a gift available to all."

"I'll soon see, Bino. I'll soon see."

Piero observed the artist approach the wall and noticed his pained expression after delicately touching two fingers to it.

"What troubles you, son?"

"Leonardo, this epic piece, it wasn't executed in *fresco*."

"No, it wasn't."

Bino understood the implication better than Piero. He understood Leonardo's mural would not last, could not last. It was as if the genius of Lombardia had rendered the piece with chalk on stone. It was destined to disappear in the storm that was time.

"What is it, Bino?"

Bino held his breath, unsure whether it was his place to explain. He would.

"Your son's mural, Piero, without the application of pigment on wet plaster, it cannot endure but in our hearts and minds."

"Leonardo is conscious of your criticism. My son, regrettably, is a restless and impatient man. It is also true the Duke may yet return and reclaim his burial vault. He and this mural were intended to leave the mortal world together."

The explanation did little to soothe Bino. Reflecting on the painting's vulnerability and unsure whether he would be invited to return, he asked. "May I remain a while? I would like to sit in the shadow of your son's genius a little longer."

"Of course. Return to me when you've enjoyed enough time in each other's company."

Bino was left alone in the silence of the great room. Thoughts and emotions stirred within and he was left to wonder, *Will I ever reimagine history so well as this?*

The artist was drawn in. It was as if the figures had noticed and invited him to table. Given recent experiences, Bino cast himself more as Judas than Peter.

Bino failed to notice a group of young religious enter the room. They gathered behind him, respecting his silence before beginning a solemn chant.

The artist didn't recognize the verse until the group arrived upon the words his mother had prayed at his bedside years before. He closed his eyes and listened to the entirety of Saint Anselm's blessing for the first time with adult ears.

> *God, teach my heart where and how to seek you,*
> > *where and how to find you...*
> *You are my God and you are my all and I have never*
> > *seen you.*
> *You have made me and remade me,*
> *You have bestowed on me all the good things I possess; still I do not know you...*
> *I have not yet done that for which I was made....*
> *Teach me to seek you...*
> *I cannot seek you unless you teach me or find you*
> > *unless you show yourself to me.*
> *Let me seek you in my desire; let me desire you in*
> > *my seeking.*
> *Let me find you by loving you; let me love you when I*
> > *find you.*

The words echoed through the hall and washed over him as a swim in the great lake once had. When the seminarians finished, all were silent and a single phrase lingered. The words were his confession—*I have not yet done that for which I was made.*

Bino opened his eyes, looked again at the mural and Christ's outstretched hands. He bowed to God and Leonardo, made a sign of the cross and returned to Piero's home. Peace and a renewed sense of purpose replaced the bitterness in his heart.

With Piero's introductions and counsel, Bino's talent was embraced and sought after by the church and its wealthy patrons. Student no more, the artist found a home within Milan's cathedrals. The clergy found in him the perfect partner, one who cared less for acclaim and gold than mythical stories expressed in vivid color on plaster walls.

Engagements of first months then years followed and a decade forward the name of the artist from Luino was synonymous with excellence. Across Lombardia, Bino's fresco work was unrivaled and prolific. The artist attracted the attention and admiration of the faithful and the envy of lesser men.

PART II

Bino

Church of San Maurizio, Milan—12 years later

Bino's arms felt heavy and he decided both his body and nature's light were done for the day. He lowered himself from his scaffold and thanked the apprentices who had earlier assisted in mixing and applying plaster to the cathedral walls. Through careful tutelage, they advanced as he once had and went about cleaning and preparing their tools for the morrow—the day the artist believed would conclude their labor.

Bino stepped back and regarded his work. After an investment of the last three years, the artist was both proud and sentimental for Piero. His friend had survived a mere four months beyond their reunion in Signor Argento's studio. And though their time together was short, Bino was convinced it was Piero's spirit and gentle whispers that encouraged free expression and distracted from his greatest demon—loneliness.

At first he wasn't sure whether to blame the demands of his craft for his not having taken a wife, or if it was simply that he hadn't met Nica's equal in vigor and beauty. Whatever the reason, he remained alone—content with solitude over what might have been a poor engagement. To those who noticed, he seemed more a priest in possession of a paintbrush than an ambitious artist committed to leaving his mark on the world. Rumored by gossips to be Piero's second son, Bino was unopposed to letting history's favor fall to "brother" Leonardo.

The artist looked at his frescos with a critical eye. He delighted in re-scripting familiar episodes within Christ's Passion and the lives of his disciples. He doubted sainthood could again be earned—*How could it be amidst such battling for influence, prestige and power?*

Bino had been the beneficiary of that influence. Piero had been well connected and his introductions, though short-lived, had been enough to secure the patronage of the church and Milan's moneyed families. *Can I be forgiven for exploiting these?*

In front of him was the likeness of Ippolita Sforza—daughter of the very house that had controlled Rome until pushed from power by Pope Alexander VI. Bino immortalized her in the company of three saints, embellishing her better features and hiding her imperfections. Ippolita had both money and influence and was grateful for the artistic compliment.

Bino recalled the wisdom of his late friend. Piero had spoken often of helping the poor while attending to the rich. "'Tis appropriate, Bino, that your soul relies upon Christ, but lean you must on the favor of the Sforza and Bentivoglio families. Lean on them, Bino, as I lean on my cane. Remember though, the cane and those in position to help you can be swept away without reason or remorse."

Bino accepted most commissions, even those on which he would have preferred to pass. He took little compensation and defended the practice with his peers by arguing bigger purses meant larger and more worrisome expectations. He refused to have his passion and talent held hostage for the coins and praise for which others cheated and lied.

The artist's San Maurizio frescos attracted the attention of visitors from Rome and Florence. Invitations arrived weekly from both cities and with these came promises of generous wages and students to support his work. He wanted little of the former and few of the latter and was attracted to a third, less conspicuous invitation. It came from an old and local Milanese church—one paying tribute to San Giorgio.

Its appeal was sincere and, in Bino, the church's patrons found a willing correspondent. "Bring beauty to our humble church, Bernardino. Make your home with us. Your prayer will be our prayer. Our table will be your table."

The artist left San Maurizio, having declined opportunities offered by privileged men in Florence and Rome. His polite rejections were misinterpreted. Those on the receiving end reasoned the Milanese fresco artist believed himself above their service. Bino neither noticed nor cared. Instead, he appeared one day at San Giorgio, entered the church unrecognized and imagined its rejuvenation.

The chapel walls and ceiling offered an open and unprejudiced canvas. Bino likened the expanse of plaster to well-tilled land awaiting a sower's seed. *What would you have me plant here, Lord?*

The artist breathed deeply and closed his eyes. He was alone again with Leonardo's inspired interpretation of the *Last Supper* and the haunting words of Saint Anselm: *I have not yet done that for which I was made.* He thought of his age—thirty-two—and the breadth of his journey. And then he thought, as he often did during restless nights, of Nica.

He imagined she was in his company and was pulled into her dark eyes. She took his hand and let it glide over her sun-kissed skin. His appetite grew and before long the swell of Nica's breast found its way to his lips and he tasted her there. He felt the tug of her hands against his hair but his hunger was of a different kind.

Bino recalled their second union and the mystery of her sex. His curiosity overwhelmed inhibition. His desire to see, taste and touch her was tangible and he trailed his lips down her flesh to explore. Nica protested until he arrived where no one had before and kissed her there. Her excitement encouraged and aroused and her aroma reminded him of his favorite boyhood place—the lake shore after a spring storm.

Nica wondered at his fascination and the maddening sensations it yielded. No person's lips had touched her sex before and she strained with her legs and arms to force him away. Her resistance only encouraged his appetite and his forearms wrapped above and below her, wresting control. She was helpless to his intrusion and an unnerving sensation of the most unexpected kind.

The poet felt her rhythm change. Nica stopped struggling against him and welcomed his exploration. He gripped and lifted the flesh of her bottom with his hands as if she were the plaster and his tongue the brush.

Nica whispered his name and they both moved with greater urgency—she not knowing where he was taking her or how the sensations in her stomach and toes were possible. She gripped his tangled hair in her hands and pulled the entirety of him to that small space. He responded by kneading her legs and hips until reaching for her hands and clasping them in his own.

Nica's breaths grew shorter and more deliberate as an indescribably pleasurable sensation coursed through her from somewhere deep inside. She gripped his hands and screamed, "*Dio mio, basta!*"

Bino felt her lift, shudder and quake. She gulped for breath and tightened the grip of her hands before the sensation repeated itself a second and third time.

"Madonna!" she screamed. It was as if one hundred candles were aglow inside her—all was light, heat and fire.

Bino's weight and position were no match for Nica's newfound strength. When she could take no more, she lifted his body with her own, drawing him onto her chest with open arms. She held fast his cheek against her heart and its rapid rhythm stilled him. She whispered words he didn't comprehend and felt the moisture of her sweat and tears.

Nica, I miss you.

A stray sound stirred him. Bino forgot where he was and looked around. He couldn't comprehend how this place of worship had suggested his most intimate memory. Though time and his labor separated him from Nica, recollections of their lovemaking were as vivid and real as they had ever been.

The artist found it impossible to set aside what had happened to her twelve years before. He was heartened by her acceptance of Piero's support and improved circumstances. What had his friend said? *Her journey isn't yours, Bino, and yours isn't to be hers.*

Months after they had parted and merely days before Piero's passing, his mentor relayed a letter from Nica. It contained only four sentences— words written with an unpracticed hand that said so much.

You know the truth. There is nothing to forgive. Reach with your gift into your soul and express what you grasp there. There, I shall also be, close to your heart.

There was no signature and no romantic allusion to a future they might share.

Nica's words challenged him and the artist focused on the blank canvas above—San Giorgio's altar wall.

Bino recalled the words of his boyhood pastor, Padre Castani, who had explained to his one-time apprentice the symbolism of the crucifix. *Accept and be heartened by the sacrifice Christ lays before us and know that He willingly shares your burden.* The priest said it was the authentic intention of the one true church and its greatest apostle, Saint Francis. To the patron of Assisi all suffering was temporary and necessary for redemption, truth and light.

Bino's answer came. *I know what I must do here.* The intention lived in him and with grace, he reasoned, it would find its way out. *Let it be so, Lord.*

When the day arrived for the artist to address those responsible for the care and beautification of San Giorgio's church, he was prepared, confident and at peace. Bino deflected doubtful expressions and rumblings while describing a collection of frescos depicting a unique approach to familiar themes.

"Wherever the mass is celebrated, we witness the cross and our Lord's human suffering. What are missing are scenes of Christ's courage—a courage born of his absolute knowledge of heaven and role in the Trinity. I propose to illustrate the wonder-filled reactions of those who called Christ son, friend and teacher. The others—those who didn't appreciate Him, won't share His courage but point to it."

Questions followed and Bino proved enthusiastic in reply; his proposal met with little resistance and permission was granted to proceed. He felt liberated, inspired and purposeful. He took careful measurements, completed sketches and prepared the larger screens—the cartoons to be pressed upon fresh plaster.

In total the artist imagined seven scenes from the Passion and Crucifixion. On the three altar walls would be frescos depicting Christ's mistreatment at the hands of Roman soldiers. Bino hoped the congregants would identify Jesus not only as Savior, but a vulnerable man, a man much like them.

Behind the altar, below the Lord's crowning, Bino imagined a large *Pieta*. He broke with tradition and added fifteen figures to the image of Mary cradling the lifeless body of her Son. Inspired by Leonardo's work, Bino illustrated the raw and physical emotion displayed by witnesses of Jesus' mistreatment and murder. Among them were an anxious mother and infant and other broken disciples, disbelieving their fate. Elsewhere Bino inserted Piero into the scene. *Wherever I share my gift, so too shall you be.*

Never distracted by the thought of what might have been in Florence or Rome, Bino made the most of his time at San Giorgio's. Free from the distractions of studio work and rigid schedules, he committed himself to his craft and improved. Alone with his tools and few assistants amid the chants of those in prayer, the artist discovered a peace unlike any he'd ever known.

When he wasn't painting, Bino enjoyed the company of the reverent monks living and working about the church. He was invited to join their morning and evening meditations and silent meal hour. He respected the sacrifices each community member made to one another and tasted the solitude he once believed existed only in scripture.

The hours and days flew by and visitors to his corner of the church marveled at his progress and the richness of the characters his brush brought to life. When asked to explain his remarkable pace and productivity, Bino made little of his talent and gave the credit to the brothers with whom he lived, ate and prayed.

Challenging work remained. The half-dome ceiling above the altar would be anchored by Christ's Crucifixion. Bino pondered the sacred image and sought to express the twin emotions his meditation revealed, grief and regret. He chose Mary and Magdalene to express the former—honoring both with halos and color-rich robes. Opposite them, Bino painted the company of soldiers at the moment they understood their culpability for the torture and murder of Jesus.

The project was faith-affirming and the irony wasn't lost on the artist. He sometimes held the heretical notion that he was recreating what he himself had witnessed fifteen centuries before. When visitors continued to marvel at his progress and inquire, Bino could only shrug his shoulders and credit God. Perhaps, he reasoned, some mysterious and beneficial force was at work.

His attitude would shift the day one of the monastic elders invited him to conversation. The prior was generous with his praise and shared his delight at Bino's seamless integration within the community of religious.

The elder priest went on to say that he believed the artist so skilled, the newest member of their community had been invited to join him as an apprentice.

Bino was troubled by the idea at first hearing. He let the priest continue and allowed the words to fill his thoughts before launching an appeal.

"Prior, I am unaccustomed to such praise and remain grateful for the opportunity to live and work among worthy men." Bino paused before continuing, "I wonder, though, whether you believe, as I do, that some men are born to instruct while others are meant to do."

"I'm not sure I understand your meaning, son."

"Forgive me. Accepting a pupil now would slow my work and handicap my crew."

"I see. Do you likewise believe, Bino, that your talent is yours and yours alone?"

"Not at all, I share it willingly through my art and…."

The prior held up a hand and began again, "We must guard against pride, Bino; I'm certain you'll little notice Brother Tomas as he develops his craft in your shadow."

There was no further debate; Bino was to accept Brother Tomas no matter how unwelcome the intrusion. The prospect of an apprentice didn't feel comfortable and the artist was forced to confront his own selfish notion. *Am I overestimating the harm? Wasn't Piero once such an observer?* Within days the artist had his answer.

The artist and his apprentice were introduced at an inopportune time. Sensitive work needed doing and Tomas put his own need for attention ahead of Bino's rapidly drying plaster. The seminarian might have waited, observed and learned but insisted he not be sidelined another day. The artist was forced off his scaffold and into interrogation.

Tomas didn't extend a hand or bow; instead he fanned his ill-fitting monastic robe from his generous waistline and asked, "Where are your people from, Brother Bino?"

Bino thought the question odd and answered the impolite inquiry by smiling and washing his stained hands in a barrel a short distance away. When he returned, he studied the newcomer. Above the young man's grey robe was a cherubic face of unusual size. Upon it were a broad mouth and too-small ears. As the morning progressed, the correlation between their sizes and deployment was not lost on the artist.

Bino began, "Brother Tomas, I'm told you wish to imitate our approach to fresco. How did you come upon this interest?"

Without hesitation, Tomas lifted his chin and said, "It was my father's idea."

Bino heard the words and cringed. "I see. Have you any natural inclination or schooling in the craft?"

"My French teachers said so and in fact often singled me out for praise."

"French? How so?"

"My father is an envoy of the church; his labors took us to Parigi and insured our safe return."

Bino was entertained by the curious confidence of the small and round seminarian and persisted in his questioning. "What caused your father to direct you to the arts?"

Tomas laughed. "Can it be that word of great discovery avoids Milan, Brother? Enlightened minds understand that our uniqueness and disposition are best framed by sacred astronomy."

It was Bino's turn to laugh. "The stars? The stars incline you towards artistic work?"

"Yes, and it would be ignorant to believe otherwise."

Bino absorbed the insult and pressed further. "Tell me more; did the Parisian church warm to your artistic tutelage?"

"For a time. I might still be in Paris were it not for its distractions; the finest artisans migrate there but would rather woo courtesans than teach monastic students. Father recognizes the community of San Giorgio as a step backward but at least free of those concerns."

Bino heard and understood. To his mind it would be difficult to overstate Brother Tomas' potential for interference and harm. Unpracticed in the arts, boorish and slovenly, the seminarian was not the pupil anyone would wish for. In subsequent sessions, his unceasing and often political chatter proved even worse. Tomas, it seemed, had traded his monastic vow of silence for a fool's vow to never be.

The artist was forced to reconsider his place at San Giorgio's and why a single student's blather so distracted from his craft. Reflecting outdoors one afternoon, the answer appeared. The sometimes poet respected and measured words with care. The value of each was weighed and understood. A word was not spoken unless, like a gold coin, its investment offered a sound return.

Bino might have better borne the burden of Tomas' commentary had it been limited to their project and craft. Instead, the apprentice considered their time together as an opportunity to blather on about private affairs and political gossip. The young monk was publicly pious, privately faithless and worse—bereft of artistic ability. He was the worst type of company and diminished Bino's enthusiasm; the productive spirit that once possessed him fled.

After several weeks of fitful sleep and little progress, Bino asked to speak with the priest responsible for Tomas' assignment. Permission was granted. Few pleasantries were exchanged and the artist wasted no time in describing his displeasure.

"It isn't going well, Prior. I'm poorly suited to respond to Tomas' needs."

"That's odd, Bino; he speaks well of you and his progress. He even suggests he may soon match your level of proficiency."

The artist cleared his throat and continued, "I mean no disrespect, but Tomas will never have the aptitude for fresco work."

With a look that conveyed more regret than surprise, the Prior took a deep breath and responded. "*La verita*—the truth, is this. We must encourage Tomas. He is not merely a seminarian but the nephew of the man who puts bread on our table. Without his uncle's favor, your commission would not be possible."

The blood drained from Bino's face; he understood the futility of his plea. Still, he wished he could take back the words next spoken to the priest.

"This cannot work, Prior; one of us must surely go."

Within a fortnight of his conversation with the priest, Bino found himself in a familiar situation—annoyed and alone on a scaffold with Tomas. It was near the end of the workday and no other members of the crew or community were below. Artist and student were applying a cartoon section to the altar ceiling. With daylight fading, time was short and the pair needed to transfer its image to the damp *intonaco* above. Failure would mean repeating the whole process from scratch.

Bino faced the ceiling and turned his back and attention from the younger man. He hoped doing so would focus his apprentice on the task at hand and deter annoying chatter. He wasn't so fortunate.

"What say you, Brother Bino, of the purer church? My father says the bishop of Rome may be forced to share his power and wealth with northern interests; they tire of his claim to their patronage. Their art and wine are superior, why not their brand of faith?"

Bino struggled to complete his section of the cartoon. Upon doing so, he rotated towards Tomas and confirmed the unthinkable. The young man had not yet begun.

With his reservoir of patience empty and with rage equal to his pulse, Bino bellowed loud enough for Piero to hear, "Enough!"

The unexpected and harsh word startled Tomas and caused him to stumble backward. His weight upset the scaffold rail and he fell to the floor seven meters below. It was an awkward drop and Bino abandoned his tools and hurried down to help. He discovered the unthinkable. Steps away from the altar, without a single witness, lay the lifeless body of his pupil.

No one, with the exception of the prior, had any reason to suspect Bino's hand in Tomas' death. The artist, it was said, never demonstrated violence nor spoke a harsh word. Still, he wondered. The words last shared with the prior haunted him: "One of us must surely go."

Tomas' moneyed family called for an investigation and the community of religious had no choice but to agree. At first, there were only whispers. Rumors and accusations followed, some suggesting Bino forced Tomas off the scaffold during an artistic squabble. If true, some argued, such un-Christian behavior could not go unpunished.

Bino's allies voiced their loyalty and support publicly while privately urging him to leave. It was suggested he travel to Monza—home to a second respected patron of their religious order. There, it was argued, the artist could distance himself from false accusations and ill will.

A letter of introduction to Monza's prominent Pelucca family was executed and shared with Bino. The note made reference to the artist's peerless skill and the soundness of his character. Bino need only arrive in Monza before the noise of Tomas' peculiar death did.

On the eve of his departure from San Giorgio, the artist was unable to sleep. Unnerved by his forced departure from what had been a comfortable home, Bino rose, opened his shutters and sought the moon. It was high above the horizon and as full as his conscience. He wished for his friend and asked, "What have you to say, Piero?"

When no answer came, Bino threw off his bedclothes in favor of those intended for his journey. So dressed, he exited his room and made his way across the courtyard where he entered the church. Habit brought his right hand to his forehead and the artist made a sign of the cross.

It was dark and Bino stepped with care. He discovered a candelabrum, lit it with the chapel's perpetual candle and used it to illuminate the way forward. He hadn't occupied the chapel at night and regretted the loss of perspective and inspiration it might have provided. In such little time, all had changed. The cold stone underfoot, the scent of incense in the air and the fresh memory of Tomas' lifeless body transformed his once-brilliant workspace into a shadow-filled mausoleum.

A chill ran up Bino's leg through his back and neck and he shivered as if in the presence of some inhospitable force. The artist dismissed thoughts of evil, took a deep breath and relaxed his shoulders. He held the candelabrum aloft and focused above. When he could see his frescos better, it wasn't pride he felt but sadness. *I'm alone with you for the last time.*

Bino's frescos came to life amid the dancing candlelight and he was satisfied with their expression and impact. His eyes roamed across the once blank canvas before resting upon the Blessed Mother and the curious change he witnessed there. *How can this be?*

He recalled painting Mary held aloft by the sympathetic arms of Magdalene with eyes closed to the horror of her Son's crucifixion. Bino was now seeing something different. Mary's eyes were open and reflecting the candlelight. Their eyes connected and Mary welcomed his pain. The grief and regret plaguing him since Tomas' death washed over him. It felt to Bino like the union of confession, penance and absolution.

The pressure within his throat dissipated and his eyes welled with tears. Bino wondered at his impatience with Tomas and fell to his knees. He rested the candelabrum on the ground and bent over in prayer.

I'm sorry, Mother. I'm sorry and grateful. You brought me to this place and it has been a worthy companion.

His prayer was interrupted by an echoing call, "Is someone there?"

Bino looked above once more, made a sign of the cross and blew out his candles. He sped away unseen—Monza his destination.

Rotto

A short distance from Monza

The retired soldier ignored the first knock upon his door. When it continued, he got angry at the intrusion and left his chair to respond. Captain de'Gavanti hoped not to find his son there and was relieved instead to see his servant. No words were exchanged, only the extension of the servant's hand bearing a letter.

The soldier didn't reach for the letter, forcing his servant to explain, "I didn't mean to interrupt you, Captain. A courier delivered this and did not wait for a reply. The sender is unknown to us—Signor Eugenio Morsi."

Captain de'Gavanti accepted the letter before returning to his seat near the hearth. He broke the wax seal, unfolded the note and studied the handwriting; the hand was unfamiliar and he knew from experience it suggested trouble. He began to read.

> *Captain de'Gavanti,*
>
> *I write to you with a mix of regret and sadness. While we enjoy no acquaintance, our sons, until recent days, shared a bond born of service—service to the very same duke who elevated your rank in recent years.*
>
> *It was during a break from their weeks-long training that your son, Amarotto, accepted an invitation from my son to join him at our farm—a half day's journey from their barracks at the edge of the city. We knew little of Amarotto*

other than the respect he deserved as your son. Please under-
stand, every courtesy was extended to him and nothing asked
in return.

These are the only facts shared publicly about his visit;
the rest of the story requires a father's discretion.

It is, of course, excusable for soldiers on holiday
to enjoy the liquid spirits made available to them. What is
impossible to excuse is the harm inflicted by those of weak
character. Captain, if you doubt the details I share, make fast
your interview with Amarotto. My son is not blameless and
was likewise drunk that night.

It sickens me to indict Amarotto, but better you know
the truth. Your son exploited his superior name and rank
to isolate and violate my son within his guest chamber. We
would know nothing of the matter were it not for the attention
of a housemaid the following morning.

All present have been instructed to remain silent. I
leave it to you to measure the truth of it and rid your son of
his unnatural inclinations.

Respectfully yours,
Signor Eugenio Morsi

The old soldier read the letter a second time—Morsi's recounting credible and damaging. There was no explanation for Rotto's appetite and worse, his son had sought to satisfy his hunger without regard to who was watching.

The Captain rose, steadied his feet and shuffled over to the hearth. He leaned towards its warmth and touched the letter to a leaping flame. He let go of the sheet, comfortable with its fate before extending both hands above the fire. Their proximity to the flame would have burned another but his calloused fingers and palms were immune to harm. When he withdrew his hands, the Captain brought them to his face and rubbed the strain from his eyes. An idea took shape behind them and he walked with it to his son's bedroom.

He rapped upon Rotto's door and hearing nothing, entered. The retired soldier looked about the room with contempt and curiosity. As a career military man, he knew only discipline; none of it revealed itself here. He wondered, *What could explain habits so foul?* Dismissing his harsh discipline and long absences, he blamed the boy's dead mother and her many indulgences.

Rotto lay prone in bed; his face was covered while unstockinged feet escaped the blanket below. His uniform and underclothes were thrown over a dusty chair and moldy apricots lay uneaten upon his table; fruit flies circled above. Completing the scene were images once familiar to him. Littering the table were sketches of that woman—*Argento's woman. Was it ten years ago? More?*

The memory of it all haunted him. The Captain had paid the artist well for her compliance—seductive images he believed would return his son to correct thinking. The day he found Rotto and the stable boy pleasing one another convinced him he had to act quickly. It wasn't enough to command his son to whip the helpless boy. No. Morale commanded each soldier to bring his lust not to his *brothers* but to the spread legs of wives and whores.

The Captain lifted one of the artist's sketches and remembered. The illustrations of the barmaid had elevated Rotto's curiosity for a while but the Captain demanded more from his son.

"We will find the girl, Rotto, and you will take her; once you've known the flesh of a whore, you won't fall prey to the peculiar tastes of half-men. You won't have my name otherwise."

A small purse was exchanged for the girl's address and a long walk commenced in the rain to the barmaid's home. His son was unable to take the lead and when commanded to consummate the forced union, couldn't do so.

That changed when the girl resisted him. Limp and embarrassed in front of his father, Rotto meted out blow after blow. Her screams distracted him and made it possible for Rotto to take her. He wasn't able to finish and the Captain, expecting the maid to choose death over repeated violation, removed his son from her wilted form.

Rotto turned upon him that night. "Are you proud of me now, sir? Are you satisfied? Or do you have another helpless girl in mind?"

Captain de'Gavanti returned his eyes to the drawing. He studied it as if seeing the maid for the first time. The woman's eyes were not fearful but strong; she looked at home in her nakedness, not wanton. It was as though she trusted the artist and cared little for poor opinion or reproach. She was beauty and peace itself and deserved better than his son. Morsi's letter was evidence of that and more.

The retired soldier was angry; the hour was late and his son slept like an undisciplined shepherd—one unaware of the wolf lurking nearby. The Captain scanned the room and identified a walking stick in the corner. He retrieved it and carried it to the base of the bed and called his son's name. When no response came, he drove the stick against the soles of Rotto's feet.

The sting was immediate and launched the young man upward.

"*Va fan culo! Per che?*"

"Ready yourself, fool."

"Why? Where are we going?"

"We leave shortly for Monza. Ambitious military men must take a wife and it is time you meet the one I've chosen for you."

Caterina

Serono ~ 1516

Caterina woke early and lifted herself out of the bed she had long shared with Isabella. She felt cold absent the warmth her sister provided and thought twice before abandoning their blankets. The stonemason's daughter retrieved her long-sleeved housedress and pulled it over her undergarments before wrapping her hands about her shoulders and massaging away the chill.

Caterina stepped into the main room expecting to see her mother and father asleep. It was Sunday and it was her father's custom to rest an hour more before chores or a visit to the church beckoned. Her parents were older now and less vigorous. Time and labor had taken their toll on once-youthful faces, backs and limbs.

Eduardo was out of bed and didn't appear to notice his daughter's entrance; she stole the moment to observe the man she most admired. He sat near the hearth fire sipping from a steaming cup—his hands as large and strong as the bond between them.

She was startled when he broke the silence with little more than a whisper, "*Buon giorno*, Caterina; it is your Saint's Day."

Caterina couldn't believe he'd remembered and stepped towards him. From behind she wrapped her cool arms about his neck and rested her nose in the thick of his grey and curly locks. "Papa, why do you rise so early?"

"I don't know. It's sometimes better to sit up and let worrisome thoughts fall from your head."

"True, Papa. Do you remember when the card reader warned us about worrying? She said it was no different than a prayer for the things we don't want."

"The old woman said that? I'm glad one of us was listening."

"I always listen, Papa."

Eduardo laughed and said, "She may be wiser than the rest of us, though a little more worrying might do her good, no?"

Silence filled the space save only for the crackle of the fire. Father and daughter were pensive. Caterina wished for nothing to change, Eduardo understanding everything must.

"Caterina, sit with me. It's better we have this moment alone."

She released him from her grasp and brought a stool closer; she positioned herself between the fire and his right hand.

"Your saint's day, Caterina."

"Yes, Papa?"

"It reminds me we cannot ignore time and certain realities."

Her eyes were focused on his and she thought it odd he wasn't looking at her. He continued.

"Your mother and I failed Isabella. We did not make a match for her at the right time and that time is gone for her."

"That can't be, Papa. Isabella is still young, pretty and kind."

Eduardo interrupted her. "Those things are not enough, Caterina. Isabella will soon be too old to have children and no one calls for her."

Her father's words made Caterina defensive. "Papa, you're wrong. I see many men look after us when we pass."

"It is you they look after, *carina*, your hair, your eyes—not Isabella."

"How do you know this?"

"This is what I wish to talk with you about. Someone has come to me."

His words were unexpected and Caterina uncurled her posture and sat back upon her stool. She spoke loud enough for her mother to stir in bed. "What are you saying, Papa?"

"A young man visited me. He invites your acquaintance."

"Who is he? Why hasn't he spoken to me?"

"That isn't how it's done with honorable girls. He is a local boy, though presently a guard in service to the church in Rome."

"What do I want with him?"

Eduardo turned towards Caterina and rested a calloused hand on her knee. "*Mi senti*, Caterina, you must have an open mind. You have twenty-four years, no? Soon you too will be beyond the age when women marry and leave their mother and father."

"Is that what you want, Papa? You want me to leave you, Mamma and this house?"

"I don't want that but it is selfish of us to keep you. Don't you understand?"

"I cannot imagine another life."

"You must. Trust me. Today you…"

"Today? What have you done? It's my special day. What gift do you make of me?"

The words stung Eduardo enough to make him reconsider his invitation. Instead he rose, rested a hand on Caterina's head and whispered.

"These twenty-four years, you have been the soul of our family. On too many days to count you inspired my work at our Lady's church and when I was vulnerable to foolishness, your voice made the correct path clear. No one can replace you in our hearts. But it's time we let you go; we cannot hold on to you as we have with Isabella. It wouldn't be fair.

A husband should know your tenderness and children should know your embrace and generous spirit."

Tears trailed across Caterina's cheeks—one hitting the top of her hand. She knew her father spoke the truth and she did one day want the family he described. Her prayers and devotion to the Blessed Mother had sustained her and now her father was inviting her to share that devotion with a man she didn't even know.

Eduardo lifted her tear-stained hand and kissed it. "The young man is to visit later today. I pledged only that you and Isabella would walk with him and make his acquaintance; his family is familiar to many; they manage the inn adjacent to the church."

"What's his name, Papa? What says he of me?"

"Giovanni. He approached me during a break from service in Rome. He was there to train with the bishop's corps and those hoping to chase the French from Lombardia. He said he spotted you at church during Advent celebrations and inquired after your name.

"I don't recall any soldiers in our church, Papa; what does he look like?"

"You'll see for yourself; and other qualities are more important."

Her father's words disappointed. *He must surely be older or severe looking. Besides, what real man of God would take up arms?* Caterina wondered if her father thought her capable of sharing affection with just any man of good character.

"Papa, you must be able to tell me something of substance about him?"

Eduardo searched for something that might allay her concern. When nothing came to mind, he resorted to sharing first impressions.

"When he approached me, he stood tall and confident while having trouble expressing his intentions. It was as though he didn't think himself worthy and invited my pardon. So if you ask me what I remember of him,

I'd say he demonstrated both courage and modesty. You may not assign much value to these qualities, but I do. No matter, your mother believes this the better option for you."

"Better than what, Papa?"

Eduardo responded with the truth. "Your mother held out hope you would give your life to the church—accept holy orders and live among the other religious."

"Mamma imagined that life for me?"

Eduardo ignored the question. He lifted her from the stool and embraced her.

"We know you enjoy a special devotion to our Lady and find peace in prayer, but I am much too selfish to sequester you behind convent walls."

Caterina responded with a ferocious hug and tender words. "*Ti voglio bene*, Papa."

"I love you too. Now make ready. Though we may one day wish to scare the young man away, let's not do so today."

Caterina left her father and rushed to her bed. *I must wake Isabella. I'll scream if she knew about this and didn't tell me.* Though ten years separated them, the pair had talked about love and marriage on many occasions and it was Isabella who explained Caterina's first bleed seven summers ago.

The cottage was a blur of activity the rest of the morning. Isabella had no choice but to rise from her slumber, fix her sister's hair and respond to more questions than there were plausable answers.

"What if he isn't handsome or doesn't say anything? What if he's boorish or unkind?"

Isabella, ever practical, smiled at Caterina's limitless curiosity and reassured her.

"We won't know until he appears. Let's see."

"I've never been so nervous."

"Don't worry. I'll be with both of you to coach you along."

Caterina embraced her. "Promise me you won't ever leave me."

"You know I can't promise that, sister."

"Promise it anyway."

"Okay, I promise I'll never leave you."

"I feel better already."

"You should; your father said Giovanni's family is a good one. And unless our soldier is blind or heartless, he is sure to adore you."

Across the village of Serono, Giovanni buttoned his uniform tight against his chest. He wished it fit better and had no alternative to improve upon his appearance. Fully dressed, he left the family inn along Via Varesina and walked the short distance to the courtyard fronting Mary's church. He stopped there and threw his gaze above where the early afternoon sun appeared frozen in the sky. The glare proved too much and Giovanni shifted his closed eyes to the ground. When he opened them, his shadow caused him to frown. Its miniature size mirrored his diminishing confidence. He had been eager for this day while also wishing it would never come. *To what question of Caterina's can I possibly be the answer?*

The memory of his brief interview with Eduardo still fresh, Giovanni stepped out of the square towards the stonemason's home. He quickened his pace, hoping to leave some of his nervousness behind.

When the cottage door presented itself, he knocked, retreated a step and waited. Eduardo opened the door with apprehension equal to Giovanni's. He was relieved to see the young man looking no different than on the day of their meeting and welcomed him into the cottage. Eduardo's wife took Giovanni by the arm and inquired after his parents.

"They are older and slower, *signora*. The inn is full these weeks before Christmas so it is good I can lend a hand."

They were interrupted by hushed voices and the well-adorned figures of Caterina and Isabella. Isabella spoke first.

"It is a pleasure to make your acquaintance, *signor*. I am Signor Eduardo's sister-in-law, Isabella."

"I am pleased to meet you, *signora*." With a nod to Caterina, he continued, "I have often seen you in each other's company. Please, call me Giovanni."

Time slowed for Caterina. She couldn't recall seeing Giovanni before and yet there was something familiar in his voice and stature. She thought him handsome and as their eyes connected for the first time, she wondered why she had ever been noticed by him at all.

Isabella moved aside as Eduardo stepped forward, "Giovanni, we present our daughter, Caterina."

Giovanni bowed slightly at the waist and spoke, "*Signorina, piacere di conoscerla*—it is a pleasure to meet you."

Giovanni wasn't so forward as to reach for her hand. Caterina noticed and extended her own. He was grateful for the gesture and grasped her fingers. She smiled and felt the warmth of his hand.

Caterina betrayed her approval with a glance to her father before returning her eyes to the handsome soldier. He was adorned in the heavy cloth and rich color of the papal guard. In his free hand was a scarlet cap; its removal had revealed dark and tangled curls.

Giovanni's gentleness put the stonemason's daughter at ease; he seemed to her more goodwill ambassador than military man. She released his hand—her own suddenly feeling empty and purposeless. A little color filled the soldier's cheeks as he stepped back and asked Eduardo whether it remained possible to accompany Caterina and Isabella for a walk.

With his daughter's approval no longer in doubt, Eduardo teased something about unfinished housework.

Caterina wasn't amused and raised her shoulders in protest. "We attended to our chores yesterday, Papa."

He smiled and responded, "You must be right. As long as Isabella agrees, you have my blessing."

Isabella was quick to respond, "Brother, it would be a pleasure to accompany Caterina and our guest for a turn."

Caterina's mother ushered the trio to the door and bid them well. Giovanni allowed the ladies to exit before joining them outside. He directed them to his left where they were less likely to come face-to-face with meddlesome neighbors. They walked in silence for a short distance before Giovanni turned to Isabella and asked a favor.

"Would you object if I make a small gift to Caterina on the occasion of her saint's day?"

Isabella responded, "No, please. It is thoughtful of you to remember."

Giovanni reached inside his coat and produced a small cloth bag bound with string. He presented it to Caterina and watched as she released the string and emptied the contents into the palm of her hand. She knew instantly what it was—pink granite pebbles linked by a braided leather cord. For years she'd had only her mother's wooden rosary beads with which to pray each evening. So fierce had been her grip that the once dark beads had paled. Because of Giovanni's generosity, she would have a stone set of her own.

Giovanni looked for clues within Caterina's clear blue eyes. Made unsure by her silence, he asked, "Do you like them?"

She looked into his brown eyes and saw genuine concern. "I like them very much. I can't imagine a finer gift."

Her delicate voice, words and smile seized him. Isabella broke the silence, "Let's continue on and not lose what's left of the winter sun."

"Forgive me, *signora*; I meant only to…"

"No apology necessary. You cannot know how perfect your gift is. My sister is sure to rescue us all with your prayer beads."

Caterina blushed. "Hush, Isabella. You know that isn't true. Our guest needn't think of me as an angel."

Giovanni laughed and responded, "I don't mind. I welcome a little of your goodness. As for the rosary, it was made by the monks we lodge with in Rome."

They resumed walking and Isabella couldn't help but notice how tightly Caterina clutched her gift against her hip. A few steps later, her smitten sister was the first to speak. "Rome, please tell us what it's like there."

Giovanni wasn't sure he should. His opinion was at odds with most people's.

"I prefer it here. It's not that Rome isn't grand or fascinating. It's both of those things. It's just an unlikely place to find Peter's church."

Caterina didn't understand. *What need would Rome have for anything beyond her church?* She said nothing while Isabella spoke up.

"We dream of visiting. Pilgrims to Serono describe its art and architecture as too remarkable to be believed."

Giovanni explained, "They don't exaggerate. It's just that the pagans' romance with the empire that was contrasted against the church that is make Rome a hard-to-govern and uncaring place. Still, it would please me to accompany you there."

Unlike Isabella, Caterina couldn't recall being anywhere other than Serono; her excitement grew. "You've seen them then—the great churches and the frescos honoring Saint Catherine and the Blessed Mother?"

"There are more than are countable. And I've seen some better and closer to home. There is a fresco artist in Milan whom the priests claim rivals Leonardo. His work fills the churches of San Maurizio and San Giorgio."

"We must beg Father to let us go, Isabella."

"One thing at a time, sister; there will be an occasion to visit Milan."

Giovanni led the group up an unfamiliar hill; it offered an expansive view of Serono and its rooftops. The setting sun played against the clouds and cast the pilgrim church in an especially pleasing light. The soldier pointed to it and commented, "You must be proud of your father; his work is good."

Caterina responded to the compliment. "It's kind of you to say so, though my father would be quick to deflect the credit."

"Modesty appears to be a family trait."

"You've noticed" replied Isabella.

Caterina added, "Papa is right about one thing. For our pilgrim church to rival the beauty and reverence of those in Milan or Rome, it must attract its own artists. How we'd love to see some color upon our Lady's walls."

Isabella couldn't resist. "Then I suggest you put your prayer beads to work, sister, so Mary will send such a person to Serono."

"I'll do it this night, Isabella."

They continued down and through the sparsely wooded plain bordering their village. The conversation drifted to Giovanni's family and the Varesina Inn. He shared stories of unusual guests who sometimes made a home there.

"We've had an entertaining collection of visitors—priests bent on inspiration, the sick seeking miracles and self-described sinners in want of redemption."

"What great theater," commented Caterina.

"It is," responded Giovanni with a warm smile. "If we weren't so busy keeping a tidy house, we'd invite the whole lot to appear on stage."

They were nearing the girls' cottage when Caterina stumbled on a rock. Giovanni reached for her hand and prevented her fall. She felt his strength and didn't wish to let go.

"Forgive her clumsiness," teased Isabella. "Caterina's head is always in the heavens."

"The fault is mine. I should have chosen a better path," Giovanni offered.

When they arrived, Isabella made easier an awkward good-bye by expressing her thanks and slipping alone through the front door. Caterina and Giovanni were left alone.

Caterina thought to inquire about his next trip home but didn't get the chance. He looked into her hopeful eyes and spoke first.

"Caterina—" *how he liked the sound of her name* "—my mother and father have many years and aren't so well. We joke the doctor will soon be a permanent guest. Anyway, before my commission expires, I hope to leave soldiering behind and relieve them in managing the inn."

"That is good—not that they're unwell, but that you can return and help them."

"Yes, yes it is. The truth is less helpful, though. The bishop's commander may be unwilling to release me."

She looked at him with concern in her eyes. "Until then, will it be dangerous for you?"

He thought it a fair question and smiled before responding.

"Why do you ask?"

Caterina blushed and reflected, *There must be a less selfish explanation.*

"Knowing how much your help means to your parents, I…"

Giovanni silenced her by reaching for the same hand he had twice held and cupped it within both of his. The gesture sent a shiver up her arms and focused her attention. He gave voice to his feelings.

"This may sound odd since we've only just met. I don't care for being a soldier but it's given me the courage to say something I must say. Still, it would make me feel better if I had your permission to say it."

Caterina was touched by his words and the force of emotion behind his eyes. She knew whatever Giovanni had to say was his truth and, for good or ill, she would hear it.

She squeezed his hands and invited, "Please, go on."

The young soldier looked above before returning his eyes to hers, "I believe no harm can come to me if I'm with you."

They were words spoken by a near-stranger but more intimate than any spoken to her before. Giovanni appreciated her goodness and reflected it back to her in a most thoughtful manner. Her eyes were wet and Caterina shed formality and placed her hands atop his shoulders.

He welcomed the gesture and embraced her. Caterina was no longer a fantasy. She was flesh, hope and maybe, incredibly, his.

Assured of the answer, he asked, "May I call upon you again?"

"Why do you ask? Didn't you say no harm could come to you if we were together?"

"Yes, I mean that."

"Well then, mustn't we be together?"

They heard the cottage door open and separated. Caterina was quick to raise a sleeve and dry damp eyes.

Eduardo looked upon them. "Caterina, it grows dark and Mamma seeks your help with supper."

"Yes, Papa."

She turned to Giovanni and spoke the first words she thought of. "The walk was wonderful. I am grateful for the beads and shall keep you in our prayers. Won't we, Papa?"

"'Tis better we leave the praying to you, Caterina."

Giovanni spoke up, "Forgive the late hour, *signor*. The fault is mine. As for prayers, Caterina, others are surely more worthy."

Eduardo said nothing more, making only a courteous wave before welcoming his daughter inside. He observed her glow and excused her so she could catch up with her mother and Isabella. He half-hoped she would reject the boy and extend her time at home; her mood suggested otherwise. *Perhaps I'll gain a son.*

Bino

On the road connecting Milan with Monza

With the rumors of Brother Tomas's death spreading, Bino sought transport to Monza. A carriage was found and with it, its well-heeled owner—Federigo. He was the handsome and charming scion of Casa Rabbia.

Bino studied his travel companion. He was fit and wore fine clothes that did little to distract from brilliant red hair and fair skin. The artist estimated his age to be near his own.

Extending a hand, his host began, "*Mi chiamo* Federigo, though I insist you call me Feder. It's a bore to travel alone so please join me if Monza be your destination."

"I welcome that if it be no imposition, thank you."

The artist introduced himself and was put at ease by his host who was quick to recount his overnight stay at San Giorgio. Bino did not volunteer the unfortunate details of his departure and wasn't asked to. Feder was satisfied to learn his guest's identity and intention—a local artist in possession of a letter of introduction to Monza's most celebrated family—Casa Pelucca.

Bino couldn't have wished for a better companion. Within an hour, he learned much of value about Monza's moneyed families and their interconnectedness. He also learned of the bond between Feder's father and Signor Pelucca. No longer a stranger to matters political and their relevance to artistic patronage, Bino listened with care.

It wasn't long before Feder shifted from teacher to interrogator; he peppered his guest with questions about art, influence and the artist's life. At first uncomfortable with his host's presumed intimacy, Bino was put at ease by Feder's self-deprecation and humor. His host made sport of Bino's humble origins and nomadic life and contrasted both with the formality of his own.

"Indoctrination, education, administration and sport," he insisted, "were the obligation of moneyed men of Lombardia."

Feder bemoaned his lack of time for creative expression and credited Bino with choosing a romantic's life. The artist and sometimes poet was amused anyone would envy his station—one light on ambition and treasure.

"You make me smile, Feder, because I've seen what it is to go without a meal and bed. It's not uncommon for my kind to worry which cleric or noble might next exchange porridge for a painting."

"True enough," responded his host. But what you lack in coin you must surely make up for with women. What of them, Bino? Do entertain me with a story or two."

The request caught Bino off guard. He turned to look outside the carriage as memories of Nica surfaced. And though it had been a while, he couldn't deny the others who'd eased his want of companionship. His conscience oft asked, *Was pleasure a sin, if it be honest and salves a desperate heart?*

Unlike most of his gender, Bino had the time and opportunity to observe women from every angle, listen to their conversations and empathize with their quiet struggles. He believed he understood them better than they sometimes understood themselves. He knew women to be clearer thinking, less modest and emotionally stronger than men credited. Bino had always been more at home in the company of women and wondered if he would find another secure enough to appreciate him.

Bino sat with female patrons and models and kept their secrets; he now had more than a few of his own. He clung to them but not without a toll. While in the company of Signor Argento, he had betrayed his own moral instincts. He sought and found redemption through Piero's generosity but gave no public credit to Leonardo's father. And there was Tomas—the dead seminarian. *I didn't drop him from the scaffold but I may as well have.*

The carriage was jarred by a hole in the road and Bino was reminded to answer the question posed by his host. He lied. "Women, you ask? My experiences are less titillating than you might expect. Painting frescos in the company of celibate monks affords me little opportunity to mingle with the fairer sex."

Feder noticed something in the artist's eyes betraying the truth. "You give those priests and seminarians too much credit, Bino; they run away from one sin or another. You're being too modest, no?"

Bino laughed and said nothing; he was learning far too much to sacrifice his ears.

For the moment satisfied, Feder continued, "Friend, fortune smiles upon us today. I like you and believe we can help one another."

Bino couldn't imagine how. With little to lose, he simply replied, "I am at your service, sir."

Feder began anew, "You'll soon make the acquaintance of a girl more intriguing than any you will have painted. She is Signor Pelucca's middle daughter, Laura."

Bino doubted the claim. Countless men and even a few priests boasted about the women they'd met and hoped to bed. Feder's claim seemed no different. Still, he thought it impolite not to inquire further.

"This daughter, what makes her unique?"

"You ask the right question, Bino. Most men appreciate only her father's wealth and fail to see what I see. There are women as attractive as

Laura, but I have yet to meet another who embraces life as she does and is second to no one in conversation and wit."

That Feder called attention to these qualities impressed Bino and bettered his opinion of him.

"You have my attention, friend."

The carriage stopped and Feder was forced to suspend their conversation. He pushed aside the coach curtain and pointed. Fronting a cypress-bordered, stone path was the gate for Casa Pelucca. Feder released the carriage door, leapt out and extended a hand to his travel companion.

His legs unaccustomed to long confinement, Bino stepped from the carriage and stumbled. He righted himself and shifted his eyes from the afternoon sun to the rich landscape before him. The artist inhaled deeply—the scent unfamiliar and pleasant, hinting of herbs and evergreen. The aroma soothed and he was grateful for the change of atmosphere.

Feder studied his companion's eyes and said, "I won't say goodbye, Bino; we shall see each other soon."

The artist moved his eyes to Feder's while reaching for his waist purse. "Let me pay you for the coachman."

"The trip is mine to give, artist. You made the journey a quicker one for me."

"It is kind of you to say so, *ti ringrazio.*"

With a nod, Feder reentered the carriage and instructed the coachman to retrieve Bino's bag before continuing home. Bino saw them off and was guided into the Pelucca compound. He entered the foyer of the main house, removed his cap and allowed his eyes to roam. What was visible to him was spacious and uncluttered. The stone and tile work beneath his feet appeared new and abundant windows allowed the light and air to mingle. The environment hinted at possibility and a new beginning.

Bino was left alone by a servant in search of his master. The artist paced about and peered into adjacent rooms. His strong visual sense attracted him to the family's art and, in particular, their wall murals. He thought their color adequate but their execution poor. The staccato of boots connecting with tile interrupted his thinking.

A young man approached. He wore a soiled jacket and riding pants and stopped a short distance away; he inspected Bino from top to bottom. With head tilted to one side, he was the first to speak. "Who are you? You're as dusty as I am."

Bino glanced below and acknowledged the wrinkled truth of his clothes. He patted his shirt and pants, stepped closer and responded, "Forgive my appearance, my name is Bernardino. I am from Luino but more recently from Milan. I come today with a letter of introduction for Signor Pelucca."

Bino retrieved the letter and offered it to the lad. The boy did not reach for it. Instead he walked around the artist, heels connecting with the floor. Stray brown hairs escaped his cap and mud pocked his cheeks and nose.

After circling, the boy stopped and remarked, "You don't overthink first impressions, do you?"

Bino didn't know what to make of the unsympathetic comment.

"Forgive me, I travelled all morning and the roads were dry and dusty. You may know my travel companion, Signor…."

The artist stopped short of completing his sentence; the young man was not interested. Bino waited to hear less offensive words and withdrew his letter of introduction. When the silence became uncomfortable, he lifted his eyes to the boy and admitted, "I am an artist seeking work."

"An artist? Look around you; do you think one is necessary?"

Bino was intrigued by the rude volleying. He measured the lad and recast his line.

"You're right, of course. I should have been clearer. I am a good artist seeking work."

The young man feigned indignation before bursting into a fit of laughter. More relieved than humored, Bino smiled.

The boy coughed and responded, "It is awful, isn't it?"

With little reluctance Bino admitted, "It is."

At the sound of approaching footsteps, the boy sped away and the artist was left alone to make his introduction.

A servant accompanied Signor Pelucca into the foyer, and leaning towards Bino with an open palm, he offered, "I present Master Pelucca; may I share your letter of introduction?"

Conscious of his appearance, Bino apologized, retrieved and relayed the San Giorgio letter. Its contents caused his host to smile and speak.

"Welcome to Casa Pelucca, Bernardino. It isn't common for us to receive artisans of merit. Was your journey comfortable?"

Bino was put at ease. Feder's description of Signor Pelucca's gentility proved accurate. His host was confident-looking, well-groomed, and wore clothes suggesting a tailor's careful attention. His weight, coloring and wrinkles betrayed generous dining and love of the sun. Better still, if any news or gossip preceded the artist in Monza, his host made no mention of it.

"My journey was better than I hoped for; I was fortunate to share the company of Federigo Rabbia."

"You were indeed fortunate. Feder's family is well regarded within these walls—walls, I imagine, that may benefit from your practiced hand."

"It would be a privilege, *signor.* I am between engagements and require little to be comfortable."

"Excellent. Lady Pelucca will be thrilled to have you spend time with us and our four children. If you agree, we'll leave the details for another day."

Bino agreed and Signor Pelucca called upon his property manager to help settle his guest. A small, seasoned and casually attired man appeared.

"Renato, please place our guest in Nonno's cottage. Find him some clothes and take the weekend to acquaint Signor Bernardino with the compound and workspaces."

Signor Pelucca returned to Bino. "Monza is not Milan but what we lack in sophistication we recover with hospitality. Be our guest for dinner on Saturday. It will be a fine opportunity to get acquainted with my wife, our children and closest neighbors. Until then, I leave you in Renato's capable hands."

Bino couldn't have asked for a more cordial welcome—one that several days forward would surely include the daughter of which Feder spoke so well. *I'll see how discerning my carriage companion is.*

Renato proved an invaluable guide. The estate servant was a third-generation staff member and knew and lived the history of the working farm. He walked the property with the artist, pointed and instructed. He made no question of the visitor's motives and appreciated the artist's lean expectations for comfort and reward.

Over his first few and succeeding days, Renato could be relied upon to detail Pelucca family history and speak to social do's and don'ts. He took such care as to accompany Bino on visits to the family's seamstress. The woman required only Renato's endorsement to replace and supplement the artist's worn clothing. Shorn of his beard and adorned with fitted clothes, the artist looked more prosperous than his purse would otherwise allow. His years within Milan's religious communities had been lean ones. The benefits enjoyed by those serving the Pelucca family were rich by comparison.

With San Giorgio at his back, Bino was hungry to create. With an open heart and mind he would satisfy the artistic intentions of his hosts and put the matter of Tomas behind him. Time and occupation would heal and nourish his creativity anew.

When Saturday evening arrived, the artist was ready. He bathed and wore the first of several shirts and trousers delivered by Renato's seamstress. He then duplicated a trick long ago learned from his brother by rolling damp rosemary between his hands and transferring its essence to his cheeks, wrists and the back of his neck.

"How do I look, Renato?"

"Almost like a gentleman, Bernardino."

"Call me Bino, please."

"As you wish, Bino."

Renato escorted the artist to the main house which was aglow with reflected sunlight. Inside, the pair adjusted to the softer light of candles and was made hungry by the aroma of grilled lamb, garlic and vegetables. It was for Bino a sensory feast—one complemented by three roaming musicians strumming stringed instruments.

Bino searched the room for anything familiar. Opposite him was a thick studded door preventing access to the dining room. Fronting it were well-manicured guests and the newcomer, despite his improved wardrobe and grooming, felt like he didn't belong.

Renato noticed the younger man's discomfort and led him by the elbow for introductions. Renato was thoughtful and well-spoken and friends and neighbors were left to wonder how someone of Bino's artistic reputation was convinced to leave Milan.

After a time, the music stopped and a servant announced the arrival of *la famiglia* Pelucca. Wife and husband entered the room. Three daughters and a young son followed.

Signora Pelucca and her husband gestured greetings to the dozen visitors along two reception lines. They proceeded slowly and Bino took his place at the tail of one of the columns. He strained to look ahead and could not identify the young man he'd met upon arrival, whom he thought to be their son.

When Signor Pelucca lingered to exchange words with the guest nearest the artist, his wife pulled at his sleeve, urging him forward.

"Yes, of course," whispered Signor Pelucca as he stepped before Bino. He smiled and spoke, "It seems the lady of the house is anxious to meet you, *signor*." And then turning to Lady Pelucca, he said, "*Cara mia*, I give you Bernardino, most recently from Milan and schooled under Leonardo."

Bino said nothing of the error—one even his mentor, Gian Steffano, wouldn't have minded. Instead, he bowed and offered, "It is an honor to meet one's patroness, *signora*."

Signora Pelucca was gracious in her reply. "It is a treat, *signor*, to have a fresco artist of your reputation among us. Is what Renato tells me true? You prefer to be called Bino?"

"*Si', signora*. I defer formality to those who care more for their influence than their art. I am called many things but prefer the simplest."

Signora Pelucca nodded her understanding before turning and presenting her children. The youngest—a son named in honor of Saint Francis, was by gender and custom introduced first. The names and respective ages of her daughters followed. They were handsome women and demonstrated varying degrees of interest.

Enza, the oldest daughter, at nearly twenty years, cared little for her mother's religious and artistic fervor and even less for any person who might feed it. Neglecting her personality, she was judged the fairest of the Pelucca sisters. Enza wasted little time in deflecting Bino's polite questions in favor of a guest she judged more worthy of her attention.

Signora Pelucca set aside her embarrassment with Enza's rude behavior and moved the shoulders of her youngest daughter forward. Valentina, at twelve, smiled at Bino and boasted, "I can draw flowers and pretty horses."

Bino took a knee, smiled at Valentina and replied, "Would you be kind and teach me? I struggle with horses."

Valentina blushed and said, "*Si'*, Signor Bino."

"Then we will be friends, *principessa*, and trade secrets."

Bino kissed the beaming girl's hand and returned to his feet.

Only the middle daughter had yet to be introduced and the artist inquired of his hostess, "I'm sorry, *signora*, the day I arrived, I met a young man resembling you."

"True? How strange," she replied. "There is no other."

The remaining daughter, at eighteen years, stepped forward with a knowing smile. "Signor Bino, I have no older brother, but I'm certain my mother would welcome your first impressions of the murals you observed the day of your arrival."

The smile, the voice, they were those of the "boy" he'd met in the foyer. Recalling their awkward meeting, Bino could only grin and search for the right words.

Before he could speak, Signora Pelucca registered her disapproval. "Laura! It's rude to ask such a question of a new acquaintance."

Laura? This was Feder's Laura? Bino's brain labored to recall what had been said or implied about her on his brief carriage ride from Milan.

"No offense taken, Lady Pelucca. I'm certain Laura intended no harm."

Laura began again, "Mamma, may I ask Renato to seat me near our guest at dinner? I'd like to learn more about his art and experiences."

"*Piacere*, forgive my daughter's curiosity, Bino. If Renato and our guest don't object, I will allow it."

Unsure of protocol, Bino responded, "I have no objection, *signora*."

Other introductions were made. Names and compliments were exchanged and forgotten. Through it all, Laura's deception distracted and humored Bino. *Was it intentional?*

The great door swung open and they were called to the dining room. Bino entered and observed the long rectangular table. He had never seen a setting so lavish. The tablecloth, ceramic plates and glassware spoke of class and privilege. The artisans and monastic religious with whom Bino had lived over the last dozen years were strangers to elegance and he appreciated it all the more.

The guests found their assigned places and Laura, satisfied with her small victory, smiled and pointed to the seat opposite her. Family and guests sat as the local pastor rose and invited all to lower their heads for a blessing. Each did so save Laura. A kick under the table alerted Bino to her rebellion.

Bino shifted his focus and observed Laura's mutinous eyes peeking from below auburn curls. Habit bid him to pray and give thanks, but her rebellion proved alluring. Laura grinned when she saw the priest respond to Bino's inattention with a frown.

After the blessing, Signor Pelucca toasted the artist, welcoming him to the broader Monza community. Dinner began and Bino acknowledged the well wishes of those adjacent to him. Laura stirred her broth and paid only polite interest to her neighbors. Noticing her disinterest, the artist searched for something clever to say. Laura caught him tongue-tied and spoke first.

"Are you always so easily distracted, Signor Bino?"

The artist was too surprised by the question to lie.

"No, I'm not. Rare is the dinner companion as equipped as you are, *signorina*, with the intention and means to distract a guest from prayer."

Laura smiled at the implication and replied, "You don't appear helpless, sir, though I reserve the right to change my mind."

"I am what you observe, Miss Laura."

She studied him with a grin before responding, "No, I don't believe you are."

Bino welcomed her candor and whispered his response, "You may be disappointed."

"I doubt that," volleyed Laura. "Bores never admit to being dull."

Bino laughed and lifted his glass in agreement.

Laura continued, "No, Signor Bino, you remind me of a gentleman we once hosted from Naples."

"Naples? How so?"

"The way you arrived, casually dressed, hat in hand, uncomfortable with formality—all attributes of the Napolitani."

"I see. Anything else?"

Laura leaned forward and motioned for Bino to do the same. He turned an ear towards her and listened. With a voice equal to her delicate charge she whispered, "Monza isn't a place for great artists to further their reputations. If you're here, it's because you have something to hide."

Bino was startled by her insight and presumption; he leaned back into his chair and looked at her across the table in silence. Laura was young but she was obviously not a child.

She witnessed his discomfort. Bino's reaction left little doubt as to the accuracy of her charge. She felt a pang of guilt and wondered, *Have I gone too far?* If the artist had a secret, tonight wasn't the occasion to remind him of it.

When supper concluded, Signor Pelucca's middle daughter sought to make amends. Accompanied by her brother Francesco, she invited Bino to the terrace. He accepted. It was a clear evening and the stars shone bright. Laura guided him towards her favorite spot and stood an arm's length away. She surprised him by pointing to constellations and naming them with what he presumed was learned accuracy.

"Do you follow the stars, Signor Bino?"

"I admire them but must admit ignorance."

"My father says young women have no need for such knowledge. Do you agree?"

Still grappling with her earlier charge, Bino wondered whether this was another test. He answered with care.

"Two things are true, Miss Laura. Your father is to be respected."

"And the other?"

"What we see above is a gift from God. Because one of those stars led the magi to Christ, knowing its name is to know a little more of heaven."

"I'm not sure I have my answer, artist. How certain are you of this God?"

Bino responded with conviction, "As certain as any mortal can be."

"What makes you so sure? What we learn from visitors speaks of war, sickness and death."

Bino looked into the night sky and did not answer.

Laura continued, "Our priest tells us only to be chaste, pray for deliverance and give of our wealth to the poor. If this is to be the explanation for God, then there is much I don't understand."

The artist studied the heavens before returning his attention to Laura. He spoke the first words that came to mind. "The cross and the stone."

Laura looked puzzled. "What?"

"The cross and stone." Bino continued, "I have spent more than half my years in churches. Each pays homage to Christ's suffering and crucifixion. Our eyes turn to the crucifix and we worship at the altar below the foot of the cross. Priests and patrons of our art even wear it about their necks."

"Go on."

"The cross bears witness to man's inhumanity to man—the torture and murder of the most innocent among us."

"What are you saying?"

"Do you agree this is what you see in church?"

"Yes, the symbol of our faith is a reminder of Christ's torture and the ugliness of this world. Am I to think differently?"

"Not at all, Miss Laura. It's simply the cross isn't all we're meant to see."

He had her attention and allowed the silence to further her appetite.

"I don't believe the cross was intended to be Christ's parting message. He means to direct our eyes elsewhere. I look past the crucifix and imagine the risen Christ shedding his death cloak. We should acknowledge and respect the cross but what inspires my faith is the shroud on the stone."

Laura digested Bino's perspective and asked, "With this understanding, why didn't you become a priest?"

Having many times asked himself the same question, Bino knew the answer well. "I'm unworthy of those shoes."

Laura said nothing while being impressed by his reasoning and candor.

"And you, Miss Laura, how large is the stone you must move?"

No one had cared enough to ask such a question before and she returned her eyes to the stars as if to find the answer there. Finding it she replied, "The stones obstructing unmarried women in Monza are immovable."

Bino was challenged by her answer, one reflecting her maturity, and answered, "Perhaps you're not meant to move it alone."

Laura shifted her attention from the night sky to the artist and smiled.

When she said nothing, Bino broke the silence. "I'm pleased to be here, but one day I will paint a different kind of church—one fully reflecting the hope and optimism of Christ's resurrection."

Laura reached for his hand and led him to a marble bench. She put a hand upon his shoulder, steadied herself and climbed atop. With Bino below, she turned his shoulders so they faced the darkest part of the sky and her favorite constellation.

"Do you see that there? Do you see its edge and shapes? I don't know its name but from now on I shall call it, 'Artist's Palette'."

Touched by her gesture, Bino spun about to face her. She sensed he lacked the words to express anything but gratitude. She smiled, put a hand over his mouth and used the other to tease his hair.

"Artist, why do you smell as if you've rolled through a rosemary bush?"

Recalling his earlier preparation, Bino laughed.

The artist from Luino was satisfied. His welcome to Casa Pelucca, Renato's friendship, and his budding friendship with Laura were worthy of a painting and poem.

Laura

Bino relished his first weeks living and working amongst the Pelucca family. He recalled months of cloistered living with San Giorgio's priests and seminarians as if a dream—one interrupted by the nightmare of Tomas's death. In Milan, the peculiar accident and accusations of the artist's complicity faded and word of the investigation failed to reach Monza.

Bino settled into his work and Signora Pelucca was delighted with the decoration of her home. She desired and the artist gave life to mythological stories and Old Testament characters. He listened well and when the outcome of any project was more his own imagining than hers, he convinced his patroness of her creativity.

Bino accepted little compensation—much less than his peers commanded when they took household commissions. The artist from Luino was satisfied with his work, his bed and growing friendship with Renato.

Apart from his fresco work, Bino was obliged to guide the Pelucca children through art lessons. Enza, the oldest of the four, thought herself above the chore and opted out. The result was time alone with Laura, Valentina and the youngest, Francesco. Bino especially looked forward to his time with Laura. These opportunities were a welcome diversion from his routine "companions"—early hours, wet plaster and scaffold climbs.

Laura's curiosity was equal to the artist's and she delighted in their verbal volleys.

"My sister doesn't appreciate art," she said during Enza's absence one morning.

Bino thought a moment before responding, "Many don't appreciate what they cannot see."

Laura threw a confused look at him. "So, you believe some find meaning where others deny it exists?"

"Yes. Why do some feel the presence of the Holy Spirit while others pretend?"

"You confound me with riddles, artist."

Bino laughed. "I don't intend to. Perhaps it's because I was raised by and among priests."

"How awful that must have been. I'm glad you're not one of them."

"It wasn't so bad," he responded. "Only a few proved true hypocrites."

"Those are the few who serve Monza," teased Laura.

Bino was anxious to change the subject. "Allow me one more riddle. What do children possess in abundance that adults pay as a toll with each succeeding year?"

"A sense of humor?" Laura guessed. "Enza hasn't had one for years."

"True, but not what I had in mind. Something more fundamental."

"Imagination? Willingness?"

"Yes! You do understand. Without a childlike imagination, few can see or appreciate what we do."

With each visit, Laura's appeal grew. The artist enjoyed her company and understood why. She was thoughtful and absent pretension. Laura's clever words were music to his ears while her auburn hair, skin and smile were food for his eyes.

She caught him staring one morning and asked, "What is it? Why do you look at me that way?"

The sometimes poet couldn't make up his mind whether it was the right time to give voice to his fascination. He was uncertain she would welcome his affection. It didn't matter; she didn't give him time enough to respond.

"Riddles aside, artist, you're not as dull as everyone else in Monza."

"I'm not sure that's a compliment but I'll accept it. If you're right, it's only because I've been blessed with unusual experiences."

"Blessed? My mother says we're blessed because we have property and farm income. You have neither of those things."

Bino thought to mention his father and brother; they had property and income. Instead he offered, "It's enough for me to be welcomed by those who appreciate beauty—a fresco where they worship, a mural in their home."

"That would never be enough for me."

"You may one day change your mind, Laura. Still, be you rich or poor, I prefer your company to that of ten wealthy men."

Laura wondered at the compliment. Privilege had been her birth-right and her parents would have branded Bino's words as heresy. She found herself at odds with them and they little appreciated her curiosity and love of the outdoors. She coped with their unflattering comparisons to Enza by stealing away and sharing hours well beyond the stable with her dogs.

Weeks, visits and words passed between Laura and the artist and her fondness for him grew. *Would Papa understand?* She was unaccustomed to trusting her feelings to anyone but Valentina.

"You care for him, don't you?" asked her younger sister one afternoon.

"Who? Signor Bino? No, well, yes; I don't know," responded Laura.

"What is it? Do you believe him too old for you? I promise not to tell Enza or Mamma."

"Old? No! What man my age has anything worthwhile to say?"

Laura reached for Valentina's hand and spoke. "Until Bino came, I never thought myself capable of giving my heart to one person. I'm too easily dispirited."

"I don't understand, Laura," replied Valentina.

"Do you know when Papa and his friends lecture us about privilege and responsibility?"

"I guess so."

"When I listen to all that rubbish, I want to scream."

Valentina laughed and squeezed her sister's hand tighter. "Go on."

"Bino embraces silence and beauty and when important things need be said, he draws your attention to them in creative ways."

"It's more than that, isn't it?" challenged Valentina.

"What do you mean?"

Valentina let go of her hand, smiled and spoke, "I've seen you watch him work. Last week when the room was warm and he removed his shirt, I saw *that* expression on your face." She mimicked the expression for her sister.

"You terrible sneak! I can't believe you were spying on us."

"If Renato hadn't interrupted, you'd still be watching him."

Laura couldn't deny the truth of it and recalled her favorite scene. She appealed to her sister.

"Aren't his arms and shoulders amazing? When he's on one foot and balancing his tools, you can see his focus and every muscle above his waist working in harmony. You get lost in the dance and forget he's drawing— until the dance ends and you see the colorful memory of his movement crafted on the wall."

Laura felt her cheeks warm and wondered at having shared such a romantic image with her twelve-year-old sister.

Bino felt the pull of Laura's admiring eyes as well. When practicing his craft, he couldn't see beyond his work but appreciated her audience all the same. *Is she too young? Does she appreciate my silence as Nica once did?* The answers didn't trouble him. What Laura lacked in years, she made up for in patience, spirit and wit.

When she wasn't present, Bino missed her and her sense of humor. *What had she said?* She had called attention to his rosemary aroma the evening they met and his obsessive artistic habits ever since.

As for the interests of other men, Bino didn't think about Feder and the fondness he professed for Laura during their coach ride from Milan. And he knew nothing of other would-be suitors eager to win Laura's heart and hand. That soon changed.

It was a beautiful morning and Bino sought to make progress before the light critical to his work faded. But with the sun at its peak, nature beckoned and he thought to find Laura and invite a walk. With the inspiration came her voice greeting him from below.

"Artist?" inquired Laura.

Bino placed his damp brush on a stool and stepped to the edge of the scaffold. Laura stood below with a serious-looking man in officer's clothing. Adorned with black hair and a full beard, Bino judged him to be no less than thirty years of age. He looked to be the kind of man who wasted little effort to get what he wanted and Bino saw something more. That something was dark and uncomfortable. *Do I know this man?*

Laura observed the peculiar look on the artist's face and began, "Signor Bino, greet a family acquaintance, Lieutenant Rotto de'Gavanti of the local militia."

Bino forced a smile while reaching for a cloth with which to wipe stained hands. He began his descent before the lieutenant raised a hand and spoke.

"Don't bother, *signor*. Miss Laura and I have a carriage waiting."

Startled by the lack of civility, Bino responded, "I see. Perhaps another time, Lieutenant."

Laura was embarrassed and began an apology when Rotto interrupted. "Miss Laura, we must be going."

As fast as they had come, they were gone. Bino threw his rag to the ground. There would be no romantic walk that afternoon. Unsettled, he concluded his work, washed his tools and sought out Renato. He found him amid the chill of the basement in the company of cured meats and casks of wine.

"Welcome, Bino. Do you come for relief from the heat or to share a taste of aged brew?"

"Neither, Renato. Isn't it enough reason to miss you?"

"Ah. What do you wish to know?"

"Why must I want to know something?"

Renato smiled while withdrawing a peg from a barrel of the prior year's vintage.

"Hold this, Bino. Being useful is the price of my company."

Bino helped and allowed the silence before backing into his inquiry.

"Renato, Miss Laura visits with an officer today—a lieutenant by the name of Rotto de'Gavanti. Do you know him?"

"And this matters to you why?"

"Something about him troubled me. It was as if we had met before without enjoying the experience. He seems a poor companion for someone I admire."

Renato stopped what he was doing and reached a wrinkled and sun-darkened hand to his chin. "I see. We are friends, no, Bino?"

"Yes, of course."

"You won't object then to me sharing a little advice?"

"No, not at all."

"Take care. Miss Laura is the second daughter to the most influential family in Monza. You must realize her affection is a prize to be won."

Bino digested the well-intended words and said nothing. Renato moved to a nearby table, lifted an empty cup and poured into it from an open jug of wine. He held the cup towards the artist. "Drink this."

Bino inhaled deeply from the cup before bringing it to his lips and sipping.

Renato frowned and explained, "An introduction was sought some weeks ago by the lieutenant's father. Retired from service, Captain de'Gavanti served our troubled duke for many years. Because he and his battalion ably guarded the roads between Monza and Milan, he sought and won Signor Pelucca's favor. Emboldened by our master's approval, he proposed a union between the son you met today and Enza. When Signor Pelucca informed him her hand had been promised to another, the old soldier shifted his inquiry to Laura."

Bino shook his head. "Am I to understand Laura's father pledged her to this man?"

"No, your patron deserves more credit than that. Master Pelucca allows Rotto to court Laura and earn the family's favor."

"And what of Feder, Federigo Rabbia?"

With genuine surprise, Renato asked, "What do you know of Signor Rabbia?"

"I know only what a *friendly bird* whispered in my ear."

"I see. Well, it seems he fancies himself the better match—one which would unite the two most prominent Monza houses."

"Does Laura enjoy his company?"

"Your *bird* seems to know precious little."

"Renato, please."

"Yes, Signor Rabbia manages to visit Laura with some frequency."

Disappointment was etched across the artist's face. The charming Feder, the ambitious Rotto, both were formidable competitors for Laura's heart.

"Bino?"

"Yes."

"You are a skilled artist enjoying the patronage of Monza's richest family. It is safer to believe yourself worthy of adding only color to her walls."

Bino didn't betray his emotions with words. He lifted his cup and gulped what remained. He returned the cup to the table and imitated a priest by motioning a cross above it.

"A flavorful brew, Renato, thank you; you are a good friend."

Free of soiled clothes and the company of others, Bino walked through the woods towards the boundary of the Pelucca estate. He found a grassy meadow amid wildflowers and sat upon the stump of a tree. The artist faced west and marveled at the brilliant blue and pink clouds above the setting sun. He was transported to his childhood and a simpler time when he could watch the light's last dance above the great lake.

Bino began to pray. *I cannot know, Jesu', whether you find favor with me—more a sinner than saint. I'm ashamed of my selfishness, impatience with fools and lust. Forgive me. If I am worthy of your daughter, Laura, give me to know and I will cherish her—mind, body and soul.*

Some days after Bino's conversation with Renato, he was guiding young Francesco through a writing exercise when he received a private message carrying the seal of Casa Rabbia. The artist excused himself and read its contents.

> *Caro Bino,*
>
> *I recall our carriage ride to Monza and wish to again enjoy your company. If your hosts can spare you for a short time, my parents invite your assistance with a domestic project. You may expect comfortable accommodations, a good wage and my entertaining company. We are eager for your reply.*
>
> *Pace e salute', Feder*

It didn't take Bino long to decide. Near to completing an important project for his patroness, the artist approached her and permission was granted. Signora Pelucca was flattered the Rabbias thought well enough of her taste to invite Bino's assistance with their own home.

Bino needed only explain his departure to Laura. How, he wondered, would she react? He thought of little else and sought her out. He found her returning from a riding lesson. She appeared as she had the day they met—outfitted with knee boots and a leather jacket, her plentiful hair tucked under a cap.

Laura saw the artist approach and directed her horse in his direction.

Bino smiled and greeted her, "Welcome back, *luce della luna*."

"Light of the moon?" she repeated. "Be that true, how be you, *mover of stone*?"

"I am well, Laura."

"And how goes your brushwork?"

"You wouldn't know because you haven't visited me in recent days."

He was right and she wanted to explain. She pointed and said, "There, Bino, walk with us." Laura dismounted, released the horse's lead rope from her saddle and led it towards a shade tree.

She began again, "My mother keeps me from our lessons; she worries I'll one day have a masterpiece but no husband."

He teased, "Your mother doesn't understand; art disappoints less than husbands."

Laura laughed before urging, "Explain this to my mother, please."

"I shall. What else keeps you from me?"

"It's dull beyond words, Bino. Enza and her betrothed accompany me and my *daily suitor* on walks or theater visits in town."

"Suitor of the day?"

"You must remember meeting Rotto, the lieutenant. He and the ever-flattering Rabbia son—Feder—are encouraged by my father to win my affection."

With an impossible-to-ignore frown, Bino asked, "How do you feel about such attention?"

"I don't care for it—though Enza insists I'd be a fool to turn both away."

Bino searched for the truth in her eyes and asked, "Is either suitor the kind of man you would wish to marry?"

"No, I mean I don't know; Rotto is condescending and willful while Feder lacks confidence and direction. I'm hardly prepared to make such a decision."

Bino said nothing.

"Am I wrong? These gentlemen need little but the favor my father's name brings."

Bino was impressed by Laura's candor and encouraged her further. "What more?"

"If you must know, neither has an imagination."

She needn't say anything else. Laura affirmed the quality uniting her spirit with his. Bino changed the subject.

"I leave you for a little while, Laura."

Her expression soured. "What? Why?"

"You needn't worry. I am gone only a fortnight or two. Your mother agreed to share me with one of your suitors."

Laura responded with genuine surprise, "How is that possible?"

"It seems Feder covets both you and your artist; his parents invite me to Casa Rabbia."

Laura was quiet in her confusion and Bino began again, "Are you all right? Would you have me relay any message to Feder?"

They arrived at the shade tree where Laura carelessly tied her horse's lead to a low-hanging branch. Her abrupt movement reflected her mood and temper. "I have no message for Feder."

She turned and thrust her hands against the artist's chest. "And you, when do you return?"

"Three weeks—four at most."

She pouted and looked him up and down in a manner reminiscent of their first meeting.

"You're a disheveled dreamer, artist, but I will miss you all the same."

"Dreamer? Dreams are all I have to keep me company."

"You may think me young, but I'm no fool, Bino. You needn't spend time with me when tavern girls are but a short carriage ride away."

With genuine surprise and a little guilt, Bino responded, "Why do you say such a thing?"

"Because nothing exciting ever happens to me!"

"Laura, you wouldn't want the excitement I've known."

"Shouldn't I be allowed to choose? And you, you never said why you fled Milan."

Bino measured his conscience and decided. He grasped Laura's shoulder and invited her to sit down. "It's time I told you. If I've been silent, it was because I worried you'd think less of me."

It was midday and they sat on the lawn under the tree's canopy. Her horse grazed nearby. Bino pulled a tall strand of grass from the lawn, knotted it and began his tale. He started with his journey from the parish of Luino, through his apprenticeship with Master Scotto and leapt to his engagement with Milanese churches. He made no mention of his time with Signor Argento though admitted to his first love.

"She wouldn't divulge her true name so we fashioned one for her— Nica. She modeled for me and we developed feelings for one another. Under the worst of circumstances we were separated and kept apart."

Laura witnessed his pain and empathized. "How terrible that must have been."

"Terrible it was. I was prepared to flee Milan and return home when I was rescued by the generous intervention of an old man of means. He invited me to look upon my situation with fresh eyes and inspired my work. I owe much of what I've accomplished since to him."

"And the woman? What became of her?"

"I cannot say for sure. Piero, the man who sheltered me, had the resources to care for her and promised to do so. I trust he kept his word."

"I would have liked to make her acquaintance. How rich her life must have been compared to mine."

"Don't say that. She placed herself in harm's way and did so to feed her fatherless son."

Laura noticed the weight of emotion in his eyes and rescued him. "These women, the ones who posed for you?"

"Yes," responded Bino.

"At first they come to support themselves, but they return for more than money—a tender word, a kind gesture or something more tangible. Don't you see, Bino? While you were drawing, these women developed feelings for you. Your attention and empathy fed their admiration and fanned their desire."

Shifting his eyes to hers, Bino whispered, "You may be right; it's a complication of the craft."

"Complication? The man doesn't exist who wouldn't trade places with you."

"I don't know. Few would be worthy of your affection."

She appreciated his humility and reached for his hand.

Bino continued his tale and concluded with his engagement at the church of San Giorgio. He reflected upon the peace he had found there and the quality of his work. "I belonged and understood what it meant to be one with my art and faith."

Bino described the tutelage of Brother Tomas and the burden it had placed on his patience and spirit. He relayed the tragic events as they unfolded. Laura's eyes widened in disbelief.

"And so I bid an urgent goodbye to San Giorgio. I confess to being in your home under false pretense. I came seeking refuge from those who would accuse me of harm."

Bino stood, brushed off his clothes and looked upon his companion; she wore an expression of concern.

"I beg your understanding and apologize. These things happened. I know not why; they just did."

When she didn't say anything, Bino continued, "If you wish, I'll share my story with your father."

She'd had enough. "*Basta, piacere!* Apology? To whom?"

Laura leapt to her feet and embraced him.

"I'm sorry, Bino, *veramente*. You never hinted at such trouble."

Bino returned her embrace and said, "I can't deny the sadness of the situation but what hurt more was not telling you the whole truth."

His candor stirred her and Laura found her head and heart occupying the same space. The glow found its way through her chest to her core and most intimate place. She silenced Bino with a kiss and then another before resting her head against his chest and feeling his heart beating there.

"Thank you for sharing your story with me," she whispered. "I've been alone too long."

The weight of his conscience fell away. The artist felt genuine absolution in Laura's arms—more than that he'd ever experienced in a priest's chamber.

He removed and dropped her riding cap and brushed his lips across her forehead before asking, "How is it possible for one so young to appreciate the power of forgiveness?"

Laura's eyes met his. "I know only that mercy should equal the sincerity with which it's sought. In any case, you did nothing wrong."

For the second time that afternoon, Laura thrust her hands against Bino's chest. She smiled a devilish smile and said, "I would have pushed Tomas off the scaffold long before you willed it to happen."

He grinned and protested, "I did not will it to happen!"

She teased, "Didn't you? You must have won favor with the same *spirit* you pray to each day."

"You make me laugh, Laura—a gift I must repay."

Laura blushed and spun around. The artist was too distracted by the curve of her figure to notice the sly smile accompanying her bold idea.

She rested her hands on her hips. "I know how you can repay me."

"How?" he replied.

"Paint me," she said.

"What?"

"I want to model for you."

"I don't know, Laura. Your parents may not approve."

"They would surely not approve."

"What makes you so sure?"

"Because I want them to know nothing of it until I'm unveiled in fresco upon our wall."

Bino wasn't sure he'd heard Laura correctly until he confirmed the intention within her eyes. It was the same look she had shared the evening they met when she whispered across the dinner table.

"Laura, I cannot."

"Can't or won't?"

"It isn't right. I respect your parents too much to hide the truth."

"What about respecting me?"

"You don't want to hurt them."

"Don't tell me what I want! Enza, Rotto, Feder—the list of offenders grows by the day. I thought you were different."

"That isn't fair, Laura."

"Think about it while you're away, artist. If you agree, I'll work out the details and craft a plan."

"I don't know."

"Will you think about it?"

"How could I think of anything else?"

Laura grinned at his honesty, stepped towards him and whispered, "I like you."

Bino retrieved and restored her riding cap. He grasped her shoulders and spoke from his heart, "So it's an imaginative man you seek?"

"I know of only one."

"And what does he imagine?"

Laura smiled and volleyed, "He imagines all bores in purgatory and the woman he loves with him in paradise."

Bino laughed and lifted her off her feet. "Anything else?"

"Yes, he's bold enough to imagine an epic fresco which truly inspires."

"And once that's accomplished what would he do?"

"Run away with me, of course!"

Bino felt liberated and expressed the affection his heart could no longer conceal. His hands moved from Laura's shoulders to the back of her neck. She yielded to his touch and he guided her. She became his canvas and his lips a generous brush. She held her breath as the artist trailed kisses from her eyelids across her brow to her ears and the nape of her neck. She delighted in his embrace and attention. When she couldn't take it any longer, Laura stood up on her toes and brought her lips to his.

Bino whispered, "I wasn't sure how you felt. You're my first and last thought each day."

He felt a tear on Laura's cheek and tasted its saltiness before returning to her ears and neck. "Don't leave," she pleaded.

"I'm sorry, Laura…I didn't dare believe you cared as I do. I'll be gone only a short while and will miss you more than I have a right to."

"What does that mean?" she asked.

"Just something Renato cautioned me about."

"Pay no mind to our old friend."

"He wants only what's best for your family."

"Then we must convince him to imagine as we do."

On the evening before Signor Rabbia's carriage was to retrieve him, Bino's conscience was heavy. *If Laura cares for me and Feder's intention mirrors mine, how can I accept his invitation?*

So bothered was the artist that he declined the cook's stew that evening in favor of a walk. He wrestled with his past and future before arriving at the family chapel and appreciating the present. He sat there and asked the Holy Trinity for what he thought he most lacked—courage and wisdom.

His mind drifted to his friend and he asked, *How would you guide me, Piero?*

He imagined the response. *What's in your heart? If you could illustrate what you feel on these walls, what would I see?*

The artist pondered the question and imagined a confusing array of characters on the wall. He saw himself, Laura and those who might object to their union—her parents, older sister and suitors. He felt powerless to overcome their objections.

Am I not worthy of a nobleman's daughter? And then there was Laura's rebellious request—"Let me model for you." *I don't know, Piero. I don't know.*

Bino's mind turned to recent projects completed for Signora Pelucca. He'd spent weeks illustrating and painting mythological characters—players in games of forbidden love orchestrated by gods against their mortal prey. Unrequited lovers became heroes through abstinence or death. Could he steal from these themes in Lady Pelucca's Christian chapel?

With the observation arrived an idea. He could cast Laura in her mother's fresco. *The scene would be reverent and better, unobjectionable.*

Bino turned to his other dilemma—how to admit the truth to Feder. He resolved to go to Casa Rabbia and find the right opportunity. Until then, he would volunteer nothing of his affection for Laura.

The next morning, she found him in his quarters and surprised him by closing the door to his room. He turned and noticed her changed. Laura looked content and carefree. Her mood was buoyed by a sense of possibility—satisfied that the man on the receiving end of her smile was capable of liberating her from her family's cruel intention.

Laura had on a new dress and the contrast with the outdoor gear she often wore earned Bino's recognition. "You look beautiful, Laura."

She smiled and pulled her hair forward over her shoulders. "You haven't seen this nest untangled, have you?"

Something about the gesture reminded the artist of Nica. She had once commented that a man could learn much about a woman's comfort and confidence by the way she styled her hair. Laura's new look affirmed both.

"Your hair is a treat for my eyes but is sure to pose a challenge for my brush."

Laura leapt forward. "So, you agree to paint me?"

He embraced her and said, "Yes, be patient with me. I have an idea which shouldn't be hard to make your mother's."

"You're learning, artist."

Their isolation, the press of her body against his and the scent of the lavender she wore aroused him. He took her face in his hands, kissed eager lips and whispered in her ear, "Had I the day, I would spend it loving you."

Laura responded by lifting her hands into Bino's hair and pulling his ear to her lips. "Haven't I been an eager student?"

Bino blushed and asked, "So you come to forgive me for leaving?"

"No, I won't do that, artist. Renato understands my forgiveness relies upon your quick return."

Lady Rabbia

Later that afternoon, Bino completed the short journey to Casa Rabbia. Though more than half the distance to Milan, the artist believed enough time had passed to suppress word of Tomas's passing.

The Rabbia family had resources, owned a good deal of property and made a show of having the entirety of its staff present to receive its guest. Bino found the servants unusually deferential; it seemed an artist worthy of the Pelucca family was one to be admired and treated with gentility.

Following a warm reception by Feder, an introduction followed to his father—a well-appointed and handsome man Bino believed more youthful than his years. Lady Rabbia was younger still and gave the impression of foreign birth. Her eyes and skin were darker than most Milanese women and her clothes tailored to flatter. She smiled and assured the artist there would be time enough for leisure before project conversations.

The artist was invited by Signor Rabbia to lodge in the main house and, as his work allowed, dine with the family in the evening. Feder made quick introductions to two younger siblings before ushering Bino to his quarters. The guest room was not far removed from those of his parents. Feder's own room, he volunteered, honored his desire for independence and was in a detached building.

"In fact, you may see it from your window."

Feder led him to the window, forced the shutters open and pointed. "I'm glad for your company, friend. I need diversion from my chores and dull conversation."

Bino responded, "Considering your generosity and that of the Pelucca family, I now understand what it is to be comfortable. Can your life here be so burdensome?"

"Allow me to answer that another time, Bino. Until then, when not occupied by my mother, prepare yourself for a hunt, starlit fires and evening debate. My father leaves tomorrow and I wish to be liberated."

Bino laughed and responded, "You entertain like no other, Feder."

"It is good of you to say so, friend. Besides, you have an ally in my mother. She insists I not monopolize your time."

After two days of merriment, wine and exaggerated tales, Feder excused himself and allowed Bino project-planning time with his mother. The artist was grateful for the courtesy and accepted his mother's lunch invitation—one he hoped would lead to an improved understanding of her expectations. He made his way to her salon where he found prepared delicacies and drink. She greeted him without the company of a servant.

Bino thought Lady Rabbia attractive and gave her unspoken credit for fashioning herself in a manner that complemented her hair and figure. She was, he estimated, ten years his senior—blessed or challenged to have borne a child when barely beyond being one herself. The artist wondered whether she, like earlier female patrons, sought to buy with coin the attention her younger self had secured for free.

Lady Rabbia was courteous and asked polite questions but there was a hint of something in her manner that discomforted her guest.

"I am pleased you accepted our invitation, Bernardino. You appear everything my son described."

"Feder is generous with his praise, my lady," he said, before adding, "Please call me Bino; I barely know the other name."

She studied him with peculiar intensity. "You're correct, Bino. Praise is better earned than given, no?"

Before the artist could reply, Signora Rabbia invited, "Take a seat and tell me, Bino, whether you are a student of Greek mythology?"

Bino chose a comfortable chair a dozen paces from his hostess, sat and replied, "Somewhat, *signora*; pagan themes entertain and instruct many outside the church; I am no exception. Why do you ask?"

"I'm fond of the story of Cephalus, Procris and Eos—the goddess of dawn. I wish to have their tale expressed upon these walls."

"I see. Their names are familiar. What more can you tell me of these role players?"

Lady Rabbia remained standing and began, "For many years the goddess Eos held Cephalus, the mortal man she desired, captive. He might have loved Eos and wanted for nothing but longed, instead, for his earthly wife Procris. The goddess relented and allowed his reunion with Procris while also giving him reason to doubt her fidelity. A proud man, Cephalus sought to prove Eos wrong.

Finding the tale so far captivating, Bino inquired, "And how did Cephalus intend to accomplish that?"

The bait taken, the lady responded, "He disguised himself as another man to demonstrate his wife was beyond temptation."

Signora Rabbia offered nothing more and took a turn about the room.

Bino grew impatient for the myth's conclusion. When the silence grew too heavy to bear, he asked, "How did our hero fare? Did Procris discover her husband's deception?"

Lady Rabbia stopped, turned towards the artist and smiled. "Fascinating, Bino. Having just heard the plot, you assume the worst and leap to his mortal wife's defense."

"No assumption was made, *signora*, I merely…"

Lady Rabbia interrupted, "Despite not wanting so, Cephalus' seduction worked. When he revealed the truth, Procris fled in shame."

Lady Rabbia continued her turn about the room until she arrived behind the artist's chair. She paused a moment before resting her hands on his broad shoulders. "I wonder, Bino. Procris was many years alone. Would you have forgiven her infidelity?"

Lady Rabbia's touch and question reminded the artist of his own isolation and loneliness and the boundaries he sometimes crossed for consolation. "Yes, I might have excused it. Did he?"

Signora Rabbia lifted her hands and delicately tugged at the back of the artist's collar before continuing her walk about the room. "Cephalus forgave and welcomed Procris home. She returned with two magical gifts—a tireless hunting hound and a target-true javelin. The dog, it seems, met its end chasing a vixen when the gods saw fit to turn both to stone. The javelin would otherwise serve."

Appreciating what courtesy demanded of an attentive listener, Bino invited her to continue.

"Jealous of her husband's mercy, friends of Procris told her Cephalus loved another. Believing them, she followed him on the occasion of his next hunt. When he stopped to rest, she positioned herself near."

The artist shifted in his chair and was hungry to learn the outcome as scripted by the goddess Eos.

Lady Rabbia continued, "Devotion wasn't enough to rescue them, Bino. Procris mistook her husband's vocal praise of nature as devotion to another woman. Full of regret, she sobbed aloud and her cry was mistaken by her husband as an approaching animal. He let fly his never-errant javelin, piercing her heart. By his own hand, Cephalus extinguished the life of his true love."

The artist weighed her words—true love—and the pleasing association conveyed—Laura. Silence occupied the room until the poet broke it. "A sad tale you tell, *signora*. And yet if we believe our souls immortal, a happy ending was yet theirs."

Lady Rabbia laughed, "I will enjoy your company, Bino. You prove yourself a romantic."

"I accept the charge. There is little merit believing otherwise."

His hostess looked out an un-shuttered window and grinned.

"You shan't be interrupted in your work, Bino. My husband and son go missing for days. As for me, I trust you'll welcome the occasional diversion from your labors."

While Bino was left to wonder at her meaning, Lady Rabbia deftly released several hooks securing the throat of her dress. She dropped her hands, turned from the window and stepped towards her prey. Feder's mother leaned into him and offered, "Stay and satisfy yourself, Bino."

Her meaning was clear and challenged him. Bino had known Laura's tenderness in recent days but there was something instinctual in Lady Rabbia's proposition. Long denied satisfaction, her appetite overwhelmed. She had cast herself as Eos and was inviting the mortal artist to set aside his romantic ambition for that which satisfied the flesh.

Lady Rabbia was no longer patroness or mother. She was the goddess whose attention soothed and flattered. She seized the moment, brushed her lips against his ear and whispered.

"Will you accept the project as I describe it, *artist*?"

At odds with his own need, he replied, "I cannot, *signora*."

Lady Rabbia was not deterred. She stood and used her right hand to retrieve a peeled apricot from a bowl at Bino's side. She lifted it to her nose and inhaled before wetting it with her tongue. He thought the fruit would find its way between her lips or his.

His patroness used her left hand to tear a panel of her dress. She exposed a pale and heavy breast and continued her seduction. She lifted her flesh upward and stimulated the areola with the wet and cool fruit.

Bino attempted to escape his chair but Lady Rabbia again leaned forward, forcing him to collapse backward.

His mind argued against his appetite. *How can I?*

Lady Rabbia stepped forcefully upon his foot with one of her own.

"You said mythology teaches, Bino. Imagine yourself at school with a generous goddess."

"I cannot, Lady; someone will surely come."

She sensed his resistance falling and moved the ripe fruit to his lips. She wet them until the artist, unconscious of the breath he held, watched her return the apricot to her mouth and take an intentional bite.

She swallowed and whispered, "Heaven or no, I wonder whether Cephalus appreciated his lost opportunity." And with those words she lifted his hand and laid it upon her flesh.

Months of celibate living collided with the artist's fealty to Laura. He rose to face his willing mistress and without care tore apart the lower panel of her dress. Lady Rabbia relished her victory and Bino's newfound hunger. She was vocal in her encouragement and delighted with Bino's ferocious response. Procris forgotten, Cephalus was without boundaries.

Afterward, Bino's thoughts were as scattered as their clothes about the floor. Lady Rabbia's skin bore the marks of repeated couplings and the artist lay exhausted at her side.

Bino projected his eyes upon the ceiling and imagined the mythological figures below. What he observed surprised. He understood the unrequited goddess but couldn't fathom the man beside her.

Signora Rabbia spoke first. "You've been well instructed, Bino. Is there someone I should thank?"

The artist was in no mood to trade tales. "Please *signora*, I beg you to say nothing of this afternoon to anyone."

"You needn't worry. The next time depends upon you."

"I cannot, Lady. The God I pray to would have me leave your home this very day."

Signora Rabbia grabbed a handful of Bino's curls and protested, "My silence, artist, relies upon the completion of our project. Until then, it would be better your god knew little of me."

Bino was anxious about her lack of discretion and soon lost himself in his labors. His conscience was at odds with her company and the pleasure her flesh might afford. He resolved to avoid time alone with Lady Rabbia and interpreted his sacrifice as argument against Renato's wine-cellar warning: *Better to not believe yourself worthy of Laura's affection.*

Feder noted his friend's preoccupation and pace and attributed the speed with which he worked as evidence of his artistic passion. So rapid and fine was Bino's progress, what else, his friend wondered, could it be? When he asked his guest if he was unwell, no answer came.

Bino admitted his vulnerability to no one and declined Lady Rabbia's invitations unless he knew others would be present. In the hours between work and rest the artist plagued himself with an unanswerable question: *Why didn't I remain at Casa Pelucca?*

His resolve proved effective until the night he and Feder returned from starlight drinking; he found Lady Rabbia waiting for him in his bed chamber. More than a dozen candles blazed and cast a glow across his mattress, desk and chair. His patroness sat upon the bed—several lengths of cord coiled at her side. He thought it strange she didn't greet him; her eyes were instead fixated on her hands. One held a bowl while the other tilted a candle above; it dripped molten wax inside.

"You've neglected me, Bino. Weren't you satisfied? Or is your hunger of a peculiar kind?"

"Lady Rabbia…"

"I bid you not to speak this night. I may be no lady but you remain my servant."

She rested the bowl and candlestick upon his desk before reaching an empty hand for the cut cords. She stood and walked towards him amidst the shadows. Her robe was open and he couldn't deny the allure of candle-light playing against her pale legs, breasts and sex.

Lady Rabbia stood before him and whispered, "You're allowed one choice this evening—one of two words. You must select one and oblige me the other."

She leaned in and brought her lips to his ear. She blew softly there and asked, "If it's redemption you seek, be it through pleasure or pain?"

Sober or no, the artist understood what he must do. He would escape, accept the risk and walk the Monza road. He reached up to gently force Lady Rabbia away but she resisted. When he released her, she leapt in front of the door and dropped her robe. "Aren't my silence and body worthy of your attention?"

Silence? Bino was paralyzed, unable to find words equal to her threat and seduction.

"I won't be kept waiting, artist. You need only choose and I am yours. Is it to be pleasure or pain?"

Drunk and discouraged, Bino chose to receive that which he couldn't render to another. "I choose pain."

Lady Rabbia studied him, grinned and said, "I thought so; you're a mystery no longer."

She allowed no time for a change of heart. "Let's begin, Bino. Pleasure is impatient and strong knots take time."

Bino woke late the following morning and wished it all had been a bad dream. His wrists and ankles bore the marks of Lady Rabbia's cords while his chest and thighs revealed the blistering of hot wax. So long neglected by her husband and society, she brought her need and scars to him. Afterward, she claimed her pleasure and taunted him until he demanded his.

I must finish and leave.

Subsequent days were nervous ones but there was one curious reward for the artist. Feder made no mention of Laura. It was as if she was forgotten. Their conversations were of a light-hearted nature and this remained true until Feder invited him to join a pheasant hunt. It would remove Bino from their home and he accepted.

Three of them set out before dawn—Bino, Feder and his servant, Nondo. Nondo was older than Feder though behaved more the part of younger brother than mentor.

Nondo readied their nets, tools and the leather sacks necessary for transporting captured game. Bino and Feder carried packs of their own; these held wine, bread and bits of smoked meats to satisfy mid-day hunger. Their march into the wilderness began.

The artist enjoyed the walk and conversation. Since departing Luino as a boy, he hadn't enjoyed uninterrupted hours outdoors and was grateful for the soothing atmosphere afforded by nature. He relaxed along ever-green corridors and within fields of wildflowers. The sights and smells invigorated and he embraced the contrast between this environment and his own—one filled with the aroma of damp plaster, lime and stain.

While appreciative of the beauty surrounding them, Bino understood the harm they might soon inflict upon God's creatures. *Better I observe than participate.* Not since striking Signor Argento had Bino raised a hand against a living thing. Still, he admired those gifted enough to bring food to his table and was eager to witness Feder's methods. Not long after, he had the chance.

Feder knew where to find ground-dwelling pheasants while Nondo's keen eyes identified their feathers amid like-colored flora. Once spotted, Bino was expected to flush the birds from the brush towards his friends.

Feder had the more difficult task. He stood opposite Bino and readied himself with a stone-weighted net. He must intercept the birds' progress and prevent flight; timing and accuracy were critical. At first, their coordination was poor and the birds escaped. With practice, the unlucky ones grew in number. Each had its neck quickly broken by Nondo before being squeezed lifeless into his leather bag.

Bino was offered a turn with the net and couldn't say no. Doing so might call into question his sense of adventure or worse, insult his host.

"I'll do it, Feder, but I fear your confidence is misplaced. A paintbrush would be more at home in your hands than this net in mine."

Feder laughed and offered, "Don't puzzle over it. Let me show you how it's done."

Feder guided him on throwing technique and direction before their walk resumed. Bino half-hoped nothing would be discovered so near to noon. Nothing was until Nondo spotted a well-hidden bird a short distance away.

"Draw closer and be ready, friend!" And with that, Feder made a wide circle about their prey.

Where only one pheasant was thought to exist, two scrambled towards Bino. Their paths didn't stray from one another and a single effective throw might bring both down.

"Now!" shouted Nondo and Bino let loose the net with all the strength and rotation his hips would allow. The net flew true, giving up one of the pair and collapsing atop the other.

Feder shouted his approval but Bino could only feign pleasure. He was proud to add to the day's bounty though he harbored some regret. He looked after the liberated bird and wondered whether it had been forever denied a companion in flight.

Feder and Nondo measured the position of the sun, estimated the time and counted their kill. Nondo shared the tally: "Six dead, seven lost and time to lunch."

Feder followed with, "So be it, Nondo. Let's eat and toast our partner."

They found a shady spot upon which to rest their gear and themselves. Nondo distributed the dried beef and bread. Within minutes these were gone and a bladder of wine was passed between them to wash their thirst away. The brew relaxed them and Nondo, who only a moment earlier had reclined beneath his cap, was heard snoring.

Little was said until Feder grew tired of the silence and began. "Bino, I am grateful to you for coming and ask your forgiveness for my parents. My father, he is forever preoccupied with the estate while my mother is left too much alone and in need of distraction."

The artist didn't need the reminder and wondered, *If you only understood how alone, friend...* Bino responded, "Your kindness is undeserved and means much to me. I'm nearly done and intend to return to Casa Pelucca as soon as possible."

"Won't you stay longer? Out time together has been short."

"Thank you but I cannot." Bino offered no explanation.

Feder looked discouraged and explained, "The wine supports my confession, Bino. When we met, I expected little more than what your acquaintance could buy with Laura's parents. I was selfish about that and didn't appreciate what more you could teach this victim of privilege."

"Victim of privilege?"

"Yes, I can explain. Shall our first lesson begin?"

"As you wish."

"I'm restless and dissatisfied, Bino. I feel this way despite having what most men desire. You, on the other hand, seem at peace with your tools, occupation and next meal. How is it so?"

"More wine is necessary to answer such a question," responded the artist.

"Drink then and answer me this. Is it your art and the sacred spaces you call home that yield the peace I seek?"

"I claim no special peace, Feder. What I can claim is one less curse than you."

"Don't tell me you have no cock!"

Bino laughed. "No, no, we share that curse to be sure. What I lack is the curse of choice. I'm too poor to suffer the freedom plaguing other men."

"Be damned! What am I to do about that when so much is expected of me?"

"It isn't for me to say. Ask yourself whether what your father commands is likely to please or disappoint."

"And when the answer isn't clear?"

"I pray, Feder. When a difficult choice looms, I sometimes pray with desperation that God reveals the better path more clearly."

"Does it work?"

"If God speaks through our intuition, then yes, it works. In the in-between moments, I admit my fallibility, take communion, and walk through open doors. There, despite trials, satisfaction can be found."

"And when there is no work, no security?"

"He keeps me company."

"Who keeps you company?"

"Men and women come and go but a friendly ghost, Piero, urges me on."

"Where does this friend call home?"

Bino considered the question and told the truth. "Piero's life ended some years ago; he still whispers to me and often has much to say."

Feder rose, walked to the edge of the wood and relieved himself. Upon returning he said, "You are different, artist. I have no ghost with whom to speak." He reflected before continuing, "Perhaps we've had too much wine."

"Perhaps, but some things defy explanation, Feder. Where you search for peace, that place, requires an allowance for the inexplicable."

"And allowing for the inexplicable, I'll want for nothing?"

"I didn't say that."

"There is something else, friend. I have a heavy heart. I once admitted to you the affection I feel towards Lady Pelucca's daughter, Laura; you're no doubt well acquainted with her."

"Yes, I'm fortunate to call her 'friend'."

"What do you think of her?"

Bino shared the truth but not the whole truth. "She is young, willful and wonderful."

"Yes, all true; there is much to distinguish her from other women."

Bino asked, "Have you told her how you feel?"

"Yes, I mean no, not explicitly anyway. We have spent afternoons together in the company of her sister."

"What concerns you, Feder?"

"She appears disinterested. When we're together, she is polite but distracted."

Bino observed and listened. His companion continued, "I was patient and hopeful until learning a local officer was similarly smitten. Her parents may favor such a match."

"I have seen him about. Are you acquainted with Lieutenant de'Gavanti?"

"No, though I'm told he's the worst sort of man—all uniform and no soul."

"I cannot deny the claim."

"What am I to do?" asked Feder before regretting the question. "Forgive me, Bino; it's rude of me to ask." He recast the question, "Were it to come down to the lieutenant or me and Laura sought your opinion, could I count on your support?"

Bino was faithful in his response. "Were my opinion sought on such a question, you may rely on my support."

The conversation ended; it was time to return home. Nondo woke, collected their things and bag of game. The trio walked towards the western horizon where the artist's attention was diverted by a sight he alone appreciated. There, in the foreground of the setting sun, a solitary pheasant creased the sky before them.

Bino's sleep was fitful that evening. Feder's final question—one inviting loyalty—plagued him. The artist was a guest in the home of a woman who had twice seduced him and a friend he was likely to betray.

It was past midnight. Bino lifted himself from bed, lit a candle and circled the room. He wished Renato was present. *I will beg his counsel.* Having no such confidant at Casa Rabbia, he prayed.

I cannot keep this secret any longer. If you're listening, Jesu, what would you have me do?

Bino's attention was diverted across the room to a cantilevered shelf. He spotted motion—a mouse lifting its nose in the air. It fixed its gaze upon him before dashing across the shelf, upsetting a cup with his instruments and making its escape below. The mouse entered a foundation crack and disappeared. Bino wished he could follow.

The artist stepped to his desk intending to restore things. As he lifted a pen he was inspired to write. Bino sat and rolled the instrument between stained fingers. He used it to stir an ink well before removing a leaf of drafting paper from a leather case. Understanding what he must say, the poet rid his pen of excess ink, touched it to paper and wrote.

> *Cara Laura*
> *In hallowed spaces I spend days alone.*
> *In the company of saints I confess my fears.*
> *With worthy men of vows I make a home.*
> *Now home is wherever you are near.*
> *I pray a higher purpose to find.*
> *As a farmer seeds to make new life.*

My tools are of a less worthy kind.
My brush may not support a wife.
Was fortune to smile on our love,
Could another lover I betray?
The caretaker does not steal away the dove.
Better I set you free some say.
You look above and give God's glory a name.
I speak of crosses, a cloak and stone.
With me there is little hope of glory or fame.
With me you shan't ever be alone.
Be nourished, Laura, by my devotion.
My heart and colors are all I have to give.
With these words I reveal the depth of my emotion.
Our kiss—the passion with which I promise to live.

Bino re-read his verse. Satisfied and too tired to notice the absence of his signature, he rolled the parchment and sealed it with wax. He wrapped the note in a handkerchief and tied the bundle with a piece of twine. To it he affixed a delivery card and indicated his intended recipient—*Signorina Laura, Casa Pelucca.*

The poet made a sign of the cross, extinguished his candle and returned to bed. When the rooster crowed at sunrise, Bino rose and relayed his parcel to a servant with instructions. Assured of its timely delivery, he sat at the breakfast table alone. He likened himself to a figure in one of his frescos—an unprepared actor within a drama he was helpless to control.

Padre Castani

Padre Castani lifted his hands and the Eucharist above the altar and shared the words he'd spoken daily in imitation of Christ for three decades: *Fa questo in memoria di me—Do this in memory of Me*. His lips completed the rest of the invocation while his mind drifted elsewhere. He looked over the heads and shoulders of the small congregation—widows alone in their grief, poor farmers praying for rain and young children gripped by mothers thirsty for an easier life. The priest saw distress and sadness and selfishly wondered whether he might ever be so fortunate as to serve those less wanting.

He heard their collective *Amen*, placed the consecrated bread on their tongues and later greeted the congregants with a sympathetic heart. "Yes, we'll bless the grave this week…the Lord is sure to bring us rain… I'll come by to lend your husband a hand."

Padre Castani retreated to his quarters with the little gifts the parishioners offered instead of coins—a few eggs in a basket, a loaf of yesterday's bread and a cup of butter. He unwrapped each with his characteristic gentleness and spoke a blessing over the gifts. He stepped to the window, threw open the shutters and considered his recent disillusionment.

Why am I so faithless? Forgive me, Father. Let me not be ungrateful.

The priest had made a habit of giving his cares to God in recent months, asking only that his heart and soul be present in his work. *If not here, Father, then in a place of your choosing.*

Excluding each birth, sunrise and harvest, Padre Castani had witnessed few miracles in his thirty years of priesthood. He had reason to kneel a day later when one disguised as a letter from the local bishop arrived. It was delivered to his door by a uniformed servant from Rome. Padre Castani sat and read the words, wondering at their unusual timing and the consequences for the faithful of Luino.

> *Brother Castani,*
>
> *Our Lady's apparition at Serono and those claiming miracles attract ever-increasing numbers of pilgrims to Her shrine. As such, the church wants for seasoned priests who can shepherd the faithful and educate young seminarians. It is the wish of our Most Holy Bishop of Rome that I commend someone to serve there. I am pleased to nominate you.*
>
> *Make fast your reply; the faithful of Luino can expect a suitable replacement for you soon after.*

Padre Castani read the invitation twice more before folding it with care and placing it in his robe pocket; his eyes welled with tears.

The bishop of Rome invites me to leave my parish and serve the pilgrims of Serono. By what magic do You make this happen, Father?

Padre Castani rose from his bench and rubbed a tired knee. He made a sign of the cross about his face and shoulders before gripping the prayer beads at his waist. He told the messenger he would have his answer in a few hours and encouraged the young man to occupy the time with a turn about Luino's lakeshore.

Excused and alone, the priest stepped back through the entryway into the adjacent chapel and looked upon it with new eyes. It was midday at the start of a new week and the sun shone brightly. He followed the light from a rear window and noted that the beam was landing upon the portrait painted years earlier by one young and gifted—Antonina's son, Bino.

The portrait of Saint Catherine was little faded and remained a fascination for old and young alike. The light played upon the saint's features and she seemed to be smiling at him.

The priest whispered to no one, "Where is the author of your portrait, Saint Catherine?"

Padre Castani and Antonina had heard infrequently from Bino after his apprenticeship and during the years when the artist was engaged in Milan. In recent months there had been no word at all. There were rumors of trouble and the priest discounted these as gossip.

More often there were accolades from those who visited the city and returned with stories of lively and reverent frescos decorating the walls of San Maurizio and San Giorgio. Villagers lifted their chins and chests upon hearing and spoke proudly of how one of their own had made good. They were generous with praise and boasted how Bino, the student, had bettered his much-lauded teacher, Leonardo.

How many years have you now, Bino? Can it be thirty and five? I pray you're shining, not as the sun, but as the moon lights the night.

The priest knelt and offered a prayer for the artist he'd sent away a boy and the community he knew he would leave behind. His mind drifted to his last and only trip to Serono. He recalled the penitent girl, Caterina. *Is she aware she possesses the courage of the saint whose portrait we so admire?* And there was her too-human father, the stonemason, Eduardo, who'd made possible his visit within Mary's church.

Wherever they be, Holy Mother, whether living or in your company, I pray You make easier their path. Il nome di Padre, Figlio, e Spiritu Santo.

When the messenger returned to his door that afternoon, Padre Castani was ready with his reply. He knew it was poor form to deny any request from the bishop.

"Come in, come in, young man."

"*Ti ringrazio*, Padre."

The priest studied the servant before him. He was handsome, tall and unpretentious. The messenger appeared to have fewer than thirty years but possessed the eyes of one wiser than his age.

The priest spoke first. "Forgive my manners. In my eagerness to read your correspondence, I failed to ask your name."

"You needn't worry, Padre. Few outside my village care. My name is Giovanni."

The priest smiled and offered, "A saintly name to be sure. Tell me, son, how were you selected for this duty?"

"Time was short. I alone was familiar with the region. In fact, before I volunteered for service, I shared an inn with my parents in Serono."

"Serono?"

"*Si'*, Padre. My mother remains there and runs the inn for those making pilgrimage."

"Ah yes. While I didn't have the pleasure of bedding there, I spotted the inn during my only visit to our Lady's shrine. And what of your father?"

"He died not long ago; his was a hard life."

"I see. You honor him with your service to Rome and the care of your mother. And Our Lady's church, are you acquainted with the pastor?"

Giovanni's cheeks filled with color as he admitted, "Not well, Padre. The demands of helping my mother and father were at odds with Sunday worship."

"I see, son. Our Lord is merciful and able to forgive much. Make your conscience lighter and speak of it when you next make a confession."

Giovanni said he would before the priest's curiosity moved the conversation in a different direction. "And Rome, what can you tell me about life there?"

Giovanni recalled the same question from Caterina and Isabella. "Rome? It is a gift to behold, Padre. It remains a monument to an earlier time, though not a Christian time, and hardly one now. I don't feel at ease there and seek every opportunity to return home."

Padre Castani appreciated the young man's sincere appraisal. "You are not the first to express that opinion, Giovanni. And yet our Lord invites us to go where He is most needed and so, it appears, shall I. You may inform those who sent you of my acceptance."

"Your acceptance is sure to please, Padre. And wonderful for those who call Serono home. In fact when you arrive, my mother will insist you spend a night at our humble inn; as you know, it is only a short walk to Mary's church."

"I won't disappoint her, son. Where are you bringing my reply?"

The courier smiled broadly. "To Serono, Padre, as the bishop is to arrive in a week's time."

Noticing Giovanni's smile the priest inquired, "Your mother's cooking? Is it what brings a smile to your face?"

Giovanni blushed a second time. "To be sure, Padre, but also a girl. You would like her. She is no stranger to Mary's church and her father, an artisan there, allows us to keep company. I hope to make her my wife."

It didn't occur to Padre Castani that the artisan and his daughter were the very souls he'd been praying for in the chapel.

"Does the young lady know of your visit and intention?"

"My visit is sure to surprise; she doesn't expect me for several weeks more. As for my intention, I am less certain of her reply."

Padre Castani took note as Giovanni grew quiet and looked away.

"What is it, son?"

"The girl, she is someone special and, I fear, deserving of someone better."

"Be at peace, son; your modesty is your prayer. 'Blessed be the poor in spirit, for the kingdom shall be theirs.'"

Giovanni made eye contact with the priest. "May it be so, Padre."

"Delay no longer. Go and share my answer. Tell the bishop I make fast my preparations and will leave Luino within a fortnight."

There was something in Padre Castani's manner and message that reassured Giovanni. He left the lakeside village pleased he would see the priest again and thrilled only days separated him from Caterina.

He would kiss her the first chance he got and not just any kiss but the sort soldiers dream of during long periods of inaction. He couldn't bring himself to think of anything save for her affection and the positive message to be relayed to the bishop of Lombardia.

Caterina

Three days later Caterina rose to the sound of anxious fowl outside her unshuttered window. She rolled over in bed and remembered Isabella had reason not to be there. She was tending to a woman before childbirth and would be a welcome houseguest before, during and shortly after the child's arrival.

Caterina felt the morning breeze against her skin and pulled her blanket higher. She welcomed the rising sun's reach through her window while gliding warm hands over chilled arms and shoulders. The sensation made her shiver and, in the moment, feel alone.

Her thoughts went to a familiar place—the wooded path she'd enjoyed with Giovanni and Isabella. She replayed the opening of his gift, his quiet expressions of kindness and her favorite memory—the embrace that made her cares fade. The significance of his embrace grew stronger with each day of their separation and she asked herself whether the depth of Giovanni's feeling was merely the wishful thinking of a stonemason's daughter.

Let it be more than this, Mary; I pray You return Giovanni safely to me.

When the wishing grew too much for her to bear, Caterina rose and prepared for the day. She washed and dressed before entering the large room adjacent to her own. Here she made her parents' bed, removed ashes from the stove and swept away the small stones and dust that had found their way into her father's work clothes. Satisfied her parents would find their home in better order, Caterina grabbed a scarf and fruit basket and exited the cottage.

Caterina closed her eyes and tilted her face toward the sun. She judged the direction of the breeze and took a less cautious breath; today the air would be unspoiled by the stench of farm animals and emptied chamber pots. The air was fresh and pure and carried only the hint of distant fires.

Caterina placed her basket on the ground and wrapped her scarf about her hair. When done, she lifted the basket and selected the path leading to nonno's orchard.

A short distance away Giovanni couldn't believe his good fortune. He'd been approaching Eduardo's cottage from the east when he spied Caterina's departure. He might have been spotted were the sun not at his back blinding her to his presence. Instead he treated himself to a generous look. With the morning light upon her, Caterina appeared otherworldly— surely lovelier than the day they parted. When she walked in the opposite direction, he allowed a safe distance and followed unnoticed.

Caterina stepped along the earthen path until it ended and a greener one began. She paused, lifted the hem of her skirt and moved with taller steps through knee-high grass until arriving at the orchard. In front of her were a dozen or more trees laden with her favorite treat—sweet apricots. Abundant sun and just enough moisture contributed to this season's generous harvest. She smiled at the bounty before her eyes, whispered gratitude and sprinted towards the most mature tree.

Giovanni heard her gleeful scream before the distance between them grew. He paused to watch a moment longer before following. He stopped when she reached her destination and heard her giggle as she repeatedly leapt as high as her legs and dress allowed.

Having succeeded, Caterina gripped a stem full of the pale orange fruit before selecting one to sample. She rubbed its furry flesh between the palms of both hands, noticing its weight and texture. She brought the fruit to her nose and measured its sweetness before touching it to her lips. She was poised to take a bite when some unexpected motion caught her attention.

The feeling in her gut began as fear but shifted quickly to paralyzing excitement. She saw someone who looked like Giovanni in the distance and wondered whether it was an apparition. *Can it be? Him? In this place?*

Without a care, her hand clenched the object of her forgotten appetite; she let the moist and pulpy residue fall to the ground.

When Giovanni appreciated her notice, he stopped. Thirty paces separated them from one another. He spoke first.

"Forgive me, Caterina. I didn't intend to startle you. I meant only to knock on your father's door when I saw you leave and followed."

Caterina had only a single thought, *I love the way you speak my name.*

She swallowed a nervous gulp before responding, "Papa didn't tell me. I hadn't any idea you were home."

Giovanni saw the surprise in her eyes before admitting, "I've not yet been home. When I saw you looking so carefree, I didn't want to interupt you."

Caterina wondered whether Giovanni had witnessed her embarrassing scream, sprint to the orchard and childlike leap into the tree. *What can he think of me?*

When she said nothing, Giovanni misunderstood. "I'm sorry; it was rude of me to say nothing."

"Yes, I mean no; you needn't worry."

"It's wonderful to see you, Caterina."

The way he looked at her made her stomach shift in a peculiar way and her face filled with warmth and color. She wanted to hear him speak the same words again but instead asked, "Do you like apricots?"

"Apricots?"

"Yes, all you see here, these once belonged to my grandfather and are the best to be found near Serono."

Giovanni smiled at what he reasoned was nervousness. "The best in Serono? I'm sure you're to be trusted in such matters. May I have a taste?"

"Yes, of course."

Caterina turned, retrieved the stem she'd dropped before and selected an apricot with care. She lifted the fruit to her nose and confirmed its readiness. Satisfied, she carelessly lifted the hem of her dress and rubbed the apricot flesh across it. When she realized her accidental immodesty, she blushed and offered the fruit in an outstretched palm.

Giovanni knew her gesture was unintended and stepped forward. Though his hunger was of a different kind, he accepted and tasted the sweet fruit before pulling her into his arms.

Caterina was overwhelmed by his embrace and offered no resistance. She wanted his kiss and he need not have asked when Giovanni placed his hands in the small of her back and whispered his request.

She tried in vain to answer without words before he delicately touched his lips to hers and then again and again with urgency. Caterina drew her tongue against his and tasted the sweetness of her apricot there. She would never see, touch or taste the fruit again without calling to mind this unexpected, glorious moment.

"You came back to me," she whispered.

"Did you doubt I would?"

"I didn't doubt you. I worried someone or something might keep us apart."

Giovanni kissed her and glided his hands from her shoulders to her hips and back again. She liked feeling him against her and stood tall on her toes so their bodies might fit better still. Here amidst the sun and the orchard, holding the object of her cascading desire, Caterina felt joy and an inclination to accept whatever he might ask of her.

Giovanni didn't wish to release her while knowing he must; she felt him shudder and relax his embrace.

"What is it?" she asked as he looked above her shoulder. "Look at me."

He did so and responded, "I came to see you, yes, but I also come to ask you and your father..."

The words barely escaped his lips before Caterina thrust her hands against his chest, forcing him an arm's length away.

"Ask me what?"

"We need..."

"Ask Papa what?"

Giovanni neglected his prepared speech, looked into her eyes and spoke from his soul. "I came to ask if you'd make me the most grateful man alive. If you'd wait for me until my service ended? If you'd be willing to separate from your sister, mother and father and be my wife?"

Since his departure, Caterina hadn't allowed herself the pleasure to imagine these questions. Now that he gave voice to them, she could do little but hold him, feel and respond.

"No, Giovanni."

"No?"

She stilled him by placing a finger against his lips. "No, my soldier, I won't wait for you. We must ask Papa to marry before you return to Rome."

Giovanni reached for the finger that guarded his lips and kissed the palm of her hand. "Are you sure?"

"Yes, I'm certain of it."

"There is something to your God, Caterina; you are the answer to my only prayer."

She hugged him tighter and whispered, "Faith is rewarded, Giovanni, and you give me every reason to believe in our Lady's grace."

"But your father, he is sure to think us reckless."

"Leave Papa to me; he will understand."

Giovanni recalled his other news. "A new priest comes this very week from Luino; I am here to share the news of his acceptance with the bishop."

"Does he come willingly?" she asked.

"If you're asking whether he comes with regret or to inspire, I'd say the latter. I like him very much, Caterina. He might be convinced, with our hoped-for approval, to celebrate our marriage."

Caterina kissed him again before pushing against him playfully, "Hope? Keep doubting me, Giovanni, and I may change my mind about you. Now help me reach my precious fruit so we won't go home empty-handed."

Rotto

Lieutenant de'Gavanti knew it was time. He would yield to his father's insistence, seek an audience with Signor Pelucca and make the case for the union of their two houses. Maybe then the nightmares would stop.

He stood unsteady and in uniform before his dead mother's looking glass and took the measure of his appeal. His left hand shook and experience taught him to grip it by the wrist with his right until the tremor faded. When he was a boy, Rotto had favored his left hand. That lasted until the local priest took his father aside and described the inclination as devil's work. The next morning and for weeks thereafter, his father tied Rotto's left wrist to his hip.

The forced use of his right hand made Rotto's writing and swordsmanship awkward. Peers made sport of his handicap and the lifelessness of his left arm. He recalled pleading with his father for relief but it came too late. It arrived only after the priest assured his father of the correctness of his discipline and victory over evil.

Rotto massaged his wrist and met his own eyes in the looking glass. He thought of Laura. He had no need or want of a wife but understood his father's financial support depended upon it. The young soldier didn't object to the company of women; he simply found more pleasure in the company and within the arms of men. When his father recognized that truth, he treated his son's heart as he would a second left hand.

Rotto lectured himself, *If it forever satisfies and rids me of him, I'll deny the truth, hide my sin and take a wife.* The words he would say to Laura's father made him nauseous but he persisted in repeating them until they were almost believable.

"Signor Pelucca, you are kind to welcome me. With your encouragement and through many chaperoned visits, Laura and I are better acquainted.

As you've learned, I'm a commissioned officer of the Guard. With your permission to wed and with Laura as my wife, I would gain access to diplomatic posts and richer stipends.

I would support your daughter and give you grandsons—one of whom I pledge will bear your name.

I have the blessing and support of my father who already conveyed a parcel of land so that Laura and I might build a home and harvest a garden."

Disgusted by his father's insistence they wed but fully aware doing so would mean little to his private pleasures, the soldier persisted in his practice. Rehearsed and certain of the outcome, Rotto sought out his aide and commanded their mounts be ready within the hour for the ride to Casa Pelucca. He wished his conscience was as clear as his path.

The sun was still rising towards its late-morning zenith when Rotto and his subordinate arrived upon the gated carriageway of Casa Pelucca. They paused when his aide called attention to a lone rider approaching from the opposite direction.

The lieutenant knew most of the travelers who had reason to cross this section of Lombardia. The posture and dress of this man were unfamiliar to the soldier. Feeling the weight of their eyes, the traveler pulled up on his reins as Rotto inquired, "You there, are you destined for Casa Pelucca this morning?"

A bit unsettled by the officer's military attire, the young man responded, "Yes, sir; I'm a courier sent to deliver a letter to a member of the Pelucca family."

"And whom do you call master, boy?"

"Signor Rabbia, sir."

"I see. We will save you the trouble as we're headed there ourselves."

"It's no bother, sir."

"Don't be foolish. I'll see that Signor Pelucca himself receives the letter. I'll be in his company shortly."

With some hesitation the courier replied, "I reason that would be all right. Only thing, sir, is that the letter isn't addressed to Signor Pelucca. It's intended for Signorina Pelucca."

With heightened curiosity Rotto responded, "I'll see it, boy."

The courier nervously produced the letter and studied it a moment before handing it over to the assertive officer.

Rotto accepted it and confirmed, with not a little surprise, Miss Laura as its intended recipient. Indifferent to the messenger's discomfort, the soldier placed the cloth-wrapped package into the breast pocket of his overcoat. "Consider it delivered, boy."

"Th...thank you, sir."

"Be on your way then."

"Yes, sir."

The lieutenant's aide studied Rotto with eyes that wondered at his motive. He was about to inquire about his companion's intentions before thinking better of it.

"Shall we continue, sir?"

"Yes, yes, lead the way."

Granted access by the gatehouse steward, the visitors soon found themselves in the company of Signor Pelucca's property manager, Renato.

Hollow greetings were exchanged and the lieutenant wasted little time in asking to be seen by Laura's father. Renato, barely masking his distaste for the officer, wished he could lie and deny an audience. His conscience wouldn't allow it. He pointed to where the junior officer could water their horses and invited Rotto to follow him to the house.

When inside, Renato said, "If time allows, Signor Pelucca will see you. You may wait here in the foyer."

"Don't delay, old man. We have important business."

"Yes, of course, Lieutenant."

Renato left the soldier. Once out of sight, he spat on the coat given to his care and took longer than necessary to locate his master.

Left alone, Rotto adjusted his uniform collar, crossed his arms behind his back and paced about the foyer. The room was circular and felt spacious owing to a domed, white-washed ceiling.

At each sixty-degree turn was one of Bino's frescos. The characters in each of six stations were expressively rendered within the mythological stories the artist recreated.

Rotto had been to Casa Pelucca throughout his courtship and was sure he had looked upon the same walls before. Still, he admitted to himself, *It's as if I'm seeing these frescos for the first time.* The paintings so distracted him he failed to notice Laura enter and just as quickly exit the space behind him. Curious at his being there and wishing to remain hidden, she positioned herself in the shadow of an arched doorway.

Rotto moved from panel to panel, marveling at the quality of the art. He would be sure to win favor with his host by complimenting his patronage of the arts.

Laura moved unseen from one foyer archway to the next. She was amused and soon bewildered by what she witnessed.

The lieutenant arrived at the last fresco where Bino's story concluded. Rotto chose the moment to remove his uniform cap and dab at the sweat beading on his brow. He turned his back on the final panel and returned to the center of the room. He restored his kerchief to his pocket and was poised to return his cap to his skull when an ominous feeling overcame him. He looked up and, spotting nothing there, returned his eyes to Bino's concluding fresco. What he saw startled him. *How can this be? By what magic is this?*

The soldier wondered if he was imagining it but as he hurried about the room looking in each direction, there was no denying the peculiar truth. Across all six panels the characters who moments earlier had been engaged with one another appeared now to focus on him. Their eyes met his with suspicion and hostility and a chill rose from his heels through the back of his legs to his core. So startled was the soldier he dropped his cap and spun about. His breath quickened and he wished he'd not sent Renato away.

Certain his eyes were tricking him, the lieutenant shut them and again mopped his brow. He stepped blindly towards the nearest wall, seeking support.

While Laura was bewildered by her suitor's behavior, it paled in comparison to what she next observed. An arm's length from the fresco before him, Rotto lowered his chin and opened his eyes to the imagined hostility surrounding him. He could take it no longer.

He pleaded, "Don't look at me that way!"

From across the room came a response. "Lieutenant, are you unwell?"

Rotto spun about with dread. There, in the center of the room, bending over to retrieve his guest's cap from the floor, was Signor Pelucca. Neither saw Laura speed away.

Embarrassed, though relieved to have company, the anxious officer stepped forward with an outstretched hand. "Forgive me, Signor, I...I was merely admiring the fine frescos you commissioned here."

"You needn't say more, Lieutenant. Since the artist's arrival, visitors to Casa Pelucca delight in these images."

Signor Pelucca handed the officer his cap. "They are quite realistic, no?"

Signor Pelucca motioned towards one and offered, "Of the six, I admit to this being my favorite. Which do you prefer?"

The soldier was at first reluctant to gaze upon the walls but felt obliged to do so. He turned his attention to the fresco to which his host pointed. Rotto lifted his eyes and was relieved all was as it had been before. The characters were no longer focused upon him and he wondered at the mystery behind imagining they were. *Damned be drink; the wine is to blame!*

Wishing he was anywhere but there, the soldier pretended agreement. "Your eye is keen, *signor*. I cannot but agree with your choice."

"I'll remember to introduce you to the artist, Lieutenant. Regrettably, Bernardino is occupied by a neighbor these days."

Signor Pelucca studied his guest and continued, "If you don't mind my saying so, Lieutenant, you look as though you've seen a spirit. Follow us to my den where Renato will pour us some wine. We can send for the doctor if you wish."

"No, thank you, *signor*, whatever ailed me passed. I would be pleased to follow you and have a word."

When they left the entryway, Laura returned. She positioned herself in the center of the room and turned about as her tormented suitor had, observing the frescos one by one. Where Rotto witnessed hostility, she found only peace. Bino's characters were human, vulnerable and forgiving. *Am I worthy of one so gifted?* She better appreciated the artist's talent and would make certain he understood as much when he returned.

Laura stepped towards the fresco where Rotto had made his emphatic plea. She lifted her eyes and saw nothing to explain the officer's distress. Her attention was drawn to an angel in the painting. She carried an infant son in one arm and a fruited stem in the other. Her hair was blonde, her eyes blue. They regarded one another and Laura searched the female figure's eyes for Bino's intention. Two words came to mind—grace and trust.

Across the compound, Rotto was made comfortable in Signor Pelucca's den. A measure of his earlier confidence returned though he surprised Signor Pelucca by rejecting Renato's wine in favor of something softer. So provided, the soldier sipped spring water and recalled the seriousness of his mission.

"Lieutenant, I was not aware you made plans to visit with Enza and Laura today. I cannot promise their availability."

"Forgive the intrusion, Signor Pelucca. I did not come to visit your daughters. I came that I might speak with you."

"I see," returned Signor Pelucca before swallowing a larger gulp of wine. "What's on your mind?"

Rotto recalled his careful preparation, set aside his water jar and stood. He held his cap at the center of his chest and improved his posture. He looked more like a cadet poised for an officer's inspection than a smitten young man seeking a father's blessing.

He began from memory. "Signor Pelucca, I have the greatest respect for you, your wife and family—all of whom reward Monza with your presence and patronage." The soldier paused before continuing, "Seeking the company of like men and women, I sought and secured a commission with the Milanese Guard."

Shifting impatiently, Signor Pelucca interrupted, "I'm sure you have, Lieutenant, but I ask you to speak plainly."

"Forgive me, Signor." His eyes met with his host's. "I come to invite your daughter Laura to be my wife. At your suggestion I…"

"Stop there, Lieutenant."

"Signor? Be sure I have the blessing of my family and the means to support…"

"That is all well, Lieutenant. Is Laura aware of your purpose for being here today?"

"No, *signor*, and…"

"I am relieved to hear it."

Signor Pelucca rose from his seat and continued, "Lieutenant, Laura is barely a woman and a fickle one at that. She is no more prepared to accept an invitation to marriage than she is to remain standing on the back of her horse."

Rotto's impatience grew. "I can accept her imperfections, *signor*."

"Take care, Lieutenant. I didn't suggest she was *imperfect*."

"I meant no disrespect. When my father approached you about Enza, you encouraged us to instead consider Laura."

Signor Pelucca couldn't argue the truth of it. And yet given what he perceived as Laura's lack of seriousness and maturity, betrothal seemed preposterous.

"You may continue to visit Laura, Lieutenant. But I remind you, it's the substance of a man that impresses, not his uniform. If you are judged worthy of Laura's affection, Lady Pelucca and I would invite you to sit at our table. Am I clear?"

Rotto understood the insult. *My name and rank are nothing to this man.* The soldier was given no choice and responded, "Yes, *signor*."

"Very well, Lieutenant. I believe we're through for today."

"With permission, *signor*? I know you to be a man of your word."

"Yes, what is it, Lieutenant?"

"Am I alone in this honorable pursuit?"

"You are not."

"I see. I trust you won't mind me sharing the details of our conversation with my father."

Put off by the young soldier's veiled threat, Signor Pelucca stood by the door and gestured with his hand, "Extend my greeting to your father, Lieutenant; you honor him with your service."

Renato had overheard the exchange and smiled. He reunited Rotto with his coat and aide and together they made a quick exit from Casa Pelucca. Few words were spoken on the journey home.

The expedition put Rotto in bad temper. There was the inexplicable nature of what he had experienced in the entryway and the embarrassment of being discovered timid and afraid. Then to have that ungrateful *swine* suggest he wasn't yet worthy to wed his *peasant* daughter—*va fan culo!* It brought to mind the many arguments he'd had with his own father and the ever-growing list of attributes of which he fell short.

Rotto disguised his injured pride until arriving home. Once there, he and his aide were met by a stable hand who guided their horses to a tie post. Anxious to make his retreat, the lieutenant made a careless attempt to dismount before his horse settled. His foot hung up in its stirrup and forced a fall to the muddy ground.

When the stable boy smiled at the lieutenant's misfortune, Rotto could abide his day-long embarrassment no longer. He leapt up in a rage and grabbed the young handler by the collar.

"You incompetent shit—you're to blame!"

Rotto withdrew his riding crop and began to whip the helpless boy across his neck, shoulders and back. The lieutenant's aide watched in horror as the officer struck the whimpering boy again and again.

Subordinates knew never to intervene in the discipline meted out by their superiors but the junior officer had seen enough and feared for the boy's life. "Sir, enough, sir!"

His plea did not distract Rotto from venting his anger and he administered several more blows before the aide leapt off his horse and stood between victim and tormentor.

"He's just a boy, sir. He meant no disrespect."

Rotto dropped the crop and looked at the nearly lifeless boy's bloody back in dismay. His left hand shook and he grabbed it with the right as if to arrest the pain he felt inside and out.

His eyes met the junior officer's and he said, "See the doctor is called. When the boy recovers, reassign him elsewhere."

"Yes, sir. Will you require the physician's attention, sir?"

Rotto ignored the question and marched towards his father's home. Outside the entrance, he labored to pull off muddy boots before throwing first one and then the other at his father's favorite dog. The dog dodged the blows and took flight.

The lieutenant moved purposefully through the house, seeking a flask of wine. Finding one, he sped with stocking feet to his bed chamber and secured the thick door behind. Rotto removed the wax seal from the flask with his front teeth before spitting it an arm's length away. He studied the bottle a moment before drawing several generous swallows and shouting for anyone to hear, "*Va fan culo!*"

Can I pretend any longer? I'm an unfit pawn in my father's game. I must have my inheritance and be gone.

Rotto paced erratically about the room. He was disgusted with himself, hated his father and angry with Signor Pelucca for making his escape more difficult. The soldier took another swallow and raised his voice to the ceiling timbers, "Signor Pelucca, you arrogant ass." *How can you think me unworthy when you know nothing of my trials and conscience?*

With another upward tilt of the bottle, he responded to his own question, "Your daughter, Laura—I will force myself to take her like that whore in Milan."

Rotto emptied the flask of wine before slamming it down on his bed-side table. Bathed in sweat, he ripped open his overcoat, causing buttons to fly in every direction. He struggled out of the coat before taking a sleeve, circling it above his head and releasing it across the room.

His angry eyes watched his coat fly. Something separated from it and fell to the floor. Rotto bent at the waist to retrieve it and the gesture made him dizzy. The room spun about him and he stumbled to the nearest wall. He supported himself against it until the sensation passed. He sat there, reset his attention and cursed his stupidity.

Judas! In his hands was the undelivered correspondence to Laura from Casa Rabbia. *It matters not now.*

He was near to ripping the package open and revealing its message when an idea—a workable, winning idea came to mind.

The lieutenant replayed his awful morning until recalling his question and Signor Pelucca's candid response. *Am I alone in pursuit of Laura's hand? You are not,* was his reply.

Rotto studied the parcel. He deliberated before resting it in his lap and reaching for the hem of his right pant leg. Lifting it, he revealed a leather knife holster. He withdrew the blade within, stood up and sat upon his straw mattress. With the tip of his blade, the soldier began the delicate process of releasing the knot holding the contents together. The twine fell away.

Rotto withdrew the rolled parchment from its cloth cover. He was disappointed to see a wax seal but relieved it revealed no monogram or crest. *I may yet be lucky.* Rotto studied the seal as if at odds with his conscience before rising and lighting a candle. Drunk and willing to chance what his sober self might not, he moved his knife blade back and forth across the flame. He then reached for a cloth rag beneath his wash basin and laid it flat upon the letter's wax seal. To both he firmly pressed the glowing knife edge.

It worked; the cloth absorbed the melted wax without marring the paper below. He repeated the process several times until all but a modest stain remained. A fresh wax seal would render it invisible. With a watch-maker's care, Rotto wiped his hands clean of soot and sat upon his bed. He opened the rolled parchment and read its curious contents.

It made no sense to him. He knew little of the Rabbia family, less still of the person he presumed crafted the poem—Feder. He read and re-read the closing verses, attempting to make sense of the message.

> *Was fortune to smile on our love,*
> *Could another lover I betray?*
> *The caretaker does not steal away the dove.*
> *Better I set you free some say.*
> *You look above and give God's glory a name.*
> *I speak of crosses, a cloak and stone.*
> *With me there is little hope of glory or fame.*
> *With me you shan't ever be alone.*
> *Be nourished, Laura, by my devotion.*
> *My heart and colors are all I have to give.*
> *With these words I reveal the depth of my emotion.*
> *Our kiss—the passion with which I promise to live.*

Rotto sat paralyzed. *Do the words betray a history of liberties taken and virtue lost? If yes, wouldn't her father give anything to hide the truth? If no, what can be made of the reference to another lover; was Feder speaking of him? And why hadn't he signed the verse? Was their intimacy so great no name was necessary?*

"Judas, is nothing easy?" he asked. Rotto was sure of one thing. The poet did not perceive himself well-worth Laura's affections. He smiled, imagined a plan and appreciated the leverage at his disposal. *The morning wasn't wasted after all.*

Bino

Within a few days Bino declared complete Lady Rabbia's commission. The artist was satisfied and greatly relieved. The mythological tale of Eos, her mortal lover and his vulnerable wife were then and forever frozen on the walls of Casa Rabbia.

When she learned of Bino's intention to return promptly to Casa Pelucca, Lady Rabbia organized a reception for her neighbors. The frescos were uncovered with much fanfare and the artist's patroness delighted in the attention. With a wink and nod, she boasted to houseguests of Bino's skill while saying nothing about what was evident for all to see. Wherever Eos, the mythical temptress, appeared, she bore the countenance, coloring and smile of Lady Rabbia.

The artist's favorite meal was prepared and served outdoors. Wine was plentiful and a fine complement to herb-infused lamb. Afterwards, guests were treated to port as musicians roamed the grounds. Guitar and flute melodies invited merriment, filling the summer air.

Bino was made uncomfortable by the attention and praise and separated himself from the group. Signora Rabbia intercepted him with a grin and invited time alone. "I may yet convince my husband of other projects, Bino. He is as pleased by your work as I am with your affection."

Her expression and the scent she wore intoxicated and called to mind their couplings. Bino's conscience and vulnerability troubled him and he made clear his intention.

"My lady, I cannot return. I was wrong to accept your company and ask only we part friends."

Her smile faded and she replied, "I don't lack friends, Bino, though it's occurred to me, you do."

"I wasn't suggesting…"

The eyes of his patroness grew dark and serious and she brought her hands to his chest. Leaning in she whispered, "You may yet require my support, artist, and I will judge you worthy of it if your brush and flesh continue to please."

No more was said and his mistress returned to the gathering. Bino stepped aside and kept walking until he found himself at a remote spot along the property's western border. He sat upon on a fallen tree, admired the new moon and thought about the morrow's return to Laura and Casa Pelucca.

One equally interested in avoiding the dullness of strangers interrupted his peace. Feder spotted his friend and inquired, "Do you mind if I join you? I'll understand if you say no."

The artist welcomed him.

"You are responsible for this madness, Bino; few reveal as much talent in five lifetimes as you produce within two fortnights."

Bino thought for a moment before responding with humility, "I can take no credit, Feder, for gifts bestowed by God."

"That may be so. Still, you've pleased at least one impossible critic. In fact, I'm not sure who will miss you more, me or Mother."

Any mention of Lady Rabbia made the artist uncomfortable and he quickly changed the subject. "I've overstayed my welcome, friend, and you shan't lack for company. If no other, Nondo will see to it you're not lonely."

"Ah, Nondo—never was there a more loyal, steadfast and passionless servant."

Bino appreciated the slight with a smile before being encouraged to follow his friend and his jug of unfinished wine. Feder led the way through the gardens, past his father's smokehouse and into a thinly treed wood.

They walked against the evening breeze and arrived at a clearing. At its center were stones and the ash of previous fires.

Feder handed the wine to Bino before rolling two tree stumps closer to the stones. The latter he maneuvered into a crude circle. Pointing to a third stump a short distance away, Feder instructed, "Rest the wine there and help me collect kindling and a few pieces of wood."

Bino did as his friend suggested before sitting on one of the righted stumps and fixing his eyes above. There it was; he spied it in the darkest part of the sky and was sure it was so—the constellation Laura had named for him. He smiled to himself and wondered whether she might likewise be looking above and sharing the moment.

Bino returned his eyes to the ground and watched as Feder assembled the kindling, dried leaves and wood. From a pouch at his hip, his friend withdrew two flint stones. He knocked them against each other until a spark settled on the leaves below. Feder cupped his hands about the leaf pile and blew softly, nourishing the flame. When it grew to modest size, he added more leaves and twigs and blew again. Larger kindling was added and the fire grew in strength. The wind picked up and carried smoke and warmth to Bino's ankles, weary arms and shoulders. Impressed by his friend's efficiency with the fire, Bino began, "You are no less an artist than I, Feder."

"You can't have had that much to drink, friend."

"No, it's true. I've watched you closely, the way you handle a pheasant net, a butcher's blade, flint stones, gifts equal or better than any I possess. *Dio mio*, you created fire in a quarter of the time it would have taken most men."

"You are kind, Padre Bino. But as you can see, a carved pheasant on the table and a fire in the hearth yield no woman for my bed."

Bino could only laugh.

His friend continued, "I don't know, artist. What is it about women that makes their appeal less only than our inability to understand them?"

"You are wise to notice. Perhaps God rendered the fairer sex both beautiful and inexplicable so men might never be without desire or purpose."

"I hope it's a joke you make."

"No, not at all. Surely you can drink to this notion. Desire motivates men to return to their beds each evening. Not wanting to lose that which satisfies the flesh, men rise each morning, work and feed the women and children entrusted to their care."

Laughing cynically Feder responded, "The dismal results prove otherwise, Bino. More men are ruled by lust than a desire to work and support the women they bed."

Silence came and Bino and Feder were hypnotized by liquid spirits and leaping flames. The artist appreciated the quiet and poured generously from the jug into his open mouth. He offered it to Feder who accepted it and did the same.

After several minutes, Feder asked the question he knew he might soon be forced to answer. "Can a man find peace alone, Bino?"

"I don't think much about it. Maybe yes. Since so much of an artist's work requires aloneness, we're better at it than most."

"I see. So what's the remedy for me?"

Bino didn't immediately answer. He gazed into the fire, watching the flames dance and the colors shift from blue to orange and back again. When words came, he said, "I think the answer lies somewhere in the divine bargain, Feder."

"What's that you say? Divine what?"

"Divine bargain. Are you willing to forfeit a bit of the security you enjoy for the thing God intends you to share with the world? We hear tales each week of men leaving the familiar to sail west. They leave their homes and families on the chance that beyond the horizon lie adventure, beauty and wealth. I cannot say whether they find it or perish. It is likely they discover something about themselves they would not have appreciated closer to home."

"The more I drink, the smarter you sound, Bino. What are you suggesting? That I steal away to *il mondo nuovo*?"

"Only figuratively; your 'new world' may be a three-day carriage ride from Monza."

"You give me reason to hope, friend. Tonight, however, we drink. Tomorrow, I'll give this notion of yours some thought."

Bino was slow to return to his guest room that morning. He wasn't certain but thought it possible Lady Rabbia would be there, eager to take advantage of her last hours with him. He was relieved to find his space unoccupied. He stepped in, secured the door and lit a candle. Bino sat upon his bed and rested his hands atop his knees. He studied the lines across his knuckles and considered the battle his craft and materials had waged there. *My hands and conscience seem those of an older man.*

His mind danced with regret; it clung to him like the smell of the woodfire on his clothing. He imagined the temptress Eos revealing her dirty secret to Feder, a mortal man whose name suggested faith and fidelity. *How badly I've repaid his kindness.*

Without undressing, Bino leaned back, lifted his feet and twisted himself so he might lie comfortably atop his wool cover. Closing his eyes caused his head to spin so he opened them and focused upon the dim candlelight reflected across the ceiling.

Why no response from Laura? Surely a note would have reached me by now.

He imagined Laura with him and relived the conversation they had shared the afternoon weeks ago in the meadow.

"Paint me," she had said. "You need only be ready when my maid comes."

The thought aroused him and he began to imagine what Laura looked like absent clothes. Beyond the physical, her appeal was hard to name and the artist reasoned it must be her quiet confidence or keen power of observation. The latter was a well kept secret—one she was willing to share with him since she judged him wise enough to understand.

It had revealed itself in her dark brown eyes across the dinner table months before. It reappeared each time they spoke when she called attention to the behavior and ideas of others—asking questions few of her feminine peers dared consider let alone put into words.

He wondered what she understood about him. Did she believe him her equal—someone who understood you could be both moral and hungry, equal in matters of spirit and flesh? He closed his eyes and thought. His fatigue and drunkenness freed him from inhibition and fueled his fantasy. Laura's whisper encouraged.

"Artist, let me touch you."

"Would I deny you?"

"You couldn't. Let me hold you, enjoy you."

Bino held his breath and focused on his pleasure. His mind danced between his awkward couplings with Lady Rabbia and the union he sought with Laura. He feared she would learn the truth and turn him away.

He imagined Laura gripping a cloak about her neck and mocking him, "How can I lay with you? You're no different than the others."

With her denial, he wanted to be with her all the more. He imagined her laughing at his weakness and sympathetically approaching. She sat beside him and with eyes intending seduction, opened her robe and gathered it at her waist. She raised her hands, crossed them and used each to conceal the opposite breast.

Laura studied his reaction before whispering, "You wish for what isn't yours, artist."

His fantasy evolved. She removed a hand from her chest and used it to play with his hair.

Laura teased while borrowing language from Lady Rabbia. "You can touch but if I'm to be your muse, you must be a compliant student."

Bino imagined Laura guiding him on the better use of his hands, mouth and tongue. His strength impressed but it was his delicate touches that won her bliss.

Bino accelerated his fantasy; his need proving too great. His lover spoke no more and he imagined her riding him to the release he needed. His resolve evaporated, his toes curled and his finish came—its intensity a surprise.

His breath slowed and he sought a happy memory—his days with Piero. Bino recalled their first visit to see Leonardo's epic mural in Milan and the prayer the seminarians had chanted there. He realized it was a prayer pointing to Laura, a prayer Saint Anselm had intended for Bino's ears to soothe his anxious soul.

Let me seek you in my desire; let me desire you in my seeking.

Let me find you by loving you; let me love you when I find you.

The candlelight danced its last upon his ceiling and the artist moved from fitful imaginings to sleep.

Laura

With his verse intercepted, Laura wondered why she had heard nothing from Bino during his weeks at Casa Rabbia. She began to think him indifferent to her affection, which was a greater emotional burden than the one her father had lain upon her. Signor Peluccca had invited her to his study several days after the lieutenant's peculiar visit and Laura recalled his discomfort. Her father had paced nervously as she sat and studied him.

Signor Pelucca had begun that morning with an unexpected question. "Laura, do you enjoy being here with your mother and me?"

Laura answered truthfully, "Yes, Papa." When he said nothing, she continued, "There are times I wish I could accompany you away from all that is familiar. I hear stories of Rome, Venice, Florence—none of these have I seen."

Signor Pelucca stood still and responded, "The road is no place for a young lady, Laura, especially in these dangerous times; daily news of French incursions arrives at our door."

"Papa, please. You don't believe us that vulnerable. I don't understand why young men are allowed to roam while young women are left home to feed sheep and milk goats. Enza may not be curious of the world beyond Monza, but I am."

"Enza is not your concern and your mother wouldn't welcome you visiting these places without the benefit of a husband."

"Husband?"

"Well…yes, perhaps it's time you gave thought to marrying."

Laura looked away; she was not surprised though it bothered her to hear her father speak the word.

Signor Pelucca softened his approach. "It is true. Enza may have too much of her mother's social ambition. You and I, on the other hand, leave too much to chance. It cannot have escaped your notice that those you keep company with express interest in such a match."

Hoping against hope that Bino had mustered the courage to speak with him, Laura questioned, "Is there a name that would surprise, Papa?"

Sensing some enthusiasm on her part, Signor Pelucca stated the obvious, "You have shared time with Rotto and Feder. Both belong to respected families and possess enough ambition to make more of themselves."

Laura's enthusiasm faded and her eyes returned to her lap.

Her father continued, "We can expect little more in name and circumstance than these men. Were you expecting someone else?"

"Yes, I mean, no. Perhaps another will come forward."

"Another? What do you say of these two gentlemen? Has either captured your attention?"

"Why must I concern myself with Rotto and Feder? They're polite and respectful, Papa. But neither speaks to my heart."

Signor Pelucca stepped towards Laura and gestured for her to stand. Taking her hands in his own, he said, "Laura, in this troubled time, the heart must follow the head. These men can provide for you, give you a home and children while putting bread upon your table."

Letting go of his hands and walking towards the terrace door, Laura spun about and spoke with a voice equal to her disappointment. "Mamma and Enza are satisfied with those things, Papa. I could never be."

Meeting her tone, her father responded, "It's easy to say so when you aren't hungry. Would you instead prefer to take vows?"

Vows! She wasn't prepared for the subtle threat and called his bluff. "Yes, I would sooner join the convent than wed a man unworthy of my affection."

"You must think differently, Laura. We can expect only so much patience from those who would call you wife."

"What if I were to select a husband of my own?"

Feeling disrespected, Signor Pelucca shouted across the room, "You don't know what you're saying. I know what's good for you and you'll marry the man I believe serves our family."

There it was. Laura had her answer. She teared up and lifted wet eyes to her father's. "I see now, Papa, where the truth lies. Excuse me from dinner this evening; I don't feel well."

Three suns had risen and set since their conversation and Laura was outside contemplating her cloudy fortune when she noticed a small carriage approaching. She recognized it right away as one belonging to Casa Rabbia. Believing it possible Bino was accompanying the coachman, she leapt up, dusted off her dress and adjusted her hair.

Across the courtyard, Signor Pelucca noticed Laura's response to the arriving carriage. Her reaction pleased him and he wondered. Perhaps his firmness three days earlier had convinced her to be more attentive to Feder.

When the carriage slowed to a stop, Renato greeted the coachman with a stable boy. The boy accepted the reins and care of the twin horses. The coachman stepped down and pivoted to open the carriage doors for its occupants. Feder and Bino stepped from within.

The travelers squinted against the bright sunlight. Bino was quick to embrace Renato who next shook Feder's extended hand. They were engaged in polite conversation when Bino noticed Laura standing at a distance.

Through an open shutter Signor Pelucca observed the artist step out of the conversation circle and face his daughter. Bino smiled and raised a hand. Their eyes met for an instant before Laura's father witnessed his daughter walk and then sprint towards the artist. She might have leapt into his chest and arms were it not for Renato's interception. He was attentive to that which protocol demanded.

Laura slowed and greeted Feder politely before turning her attention to Bino. They were near to exchanging a two-cheek kiss when their bodies collided together in more than a sisterly embrace. Feder's smile conveyed no suspicion but Signor Pelucca understood the truth. He felt dishonored and betrayed.

Signor Pelucca joined the reunion and invited Bino and Feder to the family's afternoon meal. They accepted and Renato encouraged both men to wash and enjoy the grounds before the kitchen bell sounded. Laura's father intervened and suggested there would be time for recreation after. "Feder, please join me. I wish to ask after your parents and discuss a small bit of business."

Laura looked at her father and wondered at his motives. She might have protested but was pleased to have Bino to herself if only for a short while. When Signor Pelucca and Feder were a comfortable distance away, she locked arms with the artist and led him to the terrace where they had once appreciated the stars together.

Bino felt less burdened in Laura's company and appreciated her lack of pretension. He released her arm and let her walk ahead of him through a narrow passageway. She appeared more feminine than the girl he'd left behind and he wondered at the change. Was it the absence of the riding clothes she often wore or simply the bounce of untied auburn curls against her fair skin?

"I missed you, Laura. It was a mistake to leave."

She smiled at his confession and said, "With no word from you, I feared otherwise."

He looked concerned and replied, "I wrote to you more than ten days ago; was my verse not received?"

"It wasn't. What are we to make of that?"

The artist had reason to worry. Lady Rabbia, Signor Pelucca—one or the other may have intercepted his correspondence. "I don't know."

Laura stepped into his embrace and held him. "What did you have to say, artist?"

Bino was honest. "I don't recall the exact words. I worried my affection wouldn't be enough to win your heart and your father's approval."

Laura put some space between them and stared into his eyes. "We are of one heart, Bino. And our intention grows clearer each day."

She saw doubt in his eyes and asked, "What is it? Don't you feel as I do?"

"Of course, I do. I care for you like no other and want only to be together." Bino paused, released her and looked to the sky. "Casa Rabbia, something awful happened. And Feder's parents, your father, they will want more for you than I am able to give."

"They know nothing of me, Bino. What happened?"

The artist wanted no deception to separate them; he would tell her and accept the consequences.

"Lady Rabbia, she…"

They were interrupted by Renato who spoke of Signor Pelucca's return. He urged discretion and offered hope. "Be patient; your time may yet come."

The lovers kissed and parted. Renato remained and had reason to doubt the words he'd just spoken.

When the family gathered that afternoon, Lady Pelucca took charge. Attentive to the romantic aspirations of her favored suitor, she welcomed Feder to the seat at Laura's side. Across the table, by her side, she positioned Bino. She intended to learn details of Lady Rabbia's home, hospitality and relative prosperity. If their houses were to unite, the Rabbias' successes and challenges would improve upon or diminish their own.

Bino was attentive to Lady Pelucca's inquiries and wondered at her closeness to her social rival. The artist was careful to say nothing that would put his patroness in poor spirits. "I've missed your home," Bino said with candor. "Your support and kindness are not easily replaced."

Acknowledging his friend's sentimental nature, Feder remarked with cup in hand that Bino was speaking the truth. "Never a day passed in my company when Bino failed to mention Casa Pelucca." And then looking at Laura, he continued, "There are indeed many reasons why one finds this estate appealing."

Feder was interrupted by Enza. She was calculating and not above upsetting the spirit of the afternoon. "Feder, perhaps you and Signor Bino could tell us what most attracts you to Casa Pelucca."

Signor Pelucca scolded Enza for her impertinence while privately delighting in the question.

Bino shared an uncomfortable and deferential look with Feder. His expression seemed to say, *You first.*

Feder nodded and looked down at his plate before meeting Enza's eyes, smiling and responding.

"I cannot deceive you, Miss Enza. I am grateful for the hospitality of your parents and the fortunate friendship I enjoy with your tutor, Signor Bino."

Sensing he wasn't done speaking, all were silent. Renato, who'd been helping the kitchen staff in the dining room, was equal in his attention.

"There is something else, Miss Enza."

Feder turned towards Laura and smiled. "It's your sister's company I most treasure."

Lady Pelucca beamed while Laura wasted no time in reacting to the unwelcome attention.

"I am flattered you think so, Signor, but you give too much credit where it is little deserved."

Feder responded plainly, "I can assure you, Miss Laura, I do not."

Aware of the tension in the room and dissatisfied with her daughter's response, Signora Pelucca spoke up. "You are most kind, Feder. I'm certain Laura looks with equal favor upon you."

"We haven't heard from Bino," interrupted Signor Pelucca.

All eyes shifted to the artist. He chose not to look at Laura or Feder but instead at Renato—the only one besides his lover who knew the truth of his heart. Renato was worried for his friend; he understood better than Bino the limits of his station.

Bino wished he had the courage to speak his mind, to reveal his affection and devotion to Laura. He wished he could explain she was his first and last thought each day. He wished he could turn to Signor Pelucca, kneel and make the case for his daughter's hand in marriage. He wished after doing so he could embrace Feder and beg his forgiveness for the truth—they both loved the same woman. *God, grant me the courage to say so.*

Courage failed him. Bino instead explained, "I have found peace and purpose here, Signor Pelucca—a peace akin to that I knew while painting among the religious in Milan."

The artist shifted his attention from Renato to Laura's hopeful eyes. "Your family welcomed and embraced me. Without your faith, these walls would not tell the beautiful story they do today."

Bino noticed tears welling in Laura's eyes and looked away. Signor Pelucca was unsure whether to be comforted or distressed by Bino's response. He would consider the artist's words later.

All were distracted by the ring of a servant's bell. A maid entered the dining room and announced the arrival of an unexpected guest; behind her stood Lady Rabbia.

Feder stood and greeted his mother, asking if all was all right at home. She apologized, assured him it was and said she had come to express gratitude to Lady and Signor Pelucca for Bino's three-week engagement.

Laura looked from the uninvited guest to the artist; their earlier conversation gave her reason to believe something had gone wrong at Casa Rabbia. Bino's startled expression revealed a mix of fear and sadness. Had Laura a window into his mind, she would know Bino was torn between wanting to flee and begging her for a moment alone.

Signora Pelucca calmed the gathering. She invited a seat for Lady Rabbia at her other side and spoke of Feder's kindness to Laura. Lady Rabbia smiled and assured Signora Pelucca that she and her husband held Laura in equal esteem.

Bino exchanged few words with his mistress. When he excused himself after dinner, Lady Rabbia held his hand in both of hers, nodded and said within Signora Pelucca's hearing that Bino would be pleased by their next engagement. "I've discovered a second myth worth rendering, Bino. It is sure to be more to your liking as the goddess disclaims the upper hand."

Bino escaped to his room while Feder thanked his hosts and asked whether he and his mother might visit again soon. Before Signor Pelucca could respond, his wife agreed, even naming a specific day—two Sundays forward.

"Join us at family chapel, Lady Rabbia; Bino next paints there."

"You are most kind, Signora. We would be pleased to join you."

Signora Pelucca ushered Lady Rabbia away, leaving Feder in the company of her husband.

Turning to him, Feder began, "I regret if my mother retained Bino too long, *signor*; you are kind to share him with us."

"It was no bother, Feder; we are happy to accommodate your parents whenever the need arises. Assuming you have a moment more, may we continue our earlier conversation? I wish to ask a question or two."

"Yes, of course."

Signor Pelucca's expression grew serious. "Feder, I place the well-being of my family above all else."

"Yes, that is to your credit, sir."

"Well then, you won't mind if I confirm your intention with regard to Laura."

"I am fond of Laura and would consider myself the most fortunate man in Lombardia if she felt half as much for me."

Signor Pelucca studied him and thought a bit longer before continuing. "While it's honorable to invite Laura's affection, Feder, it is my good opinion you should seek."

"I meant no disrespect, *signor*. I meant only to…"

Signor Pelucca signaled *enough* with a raised palm. "I accuse you of nothing more than being a gentleman, Feder. Can it be, though, that you're unaware others invite Laura's hand?"

Feder knew of Rotto but did not tip his hand. "Signor?"

"I was afraid so. Are you not acquainted with Lieutenant de'Gavanti's proposal?"

"No sir. Signor Bino confirmed the truth during his stay."

"Signor Bino?"

"Yes, sir. Does this surprise you?"

"Yes. Did Bino express anything more about the lieutenant or Laura?"

"*Signor?*"

"How well do you know Signor Bino?"

"I think quite well. Why do you ask?"

"You and I enjoy certain advantages, Feder; many have and will continue to depend upon us for our strength of character, discipline and loyalty."

"Yes, signor."

"Those who serve us may not always share our discipline; worse, they may not know their place."

"You needn't worry about Signor Bino; he's as true a gentleman and friend as one could hope for."

"Yes, yes, I'm sure you're correct. Still, you would be wise to demand equal candor from any man with whom you entrust your friendship."

Feder wondered at his meaning. With an uneasy feeling, he thanked Signor Pelucca for his trust and attention. "I am grateful for your confidence, *signor*. Your family may rely on me."

Caterina

Caterina waited outside her family's cottage with Isabella. They paced hand-in-hand while Giovanni, only several days home with his message from the new priest, made his appeal to Caterina's father inside. His purpose was clear—invite Eduardo's approval to wed his only daughter. Failing this, he would return to Rome an unhappy man.

Sufficient time passed and it seemed to Caterina more minutes than necessary for her father to hear Giovanni's appeal and bless their union. *This is too much to bear; what objection could Papa have?*

Caterina stared at Isabella with eyes that betrayed her concern.

"You needn't worry, sister. Your father respects Giovanni and will allow you to wed."

"I don't know, Isabella; perhaps Papa has had a change of heart."

"Hush, Caterina; don't be so impatient."

At last the cottage door opened and Caterina's mother stepped out. She met her daughter's curious eyes before lifting her lips in a broad smile that invited a hug. Caterina rushed forward and crushed her with open arms. Isabella joined the pair and the three women shared the joyful moment. When they separated, Eduardo appeared with Giovanni at his side.

The stonemason and the Roman guard stood in contrast to one another—one in uniform, the other in scrubbed trade clothes. They eyed the celebration with a mix of curiosity and pleasure before Caterina noticed them and broke free.

She ran with tears to her father, embraced and thanked him, "*Grazie Papa! Veramente, grazie!*"

Giovanni relished Caterina's joy and welcomed Isabella's kindness.

"How wonderful, Giovanni! You and I are to be *brother and sister.*"

"You shall," squealed Caterina, "and a better sister you couldn't have in the world, Giovanni."

The young soldier turned to Eduardo and gave voice to all he was feeling. "I am grateful to you, *signor*. I promise to care for your daughter."

The stonemason felt the weight of Giovanni's words and allowed himself a bit of sadness. Few would appreciate the sorrow he felt when giving up Caterina to another man—even one as honorable as Giovanni. His wife understood and sought to distract him, ushering him and Isabella inside.

Giovanni embraced Caterina and invited a walk. She said yes but wasn't sure her feet were able; her mind was a dizzying array of gratitude, gladness and questions. The soldier gripped her hand and stilled her anxiousness.

"The inn, my mother will welcome you."

"Yes, I know she will. It will make our separation easier to bear."

Giovanni embraced her and whispered, "The priest from Luino, he is to arrive in two days. I'll beg our marriage be his first within our Lady's church."

"May it be so," Caterina replied.

Padre Castani

Padre Castani concluded his journey to Serono two afternoons later. He wore a priest's cloak and arrived in a carriage without fanfare—the entirety of his possessions within a small trunk below.

As pilgrim and mule traffic increased outside his window, doubts plagued him. *What am I thinking, Lord? I am but a parish priest. Has my restlessness given way to pride and an assignment I'm unfit for? I'll correct course, return home and beg the bishop's forgiveness.*

Concern clouded his mood until he spotted the church on the horizon. With each turn of the carriage wheel it grew larger and more majestic. The sun splashed across its stone tower and calmed him as the star above Bethlehem might have calmed the magi fifteen hundred years before.

The priest's coach attracted the curiosity of travelers but Padre Castani failed to notice. The pilgrim church impressed and distracted. *Holy Mother,* he whispered, *look at what your sons' and daughters' hands have wrought.*

Soon the coachman and his human cargo arrived. He intended to spend his first night at Giovanni's inn so the priest requested his trunk be delivered there while he paused in the courtyard before Mary's church. He exited the carriage and delighted in his present anonymity. He smiled as a cornucopia of visitors, merchants and farm fowl entertained; together they would have to replace what he would most miss—the beauty, substance and simplicity of Luino's great lake.

Padre Castani recalled standing in the same spot once before. At that time he felt as any stranger would. On this occasion, it felt like home. He believed it the right place for his soul and those in want of Mary's grace. The priest made a sign of the cross and whispered a prayer of gratitude. *May I honor you, Mother, and inspire those who labor to find you.*

Padre Castani surveyed the church's progress. He had been but a child when news of Mary's miracle reached Luino. He recalled the tale of Pedretto, the mortally sick boy given up for dead. Pedretto's mother encouraged her son to pray to the Virgin, invoking Her name and begging healing grace. He had done so reverently until Mary appeared. She touched his sleeve and revived Pedretto, asking only that he encourage all to follow her Son's path and love one another.

Pedretto grew strong and honored Mary's apparition; he constructed a shrine to the Virgin at the very spot his bed once stood. Scores of pilgrims arrived each week making necessary the church. *Yes,* Padre Castani thought to himself, *something special is at work here.*

The priest's peace was disturbed by the call of a young man from across the courtyard. "Padre Castani, Padre, welcome to Serono."

At first the priest didn't recognize Giovanni; he was dressed in civilian clothes rather than the bold uniform of the papal guard. At the same time, his messenger wore the smile of a man at ease, one content to live an ordinary life within an extraordinary place.

"Your coachman alerted my mother and me to your arrival. The bishop would have greeted you himself had he not been called back to Rome. I myself must return there in a few days' time."

"Pity that, young friend. I know you have mixed feelings about your temporary home."

Giovanni laughed before responding, "You're kind to remember, Padre, but I have news so wonderful the worst service cannot tarnish it."

"Let me guess. The stonemason welcomes you to his family?"

"Yes, it is as you say and with his favor we come to make a request. Will you honor us by blessing our marriage?"

The priest envied the enthusiasm in Giovanni's eyes; it reminded him of his celibacy and the sacrifice it demanded.

"Unless the pastor objects, I'd be pleased to officiate."

"Thank you, Padre. I can't wait to share the news with Caterina. She awaits us at the inn."

Padre Castani excused Giovanni and said he would follow not long after. He first wanted to visit the church and stepped inside her doors.

The contrast between his modest chapel in Luino and this one was dramatic and he appreciated the irony. The Mother Church in Rome sought to honor the birth, death and resurrection of an unpretentious carpenter from Nazareth. That it chose to do so with ever grander cathedrals might surprise Jesus.

The priest stepped across the threshold with new eyes. He wasn't a visitor seeking a miracle but a servant invited to interpret the gospel and share its mission of hope. As he looked above and around him, Padre Castani felt small and inconsequential, surely not up to the task he believed was expected of him.

He wondered, *Perhaps the bishop's monuments to faith were intended to humble all men and women. Only then might their appetite for something bigger and more permanent grow.* It was a hunger, the priest knew, that could only be satisfied by the Eucharist.

Padre Castani readied his old knees for contact with the stone floor. He knelt, closed his eyes and offered a prayer of thanksgiving. He opened his eyes, pushed himself off the floor and looked about. The walls and ceiling were pale and undecorated and he couldn't help but recall the sentiment of his apprentice. Antonina's son had expressed casually what should have been obvious to any clergyman.

Words may not inspire those whose ears are closed to the gospel message. A story is better told with beautiful images rendered by brush and color.

You were correct, Bino. I must convince Serono's pastor of the same.

The priest left and walked across the Varesina alleyway to Giovanni's inn; he knocked upon the door and let himself in. He could hear movement and conversation nearby but said nothing while allowing his eyes to roam. The room was large, well-worn, dimly lit and dusty. It had seen many visitors and the priest could imagine them dining around three long wooden tables arranged in parallel across the floor.

The priest didn't spot his trunk so he sat at a table and waited for his hosts. What he observed made an impression. Along the walls were tributes left by those who had come to Mary's church and found healing, sustenance or an end to their isolation. There were carved statues of the Blessed Mother, Jesus, Saint Catherine and too many others to name. There were abandoned crutches and crude braces. And there were scores of sacramentals—beads and cloth necklaces that bore images of the Virgin Mother. The priest smiled; he found himself not so much at an inn but a museum of human hope.

The priest's observation was interrupted. Caterina entered the dining room from the adjacent dormitory and studied the visitor before her lips lifted into a broad smile. She approached and said, "It is you, Padre. It is you."

Wondering at the girl's words and not yet recognizing her, Padre Castani stood and replied, "I can assure you, daughter, I am no other."

The priest reflected Caterina's stare—her proximity and smile rekindling a distant memory. There was something familiar in her blue eyes, sun-washed hair and quiet confidence. *Could it be her?* Joy welled within his heart and wet his eyes.

"Are you the stonemason's daughter? Are you that Caterina?"

"The same, Padre." And with those words she ran to him, knelt and embraced his knees.

The weary priest from Luino rested his hands upon her shoulders and said, "I thought of you often, daughter, but couldn't have imagined the grown woman you are today."

Caterina had hoped she would one day meet the priest again. "You must have thought me a foolish girl those years ago—confessing my sadness and desperation. It embarrasses me to think about it now."

Padre Castani urged her up and studied her tear-streaked cheeks before responding, "Hush child. Each confession is a demonstration of courage before our Father. Your willingness to come forward inspired many others to seek mercy. I never thanked you properly and do so now."

Giovanni and his mother entered the room and looked upon the pair with curiosity. "Is it possible you know one another?" asked Giovanni.

Caterina and the priest spoke over one another before bursting into laughter. With a hand Padre Castani stilled her and launched into his recollection of their first meeting. He explained how he hadn't been given access to Mary's church and had invited pilgrims to the sacrament of confession. When no one came forward, Caterina appeared, Isabella at her side.

The priest continued, "I scarcely appreciated how a child's bravery would inspire the many? And if that wasn't enough, Caterina appealed to her father and he made possible a private tour of our Lady's church."

Giovanni didn't doubt the story. Caterina's spirit and optimism weren't wanting. These qualities contributed to her quiet beauty and he loved her for it.

An introduction was made to Giovanni's mother before the priest embraced the couple and spoke with enthusiasm about their marriage. He complimented the innkeeper on her home, expressed regret at her husband's passing and spoke with humility about his new role within the church.

Giovanni was compelled to return to Rome within days so time was short. Plans were made and questions answered. With the pastor's blessing they would marry on the nearest Sunday. The marriage contract would be endorsed at the inn and witnessed by the pastor. Giovanni and Caterina, their family and guests would then proceed to the door of Mary's church. Keeping with tradition, the priest would administer his blessing there before all entered the chapel.

Three days later, Caterina woke for the last time in her parents' cottage. She was grateful for the sunshine pouring through her un-shuttered window and was too distracted by the arrival of her wedding day to mind the flies circling above her cover. Isabella remained asleep by her side.

Caterina's mind was a mix of joy and wonder. Giovanni was a man she could stand beside, laugh and cry with and admire. Her family had known hardship, want and loss and his willing partnership meant much to her. His faith was not equal to hers but Giovanni understood all she believed and appeared capable of focusing on the possible. More than this, she would sleep in his bed that night. She would yield to his touch and know the love of another for the first time.

How must that feel? Will I satisfy him?

Isabella couldn't guide her in such matters and her mother was too uncomfortable to say more than a little. She would place her trust in Giovanni. She retrieved his gifted prayer beads from her bedpost and wrapped them about her hands. *Mary, be present with me this day; grant me the grace I need to be a good wife and mother.*

Isabella woke and asked, "What troubles you, sister?"

"I know nothing of being a wife. What if I disappoint Giovanni and his mother?"

Isabella rolled her over and embraced her from behind. "You couldn't possibly disappoint them. I've known you your whole life and can't think of a better companion."

Caterina gripped Isabella's arms about her. "Promise me you'll always be here."

Isabella knew better than to make such a promise but did so anyway. "Where else would I be?"

Her mother threw open the curtain separating the girls' bed from the kitchen and hearth. She rushed to Caterina's side and hugged her before demanding they rise and prepare for the special day. Eduardo greeted the group before inviting his daughter to the warm water he'd prepared nearby. He excused himself to allow them time to bathe and prepare.

Before he escaped, Caterina appealed to him, "Papa, wait." She ran to him and threw her arms about his neck and shoulders and refused to let him go.

He knew what she needed him to say.

"It's all right, *carina*. I will be fine and come for you when I miss my constant companion."

"I will drop everything, Papa, you know it."

"Let me go then, you three will say things only women should hear."

The stonemason fled the cottage; he didn't want Caterina to witness his tears.

While she bathed, Caterina's mother adjusted her dress. Isabella combed out her hair and braided several strands, measuring where she would later place miniature flowers. The dress of blue silk was rare and a surprise to Caterina. It was given to Isabella by a grateful mother who had no more need of it. Isabella lifted it over Caterina's head and shoulders and let it fall to the floor. It fit her well save for the waist which was pinched and secured with a beaded belt.

Her mother paused and looked with approval. Caterina reminded her of the innocence she once enjoyed. She embraced her daughter, proclaimed her the worthiest bride and crossed the nape of Caterina's neck with the same chrism her mother's priest had gifted her on her own wedding day.

"This will discourage misfortune and evil," she said.

Across town Giovanni accepted his laundered uniform shirt and trousers from his mother. He set them aside until after he'd trimmed his beard and bathed. Once dressed, he appeared in the dining room as a recruit would at his first inspection, inviting his mother's opinion. She said his father would have been proud.

Giovanni sat at table and completed what had been earlier begun. It was a marriage contract and indicated, with his mother's blessing, the conveyance of their interest in the inn to his bride should harm come to him. Giovanni knew it was a mistake for any soldier, even one who enjoyed the protection of the church, to leave undeclared his intentions. He left it to his mother to explain their decision to her family.

"Are you guided by your heart or mind, son?"

"Both, Mamma. Don't worry though—Caterina gives me every reason to live and return home."

Not long after, Padre Castani stood beneath the entrance to the pilgrim church. He heard the bridal procession before seeing it turn the corner. A trumpeter sounded the call and the blast attracted all eyes from the courtyard to the advancing parade. Four maidens preceded the group. They carried broad smiles and a silk canopy above. Below it walked Caterina alone.

Over three decades of service, Padre Castani had grown numb to the administration of his duties. Countering these were his favorites roles; he never tired of consecrating the Eucharist, making plain Christ's mercy or uniting lovers in matrimony. The latter was especially pleasing when he knew the pair shared a devotion to each other and something bigger than themselves. Many were the occasions he bore witness to faith as the salve against misfortune's pull.

The priest returned his attention to the advancing bridal party. He looked twice before recognizing the figure in blue as Caterina. With her long dress and blonde hair accented by rose-colored flowers, the bride appeared far removed from the small and innocent confessor he'd befriended years before. Behind her followed her mother, Eduardo, Giovanni's mother, Isabella and the groom.

The procession stopped and Padre Castani stepped forward. He welcomed all present and carved a cross in the air with his right hand. With this gesture the women present stepped to his left while all men, save Giovanni, stepped to his right. The groom took his place next to Caterina and her canopy was withdrawn. The symbolism was clear; from this day forward, Giovanni alone would shelter his bride from harm.

Padre Castani recited traditional words before invoking the name of Jesus and Mary—patroness of the pilgrim church and author of its miracles. The guests witnessed the priest rest his hands upon Giovanni and Caterina and speak. His words brought smiles to their faces.

The priest invited them to join hands in prayer before proclaiming them to be one body, never to be parted in the eyes of God. A cheer rose from the rear and Giovanni kissed and embraced his bride. Isabella was the first to come forward and congratulate their union.

All present crossed the Varesina alley to the inn. A generous wedding feast awaited them—its preparation a gift from those grateful for the stonemason's wages and the inn's long hospitality. The inn itself had been transformed and gone were the relics of pilgrims past. The floors and walls had been swept and scrubbed and upon once-cluttered tables lay platters of roasted peacock and boar, tureens of mustard gravy and tubs of pears and Caterina's beloved apricots. Guests picked at cheeses and nuts and quenched their thirst with generous helpings of mead and wine.

When the hour grew late, revelers urged Caterina and Giovanni to retire. Someone cried, "Carry her!" and Giovanni, without hesitation, lifted Caterina off her feet. Moved by the shared intention of family and friends, Caterina yielded to his strength. Giovanni crossed the threshold to their bed chamber, his foot securing the door behind.

The innkeeper had readied her own room for her son. Fresh blankets, candles and a hearth fire awaited them. Giovanni and Caterina stood without company for the first time that day and smiled at one another. He studied her face and noticed the blush of her cheeks. Their pink hue and the blueness of her eyes paired well and reminded him of his good fortune. He whispered something she couldn't hear amidst the noise beyond the door. He began to repeat himself when she silenced him with an embrace.

Giovanni had known the company of a woman once before—an occasion confessed to Padre Castani two days earlier. Though he couldn't explain why, the soldier was relieved to have admitted so and the priest offered him absolution and, with it, a small measure of peace. Still, Giovanni felt no more worthy of Caterina than before. She sensed his reluctance and was calmed by it. She offered her hand and playful words, "Soldier, come with me."

Giovanni smiled and accepted her hand. Caterina led him to their bed and he watched as she removed what remained of the stems in her hair and the belt at her waist. She released her braids and let her hair fall about her shoulders. She turned and made a futile attempt to lift her dress from above. Failing this, she laughed and invited his help.

His fatigue forgotten, Giovanni eased the gown over outstretched arms. He stepped back and looked away. Caterina removed her underclothes and held them across her waist. She invited him to look and Giovanni lifted his eyes. She wore a delicate smile and the hearth light played upon the backs of her hands, fair skin and breasts.

"Do I please you?" she asked.

Giovanni didn't have words equal to his appreciation. He stepped closer, smiled and cradled her hands in his own. The material separating them fell away. Caterina's flesh rose and she was the first to say something. "I'm cold, Giovanni."

"Forgive me," he responded and made quick work of the hooks securing his uniform shirt. He opened and removed it and drew it across Caterina's shoulders. He could wait no longer and pulled the cloth towards him until no space remained. It was the moment Caterina had dreamt about since Giovanni's unexpected return and the intimate gesture would long sustain her.

Caterina pressed her cheek against her lover's chest. With the din beyond their door faded, she believed she both heard and felt Giovanni's beating heart. She wrapped her hands about his waist and whispered gratitude.

"Thank me?" he asked. "You don't understand, Caterina, do you?"

She stilled his lips with a finger before rising up on her toes and kissing him. "I am yours, soldier; now and always."

Giovanni's desire became urgent. He lifted her off her feet and laid her upon their bed. He removed the rest of his clothes and joined her.

Caterina watched him and gave no thought to her morning apprehension. Her concern yielded to sensations of an imagined kind—his lips and breath on her ears, neck and breasts and the gentle rotation of his free hand across her belly and thighs. When that wasn't enough, she guided Giovanni to her center.

He waited until her eyes met his. He read acceptance there and joined her. Caterina welcomed him and he responded to each soft cry with slower and more deliberate movement. She reassured him with words and a kiss and he responded with pace and purpose. Caterina wrapped herself about him; certain of her desire, Giovanni abandoned control.

She pulled her lover's head to her beating heart and shifted her legs in a manner that eased her discomfort. A different and pleasurable sensation grew within her and her breathing became shallow and more frequent. Caterina had heard tales of physical bliss but didn't imagine it possible. The sensation intensified and she wondered whether Giovanni felt it too.

He removed all doubt with sudden and rapid intensity. Her soldier inserted a hand below her core and lifted her into his thrusts. Caterina grew dizzy with feeling and shuttered at what she believed was his soul pouring into her.

She absorbed his warmth and weight and embraced his exhausted frame. He withdrew and she hesitated before releasing him to her side. Caterina twisted her body and rested her head upon Giovanni's shoulder. He curled his right arm about her and held her until his breath slowed and he yielded to sleep. She listened to his breath and felt secure.

The new bride rose and went to the cupboard. She retrieved a night dress, lowered it over her body and knelt at the side of the bed. It didn't occur to Caterina to alter her daily habit so she made a sign of the cross and offered a prayer of gratitude. She asked Mary to look after her soldier and return him safely to her. Ordained by marriage, the new innkeeper rose and returned to Giovanni's side. Too full of wonder to sleep, Caterina revisited the day and its wonderful conclusion.

"*Ti voglio*," Giovanni whispered.

"I love you too," she replied.

The candlelight faded and her eyes adjusted to the darkness. It was then Caterina noticed a crucifix hanging above the door. Like the one which hung above Isabella's bed it was a small thing that meant a lot. It united this place with the only home she'd ever known.

Bino

Bino resumed his routine and Signora Pelucca was quick to arrange a meeting with him. She wished to review her intention to decorate the family chapel. With guests planned within a fortnight, the artist would have to respond quickly. The June solstice had passed and the days were growing shorter.

Before his visit with Lady Pelucca, Bino sought Renato's company and counsel. He found his friend in the kitchen and apologized for the intrusion. Renato greeted him with a smile and inquired after Bino's health. Satisfied with the answer and sure his young friend would reveal what was on his mind, Renato filled the silence.

"It's good to have you haunt our home again, Bino. Join me for a little while. The distraction is welcome and I tire of making sense of Signor Pelucca's ledger. There is much expense and too little income to balance within an estate of this size."

The artist could only smile. "I understand little of what you say and less of what you do, Renato. I am sure you've earned our Master's trust for such things."

Renato studied Bino for a moment before returning his eyes to the numbers and saying, "I sense something didn't go well for you at Casa Rabbia."

Bino was taken aback by Renato's intuition and said nothing. Piero had also had this gift and the artist reasoned it was one source of Leonardo's genius. His old mentor had understood the questions which needed asking. It was the substance of Piero's questions that made the answers easier to discern.

Renato replaced Bino's silence. "You needn't tell me, son." And then suspecting the source of Bino's dour mood, he continued, "Lady Rabbia, rare is the man able to escape her cunning and appetite."

Bino betrayed his relief by gripping Renato's shoulders. "I needed your company, friend. I was weak and didn't do enough to discourage her advances. Will she make trouble for me?"

"We are servants, Bino; we serve."

"My conscience isn't clear, Renato. I welcomed her attention."

"Is she so different? She has rank and privilege and a thing far worse, neglect. Confess your sin to God if you must but Monza is not heaven; here we answer to those who purchase redemption with power and treasure."

"And what of the priests? They argue we are equal in God's eyes."

"Don't be naïve, Bino. Enza meant to embarrass you the other day; you were wise to respond with care."

"I'm less satisfied than you, Renato. I couldn't muster the courage to speak the truth."

"Courage is a luxury a poor artist can ill afford."

Bino's expression turned serious. "There is more, Renato." The sometimes poet paused before continuing. "Before departing for Casa Rabbia, Laura and I declared our affection for one another. I know she is young, but she has wisdom and conviction beyond her years. We want to be together."

"I was afraid you might say these things, Bino. I wish happiness was mine to give. Instead I must tell you her father would never agree to such a union."

Bino's shoulders sagged. "Haven't I done everything asked of me? Haven't I proven myself worthy in all ways excluding title? I come to you for encouragement, Renato; you offer only gloom."

"Forgive me, son. I have known the pain of impossible love and put it far from imagining. You would be wise to do the same."

"I'm a humble artist; my eyes, hands and brush are the tools I rely upon. These tools have not failed me because they respond to God's spirit. Now, you ask that I deny this Spirit in deference to station. I can no more walk away from Laura as paint without color."

"And what of Feder? Is he aware of the depth of your feeling for the woman he wishes to make his wife?"

"No, no, this plagues me. Feder is a good and caring man. Were it Feder Laura wanted, I would honor her choice and step aside."

"Tread carefully, Bino. Artists and servants are easily replaced. The French have long arms and we are one declaration removed from war. Without the patronage of Signor Pelucca, we could find ourselves seeking refuge within a corps of mercenaries."

"I can be patient, Renato. Time may grant the change in attitude Laura and I require to make our union possible."

"What would you have me do until then, Bino?"

"Pray I have the courage and wisdom to influence Signor Pelucca towards this end. Can you do that much for me?"

"You are the artist, Bino. You paint a picture and ask me to appreciate it."

Renato rose from his chair, turned about and embraced Bino. "I will do this for you."

Bino left Renato's company and waited in the family chapel for Signora Pelucca. Upon arriving, the artist was pleased to learn of her interest in dedicating the space to the saint he had been inspired by as a boy—Saint Catherine. Bino recalled and retold the stories his own mother shared with him at bedtime. He made no mention of his portrait—the mystical image of Catherine he had painted on a discarded door for the parish of Luino.

The Saint's legend meant more to him now. Catherine renounced a royal proposal of marriage, instead affirming her devotion to another, Christ. Her refusal to wed any man less worthy led to her cruel martyrdom and a permanent place in church lore. Bino imagined a scene with such clarity that he interrupted Lady Pelucca mid-sentence. *How can I make my idea hers?*

Thinking quickly, the artist stood, cupped Lady Pelucca's hands within his and expressed enthusiasm.

"Yours is a wonderful idea, *signora*."

He released her hands and gestured with a sweeping motion towards the altar wall.

"Guests will marvel at the ritual of Saint Catherine's burial. We'll clothe her in royal robes and have her transported to her tomb by a team of winged angels. Sky and clouds will mark her glorious and eternal home."

Bino provided additional detail until the eyes of his patroness revealed a familiar look. Lady Pelucca accepted responsibility for his ideas and invited the artist to proceed. She made only a single demand; the fresco be completed in time for Feder and Lady Rabbia's return.

"I won't disappoint you, *signora*, and will begin after the morrow. I'll prepare the drawings and find hands to ready the walls, apply the cartoon and wet the plaster."

"Renato will reassign the help you need. Anything else?" she inquired.

Bino indicated "no" while understanding he wasn't yet through with her. Signora Pelucca thanked him and was steps away from leaving the chapel when the artist casually called her name.

"Yes, Bino?"

"*Signora*, forgive me; I had a thought. Would it be possible for Enza to sit for me? A young woman's features would improve my execution."

Bino believed Enza absent and was eager to hear her mother's reply.

"I'm sorry, Bino. Enza travels with her father today and tomorrow. Would Laura do? If yes, I'll insist she make herself available."

Bino smiled. "Miss Laura would be perfect, *signora—ti ringrazio!*"

Laura joined him later and her mood was much improved. She studied him while overflowing with curiosity. She wondered aloud how the artist had won her mother's agreement without a single objection.

Bino was prepared to respond but was distracted. Laura's hair fell loosely upon her shoulders and her borrowed robe did little to conceal her figure. Her eyes and smile betrayed the affection she held for him.

"You are not the same girl I left several weeks ago, Laura. You are a beautiful woman."

His unexpected compliment brought color to her cheeks. He reached for her hand with his left while his right gently lifted her chin. He explained how during his final hours away he'd arrived at the idea of making this sitting her mother's idea.

Laura listened before responding. "I should never have doubted you, Bino. Father expects me to marry soon and your magic would help."

"Renato says I dare not consider such a thing. And yet, lately, it's the only thing I think of."

Laura looked about to confirm their privacy before folding herself into Bino's arms. "Say so again, Bino."

He did so before expressing himself with a kiss. "Time and light are precious, *Saint Catherine*; let's get started."

Bino had Laura lie with eyes closed upon a table. He placed a folded cloth below her head to make her comfortable and redirected a portion of her hair across her robed shoulder. The rest of her hair remained suspended from the tabletop. The artist was delighted by the way her loose curls resisted gravity and seemed to spring away from the floor.

Laura wished to speak as he touched pencil to paper but he argued against it.

"Try to remain silent. I must imagine you as Catherine now. Twould be better for you to channel her faith and feeling when she argued against a loveless marriage."

Laura lay still. She listened to the man she loved and felt at peace in his company. She wasn't inclined to prayer but considered Saint Catherine and solicited her help. She felt heard and slipped into a restful sleep.

Bino noticed a change in his subject and whispered Laura's name. When she didn't respond, he closed his own eyes and imagined her figure upon the chapel wall. He saw the angels accompany Laura there and hover as if reluctant to place her in the tomb. The vision pleased and he understood. Laura would not enter any tomb without having first been loved by him.

Bino opened his eyes and moved his pencil across the paper. His execution was rapid and flawless. The artist lost time consciousness and when finished, looked over his shoulder and imagined Piero seated there—his cane leaning to one side. The bearded ghost looked satisfied and expressed as much in a soft voice only the artist could hear.

You've done well here, Bino. It's time to leave.

"What is it you say? I've just returned and this woman, we are in love."

You must go all the same.

"Why? I'm tired of fleeing and wish to take a wife."

You must first answer a different call.

"How can I? I can't. I won't."

It isn't for you to decide.

When he woke, Bino wasn't drawing in the chapel any longer; he was lying in his own bed, recalling Piero's words: *You must go all the same.*

Be damned, Piero. What good can come from abandoning Laura and this place?

No response came.

Rotto

It was the end of his workday and Renato walked the perimeter of the Pelucca grounds enjoying the dry warmth of late summer. He wasn't a superstitious man but he had cause to wonder what might be foretold by a cloud of ravens transiting the sky.

It was the Friday preceding Signora Pelucca's chapel opening. Bino's tribute fresco to Saint Catherine would be unveiled on Sunday. Neighbors, parish priests and a coveted son-in-law, Feder Rabbia, had been invited to share the occasion. When he confirmed his exclusion from Signora Pelucca's guest list, Lieutenant de'Gavanti was prepared to act.

The weeks following his disappointing visit with Signor Pelucca did little to soften Rotto's resolve. Equipped with Bino's pirated poem—one he believed penned by Feder, Rotto contrived a plan to restore his good standing. He would appeal to Laura first before threatening to bring embarrassment upon the family.

Rotto bathed, trimmed his beard and mustache and donned his dress uniform. He sought out his aide and together they arranged for their horses to be readied for their return to Casa Pelucca. Their journey began, Rotto confident of the outcome.

Nearer their destination, the would-be husband halted their progress. The horses strained to reach grass upon which to graze while the Lieutenant pointed to a clearing on the horizon. He directed his companion's attention to the Pelucca property, grinned and remarked, "Look there; soon that will serve as our second home."

They pushed forward and within the hour, the pair trotted through the open gates of Casa Pelucca. Spotting their approach, Renato moved briskly from the edge of the wood to the courtyard. He hoped to intercept and reverse their course.

Renato wasn't merely wary of Rotto's unannounced visits. The caretaker looked poorly upon any person, especially one he thought capable of cruelty, who might purchase his master's good opinion.

With polite and cold resolve Renato greeted the visitor. "Good morning, Lieutenant."

"And you, old man," offered Rotto. "Would you lead my aide to wherever water can be had for our horses?"

"Of course, Lieutenant. And yet I wonder whether Signor Pelucca expects you this morning? He is busier than usual and requested I avoid interruption."

Rotto heard the disdain revealed by Renato's message and resolved to one day rid him of it and his position.

"Signor Pelucca will want to speak with me as the subject concerns his family. Still, I will yield to his schedule and visit with Signorina Laura first."

"Does she expect you, Lieutenant?"

Rotto felt his left hand tremble. He steadied it with his right and responded, "I don't enjoy the luxury of a social secretary, old man. She does not expect me."

"We'll do the best we can, then. Follow me to the foyer where you can wait for Miss Laura."

Mention of the reception hall brought to mind the mysterious anxiety he experienced there. The officer dismounted and handed the reins to his companion.

"I prefer to wait outdoors if it would please Miss Laura to join me for a stroll."

"As you wish, Lieutenant."

Renato left him and guided Rotto's aide to the estate stables.

Laura was full of expectation for the weekend. She was impatient to see the chapel fresco while marveling at the irony. She believed herself unworthy of the saint and yet would soon be revealed as her unholy substitute.

With the artist's encouragement, an undeniable peace washed over Laura. She felt less anxious about the future, her father's intentions and the attention of other men. She trusted Bino and his unshakeable faith that all would somehow work out. Laura even began to pray; if God was responsible for injecting so thoughtful a lover in her life, why shouldn't she bring gratitude and a thirst for understanding to Him. Her solitude was interrupted by Renato's knock upon her door.

"Yes?"

"Forgive me, Miss Laura. Lieutenant de'Gavanti is here and wishes to visit with you."

"Him, now? Can he be put off, Renato?"

"May I speak with candor, Miss Laura?"

"Yes, of course."

Renato entered and paused before proceeding. "Bino has taken me into his confidence, Miss Laura, and shared his affection for you. While I don't presume to know whether you return his feelings, if you do, I think it better for you to express your respect and disinterest with the lieutenant sooner than later."

Laura was surprised and glad for Renato's honesty and regretted not having invited his counsel sooner. She rose, stepped towards him and reached for both of his hands.

"*Ti ringrazio*—thank you, Renato. You're right, of course. I've been foolish to keep my feelings to myself for so long. Tell the lieutenant I'll join him."

"Yes, Miss Laura."

"And Renato?"

"Yes, Miss Laura."

"I am grateful for the friend you are to Bino."

"You needn't thank me, Miss Laura. He's the closest thing I've had to a son these many years."

Laura changed her dress and ran a comb through her hair before joining Rotto outside. He wore his pressed uniform and a formal expression; Laura thought his hair unnaturally dark and tame. He forced a smile and reached for her hand. She offered it reluctantly and bit her lip when he brought a kiss to it.

Rotto invited her for an unchaperoned walk. He wanted her alone and reasoned their visibility would prove enough to defend against an accusation of impropriety.

"It is good to see you again, Miss Laura."

"It's kind of you to say so, Lieutenant. How have you and your father been?"

"We are well but concerns grow about Monza now that the French occupy Milan. Landowners have reason to worry. Threats of confiscation and taxes follow this regime."

"Do you worry about these things, Lieutenant?"

"Please, Rotto will do. You ask the correct question, though. Father doesn't worry since he is fortunate with his connections and I will soon command a squad in the Monza Guard."

Rotto spoke the truth. His father confessed no loyalty. His only concern was which side bore the larger purse.

Laura feigned ignorance and interest. "It's all confusing to me, Rotto, though we are pleased for your promotion."

The soldier shifted uncomfortably, ignoring Laura's words in deference to his own agenda.

"May we stop a moment, Miss Laura? There is something I wish to talk with you about."

As Laura halted and readied herself, Rotto thought only of his father, the escape marriage would allow and the private pleasures he would seek elsewhere. He spoke memorized words without feeling.

"All is well for me, Miss Laura. What would make my happiness complete is your willingness to join me as my wife. I spoke to your father and he asked I prove myself worthy of his blessing. A positive word from you would surely help."

Laura raised her eyes to his and her expression registered little surprise. She thought of Renato's counsel and was pleased to answer Rotto's invitation without doubt.

"You flatter me, Lieutenant. I have been unfair and less than candid about my feelings."

"That may be true, *signorina*, but I understand more than I'm given credit for."

Her response was immediate. "I'm not sure of your meaning, Lieutenant."

Flustered by her avoidance of his name, Rotto misspoke. "I meant only to say I'm prepared to overlook your indiscretions."

Laura's demeanor shifted with the accusation. "Indiscretions? What are you referring to?"

"I don't wish to offend, Miss Laura, but do you deny being careless with your affection?"

"You insult me, sir. But since I'm accused of impropriety, to whom are you referring?"

"Don't play the fool. Do you deny your unfortunate attention to Signor Rabbia?"

"Signor Rabbia. Feder? What do you suppose about the company we keep? He is nothing if not a gentleman."

The soldier's left hand began to quake and reason abandoned him. He wanted nothing of Laura but even less of the father he loathed. There was no escape other than the one a marriage to Signor Pelucca's daughter made possible. The ferocity of his attack would convince her.

Rotto raised his voice and responded, "You're no doubt familiar with the stories. Can Feder be at all different from his whoring mother? And yet you deny the affair! I am unafraid to alert your father and will do so unless you accept your place with me."

Laura couldn't fathom the soldier's words. *What could he know of me and Feder that hinted at liberties taken? And believing so ugly a rumor true, why insist I take a place at his side?*

Laura's confusion turned to fury and her fury to tearful expression.

"I reject your proposal, Lieutenant. Any regard I may have had for you and your misplaced feelings are lost. Feder has behaved honorably and you insult both of us by suggesting something to the contrary. I would no more marry you than swear on my mother's life."

Rotto lifted a hand to strike her and was close to doing so before sense dictated otherwise. Instead he stilled his left hand by using it to grab her wrist and pulling her towards him. "Don't be a fool, *signorina*. You'll have no suitors when the truth is told. You'll beg my forgiveness when all might have been transacted quietly."

He's mad. Laura knew she must escape and used her free hand to push against his chest while wrenching her captive arm from his control.

Rotto relented and laughed at her weakness. "*Putana*, whore! We'll see who smiles last."

My father thinks you're the one to change me. He's made that mistake before.

Laura backpedaled while pointing a finger in his direction. "Two things are true, Lieutenant. I don't understand you and I do not fear you. How could I ever marry a man capable of such cruelty?"

Laura turned and ran from him towards home. She hoped to never see Rotto again.

He remained there confused by Laura's denial, one at odds with the pirated poem in his possession. What was she thinking and why would she prefer the son of a whore to the security he offered? Her father must convince her.

Renato witnessed Laura's return and the pained expression upon her face. He wondered whether she had communicated the truth and whether the soldier had taken the news badly. Before he could follow and satisfy his curiosity, Rotto intercepted him—his own face betraying disappointment and anger.

Renato inquired, "Is all well with you and the *signorina*, Lieutenant?"

"No, old man, but little a father's intervention won't resolve. Tell Signor Pelucca I wish to visit with him."

Renato found his master agreeable and invited the lieutenant to follow him to Signor Pelucca's study. Quick greetings were exchanged and Renato asked Signor Pelucca if he wished to have him remain and attend to their needs. The request surprised and annoyed Rotto who never tolerated intrusion from staff. Signor Pelucca was gracious in his reply.

"We'll be fine, Renato, but please bring two cups of pressed cider."

Shifting attention to his unexpected guest, Signor Pelucca began, "What inspires your trip across Monza this morning, Lieutenant?"

Rotto cleared his throat, stiffened his posture and replied, "When we last visited, Signor Pelucca, you asked me to prove myself worthy of Miss Laura. I come this morning with that in mind. In fact I came to express my intentions to her directly and to protect both her and your esteemed family from what is sure to embarrass and offend."

Signor Pelucca had since resolved that Laura wed Feder Rabbia. He neither liked nor trusted Rotto and found his manner calculating. So convinced was Laura's father that when alerted to the lieutenant's visit, he intended to greet her suitor and dismiss the possibility of uniting their houses. Yet now the man he intended to reject claimed to be in a position to rescue *famiglia* Pelucca from imminent embarrassment.

"You have my attention, Lieutenant."

"I won't waste your time, *signor*."

Rotto paused before launching into his deception. "Some days after our last visit, a stable hand brought a letter to me which he intercepted at a local tavern. It seems one of your neighbor's servants was offering the note and its compromising details to the highest bidder. The lad was removed from the tavern and threatened before admitting he stole the note from Signor Rabbia's courier. The courier intended to deliver the letter to Miss Laura."

Rotto paused and lifted his eyes to the ceiling; he'd forgotten how to embellish the great lie.

Signor Pelucca found the lieutenant's posture and tone unusual but urged him to continue.

"My servant took possession of the letter and read its contents before sharing both with me. He was punished for reading the letter and pledged to speak no more about it."

"This is indeed troubling, Lieutenant. I must say though, it appears the tale does more to damage the reputation of your house more than mine. Wouldn't you agree?"

"I would say yes, Signor Pelucca, was it not for the content of the correspondence. I'm afraid it hints at liberties taken and virtue lost."

The words stung Laura's father more than an open hand across the cheek. "Take care, man! Is the letter in your possession?"

"It is."

"I insist on seeing it."

Rotto produced the unsigned page from his coat and handed it to Signor Pelucca. He moved with it towards an open window and held it at arm's length. He quietly read the words purportedly written by Feder to Laura.

> In hallowed spaces I spend days alone.
> In the company of saints I confess my fears.
> With worthy men of vows I make a home.
> Now home is wherever you are near.
> I pray a higher purpose to find.
> As a farmer seeds to make new life.
> My tools are of a less worthy kind.
> My brush may not support a wife.
> Was fortune to smile on our love,
> Could another lover I betray?
> The caretaker does not steal away the dove.
> Better I set you free some say.
> You look above and give God's glory a name.
> I speak of crosses, a cloak and stone.
> With me there is little hope of glory or fame.
> With me you shan't ever be alone.
> Be nourished, Laura, by my devotion.
> My heart and colors are all I have to give.
> With these words I reveal the depth of my emotion.
> Our kiss—the passion with which I promise to live.

Signor Pelucca knew at once the author of the poem and dismissed Rotto's interpretation. He chose not to share the truth. He read the verse twice more. The words were honest and imposing.

Bino was sincere in his affection while guilty of exploiting his place at his patron's table. If there be shame, it belonged to the artist, to Bino alone. Signor Pelucca returned his attention to his guest.

"Is Laura aware of the letter, Lieutenant?"

"Not by my voice, *signor*. I invited her to be candid with me about her relationship with Feder but she denied wrongdoing and belittled my efforts to quiet the affair."

"What is it you mean by 'your efforts,' Lieutenant?"

"Before her honor is called into question, I remain willing to make Miss Laura my wife."

With masked sarcasm, Signor Pelucca responded, "How generous of you, Lieutenant!"

His host paced about the room, leaving Rotto to wonder what might be said. He was poised to open his mouth before thinking better of it.

Signor Pelucca moved to the hearth and removed a long wick from a wooden box above. He leaned over and touched the wick to the flame below until it glowed. He withdrew it and brought it to the edge of Bino's verse until the page ignited. Rotto realized too late what was happening.

"I recall a day, Lieutenant, when one could rely upon the privacy of one's correspondence. While I am grateful for your candor, I am much grieved that your servant read the intercepted letter and shared its contents."

"But, *signor*..."

"You needn't concern yourself with my daughter's reputation; she remains the innocent."

Signor Pelucca released what remained of the page above the hearth flame. He turned and refocused on the scheming officer.

"I wonder, Lieutenant. If your interpretation of the verse had been correct, why would you have been willing to overlook my daughter's tarnished reputation?"

Rotto wasn't prepared for the question and upset at having overlooked so obvious an inquiry. The truth wouldn't serve him. He couldn't admit he'd be better at exploiting Laura's surname than her father or that Laura could be taught to overlook his unusual lust—the thought of her finding him with another man arousing his senses.

Rotto met Signor Pelucca's eyes and lied, "Because despite every-thing, *signor*, I admire your daughter."

"Claims of love blind many men from prudence, Lieutenant. I need to think this through."

"Excuse me, *signor*?"

"I'll consider your proposal and let you know what I decide."

"Very well, *signor*, but I don't know how much longer I can threaten against village speak."

Laura's father understood Rotto's unsubtle threat and was disgusted by it.

"Tread carefully, Lieutenant. I value discretion above all else and we must be better than those who choose gossip over the substance of their neighbors' character. We have many years and loyalties in Monza; it is well for you to remember."

Rotto pretended respect, bowing at the waist and bringing his heels together. He felt no more satisfaction than on the occasion of his last visit. Laura and her father would not bend to his will and he was left to wonder. The Lieutenant was unaccustomed to denial from anyone other than his father and was impatient for an answer. He understood what he must do.

What deception am I missing? I'll force their hands and bring the accusation to Feder. Once accused, he is sure to challenge me to a public fight for Laura's honor. He cannot match my swordsmanship and I'll claim her over anyone's objections.

Signor Pelucca's thoughts were conflicted, unsure of how to pro-ceed. Interest in a man's daughter was normally a good thing. Negotiations would follow and concessions won. This situation was far from normal. He considered himself three-handed. On one hand, the artist was exploiting his generosity by seeking an advantageous marriage with Laura. Bino's lack of position and influence disqualified him and yet there was something reverential in his poem that softened the blow. On the other hand, Rotto had rank but a transparent thirst for power. Once married, he would prove impossible to manage. Worse, he cared so little for Laura he was prepared to publicly embarrass her. Finally, there was Feder; he offered pedigree and could be molded. With time Laura would forget her infatuation with the artist and admit, as her mother once did, that security is a prize more valued than passion.

The choice was clear. The heir to Casa Rabbia was his best option. *How to proceed?* Laura was a temporary obstacle; she would yield to his will or face abandonment and disgrace. The problem would be her suitors. Signor Pelucca would alter the game—one which Feder alone could win.

Bino

Dusk settled over Lombardia and Bino, unaware of the day's events, reclined on his straw mattress. He wasn't suffering the physical aches that accompanied fresco work and he reasoned it was his subject. Even as she lay still, Laura was radiant as Saint Catherine. Lady Pelucca would see and reveal both the day after next.

As the central figure, Laura was sure to raise eyebrows. He remained focused on the chapel and the positive reaction of those attending. *Won't public acceptance and praise make it possible for me to approach her father?*

Bino extinguished his evening candle and was near sleep when he heard several soft raps upon the door. It opened and the artist witnessed a glowing ember float through. There was a shuffling of feet and for a moment Bino thought it possible Lady Rabbia had gained entry. *She'll have me no more.*

The artist bolted up in the darkness and demanded, "Who's there?"

The intruder stilled, closed and stood against the door. An unrecognized voice whispered, "Forgive me, Signor Bino; it's Rita—Miss Pelucca's maid."

Bino misunderstood and rubbed his eyes before they adjusted to the light. "Is Lady Pelucca unwell?"

"No Signor, forgive me. It's Miss Laura. She asks if you will come quietly."

Surprised and fearful, Bino said nothing and measured Rita's resolve.

"I don't know if that's a good idea, Rita."

"Miss Laura thought you'd be unsure, Signor."

When the artist said nothing, Rita continued, "There is much I cannot say, Signor Bino. My conscience allows this. I believe you to be an honorable man—surely one worthy of my confidence. I fear if you don't come, Miss Laura will flee this house and place herself in danger."

Bino was consoled and troubled by Rita's words. *What would suddenly cause Laura to flee?*

"I'll come, Rita."

They walked quickly and silently across the moonlit courtyard to reach the main corridor of Casa Pelucca. Upon reaching Laura's bed chamber, Rita knocked softly and motioned for Bino to enter. Bino studied Rita, whispered thanks and entered the room. She closed the door behind him and slipped away.

Bino stepped forward into the dimly lit chamber. He closed his eyes and inhaled deeply. The breeze from an open window hinted of cut flowers and perfume. He opened his eyes and saw Laura framed by the moonlight.

"Are you angry with me?" she whispered.

"Angry? No, I think you're mad to invite me here. What would your father do if…"

"I don't care. Don't you want to be with me?"

"Yes, and I…"

"Enough. Don't you see what's happening, Bino? Feder, Rotto, my father, they're all conspiring to steal me away from you. I don't understand where the lies are coming from, but if we don't act soon, our hope of a future together will be lost."

Laura turned her back to the artist and began to cry.

Bino hadn't expected this. Her words stung and his gut clenched. He stepped towards her, grasped her shoulders and pulled her into his chest. She resisted until he reached around her, cupped her hands in his own and drew them towards her belly.

Laura felt his beating heart against her back. Her head, tilted to one side, found its place under his chin. She whispered, "Forgive me for waking you. I'm frightened."

"I wanted to come. I should have been honest with your father from the moment I knew you felt as I did."

Bino relaxed his grip and turned her so she was facing him. He read the mix of sadness and fear in her eyes. "What happened today? Did you speak with your father about me?"

Laura told him about her visit with Rotto, his arrogance and her alleged impropriety with Feder. She described his intensity, false affection and violent manner. She rubbed her sore wrist before continuing, "He's a troubled man, Bino, and I want nothing to do with him."

He lifted her bruised arm out of a shadow and recalled the evening he'd found Nica cowering in the moonlight. His anger returned. "He hurt you?"

"I don't think he meant to, Bino. He seemed desperate and afraid. Worse, Renato tells me he brought his accusation to Papa."

"Did you speak to your father?"

"No. He speaks only of names, position and suitors' ability to put bread on my table."

"You underestimate him, Laura; he wouldn't tolerate this. And he shouldn't be faulted for caring about your well-being."

"How can you say that when we're meant to be together? Luxury could never fill the void in my heart."

Bino embraced her and offered, "I will ask to speak with your father in the morning; I won't let another moon rise before doing so."

Laura studied him and brought her lips to his. She trembled in equal measure to her desire.

The artist's conscience was conflicted. Laura's nightdress did little to mask the fullness of her breasts or the beating of her heart. Bino appreciated the peril at being discovered alone with Laura and doubted the worthiness of his words against Signor Pelucca's intention. He suspected Laura would object to his course.

"Let me go, Laura. I know what I must do and I don't wish to jeopardize your parents' good opinion of me."

Her body responded first and Laura strengthened her hold.

"You may have buried Saint Catherine, artist, but I won't be put so easily to sleep."

Bino smiled. He appreciated her wit and recalled how Feder had brought it to his attention during their first carriage ride.

He sighed and spoke, "If I stay a moment longer, I'll never leave."

"Stay then."

"I'm no saint, Laura, and I want you more than I can deny. You're worthy of that denial and I won't rest until no option remains."

Laura spoke before sealing her request with a kiss. "Be gone then. Return only to take me away."

Bino left Laura and was reversing his steps across the courtyard when the moon got his attention. It was full and remarkably bright—bright enough, he thought, to paint a fresco-starved wall.

Bino sensed another's presence. He spun about but saw no one. An ominous feeling occupied him and he recalled Piero's words. His friend had told him to *leave this place.*

Why Piero? Why must I leave the one I love?

Piero often resorted to riddles during the time they shared; would this forever be one of them?

If leave I must, I will take Laura with me.

The artist's moonlit meditation was interrupted by a distant sound. It was faint and faded before strengthening in the quiet of night. It was the sound of galloping hooves on the gate pathway.

A solitary rider approached. He was a man in a hurry, one carelessly clothed and eager to communicate an important message. The messenger slowed and reined his horse nearer the artist's cottage. Bino recognized him as Nondo—Feder's servant and fellow huntsman.

Bino ran towards the cottage, wishing to intercept Nondo before others were startled from sleep. The visitor spied him and tugged his reins rearward until his horse halted in front of the artist.

With an urgent tone, Nondo began.

"Signor Bino, what good fortune! I was sent to retrieve you and didn't believe I'd meet with success."

Bino responded with concern. "What do you have to report, Nondo? Tell me plainly if your master is unwell."

"I cannot be sure, *signor*; Feder relays news of the worst kind. Lieutenant de'Gavante accuses him of stealing Miss Laura's virtue and challenges Master Feder to a sunrise tournament."

The words confirmed Laura's fear while raising many questions. *What nonsense produced this dangerous accusation?*

"How is this possible, Nondo?"

"We know nothing of the source. Master asks only if you'll come, if you'll honor him and serve as his second."

Bino thought only a moment before replying, "What good am I to Feder? I know nothing of fighting and honor tournaments."

Nondo continued, "You needn't worry, Signor Bino; he is well-schooled in sword play. Master won't take the lieutenant's life should he yield and withdraw his complaint."

"And if the lieutenant refuses?"

"Then he will die and deserve to."

"Where do we ride, Nondo?"

"Piazza di Monza."

Bino begged a few moments to prepare. He entered his cottage and removed his night clothes. He replaced them with pieces absent the stains of his occupation— the shirt he had intended to wear Sunday for the unveiling of his chapel fresco. Atop clean leggings he laced up calf boots. He knotted these across his ankles thinking nothing of the hour or his fatigue.

Once done, Bino stood and surveyed the room. He was reminded of the night he'd fled Milan—the ghost of Brother Tomas urging him away. The artist was near to exiting when instinct told him to leave word for Renato. He moved to his desk and scribbled his destination, describing what was about to happen. He concluded the note by signing, *Piacere, come if able, friend. Bino.* He slid the note under his neighbor's door and returned outdoors.

The artist found the moon higher in the sky. The evening seemed too beautiful for the ugliness scheduled to follow. Nondo returned to his horse, mounted and assisted Bino in taking the space behind him. The trip to Monza would be brief and with an abrupt kick to the horse's ribs, the pair departed.

Throughout their ride Nondo served as coach to the artist. He instructed where and how Bino, as his Master's second, should position himself and behave.

"Be silent, Bino, and only come to Master Feder's aid if he requests."

Nondo may as well have spoken the words in French; it all sounded alien to the artist who had but a single occasion to deliver a blow and that to the helpless figure of Argento.

"Remain calm, Signor Bino; the lieutenant knows nothing of master's proficiency with swords. We shall have the element of surprise."

All was quiet when they arrived upon Piazza di Monza. Saturday's sun had not yet crossed the eastern horizon and the moon appeared unwilling to relinquish its place in the sky. A chill lingered in the air and both servant and passenger lifted their collars against the cold. Bino said nothing while mindful of the situation and the ill feeling in his stomach. *What can I offer here?*

At Nondo's prompting they dismounted and walked with his horse to the stone well-head nearby. The servant offered a cup of water and the artist refused. He was too anxious to put anything down.

They weren't there long before a rider was heard approaching from the south.

Nondo recognized the cadence and said, "That will be Master Feder."

Feder arrived with the sun and the appearance of both made Bino more hopeful. He rushed towards his friend and offered a concerned greeting. Feder jumped to the ground and embraced the artist before giving voice to his conviction.

"I accept this challenge, Bino. What can be more important to me than Laura's honor? It will prove the most worthy act in my otherwise unremarkable life. I am grateful you stand with me."

Bino was speechless. The sometimes poet couldn't find words equal to the occasion. Instead he wondered aloud, "What can the lieutenant know of you and Laura? Can't you make him understand this isn't necessary?"

"Rotto claims to be in possession of an intercepted letter written in my hand. I know nothing of such a letter but see no reason to deny it. You needn't worry, Bino," continued Feder, "I don't intend to press my advantage too far."

Bino knew it was time to reveal his feelings for Laura.

"Friend, we must talk. The intercepted letter was mine."

Before Feder could digest Bino's confession, they were interrupted by two horses entering the square from the north. Mounted upon them were Rotto and his aide in full military regalia. The lieutenant sat tall, silent and expressionless. When he recognized Casa Pelucca's house artist as Feder's second, he smiled.

The challengers reined their horses to a stop and dismounted thirty paces distant from where Feder, Nondo and Bino stood. The junior officer accepted Rotto's riding gloves in exchange for a leaner pair. He then led the horses to a tie-post and secured them. Before a word was spoken, he withdrew a scabbard linked to Rotto's saddle and rejoined his superior.

Rotto began the verbal volley and demonstrated disrespect by using his opponent's common name. "Judging from your company, Feder, I wonder if you've come to duel or decorate the square."

Bino interrupted, "You misunderstand, Lieutenant."

Unsmiling, Feder raised a hand to quiet the artist and responded, "I come only to silence those who deal in lies, Rotto. Do you wish to reconsider and apologize for your folly?"

Rotto ignored the invitation, turning instead to his aide with an open hand. The junior officer required no explanation; he withdrew the lieutenant's rapier from its scabbard and placed the decorated grip in the palm of Rotto's hand.

The lieutenant weighed his weapon, held it high and forward, making small circles in the air. He appeared to be writing in the sky.

Rotto's seriousness troubled Bino but did nothing to diminish Feder's resolve.

Rotto pointed his sword at the pair and spoke, "You seem anxious for embarrassment, Feder. 'Twould be a pity to orphan your parents before their time. Bow now, acknowledge your shame and leave Laura to my care. In return I'll let you live to inherit an undeserved fortune."

"You are unworthy of Signorina Pelucca and underestimate me, Rotto. You need only know I would never dishonor the woman I love."

Bino was poised to leap forward and argue in behalf of his friend when he felt Nondo's gentle tug on the back of his shirt, "Say nothing, Signor Bino."

Rotto's laugh reminded Bino of his culpability.

"You seem to favor poetry and romantic words, Feder. Words, however, are no match for deeds. Be you brave enough, draw your sword and settle this properly."

Nondo released Bino's shirt and delivered Feder's scabbard to his outstretched hand. Feder withdrew his rapier from its case and handed the latter back to Nondo. Nondo offered a second sword to Bino and it was reluctantly accepted. The artist studied the instrument and felt less empowered.

Outside the participants' notice, a growing group of villagers formed a perimeter about the square. Word had spread of the honor tournament and those thirsty for blood and gossip were taking their places at table.

As Feder and Rotto approached one another, three additional spectators arrived from opposite points of the square. Renato came accompanied by Signor Pelucca while Lady Rabbia arrived alone.

The dueling pair touched swords as their appointed seconds glanced nervously at one another. Someone punctuated the silence with support for the soldier and the lieutenant seized the moment to take the offensive. He delivered a sharp sequence of blows meant to overpower Feder but even Lady Rabbia's loud plea to "stop" did nothing to diminish her son's focus and defensive footwork.

Signor Pelucca watched with concerned amazement. *How had it come to this? And why had the artist been invited to second the man he intended for Laura?*

Feder's pulse quickened and he called upon his years of tutelage in sword-craft. He circled about his angry opponent, sidestepping blows. He used his rapier to deflect Rotto's energy up and outward where fatigue was likely to follow.

Rotto impressed the crowd and confused his opponent. His custom-made sword flew from his right to left hand and back again. He appeared tireless and smug and nodded towards Signor Pelucca at each opportunity. His own father wasn't present but he used his hatred and disdain for the man to fuel his attack. *Feder would yield or die.*

Renato sought to connect eyes with Bino and failed. The artist could not be distracted from his responsibility and the anxiousness he felt for his friend. Instead, Renato was distracted by a solitary dove circling above the square; he followed its path until it perched atop other viewers within the cathedral bell tower.

Shouts for and against attracted scores to Piazza Monza. Rotto, sensing weakness, increased the ferocity of his blows against Feder's parries. When her son absorbed a particularly weighty thrust and stumbled, Lady Rabbia screamed and fell into the arms of others.

The artist grew more nervous with each deflected parry and looked to Nondo for reassurance; Nondo met Bino's eyes and nodded twice with confidence.

A strong wind blew through the square and Renato noticed the dove resume flight. With the wind came change. Rotto's bullying turned the crowd against him and chants in support of the perceived underdog grew more frequent. Feder found the strength to thwart Rotto's aggression while the lieutenant confronted tightening muscles and the weight of his instrument.

Feder sought an opportunity and seized the moment when it arrived. With quickness surprising everyone but Nondo, Feder dodged a high volley, dropped low and reversed his swing. With momentum and a terrific twist he connected his forearm with the area behind Rotto's knees. The blow upended his opponent and the lieutenant fell back-first into the packed earth.

Feder leapt upon Rotto, paralyzing a shoulder with his left boot. He placed his blade tip against the lieutenant's neck and bellowed, "Yield!" Rotto would not have it and continued to struggle until a glance from Feder's weapon shed the morning's first blood.

The lieutenant's aide moved to defend, his sword at the ready. Before he'd taken two steps, Feder shouted him back and held aloft his left hand. "Steady, second; I have cause but do not intend further harm to those in service of the duke."

Some in the crowd objected but Feder would not hear it. He identified and smiled at someone before connecting with Signor Pelucca's sober eyes. He was relieved to see Laura's father holding his mother aloft.

The victor spoke loud enough for all to hear, "The lieutenant is free to go. He need only retract his lie and any claim to the woman I love."

Escaping everyone's notice was the young woman herself. Alerted to the tournament by her maid, Laura could not be dissuaded from attending. Disguised as a lad and shielding herself from those who might recognize her, Laura delighted in Feder's victory but not the implied claim to her hand.

Rotto understood the futility of his position. He masked his rage with a tepid response. "I yield."

"I don't think anyone heard you, Lieutenant," responded Feder.

"I yield!" repeated Rotto.

"So be it," allowed Feder. "I remit you to the duke's service."

Feder removed his boot from Rotto's shoulder and stepped away. He approached Nondo, transferred his weapon and embraced Bino, who happily discarded his own blade to the earth.

The crowd applauded the outcome and quieted until the once-proud lieutenant fell while lifting himself from the stone below. Rotto mistook the rumbling for mocking laughter and exploded off the ground.

Bino observed what few were in position to see. The officer seemed intent on avenging his embarrassment and only the artist, were he quick enough, could prevent it. Rotto let loose with a great yell and sped toward them. He slowed only to retrieve Bino's sword from the earth before others shifted their attention.

With only Bino's horrific expression and tardy gasp to warn him, Feder absorbed Rotto's penetrating blow between his shoulder blades. Unable to breathe, he collapsed to the ground.

Bino and Nondo dropped with Feder to the earth and shouted words of hope to their dying friend. In the ensuing chaos, Rotto fled through the crowd.

Feder's eyes were wide and his tongue twisted. Blood spilled from his mouth and wound and pooled below as his skin paled. Shouts and commotion followed before all were silenced by Lady Rabbia's wail.

She pushed her way forward with Signor Pelucca and Renato and fell to her knees at Feder's side. Wild with emotion, she thrust her palm against Bino's chest accusingly. "You! You were chosen to protect him. Instead my son is slain with your sword."

Bino fell backward in disbelief. Lady Rabbia cradled her son's head and shoulders in her lap as Renato and Nondo spoke in his defense. Neither witnessed Laura appear.

Renato began. "Signora, you're mistaken. The coward acted too quickly..."

Lady Rabbia silenced him.

She pointed to Bino and challenged all within hearing, "How well do you know this man? He took liberties with me under my husband's roof, and fearing Feder's discovery, left him unprotected."

The cruel accusation opened Feder's eyes and he looked to Bino for a denial. The artist motioned no to his dying friend but would not indict Lady Rabbia publicly. Feder misread Bino's silence as guilt. With his last breath, he uttered but a single word: "Why?"

Laura remained quiet no longer. "She lies, Feder! Bino could never do such a thing. Tell them, Bino. Tell them."

All eyes turned to the lad in their midst. Feeling the weight of their stare, Laura removed her hood, drawing gasps from the villagers and a rebuke from her father. Betraying his anger, Signor Pelucca commanded, "Leave at once, Laura!"

Renato rushed to Laura's side intending to protect her from further criticism but she pushed him away and leapt to the artist's side. "Say something, Bino. They don't know you."

Bino gripped Laura's shoulders for the second time that morning and whispered words she didn't understand, "I cannot speak it here, Laura, not with Feder so cruelly disposed."

Feder exhaled his last. No one observed the dove as it circled and escaped the piazza below.

Signor Pelucca lowered himself to a knee and laid a hand upon Lady Rabbia's shoulder. He offered words of sympathy and purpose before standing and joining Rotto's aide and interested citizens.

"Find and capture the lieutenant; he will pay for this injustice with his life."

He dismissed them and turned his attention to Bino. "Leave us, artist. Leave Monza and never return. I regret ever welcoming you into my home."

Laura rushed to her father and threw her fists against his chest. "You cannot send him away, Papa. He's done nothing wrong and was a friend to Feder and our family. I love him."

Signor Pelucca would not hear it. "Renato, return Laura to her mother at once. I will accompany Lady Rabbia and her son home."

Renato was again ready to speak in Bino's defense when Laura interrupted. "I won't go, Papa! Tell him, Bino. Tell him we intend to wed."

Gasps and chatter sprung from the crowd until Bino gave voice to the truth. Signor Pelucca tried to quiet him but he wouldn't be denied.

"You must hear me, *signor*. If I failed Feder, it was for lack of experience. He was an honorable man, my friend and his feelings for Laura true."

"Silence! You haven't earned my ear."

Bino paused and rubbed his bloody hands across his pant legs before continuing, "You must listen, Signor. I came to Monza expecting little. I accepted Feder's friendship, the generosity of your family and Laura's inspiration. I cannot explain the evil we witnessed today. I know only my heart belongs to your daughter and forever shall."

Signor Pelucca put an end to Bino's confession. "Enough! I'm to believe you over a trusted neighbor? Renato, Nondo, escort Signor Bino to the edge of the village. I grant his freedom and nothing more."

Laura extracted herself from Renato's grip. "Take me with you, Bino! This cannot be my home any longer."

The artist reached for her hands and spoke, "Not like this, Laura. Our promise, this morning, remember."

Tears streaked Laura's cheeks. "What are you saying? How can I remain without you?"

Signor Pelucca had had enough. Embarrassed and insulted by one of his own blood, he grabbed Laura's arm, struck her across the face and pledged aloud, "If you won't return home, you'll go to the convent and soon!"

Bino leapt to rescue Laura but was restrained by Renato. "Come away, son. It's no longer safe for you here."

Bino understood the urgency of his plea. *How had everything gone so wrong?* Haunted by Piero's words, the artist pondered what might have been avoided by leaving sooner. *Feder lay murdered, alerted at his last breath of my infidelity. I failed to protect the only man Signor Pelucca believed worthy of Laura and worse, I'm breaking my midnight vow and fleeing Casa Pelucca without her.*

Dio! What must I do, Lord?

Renato dragged the numb artist from the crowd amid slurs and scornful eyes. The pair walked in silence, disbelieving the ugliness left behind—neither appreciating the path of the dove.

When they reached Monza's border, they stood in silence. Renato embraced the younger man as a father would a son. Bino welcomed the gesture and asked, "How can I leave without her, Renato?" He wanted to ask if he would be forgiven for doing so.

As if a mind reader, Renato reassured him. "If she's sent away, I will follow and explain everything. Laura will understand and forgive."

"And me, Renato? Can I forgive myself?"

"You must."

"And until then, where shall I go?"

Renato thought before responding, "*Forse e' meglio*, maybe it's better you go home. Luino won't have changed much. Perhaps she has something to say to you."

Bino's heart lightened. "I will miss you, Renato. You give me reason to hope."

Renato embraced him a second time before removing his coat and giving it to the traveler. The nomadic artist accepted it and looked down the eastern road.

"The path is clear, Renato. And I won't travel it alone. I know a friendly ghost who it seems has something left to teach me.

PART III

Caterina

I don't want anyone's pity. Caterina withdrew her fingers from her infant son's hand and wiped away tears. Her other hand clutched her baby to her chest while Padre Castani's blessing swirled about her like dry leaves in the wind.

The new innkeeper couldn't believe her turn of fortune—*Mamma and Papa taken in so little time and still no word of Giovanni.* Fever was claiming a harsh toll from Serono's most vulnerable citizens and she and Giovanni had buried his mother and her beloved father before her soldier had returned to service three months ago. This day marked six weeks since any word from him and Caterina's mother now lay cold above the December earth.

The joy of her wedding day seemed a distant memory. It had yielded to fear and faith—fear that Giovanni had been mortally wounded in action against the French, fear the son she bore him couldn't be protected from fever, and faith that Mary, the author of uncounted miracles in Serono, would restore Giovanni and health to this inhospitable place.

How can I survive? In moments of despair, she wished she was among those taken, and immediately felt guilt for seeking Giovanni's feared fate—death and peace. These were the gifts of a difficult age though Padre Castani told her it was a sin to think that way.

Mattia's cry stirred her from her somber meditation. Those surrounding her mother's coffin whispered until an older woman in a grey robe approached and asked Caterina if she'd prefer a moment alone.

"Let me take the child," the woman offered.

"No," said Caterina abruptly, quickly regretting her rudeness. *They don't understand; I want nothing taken from me anymore.*

"Padre Castani, I must return home with Mattia."

"Very well," he replied, motioning for the men at his side to lower the baby's grandmother into the earth. Near them, Isabella wept for the loss of her elder sister.

The graveyard exodus began and Caterina took the first step toward home and an uncertain future. The rising sun was at odds with her mood and feelings of despair. Her parents were gone, her husband was missing and his extended family was too full of cares to offer assistance.

As she walked with her son and Isabella, Caterina set aside her mother's passing and thought of Giovanni. She gripped his prayer beads and brought to mind his strength and quiet confidence. *What if he never returns? I am so frightened, Mary.*

Daughter no longer, Caterina owned the cares of a new mother and innkeeper—each role as unfamiliar as the disease gripping Lombardia. She pledged her steadfast faith...*If only this fitful chapter would end.*

When Giovanni's mother died, he had shared the surprising truth of his father's heritage. Generations before, his family had won the loyalty and favor of *famiglia* Visconti—the moneyed family that forged progress and first governed the outpost of Serono. As a gift to Giovanni's ancestral family, the Viscontis had awarded the stone, multi-room cottage along Via Varesina. Succeeding generations had passed the property to each first-born son until the cottage became Giovanni's.

Caterina was, therefore, doubly grateful for her child—a healthy son and legitimate heir. She hugged Mattia a little tighter and whispered a prayer of thanksgiving in his ear.

They had named him Mattia before his Christening, when Padre Castani had shared the saint's little-known story. In the aftermath of Judas' betrayal and Christ's crucifixion, Peter and the remaining disciples sought to add a twelfth member to their community. Candidates were proposed and from the final pair Mattia was selected. He would forever be the only disciple not chosen by Christ but by the mortal men inspired to follow Him.

With her soldier's survival in question, Mattia was all that stood between Caterina and homelessness. Giovanni's cousins understood this and inquired often after the baby's health. Among them were other first-born sons, eager and able to claim the inn. Caterina guarded Mattia's health and, by extension, her home. If her husband failed to return, their son and cottage would serve as his legacy.

The innkeeper arrived at her door but did not enter. Instead she looked across the alley. Her home faced the sanctuary of the pilgrim church. It remained her favorite place of reflection and a persistent reminder of her father since it bore the happy evidence of Eduardo's masonry. She referred to the church as her *stone garden* and found peace within its walls. *Maybe I ask too much of you.* The innkeeper's daily visits and prayers for Giovanni's return were so far unanswered.

Caterina touched her head and shoulders in a sign of the cross before entering her home. Isabella accepted the baby and followed. No words were spoken. When they settled, Caterina nursed Mattia and laid him to rest.

They set about busying themselves, sweeping the walls and scrubbing the floor. They labored while ignoring knocks upon the heavy wooden door; meddlesome neighbors and guests were not welcome that day or the next. At dusk, Isabella hugged Caterina and repeated her belief that

Giovanni would return. Without waiting for a reply, she began the short journey to the cottage where she and Caterina had known happier days.

Alone with her sleeping son, Caterina put propriety aside and unwrapped all the candles Giovanni had left behind. She appreciated the irony. He so liked the light but had left her with a heart filled with darkness. She lit a single wick from the hearth before touching eleven more in her bed chamber. The totality of loss washed over her and for the second time that day she wept.

Am I faithless? The question caught her by surprise. *Why no word? Does every soldier's wife accept the unthinkable?*

I'm frightened, Giovanni. How can I manage the inn and shepherd Mattia without you?

She wiped a tear from her cheek and whispered, "If only you were here to enjoy our candlelight."

Mattia stirred and began to coo. She went to him and withdrew him from his crib into her arms.

She studied him and spoke softly, "Papa isn't here because he's protecting us."

To settle him she waltzed about the room. Mattia smiled; it was a magical moment that relieved a little of her pain. When she tired of the dance, she extinguished the candles in succession. At each she whispered a name. This one's for Papa, this one for Nonna, Nonno, Isabella, Padre Castani, and on until concluding with the holy family—Joseph, Mary and Jesus. Mattia delighted in the ritual before closing his eyes and reclining with Caterina on her bed.

Caterina retrieved Giovanni's prayer beads from her headboard and repeated the devotion spoken each night of her life. *Mary, full of Grace, the Lord is with Thee.*

Beyond her notice, the scent of candlelight and glow of good intention settled upon them. Sleep came and with it a return on her spirit-full investment. Caterina's appeal penetrated earth and sky and from these flowed a generous wellspring of heaven's most underappreciated gift—grace.

Winter days came and went. Their brevity contributed to the innkeeper's sense of isolation. Worse, exaggerated rumors of fever and death reduced visits to Serono. Fewer pilgrims meant fewer lodgers and reduced income for the inn.

What can I do? Caterina woke with the question one morning.

Mattia cried and she reached for him. She warmed him with her arms and rested a cool cheek against his before opening her nightdress and allowing him to suckle at her breast. He nourished there while she hummed a familiar melody and considered to whom she might turn for help. Older and more comfortable than most first-time mothers, she invited little sympathy from neighbors.

On her behalf, Padre Castani reached out to the Bishop for assistance and was frustrated by his response. When the parish priest asked for an explanation, the Bishop spoke of Giovanni's uncertain status. "We don't yet know whether Giovanni served Rome nobly. Return to me when we have word of his death, capture, or, God forbid, desertion. Without evidence, the church cannot offer widows' alms."

Caterina put anxious thoughts aside and began her day. With Mattia satisfied, she visited the well-head and returned with fresh water. She lit a fire, hung the water above it and counted the coins remaining in her purse. Without a regular guest or the generosity of Giovanni's family, her resources would be inadequate to see them through January.

Caterina carried a portion of the hearth-warmed water to a corner of the room. She straddled a wooden basin there and used a rag to rinse herself and the baby. With their bath complete, she lifted a robe over her shoulders, dried and dressed Mattia. She returned to the tub of warm water and used it with butcher's soap to scrub Mattia's soiled clothes. These were wrung out and hung in preparation for the next day.

Caterina felt hungry and tore several pieces of stale bread from Sunday's loaf. She offered a blessing over these and washed them down with warm milk. When satisfied, the innkeeper dressed, lifted a comb and began the daily task of untangling her hair. She recalled Giovanni admiring the ritual as she collected a fistful of hair in one hand while teasing it straight with the other.

Her blonde locks attracted unwanted attention from men and the envy of women. She paused in front of her looking glass and wondered.

What might the wig maker offer? Be it too soon to think that way? Giovanni would surely not forgive me.

With her morning ritual complete, Caterina pulled a coat over her shoulders, wrapped Mattia in a wool blanket and checked the fire. Assured the cottage was in order, she left home with the baby and walked across the alley into the church. Once inside, she paused to her allow her eyes adjust to the lesser light.

The innkeeper inhaled, filling her lungs with a unique and welcome aroma—a rich mixture of candle wax, incense and wood. The scent transported her to earlier days when she had entered this place enthusiastic about her first sacraments of reconciliation and communion.

She stepped forward with her son and noticed others seated or kneeling in prayer. She wondered whether they had come as she had, seeking refuge from painful circumstances or simply the cold. She gripped Mattia to her chest and approached the offertory chapel. Her father had completed his work there only weeks before his death. She was grateful to Padre Castani for calling attention to it at his deathbed anointing.

She lit a candle before lowering herself to an adjacent kneeler. The stiff and cold wood felt uncomfortable against her knees and she reasoned it was what kept others away. She thought of Giovanni and spoke to him before making her appeal.

Give me courage, increase my faith and let me not be ungrateful for the blessings you share. Caterina thought to say more but instead asked forgiveness for the uncharitable feelings she harbored towards Giovanni's family. She rose from her knees and took a few steps away before returning and genuflecting. *I will return each day, Blessed Mother, and offer a candle until the path you choose for me is clear.*

The innkeeper repeated her daily visitation. The winter rains did not interrupt her visits. When she felt especially vulnerable and discouraged, she left Mattia with Isabella and remained in the chapel for an extended period of time.

The way forward remained cloudy and infrequent lodgers yielded only subsistence wages for her purse. It was enough to purchase bread, milk and fruit, but the innkeeper knew other levies were looming. She would be forced to seek credit or make a pride-swallowing appeal to Giovanni's cousins.

Awful rumors reached her ears as well. More than a few village women withheld greetings and attributed absent husbands to Caterina's physical charms. *Her door and legs are open,* they gossiped, *for soldi piccoli. Were she honorable, she would bury her husband and take another.*

The thought occurred to her during her weakest moments. It was then she felt vulnerable to behavior from which Isabella, Padre Castani and prayer distracted.

Mary, give me courage. Save us from despair.

Loyalty and reason sustained her. Without evidence of Giovanni's death, taking a lover would betray her vow and a loveless marriage might come at the expense of the independence she cherished.

Eight weeks of offertories brought Caterina no closer to the resolution for which she prayed. She fell to her knees one April morning, studied the blank church walls about her and closed her eyes. It was time; she would relinquish the inn to Giovanni's family, live in more modest circumstances and survive on the rental income it might provide until Mattia could claim it as his own. She would shed her pride, visit her husband's cousins and make the offer.

You lead me here, Mother. I'm at peace with it.

Caterina rose from her prayer with a sense of finality, turned and was poised to exit when a familiar voice hailed her.

"*Cara* Caterina!"

She spun about and was pleased to see Padre Castani approaching.

"*Buon giorno*, Padre. Are you well?"

There was a brief and awkward silence during which she felt the priest's kind and admiring eyes embrace her.

"Yes, yes. Forgive me," he began, before searching for better words.

Color came to the priest's cheeks and he appeared too confused to speak. He'd met Caterina when she was a child and again on the eve of her wedding. Then and now, he believed her faith and kindness rivaled only by her soul-piercing, blue eyes. Accompanied by her smile, they mirrored her affection and pleased Padre Castani in all ways save one. Caterina was for him a tangible reminder of his priestly sacrifice. He brushed the realization aside and cleared his throat before resuming the conversation.

"I see you here each day, child, and am moved by your devotion to our Lady. Like you, I'm pained by Giovanni's absence. I know no finer man or nobler servant."

A long pause followed during which the priest measured his words. "Caterina, it may be time to allow our soldier's soul rest."

Caterina attempted to hide her tears by lifting her eyes to the chapel ceiling. "*Non so.* I don't know, Padre. How can I bury Giovanni when my heart believes he will come home?"

Her conviction and sadness stirred him in a way he hadn't thought possible. He reached for her shoulders and gave them a reassuring squeeze.

Caterina looked down upon the floor. "I worry for my faith, Padre. As things are, I cannot hope to feed my son and keep the inn. I come each day to pray for our Lady's direction and am now resigned to the answer. We will vacate the inn and invite a share of its income from Giovanni's cousins."

What he said next surprised her. "I wish I was as courageous and faithful as you, Caterina."

Curious at his meaning, she whispered, "How can that be?"

"When I was your age, I had other notions about the man I could be. I grew and moved in several directions but wherever I turned, fear paralyzed me. Having nowhere to bring my fear, I brought it to God and became a priest."

Padre Castani paused before continuing, "In the end, I wasn't willing to sacrifice security for a chance at bliss. But you, you step forward day after day, open to the message of the Holy Spirit. Rejoice in this and do not abandon hope."

The priest rested an open palm across her joined hands and brought warmth there.

"Pray with me, Caterina. Mother of graces," he began, "look upon your servant with favor. Reward her faith, bless the bodies and souls of her husband and son and grant unto them their daily bread. Open her eyes to your message of abundance and forgive us both our moments of despair. We ask this in the name of your Son, our Lord, Jesus Christ."

Caterina relaxed her shoulders and exhaled the words, "*Grazie tanto*, Padre Castani."

"*Prego, signora*. Giovanni may yet hear our prayer."

Caterina was lost in a dream that night. Giovanni crawled into bed and wrapped himself about her. He bore no scent of battle or the road—odors calling to mind places and violence to which she would never grow accustomed. His embrace forced the air out of her lungs and she felt protected. She buried her head under his arm and shifted a leg between his.

"You've come back to me," she whispered. "I've been so alone."

"I never left you, Caterina."

"You did and now I'm afraid."

"You don't understand. You are much stronger than you know."

"I'm a soldier's wife and the mother of your son. I am nothing else."

"You are more than these."

"I will lose your home and throw myself at the mercy of your family."

"You won't do this. Trust."

"Enough words. Don't you want me?"

Caterina reached for his warmth but where she once found him aroused, there was nothing. She woke fitfully, calling his name, "Giovanni, *non mi partire!*"

Padre Castani

The following morning brought hints of spring and mild temperatures. Eager to leave winter behind, Padre Castani presided over sunrise mass and returned to the rectory. He requested the opening of its shutters and welcomed fresh air into his rooms.

Something of the breeze reminded him of home and he wondered for a moment about the Luino parish he'd left behind. He didn't regret the move despite its poor timing. How could he or anyone have imagined the steep price fever would exact from Serono's most vulnerable. *Lord, shepherd the souls of the lost and lift the cares of those left behind.*

The priest threw himself into prayer and contemplation and was poised to begin some letter writing when a seminarian knocked upon the door.

"You have a visitor, Brother Castani. He won't share his name though says he comes at your request."

The priest didn't respond quickly to the unwelcome intrusion and the seminarian continued, "Was it up to me, Padre, I would turn him away; his appearance is wanting. He smells of the road and made no effort to comb his hair and beard."

Padre Castani didn't share the pretensions of the bishop's staff and was charitable.

"Brother, we're not all blessed with a looking glass and calling coat; I'll meet our guest in the parlor."

"As you wish, Brother."

When the priest entered the parlor minutes later, he spied the visitor's broad back. A worn and ill-sized cloak hung about his shoulders and swung from side to side as he moved to review art on the opposite wall.

Despite sensing the priest's arrival, the pilgrim remained focused elsewhere and inquired, "You are Padre Castani?"

"I am."

"You come to Serono from the parish of Luino?"

"I have."

"How are things there, Padre?"

"Forgive me son, why do you ask?"

Bino turned and faced the priest. His childhood mentor appeared smaller and rounder with less hair and fuller brows but the eyes and posture hadn't changed. The artist relaxed and studied his curious host.

"I ask because many years ago a kind priest made possible my escape from a proud mother and doubtful father. Before this moment, I never expressed the fullness of my gratitude and regret."

A chill rose through the old priest's robe and he reached instinctively for the prayer beads hanging loosely from his waist. Padre Castani stepped closer, tilted his head and looked through the visitor's weary mask for something familiar. And in so searching found it.

"Bino?"

There was no response, only a softening of the artist's posture and the closing of his eyes.

"Before the saints and angels, is it you?"

Bino looked upon the priest and answered, "Yes, Padre, it's me."

The good shepherd's eyes flooded with tears and he leapt forward to embrace his lamb. Bino returned the full force of the priest's hug, lifting him off his feet.

"My letter found you. You came."

"I did and am glad for it."

Bino delighted in the joy of their reunion. Since the day fifteen months earlier when he abandoned Laura and bid Renato farewell, the artist had known little beyond sadness and doubt. Not a night passed that he didn't weigh the cruel price of Feder's blood. There had been many casualties—the woman he loved, the friendships he shared and his passion to create.

When they separated, Padre Castani noted the sadness in the artist's eyes and invited him to sit down.

"Are you hungry or thirsty? Are you in want of a bath? Tell me where you've been, son, and what injury the Father and I can mend."

Bino accepted a chair and pondered the invitation to the sacrament he most required, reconcilliation. A bath could wait.

"I'm not sure where to begin, Padre. The day is short and my sins too numerous to mention."

"I have nowhere to be, Bino. And recall what I once told you; it's in the recounting of a difficult story where the seed of redemption lies."

"I've missed your wisdom, Padre."

"And I your candor."

A comfortable silence filled the space between them and the priest resisted the urge to speak first. He would not rush the telling of a difficult tale.

Bino closed his eyes and relived his chaotic journey from Luino to Milan to Monza as if it was an expansive mural on a cathedral wall. The beginning and middle were clear. Clouding the end was the Pelucca chapel fresco. He hadn't been present for the big reveal—the *Burial of Saint Catherine.*

Will I ever be privileged to see it or Laura again?

"I'm not proud of myself, Padre. I will tell all of it and pray you won't think too poorly of your student. I have little in my purse and no home."

The priest appreciated his words and said nothing. He remained an attentive listener for the succeeding two hours.

"You left me under the care of Master Gian Stefano Scotto," began Bino. "He welcomed us to Leonardo's studio. Another student, Gaudenzio Ferrari, and I furthered our skills in the company of others before bettering them and being apprenticed elsewhere. I left Scotto's workshop and my troubles began."

Bino read empathy in Padre Castani's eyes and continued. He spared no uncomfortable detail. He spoke of Signor Argento and their twisted patron—one delighting in ever-more vulgar images of women. He described his first love, Nica, and the violent misfortune visited upon her. He introduced his mysterious benefactor—Piero, and elicited a wide-eyed response from the priest when identifying him as Leonardo's father.

"It was through Piero's patient counsel and connections I found work in Milan's finest churches. My frescos improved in substance and quality until I was commended to mentor a seminarian at San Giorgio's."

Bino rose and paced the room. He spoke of Brother Tomas's death, his own culpability and flight to Monza.

"I hid at Casa Pelucca. It was there I met the woman I wish to wed and accepted the generosity of her father and *famiglia* Rabbia. I fell in love with Laura and lacked the courage to give public voice to my affection. A great misunderstanding followed between Feder, a gentleman worthy of her hand, and Rotto, a soldier worthy of damnation."

Bino returned to his seat before recounting the awful details of his seduction at the hands of Lady Rabbia. "My sin is equal to hers, Padre. I could have run and owned my loneliness; my lust proved stronger."

Bino concluded with a description of the honor tournament and its aftermath. "I saw the villain coming and did nothing. I watched as Rotto thrust my sword into Feder's back."

Bino raised his voice before continuing, "As Feder lay dying, I could say little to counter the truth shared by his mother. My betrayal was complete. I fled Monza, cloistered with some religious and returned to Luino. Your successor relayed your letter. And so here the prodigal son awaits your judgment."

Padre Castani breathed deeply and digested Bino's words. Had another spoken them, he would have reasoned them too fantastic to be believed. His own spiritual journey convinced him otherwise. *Faith demands respect for mystery.*

Contemplation was the first and best reaction to a journey as remarkable as Bino's. There was the undeniable genius of the artist's hands— hands the priest had encouraged to leave Luino. Juxtaposed against such genius was a long list of misfortunes—an assaulted innocent, a dead priest, infidelity and a murdered nobleman.

Padre Castani judged his own words insufficient to the task. Instead he looked at the artist with an affectionate heart, rose and stepped towards a nearby bookshelf. He searched it before selecting a volume and returning to his seat.

The priest thumbed through the pages until arriving at the desired passage from Mark's gospel. He read it aloud.

Anyone who wants to be a follower of mine has to put self aside, shoulder their cross, and go the way that I go. Whoever holds onto their life will lose it. But whoever lets go of their life for my sake and the Gospel's will save it.

"I've heard your story, son, believe you contrite and so with God's grace absolve you from your sin. You shouldered your cross. You left us a child and struggled through dark passages before returning home. It is time for you to leave the desert and serve as witness to Christ's resurrection."

The priest put the book down, rose and sat adjacent to Bino. He covered the artist's clasped hands with one of his own.

"You were given a great gift and when invited, used it. You used it as you once challenged me, to inspire seekers to the faith. That bad things happened to you is not unusual. But redemption is a cruel mistress. She commands us to rise, ignore ignorant criticism and move forward."

"Can it be that simple, Padre?"

"If your friend Piero was here, would he not say the same thing?"

Bino knew the answer. It was as if Piero and the priest had conspired to rescue him from his despondency.

"He spoke to me in a dream one evening, Padre. He said I must leave Casa Pelucca. I was selfish and would not leave without Laura."

"Are you so sure of his message?"

"I am today."

"*Senti*, Bino. Even if you're correct, when God intends a marriage for us, we must accept it on His terms. Isn't it possible Laura learned the truth and prays for your return?"

The artist shook his head in disagreement. "Hope is a dangerous thing, Padre. A man can long hope for a thing that won't ever come."

"You claim Laura loved you; love cannot exist absent mercy. It is yours for the asking and I suggest one path."

"And what would that be?"

"You'll have my answer tomorrow. Wash, rest and enjoy a meal with your old friend; my company and prayer are your penance for staying away so long."

Bino smiled and accepted. He trusted the priest to guide him towards a resolution.

"And where shall I stay, Padre? Have you room enough for me here?"

"Remain with us tonight, Bino; I have something else in mind for the remainder of your stay."

The priest invited the seminarian back into the room and asked him to play Samaritan to the road-weary traveler.

Padre Castani excused himself after an enthusiastic embrace. "Remain faithful, Bino. We shan't lose each other again."

Caterina

It was late in the afternoon and the sun was falling below the western sky. Isabella and Caterina were attending to departing lodgers when the priest knocked upon their half-open door. Padre Castani was in a good mood and without being asked offered the lodgers a blessing and travelers' prayer.

Caterina wondered at the priest's elevated spirits; she hadn't seen him this animated and looked forward to an explanation. The women invited him to stay for supper and he thanked them before declining.

"Forgive me. A dear friend from home expects me at the rectory. Our cook isn't as capable as you so our stomachs must suffer the consequences."

Isabella mirrored the priest's good humor. "We'll suffer too, Padre. Who will hear our confessions, bless our bread and make us merry with stories?"

The priest wouldn't hear it. "The day you two seek absolution, Mary's church will have want of a better priest."

Padre Castani sat with Caterina and Isabella and described the Lazarus-like return of his long-absent friend. He spoke of Bino's childhood and eventual mastery of fresco. He made no mention of the artist's trials and damaged confidence. He spoke instead of his intention.

"Before writing to Bino, I sought and received approval from the bishop for the beautification of our Lady's church. The stipend isn't generous but I'm confident Bino will accept the commission and remain with us a short while."

The innkeeper appreciated the priest's intention. He and Giovanni had often lamented the dull interior of the pilgrim church with its pale and lifeless walls.

Padre Castani continued, "Bino is sure to transform the chapel. Word of it will replace inaccurate accounts of sickness and inspire pilgrims anew. They will return to Serono, rekindle their faith and lodge at your inn."

Isabella spoke for both of them. "Hopeful news, Padre; we pray the inn can survive until the artist's work is complete."

The priest grasped her arm with tenderness. "You don't understand. I want my friend to remain here with you; Rome will compensate for his room and board."

Failing to comprehend, Caterina repeated his words. When Padre Castani made clear his message, she leapt to embrace him. Isabella looked on as the priest's cheeks turned crimson.

"Better I go now and settle the details. I must convince Bino of the merit of our plan."

Caterina stopped him, looked about the room and gave voice to her concern. "Padre, what if our circumstances are too modest for such a gifted artist? He is sure to seek better accommodations. And what of Mattia? A crying child will interrupt his rest."

The priest gripped her hands within his own, smiled and reassured her. "He is nothing like those pampered few. He will appreciate your son and many kindnesses."

Caterina began the next day with a smile. After completing her chores, she walked to the church, lit a candle and offered thanks to Mary for what she believed was Her response to months of prayer. Giovanni's absence remained a heavy burden but she had a quiet confidence about his well-being and a renewed sense of possibility about the inn.

Meals needed planning before the priest's special guest arrived so Caterina invited Isabella to join her and Mattia for a turn about the village.

The women were unable to conceal their nervousness and they agreed the Serono market would prove a welcome diversion.

They weren't wrong. The plaza was a brilliant collage of merchants and shoppers. There were voices, colors and aromas that were at intervals awful and appetizing. The former resulted from farm animals and unwashed patrons, the latter from hot coals grilling boar and lamb.

Isabella delighted in Caterina's wide eyes as both were entertained by aggressive peddlers standing before their carts, boasting the finest in local food, textiles or jewelry. One such craftsman moved quickly towards the innkeeper with necklace in hand. Before she could protest, it was about her neck and clasped from behind. A looking glass was thrust towards her by a second person and she heard the words, "Surely this was made for you, *signora*."

Caterina couldn't deny its beauty or justify its purchase. *When would I ever wear such a thing?*

Isabella complimented, "You look like that famous portrait, sister."

"Ah," said the merchant. "This one is as wise as you are beautiful, *signora*."

Caterina set aside her cares and stared into the glass. The silver strand with blue gemstones fell comfortably about her neck and called attention to her like-colored eyes. *Is it wrong to desire such a thing?*

The question came and went. Even if coin enough existed, a soldier's wife with little means of support could never justify such indulgence. She unclasped the necklace and returned it to the merchant's hand. With a wink to Isabella and a smile that masked her disappointment, Caterina offered, "When my husband inquires, I'll tell him of my reward here."

Moving further into the crowd, Isabella was attracted to a small group gathered about a long wooden table. Seated behind the table was a worn and wrinkled woman. She was unfamiliar to them and wore a flowing robe of many colors. Her large brown eyes betrayed kindness and wisdom.

Isabella pressed her way forward until arriving at the table's edge and the elder woman's left hand. Caterina called after her before giving up, tightening her hold on Mattia and excusing her way through the crowd. When she reached Isabella, she tugged at her sleeve and urged, "We must go."

The mistress of the table raised her eyes and laid a gentle hand on Caterina's arm before offering, "Let her be, all is well with your sister."

Caterina released Isabella. The mysterious woman lowered her eyes and resumed the laying of stem flowers on the table. When finished, she reached into the fold of her dress and withdrew a collection of painted cards. She fanned these out as if to cool herself before turning her wrist and revealing them to the audience. She selected a dark-skinned pilgrim in the crowd and began her presentation.

"*Signor*, observe the cards. Do you agree each is unique?"

He verified her claim before she shuffled them and laid them painted-side-down within the stem-bordered shapes on the table. There were two dozen cards in all and their random placement added to the crowd's curiosity.

"What is to come?" shouted someone behind Isabella. Another bellowed, "*Strega!* Prove yourself."

The gypsy closed her eyes. Her arms swept the air vertically in a circular pattern before her fingers united above her head and descended slowly into her lap.

To a child at her right, she spoke clearly for all to hear. "Where is the sun today, little one?"

"It is behind the clouds, *signora*."

"True," the woman responded. "Where is it on the table?"

"I don't know, *signora*."

"But you do. Select one card from the triangle and hold it up for all to see."

The boy thought a moment before picking one of several cards in the triangle. He brought it quickly to his chest before allowing himself a look. A smile crossed his face before he thrust the card outward and upward. The card displayed an image of the sun behind a shadowy cloak of gray. The audience voiced its approval and the commotion attracted more pilgrims to the table.

The gypsy quieted them with her hands and motioned twin brothers forward. "Which of you will pick a card?"

"I will," announced the smaller of the two.

"Be you brave, select a card from the square."

The boy reached forward for one card before changing his mind and selecting another. He chose not to look at it before thrusting it above his brother's head.

The crowd erupted in cheers. There for all to behold were *gemelli*—the zodiac twins.

"What is to come?" repeated a hostile voice from behind Caterina.

The card mistress responded without emotion. "The cards, they do not reveal what is to come. The cards reveal what is and what could be."

From below the table the card mistress raised a silk-lined basket and asked that it be passed among the audience. "*Con piccolo soldi mi potete aiutare*—a little money will help me."

The gypsy witnessed Caterina shake her purse. Though no sound resulted, the innkeeper reached in, selected one of several coins and handed it to Isabella to contribute.

"You mustn't," Isabella began.

"It's okay. We can all part with something."

Isabella released the coin.

"My turn," shouted the drunken heckler. He stepped forward with a silver piece in hand and made a show of dropping it in the box.

The woman studied him, offered gratitude and asked, "Are you certain, traveler?"

Unrecognizable to anyone present, the dark-eyed and presently clean-shaven Lieutenant de'Gavanti mocked her. "You have your money, witch. Yours is a game of chance; what have I to lose but a remnant of my fortune?"

She studied before responding, "Sometimes a thing more precious than we realize."

The wayward officer ignored her reply and asked, "Where shall I pick?"

"Your path is in the circle," responded the table mistress.

Rotto thought to challenge her direction but relented. The outlaw thumped his chest with his right fist and reached into the circle with his left. He lifted a card and brought it to his eyes. Only those closest to him were able to see. Illustrated there was a bewildered figure chained at the ankle to a stone. His free leg was suspended in the opposite direction in a futile attempt to escape from fire.

A woman at his side gasped while Rotto turned crimson with anger. "Strunce! Piece of shit."

Rotto tore the card in half and half again before throwing the pieces at the gypsy. Murmurs filled the silence while the fugitive fled.

Isabella was frightened and Caterina reached for her sleeve to force their departure. When she did so, the table mistress interrupted and urged, "Sister, take a card, please."

Caterina connected with the gypsy's eyes. "I am a Christian woman, *signora*. I assign little value to such things."

The woman regarded Caterina with humility before pointing to a spot on the table. "Then you needn't fear me."

Caterina moved her eyes to the same circle from which Rotto had chosen and selected a card. Unlike the others, she handed the card face-down to the gypsy. Without looking at it, the woman turned to Isabella and said, "Your sister chose well."

To the disappointment of all present, the table mistress removed a small cloth from her sleeve, folded it about the card and presented it as a gift to Caterina.

"Take this with you; it is yours alone."

Isabella and Caterina studied the small package before expressing gratitude and accepting it. Arm-in-arm they sped away.

When their shopping concluded, they returned to the inn with Mattia. The baby was fed and put down for a nap. Isabella would not normally remain but did this day and Caterina required no explanation. When her sister began other chores, Isabella protested and demanded she open the gypsy's gift.

"I don't think I can; what if it's a bad omen?"

Isabella offered to open it for her and reminded the woman had said she chose well. "Why would she say that if you had something to fear?"

Caterina retrieved the small package, made a sign of the cross and unwrapped the object. She held the image in the light and wondered at its meaning.

Illustrated was a pair of lovers sitting below a tree laden with fruit. It called to mind her unexpected reunion with Giovanni.

"What can it mean, Isabella?"

"It means Giovanni will return. Mother will restore him to you."

"I don't know."

Isabella accepted the card and pointed. "See here, they hold hands and sip from a glass of amber wine."

"Serono knows no such colored spirits."

Isabella hugged her and responded, "Then you and Giovanni shall make it so."

Bino

That same afternoon Bino entered the pilgrim church with Padre Castani. The priest was eager and proud to show off his improved circumstance to his one-time student from Luino.

Bino was gracious in his reaction. "She is a worthy church and fortunate to have found you, Padre."

Bino won the smile he wished for and was a patient listener as the priest chronicled the church's history. During a quiet moment, Bino looked above and inhaled. The aroma was a familiar one and he was transported back to his experiences among the cloistered brothers in Milan. Until the tragic episode with Tomas, creativity and peace had sustained him. Now Laura's company alone would satisfy.

The artist admired and missed her and recalled the many instances she had humored him with clever words and gestures. He recalled her scent, her touch and her commitment to him. *Would it hold?* Twice she had expressed her willingness to shed her name and wealth to be united with him.

His wondering was interrupted by Padre Castani. "Come see, Bino."

The pair moved towards the altar and arrived at the anti-chapel. Here there were broad and plain expanses of wall. The priest grabbed Bino about his shoulders and turned him to face one side and the other.

Padre Castani needn't have spoken. Bino understood his intention.

"These walls, these are the path you propose for my redemption?"

"Yes. Why else would we arrive here together in this place? So near our home and yet so far."

"I cannot say, Padre. But what can be accomplished here that hasn't been done a dozen times before throughout Lombardia?"

The priest invited him to listen. "*Mi senti*."

Bino tilted his head upward and closed his eyes.

"We owe Christ to God and his chosen daughter Mary. This will forever be Her church. Make it Hers, Bino. Do what has never been done before; reveal Christ through his mother's eyes and story. Doing so is sure to inspire many and teach you something that must be learned. This is why you are called to Serono."

The artist digested Padre Castani's words, dropped his head and stepped to the wall. With eyes still closed, he ran his hands forward and back, feeling its texture and imperfections. It felt right to him and he replayed the routine along the opposite side.

Bino opened his eyes, faced the priest and asked, "May we do it our way, Padre?"

The priest smiled, "Bring your ideas to me and I'll convince the bishop they were his."

"Are there able assistants and models to be found?"

"What we lack in wages, we make up for with strong shoulders and handsome faces."

"Let it be so, Padre."

Padre Castani embraced him and expressed gratitude. He next explained his plan to house Bino and a drawing table across the Varesina alley within Caterina's inn.

"You will find the accommodation comfortable and the innkeeper kind beyond compare. You may rely on her discretion and she may rely on the bishop's purse."

"She won't mind me then?"

The priest laughed. "The innkeeper hasn't had an easy time and fears for your comfort. Fever claimed her father and mother, and were that not enough, her husband, while in service of the church, has gone missing; his disappearance vexes us all. Accommodating you will be a healthy distraction."

The artist appreciated his own diversion. "Padre, I need no compensation other than what the innkeeper requires to house and feed me."

"Hush, Bino. I won't have the saints repeat your words; the bishop would no doubt exploit your generosity and pay you less than deserved."

Early that evening, Bino arrived at the inn with Padre Castani. He wore borrowed clothes and a trim beard. Together they carried baskets of day-old bread and ripe fruit the priest had claimed from Sunday's offertory.

Isabella greeted the pair and explained Caterina would join them after feeding and bedding Mattia. When she appeared, the priest concluded introductions. Aware of Bino and Caterina's nervousness, he carried the conversation.

Isabella did her best to assist during awkward silences. She recalled the doubts Caterina had expressed before their guests arrived. *Will it be all right having a stranger so long with us? And he an unwed man, would Giovanni approve?* Isabella had reassured her, "Padre Castani wouldn't invite someone of ill temper. And the bishop's coin would replace any concern Giovanni might have had."

Dinner commenced and with it the flow of wine and the priest's pilgrim tales. Smiles were exchanged throughout the evening with Caterina speaking little and Bino only in response to questions. When it was time to leave, the priest invited Isabella to show Bino his bed and illustration room. He was surprised to learn the innkeeper had sacrificed her own.

"Why, child?" the priest asked.

Caterina's eyes met the artist's and she responded, "The light is better there, Signor Bino, and you won't be interrupted when I need access to the kitchen or alley."

Bino sensed she wouldn't accept a different arrangement and replied, "It is kind of you, *signora*."

Satisfied and wine-weary, Padre Castani bid good-night to the artist and his hosts and pledged quick delivery of the materials the artist sought for his work.

"And the models," Bino asked. "Do you have candidates in mind?"

The priest apologized and explained his seminarians were seeking women and men to fill the critical roles of the Holy Family. "There is no shortage of souls eager for the privilege. We'll send the better prospects for the part of Blessed Mother in the morning."

Bino followed Isabella to his room. He entered and took note of the bed, hearth fire and generous candlelight. He felt welcome and witnessed more evidence of the innkeeper's attention—a drawing table positioned to take best advantage of the south-facing window and each day's light.

When his host and Isabella excused themselves, Bino extinguished several candles and sat upon Caterina's bed. He smoothed his hands over the wool blanket and appreciated the loneliness she must feel at her husband's absence. He replayed the evening's conversation; the innkeeper had made no mention of Giovanni, the loss of her parents or any selfish desire. He thought her of like quality to his own mother and his past inattention made him hungrier to serve.

The artist thought of the noble men and women in his life and drew a conclusion. Padre Castani, Piero and Renato guided with words. Antonina, Nica, Laura and, it seemed, Caterina guided with deeds. *Was either method superior? Better I answer another day.*

Bino removed his boots and reclined atop his blanket. He closed his eyes, thought of Laura and whispered a prayer-Saint Anselm's words recalled.

Let me seek you in my desire; let me desire you in my seeking.
Let me find you by loving you; let me love you when I find you.

Sleep came and with it, much-needed recovery. Still dressed, Bino woke ten hours later to a gentle knock upon the door. Caterina peeked in and said the priest's candidates had begun to arrive. The artist was confused until the innkeeper explained with a smile.

"The young women wishing to pose as the Blessed Mother—they come to win your favor. I'll bring some fresh water for you to make ready."

Bino laughed and begged forgiveness for their intrusion. The innkeeper dismissed his apology and offered that the women were entertaining one another.

With neither a comb through his beard nor fresh clothes upon his lean frame, the artist wasn't long in entering the dining room to greet the women. There were four present and each regarded the wrinkled artist with surprise. Bino studied them. Their manner and dress displayed a consciousness and style at odds with his view of Mary. He was so humored by the seminarians' choices, Caterina witnessed him twist and translate a giggle into a cough. The innkeeper thought as he did and failed to conceal a smile of her own.

Bino wondered at others' lack of vision—their inability to see as he saw. The dividend from his thirty-year investment in his craft was intuition. It was the reward for hundreds of sittings, portraits and imaginings. It wasn't the physical attributes of a model which inspired but something intangible and impossible to put into words.

The artist circled the women and recalled his first experience with model selection twenty-five years earlier. Then the girls had been selected by Argento and he had been aroused by their mystery. The women before him this morning failed to stoke his curiosity.

Caterina was relieved when the group was excused. When they'd gone, Bino pulled at his beard, looked at her and said he would speak to Padre Castani. "The next group will prove better."

Caterina shook her head and shared a doubtful smile that triggered contagious laughter.

Subsequent days failed to produce a young woman suitable for the artist's critical role. Frustrated, Bino told Padre Castani to suspend the effort. The artist would instead sketch ideas for the four frescos his commission required.

During that time, Bino was invited by Caterina to share dinner with her, Isabella and two former guests in need of a meal. Over soup the guests described their passage to Serono via Monza. Bino's attention was noteworthy. *Might you they have news of famiglia Pelucca?*

The pilgrims shared details of a much-discussed honor tournament in Monza the year before. Caterina knew from the priest, though did not volunteer, Bino's recent engagement there. The artist's sudden discomfort was as plain as her empathy.

The travelers titillated with details of the scandal and its damaged participants. Caterina and Isabella learned of the compromised reputations of Monza's first families—one suffering the rejection of a much-courted daughter, the other coping with the cruel murder of its only son. Less aware of her audience, Isabella wasn't shy about inviting detail. The guests were too lubricated with wine to withhold any real or imagined embellishment.

When quiet settled about the room, Bino looked up from his plate and asked, "You mention a daughter. Some must have thought her noble. What became of her?"

The visitors looked at one another before one spoke. "The family is silent. Some say she did herself harm; others say she fled to find her lover, an artist who betrayed her father."

Bino interrupted, "And the murderer?"

"He was a member of the Monza guard. He fled his post and hasn't been seen since; *famiglia* Rabbia may never know justice."

News of Rotto's escape stung the artist and he excused himself from the table. Caterina recognized his pain and brought the conversation and evening to a close. She thought to follow Bino and invite a conversation. *If I share my loss, will his own be easier to bear?* She left him to his thoughts.

The artist entered his room and closed the door. Full of emotion and too restless to sleep, he sat at his drawing table and reached for parchment, pen and ink. *It is time. I must know.*

Cara Laura
I pray it's not too late; love is meant to last.
I'm not uncaring; under your spell I'm cast.
My silence and choices, for these I am to blame.
Rejection and insults you've borne alone;
    I'm ashamed.
I didn't see what you saw, a future removed
    from there.
Loss of family, fortune and influence, you little cared.
You needed a partner to share beauty and dis-
    tant lands.
I was a slave to tradition and failed to extend
    my hand.
Laura, you are the student no longer, the teacher no
    longer me.
I promise to find and follow you and learn what joy
    can be.
Let's begin again in a place apart and time.
My hand and heart are yours if still you wish
    me thine.
So whisper your invitation to the dove and release it
    with haste to me.
I shall kiss the hand that sent it and forever true to
    you be.

The poet signed and sealed his letter. He addressed it and an accompanying note to Renato at Casa Pelucca. *He will know where to find you.*

Satisfied, the artist removed his clothes and retired. Tomorrow, he reasoned, would bring him one day closer to the woman he loved.

He woke before sunrise, exited the inn unnoticed and delivered his correspondence to the praying figure of Padre Castani. He asked the priest to forward his letter via the surest courier to Monza and then only to the hand of Renato. "I trust no other there."

Padre Castani pledged his assistance and waved the artist home. Bino left the church and delighted in the sunrise with an eastward walk. For the first time in months he felt he was where he needed to be. *Positive intention and Renato's favor may welcome Laura home.*

Bino felt the sun upon his face and slowed to absorb its penetrating rays. Nature, he granted, was far more spirit-filled than any image he was capable of creating. The warmth inspired gratitude and imagery and he rushed home to draw before the feeling left him.

He retraced his steps along the Varesina road, wondering whether he would find a model worthy of the Blessed Mother and his ideas. This was his focus as he slowed and opened the inn door. He did so with care so as to not wake Mattia. Caterina failed to see him enter.

The artist's pulse quickened when the woman he sought revealed herself. Before him, bathed in golden light from an un-shuttered window, nursed the reverent, fair-haired innkeeper. He stood speechless, calmed by Caterina's grace and unpretentious beauty. Bino had found *his* Mary.

Renato

Casa Pelucca, Monza, 1525

Renato woke early and began the day as he had the previous thousand. He lay in bed and inventoried the places his body hurt after a lifetime of service. He felt the tightness in his neck, the ache of a hip that predicted wet weather and knees that begged him to remain still a while longer.

The house and compound were quiet and he missed the busyness that was once a source of pride and entertainment. More than these he missed Bino, and Laura—the daughter he had cautioned the artist not to love. *Why did I ever do such a thing?*

The tragedy of the last year replayed in his mind and Renato questioned his part in it. *Did I betray the family by not speaking up sooner?* And Laura. *So fearless she chose exile over compromise.*

After the murderous tournament, Signor Pelucca confronted his daughter, demanding to know the truth about her relationship with the artist. Laura responded with hopeful care. She assured her father of her chastity and depth of affection. When his criticisms of Bino and her foolishness persisted, she could take it no longer.

"Papa! You would have had me wed the lieutenant, a man I couldn't love. He proved himself a villain and may never face justice. At least Feder was honorable; he deserved a bride who shared his devotion. I wasn't that woman."

Signor Pelucca insisted she stop. "Be silent, Laura!"

"Silent? Silence cost me the only person I ever cared for. I will not be silent any longer."

"Enough!"

"What of your silence, Papa? I'm told you knew of Lady Rabbia's appetite and spoke none of it to Bino. Could you have resisted her twenty years ago?"

"I warn you, Laura; be silent."

"You put Bino at risk in her home and pretend dismay at the consequences. Worse, you chased him away. You need only see his frescos to understand the truth of his heart. It was Bino who urged me to be patient with you and respect your place. He refused to believe me when I told him your mind couldn't be changed, that your regard for me wasn't as great as your desire for wealth and influence."

Signor Pelucca stepped towards her. "I warn you; I will send you away."

Laura's eyes welled with tears and her voice grew stronger. "You couldn't convince me to stay."

His backhand slap was too quick to dodge. It stung and left her full of rage and empty of words. Signor Pelucca was the last to speak.

"You dishonor our family and are no longer daughter to me. The convent in Lugano will be your home. They can do with you as they wish."

Renato recalled the wails of Lady Pelucca and her futile attempts to alter her husband's decision; he was not swayed and his harsh sentence proved final. Laura left within days. No word of her was permitted in his presence.

Renato put aside his dark memories, rose from bed and prepared for the pain accompanying his first steps of the day. He accepted these with a grimace and a sign of the cross before relieving himself and dressing.

Renato stepped into the courtyard, inhaled deeply and moved towards the small family chapel where Bino had spent his final days. The old servant opened the door, entered and was surprised by the stagnant cool air. He lifted his right hand and pinched the collar about his neck, insulating his chest from the cold.

Why haven't I come sooner? Renato pondered this until sitting on one of several benches facing the altar. He rubbed the chill out of his knees, smiled and whispered, "I'm the sole mourner at your funeral, Bino."

From behind him the rising sun focused a beam of light through a narrow window. He watched as the light traced a diagonal line across the room, illuminating a cylinder of drifting dust in the air. The beam settled upon Bino's unappreciated fresco. The artist's treatment of Saint Catherine's burial held new meaning for Renato. Adorned with wings and gilded robes of green, pink and violet, three angels bore the body of the saint to her tomb. When Lady Pelucca had agreed to let Bino model the saint after Laura, she could not have imagined her husband would within a fortnight declare Laura *dead* to them.

Renato couldn't pull his eyes away. Six angelic hands cradled Laura amidst billowy clouds; she looked at peace and royal in a crimson burial robe. *You have an imaginative soul, Bino. Wherever you be, I pray you believe Laura endures for you.*

An unexpected knock woke the servant from his meditation. "Yes," he called to no one.

A courier entered bearing a small leather pouch. "I was told I might find Signor Renato here; are you this man?" the young traveler asked.

"I am," responded the servant.

Something in the courier's eyes expressed doubt. "I don't mean any disrespect, *signor*; it's just I've been instructed to relay a letter to Signor Renato and no other. So forgive me if I ask again, are you Renato—servant to Signor and Lady Pelucca?"

Renato rose from the bench with more dread than impatience. "Yes, I am servant to Casa Pelucca. My name is Renato."

"Very well, I deliver these to you and now return to Serono."

"Serono? Wait young man, who…"

The courier didn't turn or offer an explanation; as quickly as he had come, he was gone.

Renato sat and looked at two sealed letters resting in his hands. He was about to break both wax seals before noticing each carried its own external inscription. He lifted each in turn at arm's length so his eyes might better see what was written there. His name appeared on one, Miss Laura's on the other.

With hope, enthusiasm and a thumping chest, Renato broke the seal of his letter, held it aloft in the light and read. He recognized Bino's hand. When finished, he read it twice more convincing himself it was true. Dio mio. *You are well and engaged in Serono, friend. You've made your confession and are creating again. And mystery of mysteries, you haven't given up on Miss Laura.*

Hope is a dangerous thing. He had once spoken those words to the artist and was pleased Bino's letter was evidence of his rebuttal. Renato's attention shifted again to the chapel fresco. Saint Catherine proved difficult to kill and her marriage had survived death itself. Surely, she had inspired the artist to act.

With renewed spirit, Renato rose, bowed and spoke. "Wake Laura, I've a message for you from your lover."

Rotto

Lieutenant de'Gavanti woke from a drunken slumber and wondered for a moment whether it all had been a bad dream. A mere twelve months before he'd had rank and resources and an infirm father who was sure to increase both. He never counted on the ugliness which followed—his underestimation of Signor Pelucca, loss to Feder and his own unfortunate retribution. *What was it for?*

His left hand shook violently and he recalled the priest telling him it was the demon within fighting for recognition. He stilled the tremor with his right hand, lifted the left as if it were an object to be measured and bellowed, "I will rid myself of this evil for good!"

Rotto stood up and searched for his sword. Finding it he stumbled to a table, slammed his left palm upon it and raised his weapon above. With a scream and sweeping motion he brought the blade down, severing the tips of his middle fingers. He lifted and stared at the bloody mass and bellowed, "*Va fan culo*, Papa!"

The fugitive thrust his injured hand into a wash basin and recoiled at the pain. Sobriety followed and with it a successful search for his field bag and the herbs and rags within. He dressed his throbbing hand and drank generously from the leather wine pouch retrieved from a hook upon the door.

The pain exceeded anything Rotto had yet experienced. It stilled his errant hand but not his soul. The fugitive recalled his father's intolerance and errant judgment and the many instances of mistreatment so many years before. Mindful of his abuse and that of the priest, he returned to the table and gathered the severed tips of his fingers. *I'll find a courier.* "One for you, Papa, and the other for the priest." *You'll have them with your foolish drawings. Where are they?*

Rotto lifted one of two loose bags that had accompanied him from Monza and emptied its contents on the floor. From it came a pair of uniform trousers, a length of rope, his mess kit and a parchment roll. He pinched the latter between his left elbow and hip and unfurled it with his right. "Have you now, girl."

Bino's illustrations of Nica's figure were little faded. He recalled his father lifting each crude image in turn and berating him for his indifference. The artist had rendered the woman as his father commanded—bare and vulnerable.

He remembered her screams when his father brought him to her. *What had she said then? She'd given that life up.*

Rotto recalled getting aroused and thinking how poorly his father understood him. *If I couldn't find pleasure wherever I'd like, why should a whore stop being a whore?*

Soon the throbbing and pain of his left hand became too much to bear. Rotto finished his wine, collapsed upon the bed and slept. When he woke hours later, his empty stomach compounded his discomfort and he searched his scattered room for something to eat. There was nothing to satisfy and a purse with too little inside.

"Judas!" he screamed.

"Quiet!" replied a voice from an adjacent room.

Rotto paced like a distressed tiger, wondering at his next move. He could not return to Monza; he was sure to be arrested and hung for killing

Feder—*too many witnesses and too little sympathy.* He could continue to steal but the Serono merchants had come to associate him with missing coins and bread.

Where do desperate men go?

The answer occurred to Rotto and he smiled. He reasoned it would work and improve upon his failed deceptions. The fugitive dressed and abandoned his quarters.

Padre Castani

All was quiet. The priest was drafting his monthly report to Rome when a seminarian's knock came.

"Brother Castani, a pilgrim wishes to see you for absolution. When I told him to return in two days, he claimed he'd harmed himself and would do so again."

The priest reflected on the absence of such drama in the small parish of Luino before agreeing to hear the traveler's confession a short while later. He finished his letter, sealed it and relayed it to a courier before making his away across the alley to the chapel. He entered; few were present save for Bino's crew and the curious-looking traveler. The visitor spotted him, stood and approached with purpose.

The priest thrust his hands into his robe and searched. He coped with nervousness by gripping prayer beads and needed to hold them now. He was relieved to find them and circled the string of stones about his right hand.

Rotto approached. He stopped an arm's length away and the priest observed his ragged dress, neglected hair and hollow eyes. If the lieutenant greeted him, the priest was too distracted to hear. He did feel a curious charge trace his spine and heard himself say, "Please sit, son."

The fugitive claimed a seat and the priest, despite his discomfort, sat close enough for their knees to touch. What Padre Castani observed puzzled—a poorly bandaged hand and half-sunned face pale of the beard removed below. And then there were the traveler's eyes—absent emotion and gray. Neither wished to speak first and the silence expanded until it grew too heavy for the clergyman to bear.

"What have you come to say, son? I was told you seek our Father's mercy."

Rotto mumbled something unintelligible before launching into an exaggerated tale of woe. His fabrication included parental loss, abuse at the hands of caretakers, petty crime, servitude and a bigger lie—conscription by French aggressors. If half of what Padre Castani heard was true, the priest reasoned it lucky the traveler was alive.

Nearing the end of his story, Rotto feigned emotion, tears and dread. "The worst of it, Padre, is I deserted my squadron; this will seem cowardly to some but I can no longer use my injured hand to wage war."

The priest quieted him; something was missing. Rotto's story fell short of believability. Padre Castani had heard thousands of confessions before; the soldier's tale lacked humility and genuine regret. *And yet isn't mercy withheld the greater sin?*

The priest moved to rest a hand on Rotto's knee and witnessed the confessor recoil.

"I'm sorry, Padre. I'm not yet comfortable with the touch of another."

The priest withdrew his hand. "Forgive me, son. Be you contrite, absolution is yours for the asking."

"Yes, of course, Padre, but I worry for my soul. I'm alone, hungry and desperate for work. Prayer led me to you and I was told you wouldn't let me down."

"I don't understand, son. Why not return to the place of your birth and invite the forgiveness of those who till our Father's soil? Surely they can accept your betrayal of the French."

Rotto was quick to respond. "No! I mean that's impossible. I can never return there—the memories are too painful."

The priest reached for and opened the small purse at his waist and removed several coins. "Take these and enjoy a meal; I cannot promise more than prayers but will consider those in need of an able hand."

With a forced smile and deferential posture, the fugitive responded, "You offer too much, Padre; give me but one coin and I'll return after the morrow. By then you will have shared my appeal with others."

The priest was made uneasy by Rotto's transparent manipulation. "Is there more?"

"I don't understand, Padre."

"Is there something more you wish to confess, son? Don't hold back; our Lord's mercy knows no bounds."

The not-so-subtle implication sparked Rotto's anger. He stood up from the bench and clenched his hands, reigniting the pain. A moment longer and his temper would betray his lie. Instead, the fugitive exhaled, looked over the priest's shoulder and offered, "With God's mercy, my conscience is light."

Unconvinced of the truth, Padre Castani granted Rotto absolution and sent him on his way. "You may visit us in two days' time. If I have something to report, I'll share it with you then."

The fugitive bowed and departed with his coin. The priest looked above and whispered, "Some of your children, Mary, stray too far from home."

The priest remained in prayer before sitting back and enjoying the fluency with which Bino directed his team. There were to be four frescos and the priest remained gleeful at Bino's participation and their shrewd navigation of the approval process with Rome. So pleased had been the pope's treasurer with how little Bino required that Padre Castani's unconventional intention for the church had mattered little.

What made their proposal unusual were the subjects of the four panels—all scenes from Mary's life. These included *The Marriage of the*

Virgin, The Adoration of the Wise Men, The Presentation of the Christ Child in the Temple and *The Disputation*—Mary finding her adolescent son debating with temple scholars. Such a collection had never been attempted and if well-executed, would serve for centuries as a reminder of Mary's humanity. *If we fail, Bino, the folly will forever be ours.*

The priest's meditation was interrupted by Isabella. "Good morning, Padre, forgive me for intruding upon your prayers."

Padre Castani raised his eyes to find Caterina's constant companion. He believed her attractive and too good-natured to be alone. Though too old for marriage, Isabella was undeniably comfortable with solitude. Rare was the person who witnessed her without a smile.

"We were cooking this morning for Bino's crew and we've enough to share with you. I bring you something to eat."

"That is kind of you, child. At every turn of the sun, you and Caterina recreate the miracle of the loaves and fishes."

"You give us too much credit, Padre."

"I don't think I do."

The conversation continued until the priest was reminded of his uncomfortable and earlier commitment to the visitor.

"Isabella, a troubled soul visited me this morning in search of work. I presently have nothing for him. I've thought of asking whether Bino requires more hands but don't wish to distract him from his progress."

Isabella interrupted him. "Yes, Padre."

"Excuse me?"

"Yes, we can use him. The wage is modest but Eduardo's apricot grove requires attention. With the inn full, the effort to harvest the fruit and trim the trees is too much for us."

The priest was upset with her response. It wasn't what Isabella said but what it implied. It meant Caterina no longer relied upon Giovanni's return. Like her the priest had held out hope Giovanni would find his way back to them.

Noticing his change of mood, Isabella asked, "Is something wrong, Padre?"

"What? No, your kindness does you credit, Isabella. With your permission I'll direct the pilgrim to your cottage tomorrow."

"Does he have a name, Padre?"

"Strange, child, I forgot to ask."

Bino

Bino looked across the chapel and made eye contact with Isabella. It wasn't unusual for her to look in on him and his crew. Whenever he turned, she seemed to be there with a flask of water or piece of bread. Her sister, instead, chose to stay away. Caterina oft repeated, "I wish to see your work when it's complete."

Bino recalled the day his soul had committed to the Serono project. It was the day he walked in on Caterina nursing Mattia. The morning light was at her back and the sun appeared as if it were a halo over her shoulder. The scene and delicate light were emblematic of the Blessed Mother he wished to portray—a woman of this world invited to inspire mindfulness of the next.

The bewildered innkeeper shifted that morning under the artist's notice. "Forgive me," Caterina said. "Would you prefer that the baby and I move so you may take better advantage of the light?"

Bino swallowed and replied, "Where and as you sit, the advantage, *signora*, is all mine."

Color rose in Caterina's cheeks and she adjusted the cloth shielding her breast and suckling son. Bino retreated before lifting his eyes to face his host again. The sometimes poet smiled and continued, "I've been blind, *signora*. You, you alone are the one."

"I don't understand your meaning, Signor Bino."

"These weeks…the scores of young women, none so right as you. And there you were with Mattia each day."

"What are you saying?"

Bino approached and rested upon a knee. He reached for the inn-keeper's free hand and lifted his eyes to hers. "I wish to say nothing. I wish only to ask if you and Mattia will serve as inspiration for the Blessed Mother and the infant Christ."

Bino's place and posture reduced the once-intimidating artisan to someone at once familiar and worthy of trust.

Caterina shook her head in disagreement. "Such a thing is impossi-ble. Do you understand what you're asking, Bino?"

It was the first time she had referred to him by his common name and it caused him to smile.

"I'm asking if you will be *our* Mary. I want your face, your eyes, your heart for my portraits and frescos."

"You don't mean that. I'm unworthy of such an honor."

"Your reluctance, Caterina, is precisely what I would expect and wish for."

Caterina cradled her sleeping son in her arms. She heard Bino's words but was reluctant to accept the invitation.

"Better to confess such madness to Padre Castani. He is sure to take exception. Explain to him that you wish Mary to bear the likeness of the stone cutter's daughter."

"I'll grant it's unusual but he is sure to agree. Think of me as a wing-less Gabriel. You, dear innkeeper, are the one."

Bino's conviction stirred her somewhere deep inside and she was reminded of Giovanni's affection. *My soldier, what would you say to such a request?*

The silence grew awkward and the artist broke it. "You're thinking too much. Let your heart dictate your destiny."

Destiny—the word froze Caterina in place. She recalled a different day, the day she and Isabella had visited the gypsy in the market. The mys-terious woman convinced her to select a card from the table. She did that and handed it unseen to the woman who wrapped it with care and presented it as a gift to her. *Where did I put it?*

Caterina rose and rested her son in his crib. She paced about the room before stopping, opening a cupboard and retrieving something from the highest shelf.

Bino watched her with curiosity as she brought a small package to the dining table, sat and unwrapped it. Her breathing quickened and her shoulders rose and fell. The innkeeper's eyes welled with tears before her lips lifted into a smile.

Bino rose from the floor and approached her. He leaned over and retrieved the card from the table. He saw what appeared to be lovers in the shade of a fruit tree. "What does it mean? Be this you and Giovanni?"

Amidst tears she answered, "I think yes. I think I'm meant to do this thing for you and then maybe, just maybe, Giovanni will return."

Her faith stirred him and filled him with admiration and something more. It was love—not the love he held in his heart for Laura but that which love relied upon—mercy. He understood why Piero's spirit had bid him to leave Monza. He needed to reconnect with his past, accept Padre Castani's absolution and witness the innkeeper's grace.

Caterina lifted her eyes to his. "What you ask, Bino. There is no greater compliment—one I can never repay."

"You already have, *signora*. I believe you understood my part in the tragic Monza tournament described by your guests. I came to Serono without purpose and little hope of a reunion with Laura. Because of you, I believe both are possible."

Caterina's acceptance was greeted enthusiastically by the community of faithful—less so by those jealous of her influence with Padre Castani. He encouraged her to think only of Mary and the joy she must have for her servant.

The innkeeper's commitment meant more hours in the artist's company. They spoke, laughed and shared stories while he choreographed her scenes. He learned about her affection for her father, childhood introduction to the priest and brief courtship with Giovanni. Bino marveled at her many kindnesses and fealty to a man most swore would never return.

The gypsy's card remained upon the table. Each day the artist witnessed Caterina lift it and whisper her intention. The illustration inspired warm feelings and something more—her attention to the pictured glass of amber wine. Caterina recalled mixing a like-colored spirit with her father many years before. It was strong and sweet and Eduardo proudly shared it with his favorite guests. *God willing, I'll recreate some as a treat for Bino.*

Caterina delighted in Bino's company and insisted he be less formal. The artist responded in kind; no longer burdened by secrets, his relaxed and thoughtful manner made Giovanni's absence easier to bear. As for his obvious talent, Caterina reasoned it a gift from God. What else, she wondered, could explain his intuition, speed, and willingness to sacrifice a year for so little reward?

Others thought the same. Bino's crew and observant neighbors couldn't fathom why an artist of his merit had sidestepped the notice and treasure of the art centers—Florence, Venice and Rome, for the anonymity of Serono. They and his resentful contemporaries failed to appreciate Bino's character and motivation. He thought nothing of his purse. He wanted only to create soulful images upon walls thirsty for meaning and light.

Bino was gracious in accepting their compliments but had no patience for those wishing to deify him. *If they only knew my path.* He found his work redemptive and there was no Brother Tomas to upset his peace and creativity.

Rotto

At the suggestion of Padre Castani, Lieutenant de'Gavanti rose and sought out Isabella. He was told she could be found at the Varesina Inn—where Padre Castani implied, angels dwell.

"Could I lodge there, Padre?" questioned Rotto of the priest.

The priest answered with an emphatic *no*. "You'll be offered food and drink all the same."

Rotto feigned gratitude and left the rectory. He approached Caterina's inn via the alley bordering the basilica, paying little attention to the artist and several men walking in the opposite direction. Their paths crossed and Bino noticed the fugitive, dropped his head and abruptly looked again. Unaccustomed to Rotto's beardless appearance and civilian dress, no connection was made. Still, there was something in the person's gait and posture that seemed familiar. Bino looked after the visitor and noticed his intention to enter the inn. *I must remember to ask Caterina about him.*

Isabella greeted Rotto and introduced herself. He explained he had been sent by the priest and was pleased to learn the handsome person beckoning him inside was the very woman in need of assistance.

Rotto entered and stared at Isabella. She resembled an illustration of his mother – someone he had never known. In her absence he endured his father's endless criticism of her gender and taught to expect little from a wife beyond a meal and open legs. Isabella's words were lost to him; only her naïve invitation mattered. When his focus returned, he found her staring at his wrapped hand and eager for a reply.

The fugitive pretended regret and said, "Forgive me, *signora*, waging war cost my brothers their lives and me my hearing. What is it you ask?"

"Your damaged hand, are you able to help us? My sister and I must harvest our apricots. Ladders and tools we have; strength and hands we lack."

Rotto dodged the question, instead asking, "Have neither of you men, *signora*?"

Isabella thought to mention Giovanni before thinking better of it and responding, "No, I'm afraid we find ourselves alone."

Her answer pleased him. "It is right to be afraid, *signora*. There is danger aplenty within even the most traveled woods."

Isabella had no reason to believe their grove unsafe and was made uncomfortable by the implication. She dismissed the traveler's comment as cautionary and let it pass.

"Forgive me; you know my name but I don't know yours."

He was caught off-guard and responded with unnecessary candor, "Rotto, though few know me by that name."

She again looked at his bandaged hand and continued, "We cannot pay much, but if you're healthy and join us, you'll earn something and be well fed."

Rotto laughed. "I'm sure I shall." *Very well fed.*

Isabella put aside his awkward manner and her discomfort. She and Caterina required help and time was short. She explained the location of the grove and when she expected him. He left with a wrapped lunch and bid Isabella farewell until the morrow.

That evening Bino questioned Caterina about the visitor; she was unable to help. "Padre Castani sent the pilgrim to Isabella and he did little to ingratiate himself. Still, we're desperate for assistance and cannot afford to turn able hands aside."

"And his name and circumstances?" inquired Bino.

"I didn't ask her, but I shall. Do we have reason to worry?"

"No," he responded candidly. "My objectivity is clouded by experience; the help will be good for Isabella."

Renato

Renato's carriage crawled along the wooded hills marking the passage between Lombardia and the lake region. He had heard tales of snowcapped peaks, blue glacial lakes and green river valleys, but the career servant never expected to leave Monza long enough to experience them first-hand. With little fanfare or explanation he sought and received permission from Signor Pelucca for a brief break from service.

Breathtaking vistas greeted Renato with each trail turn. They distracted from his primary purpose—finding Laura and delivering Bino's letter. Romantic fulfillment was never his to savor but it wouldn't prevent him from making it possible for other worthy souls.

Renato hoped his intelligence was sound. All the old servant had to go on was a conversation overheard between Signora Pelucca and her eldest daughter. While Enza didn't miss her sister, she was curious to learn to where Laura had been banished.

The convent in Lugano was all Signora Pelucca had chosen to share.

Renato's arthritic frame absorbed one bump after another as the ride extended from Monza's temperate climate through cold alpine passes to the autumnal-colored valleys on the other side. When the coach emerged from the trees, he spotted Lugano's great lake. Descriptions failed to do it justice; it was broad, unimaginably blue and clear. Renato better understood why so many sought this territory for themselves. *Why wouldn't Rome and her church welcome this land too?*

The carriage stopped and Renato emerged from his punishing days of travel. He gathered his few possessions and sought a place to rest. He was directed to a local rooming house and was granted its last bed. It was a minor victory but one which fed his hoped-for outcome.

Rain the following morning did little to diminish his spirits. Renato ventured out of the rooming house carrying three things—his coat, prayer beads and Bino's letter to Laura. The servant limped along the lake shore stopping only to inquire of passersby, "Where can I find the home for women religious?"

Few villagers were willing to say much to a stranger about the church and its servants until one took pity on him.

"I was once a resident there myself," volunteered a mother escorting young children. She pointed away from the lake shore up the hill and said, "The convent is a good walk from here. Unless you're planning to stay, t'would be better to go another day."

Renato thanked her and persisted with his journey all the same. Up the hill he climbed in the worsening rain, stopping only to shake his coat of its moisture and relieve himself amidst the trees bordering the footpath. He felt the pull of purpose; if Laura was near, it would warm his heart to see her smile again.

Near breathless and wet to his core, Renato arrived at the convent gate. It was dusk and behind the fence posts, fog shrouded the convent's stone facade. The old servant immediately thought it an inhospitable place for someone of Laura's temperament and spirit. *Come home, daughter, or better, come with me.*

Renato peered through the gate, searching for signs of life. He saw no one and was close to launching an ill-advised climb before a voice from beyond his sight shouted, "We don't serve the poor at this hour, be gone!"

Renato attempted to speak but could only manage a series of coughs. When his presence and coughs persisted, the guard thrust his staff through the gate. It met Renato's retching chest, knocking him backward onto the hard wet stone.

The weary traveler attempted to right himself but lacked the strength to do so. Instead from a sitting position he reached into his coat and held Bino's letter above his head so the guard might see. As quickly as he did so all went dark; letter and carrier fell to the earth.

When he woke the next day, Renato believed himself to be in purgatory—a place the Monza priest had spoken of as heaven's kitchen. *Only souls readied by God would win an invitation to His abundant feast.* He was burning with fever and candles adjacent to his bed illuminated walls adorned with a wood crucifix and carved statues of the saints. Renato witnessed a wingless angel swab his head and cheeks with a cool cloth while a second placed a glowing stone under his bed.

This scene replayed itself throughout his delirium until the fever left him and he woke to observe the rising sun through an open shutter. An older woman sitting with eyes closed and grasping his prayer beads heard him stir and rose to take his hand in hers.

"Mother Mary, you survived," she said.

Her smile gave the servant hope he'd graduated from purgatory. And yet if this was heaven, he reasoned, it held little advantage over Casa Pelucca.

"Be I in heaven?" Renato asked.

The woman squeezed his hand, smiled and said, "No."

"Then where am I?"

"We found you outside the gate. You're home with our Lord's servants in Lugano."

Her words made little sense until the memory of his ambitious journey returned. With a start, he lifted his head and shoulders from the straw mattress.

"There was a letter. Did you find a letter in my company?"

"Aye, we did. And our Mother took great care to read it."

"Your Mother?"

"Yes, our sisters cannot accept visitors during their first years nor send or receive communication from outside; *nostra* Madre Superiore intervened. She judged the content of your message inappropriate to our mission and the spiritual well-being of its intended recipient."

Despite his fatigue, Renato gave voice to his frustration. "She read another's correspondence? How can the mission of this convent forbid private communication? I beg you, sister, as I've traveled far."

"Do not trouble yourself, *signor*; your health is too fragile to argue. Stay with us a little longer; your letter shall be restored to you."

He lacked the strength to challenge his nurse further and softened his tone.

"Laura, Laura of the Monza Pelucca family, she is here, then?"

"Yes, though she goes by the name Mother chose for her."

"Can you tell her I've come?"

"We think it unwise. 'Tis better she focus her mind and prayer in the service of God and her vow."

Appreciating the futility of his plea, Renato nodded his agreement and didn't argue his intention further.

He drifted off to sleep, comforted by a solitary thought. *I will regain my strength and travel to Serono with news of Laura's whereabouts; Bino can rescue her from this place.*

Bino

As if intentions had wings, Bino stirred from his work in Mary's church, thinking of Laura. Of the four frescos commissioned by Rome, one remained and it would prove the hardest. It was to be his imagining of Mary's wedding to Joseph and he couldn't help but want the same for himself. That he loved and wanted Laura he was sure. Less certain were her feelings for him.

The question saddened him and he set it aside, choosing instead to dismiss his crew and use the day's remaining light to clean his tools. He plunged them with stained hands within barrels of fresh water. He freed his brushes of color while imagining his conscience scrubbed by months of service, contrition and prayer. The artist recalled Padre Castani's words. *You'll know God's forgiven you, when you've forgiven yourself.*

His work complete, Bino exited the church. Indoor shadows yielded to brilliant afternoon light and the artist regretted such light couldn't be harnessed to illuminate his late afternoons and night. He entered Caterina's inn looking forward to the evening meal they would share when he spied her sweeping the floor. He watched and smiled. *She makes even a broomstick a handsome dance partner.*

He shouted a greeting and teased, "My next fresco will prove Mary bettered Joseph's home."

Caterina pointed her broom towards him and responded, "Was I the mother of Jesus, I would have insisted upon a miracle making it forever unnecessary."

Bino laughed and offered to relieve her of the broom. She accepted, sat and observed him make quick work of the chore. *A thoughtful husband you'll be.*

"Is Isabella to join us this evening?" Bino asked.

"No, she's in the grove harvesting the last of the fruit. There's plenty on the table if you're hungry."

Bino rested the broom against the wall and moved to the table. At its center was a wooden bowl holding the apricots he'd helped harvest a week earlier. He had gone to the grove often in recent months. He found it an ideal place to clear his head, imagine and improve his execution of land-scape drawing. The artist borrowed generously from the grove's features within his nativity fresco.

Bino selected several apricots and juggled them for the innkeeper's entertainment before sitting and passing the ripe fruit between his outsized hands. Marveling at their velvety texture, he selected one and plunged his teeth into its soft yellow flesh.

Caterina watched him devour each in turn. She then approached and collected the apricot kernels, setting them aside in a bowl.

"What will you do with these?" he asked.

"If I remember well, they'll flavor a liquid treat. If I fail, nothing at all."

His appetite sated, Bino found his host an eager listener. He spoke affectionately of Piero, his mentor's unsatisfying relationship with Leonardo's mother and pursuit of redemption. The artist spoke of the generous quality Caterina and Piero shared and something else.

"Like you, Piero inspires my work. You won't be surprised he's found a home with you in my frescos. You'll know him by his beard and the wisdom reflected by his eyes."

Caterina allowed his compliments to settle before announcing a change of mind. "It's time, Bino."

"Time? Time for what?"

Caterina rose, pressed her hands into the belly of her housedress and said, "It's time to put my fear aside and see your work."

Something shifted between them; it was familiar and comfortable. Bino got up from the table and met her eyes. They regarded one another, she trying to decide and he understanding her pain. The loss of her parents and Giovanni's long absence had exacted a large toll and before her was the salve for her cares and isolation.

Caterina rushed forward and threw her arms about Bino's neck and shoulders. He returned her embrace and offered strength and reassurance. To the artist it was as if all that was good and worthy had stepped out from his fresco and demonstrated Mary's humanity. To the innkeeper Bino was her father reincarnate, present to heal.

Caterina spoke first. "I've been so alone, Bino. Am I wrong to wait?"

He allowed some room between them and answered, "I cannot say, Caterina. But somewhere I hope Laura's asking the same question and being urged to trust. Be Giovanni among the living, your light will guide him home."

She smiled, wiped a tear away and whispered gratitude. "*Ti ringrazio.*"

Bino extended a hand. "Accompany me to the church while there's still light. I wish to show you what Giovanni returns to."

They made the short walk and entered the church. While cradling Mattia, Caterina nervously approached the space where curtains hid Bino's frescos. Time and again she had declined to spy beneath. Reassured by the artist, her feet carried her through the first veil.

There, not far above eye level, she discovered his nativity fresco. Despite knowing it would be so, Caterina was startled to see herself robed in blue, cast as Blessed Mother. Kings were kneeling at her feet and presenting gifts to Mattia, who was seated upright on her lap. Excluding delicate halos all appeared human, simple and of this world.

Caterina handed Mattia to Bino so she might enjoy a better look. Before her was Santa Maria not as goddess but humble servant and caretaker to a most precious Son. At her left shoulder Joseph stood with shepherd staff in hand, farm animals and kings equal in their reverence. Above the manger, the caravan of camels and kings' servants was not drawn ascendant to a throne but descendant to the Holy Family where Caterina's likeness sat with humility and bittersweet expectation.

"It's beautiful, Bino. I'm so grateful."

Her thoughts returned to her father. *Papa, I pray you see this. What say you of Bino's gift—a hand so true it reveals my heart?*

The failing light cut their visit short and Caterina promised the artist she would return with him the next day and again thereafter. "It is better we go slowly."

They returned home and prepared supper; Caterina was aglow and Bino more confident that she could accommodate newfound celebrity. He reiterated his appreciation for her sacrifice of time and space. "I must also thank Isabella for making quick work of the apricot harvest."

Caterina nodded and replied, "That was true until today, Bino. When I visited the grove this morning, all but one of her helpers was absent. It was as if someone told them not to come."

Bino wasn't sure he'd heard correctly. "What did you say?"

"Only the traveler sent by Padre Castani was present this morning; the others failed to come."

Caterina read the concern etched upon Bino's face. "What is it?" she asked.

"His name—did Isabella share his name?"

The innkeeper looked above as if searching for an answer. "I don't recall."

"Try, please," he implored her.

Caterina turned toward the artist and spoke.

"It was something unusual—Ro...Rotto, I think."

Before she could speak another word, Bino exploded out of his seat and searched about the dining room. Dissatisfied, he reached for the broom and with a wild swing slammed its straw head against the edge of their dining table. It snapped there, creating a jagged edge.

Caterina stumbled backward and cried out; she couldn't fathom Bino's unexpected rage. She lifted a hand over her mouth and backpedaled farther as he approached.

He stopped and spoke. "Isabella is in great danger. Tell the priest and pray I'm not too late."

The artist bolted from the inn and sprinted up the alley towards the edge of the village.

The innkeeper was left to wonder at Bino's recognition. *Who is this man to him?*

Mattia drew her attention with a wail. She lifted and embraced him and said, "We must rush to Padre Castani and beg his help."

Rotto

The sun was twenty degrees above the western horizon when the last of the apricot trees shed its fruit. Isabella was atop a ladder, her arms heavy and her hands sore from hours of labor. She descended to the earth still angry at those who had promised to be here and weren't.

Rotto enjoyed the view from below. Isabella's flesh sparked a familiar need within. It was a need he normally brought to a subordinate; his desertion from the guard and society gave him no choice but to seek satisfaction when circumstances allowed. *Or forced.*

The afternoon heat had caused Isabella to shed a layer of clothing and her bare calves and unwrapped figure drew his attention. As she stepped away from the tree, she turned and caught Rotto staring. While accustomed to the unwanted attention of pilgrims in the square, her present isolation made Rotto's attention threatening.

He spoke, "I give you credit, *signora*. Your effort was close to my own today."

Believing she might have misjudged him, Isabella returned the compliment. "I commend you too, Signor Rotto. At least you honored your pledge and came."

The fugitive rose from his seated position and dusted off his clothing. "*Prego, signora*. You ought not misjudge those who didn't come."

Isabella hadn't expected his charitable comment and asked, "Why is that, *signor*? They wasted the day and wage while we chose to work."

The fugitive surveyed Isabella from bottom to top before responding, "I insisted they not return."

She wasn't sure she'd heard him correctly. "What's that?"

"I gave them my wages from yesterday and explained your preference to finish the project alone."

Isabella's stomach lurched and her pulse quickened. She backpedaled and raised her voice. "You're a dishonest man, Signor Rotto. I'd like you to leave now."

"I'll leave once I'm paid, *signora*, no sooner."

Isabella stepped quickly towards her belongings and retrieved her purse; she found it empty. Alarmed and frightened she turned to face him and demanded, "What have you done with my coins?"

Rotto's eyes narrowed and his smile disappeared. "Are you suggesting I'm a thief, *signora*? What proof have you?"

Isabella met his resolve with her own. "Leave now and I won't report you to the Serono guard."

Rotto shook his head from side to side and took a step towards her.

"You and I have this grove to ourselves. I have nowhere to go and will remain until paid."

Isabella raised her voice, hoping against hope she might attract attention. "How can I pay you when you've taken my coins?"

"I'm sure one of us can think of a way, don't you?"

His ugly intention made clear, Isabella's heart pounded; she knew she must act quickly. She spun away from him and began to run as fast as her feet allowed. She hadn't gotten ten meters before Rotto dove for the hem of her dress, seized upon it and caused her to fall.

Amidst her screams the fugitive spun about, squatted and grabbed her ankles roughly. He stood and pulled her towards the base of a tree.

Isabella appreciated the seriousness of her situation and was caught between shock and an intention to fight. She grasped at the earth below, hoping to slow his progress or find something with which to battle. A handful of stones was all she could muster.

When he reached an evergreen at the edge of the clearing, Rotto dropped Isabella's feet, faced her and pointed a finger. "You're no better than the whores who refuse what they're asked. Shall we agree on the proper punishment?"

Isabella lifted herself onto her hands and knees before absorbing the full force of his kick into her side. The pain was sudden and sharp and stole her breath away. She collapsed, wondering at the horror he would next visit upon her.

Her assailant's bruised hand began to quake and he stilled it with a firm hold upon Isabella's wrist. He pulled her limp form up and she stumbled a short distance away before releasing her fistful of stones at Rotto's face. The pain it inflicted was immediate.

"Judas!" he screamed, as cuts opened below his right eye, neck and nose. Rotto's hands covered his face as he approached and swung wildly at her. The back of one hand connected with Isabella's cheek and she again crumpled to the ground.

The fugitive pulled at the bottom of his work shirt to stem the bleeding above. Having done so, he lifted Isabella from the ground and leaned her chest forward against the tree. He circled her arms about the bark and secured her wrists with the rope released from around his waist.

Isabella couldn't fathom how quickly he had gotten the better of her. "*Piacere, Maria!*" she bellowed. "Please," she begged. "If it's money you want, I can pay you."

"Your money I have, *signora*. Better I take my pleasure."

Rotto tore open the back of Isabella's dress. She pulled at her wrists and forced her feet together, the unwelcome sensation of evening air against exposed skin. She appealed again, "Stop, please, no!"

Her words inspired greater aggression and he left her alone for a moment to search for a tool with which to tease. Rotto returned and paced about the tree deliberately. He held a harvesting pole—a two-meter staff with a blacksmith's treble hook spooled tightly about its end.

"What better to harvest fruit with, wouldn't you agree, *signora*?"

"Mother of God, please!"

"It would please me if you were a man, *signora*, but you'll do."

Rotto rested the hook at the base of her skull and brought it down her spine with delicate pressure. He tugged at her undergarments until each released and teased the surface of her skin. Soon she wore only boots and the marks of his torture. Isabella persisted in her struggle and calls for help.

"Look at you. A lady wouldn't pose like this. You're not so proud now are you?"

Rotto raked the sides of her breasts with the tool before using it to force her legs apart.

"It'll hurt less if you make room for me, *signora*."

Bothered by her screams, the fugitive stepped back and removed his boots. He pulled his stockings from his feet and wrapped one about her mouth; the other he used to reinforce her wrists before restoring his boots to bare feet.

As Isabella's muffled pleas grew more urgent and guttural, Rotto's descent into madness was complete. He had none of the things he once wanted: independence, influence and subordinates to satisfy. It no longer mattered. He reasoned his sins indistinguishable from those who misused him. His father and the priest had been harsh, unforgiving and dark men; he imagined their welcome to the indulgent, regret-free place they dwelled. Rotto's intention to be apart from such men might have once led him to pity Isabella—no longer.

"Beg me to punish you or I'll retrieve your sister so you can enjoy this together."

Isabella sobbed. Her thoughts flew to Caterina and Mattia and the horrors Rotto could visit upon them.

"Leave them. Take me!" she screamed.

Some distance away, his pace quickened through the forest and he stopped to listen. *What is it? The call of a bird, a lame vixen?*

All was silent and he resumed walking.

Twenty steps later, he heard it again. The call was softer and he didn't bother to stop. His focus was singular, his urgency bordering on extreme. He pressed forward, burying his fear. *Will she be okay? Could our lives begin again?*

Exhausted and unable to distinguish one trail from another, he wondered if he was lost. He stopped, breathless, and looked about for a sign, anything that might confirm his location beyond Serono. He inhaled with purpose and the hint of *it* was there. It wasn't visible yet there was no mistaking its presence.

He was relieved and delighted at his good fortune. He measured the direction of the wind and stepped quickly toward its source and the path he was sure to find there, there amidst the essence of maturing fruit.

Several hundred meters further the aroma of ripe apricot was clearer and so was the chirping he had heard before. *It isn't a bird or injured beast; it's a voice, a voice in distress.*

He sprinted towards it.

Rotto circled about Isabella. The moon was full and reflected sufficient light to reveal his victim's red and swollen flesh.

"Enough of your cries, *signora*. You must be quiet if you want compensation for today's labor."

Rotto lowered his stocking from her mouth to her neck and pulled until she could scream no more. Her abrupt silence reminded him of the unconscious whore he and his father had enjoyed in Milan years before.

The fugitive positioned himself behind Isabella and grabbed her hips with both hands. Her flesh was hot from the bruising inflicted there.

"Pity you can't tell me how you like it. Shall I try the tool first?"

Bino

Equipped only with a broken broom handle, Bino fled Caterina's inn and sprinted towards Isabella's cottage. He hoped she had escaped harm and had gone home to bathe before making her way to the inn. When he found her cottage empty, his heart sank and pulse quickened. He began his sprint to the grove.

As he ran, ugly memories invaded Bino's mind. He couldn't help but inventory the list of awful outcomes for which he held himself responsible. First was Nica; he felt dishonest about his work—drawings he reasoned had led to her exploitation at the hands of someone wicked. Second was his perceived betrayal of Piero's intention.

You rescued me from self loathing and convinced me to use my talent wisely. I might have honored your legacy and treated Tomas with patience. Instead he lies cold under the earth.

The artist thought next of his escape and chance meeting with Feder—a gentle soul and worthy friend. Bino reasoned his silence had cost Feder his life and Signor Pelucca a daughter well-married.

I bear a heavy burden for my silence. But how can it be the lieutenant follows me here and harms the innocents sheltering me? Be you a merciful God, or a cruel puppeteer?

Bino entered the clearing between the forest and grove. It seemed an entirely different place since the mornings he had joined Caterina to draw.

He'd come to sketch the landscape in order to use portions as background for his nativity fresco. Those occasions were happy ones; there were friends and laughter. Now there were only silence, shadows and dread.

Bino thought he heard a man's voice and called loudly, "Isabella, Isabella!"

Alerted by the intruder, Rotto bent at the waist and lifted the harvesting pole. He heard the crush of leaves and saw an advancing shadow.

Illuminated by the moon, the sight before the artist confirmed his worst fears. He rushed towards Feder's killer, yelled something incoherent and swung his broomstick with all the force he could muster. Rotto was prepared and squared the harvesting pole in time to absorb the blow.

The suddenness of the battle and declining light prevented the fugitive from identifying his opponent. The anger and advantage belonged to Bino, who continued to pound at Rotto's cross-checks.

The dueling pair moved in a circle, the soldier on the receiving end of the artist's blows and words. "Why, why did you kill Feder when he showed you mercy? And such unspeakable cruelty to Isabella. You've wagered your soul, Rotto, and lost it!"

With those words, Rotto recognized his assailant and felt better about his chances. His opponent was passionate but unskilled; an opening would come. "Let's drop our weapons, artist, and help the girl."

Bino ignored the false appeal and pressed on, meting out blow after blow until his broomstick snapped in half. Rotto seized the opportunity and shifted from a defensive crouch. He turned the sharp edge of the harvesting pole towards the artist and advanced.

Bino scanned the turf, searching for anything that might deflect his assailant. Finding nothing he shouted, "Fear not, Isabella, help is coming!"

Rotto laughed. "It will be too late for both of you."

With that the fugitive lunged at the artist, forcing him to retreat towards the grove. A root caught Bino's boot and he tumbled backward to the ground. Acting quickly Rotto pressed the edge of the tool against the artist's chest. An unexpected voice took them both by surprise.

"You there, why do you threaten this man?"

Rotto turned and observed an odd-looking man in a well-worn, though familiar uniform. It was the uniform of the church and carried its bishop's seal. One hand sat atop the scabbard of his sword.

Rotto pointed towards Isabella. "See there; this man assaulted the woman bound to the tree."

His back pinned to the earth by the tip of Rotto's tool, Bino argued, "Believe nothing this man says. Protect yourself and save the girl."

The Roman soldier weighed their words, withdrew his sword from its scabbard and raised it up. He pointed its tip at Rotto and said, "If what you say is true, release the girl and bring her to me."

Rotto feigned consent, removed the harvesting polefrom Bino's chest and moved in the direction of Isabella. Not two steps further he swung the tool and connected with the soldier's blade hand. A wound opened upon contact causing his weapon to fall to the ground.

Bino launched himself off the earth and attacked from behind. The fugitive was caught unaware and dropped his tool. The pair fell to the ground and wrestled for control. Together they rolled over tree roots and moist fruit, the sweet smell at odds with the harm each intended.

The Roman soldier, weakened by capitivity, hunger and his journey from France, could only watch the battle unfold before him. He fell to his knees and grabbed at his sword hand, still throbbing from Rotto's direct blow.

The artist's strength overwhelmed Rotto who soon found his back against Bino's chest, a thick forearm around his throat. The fugitive knew he had but one chance at freedom. He lifted a heel and swung wildly for Bino's groin. It wasn't a direct hit but proved enough for him to roll out of the pained artist's grasp and scamper towards his weapon.

Bino was slow to respond and with a cloud before the moon, lost sight of his assailant. He spun about in vain until the sound of rushing footsteps alerted him to Feder's killer once more. The artist dodged the sharp end of Rotto's tool twice. The fugitive's third attempt connected with Bino's chest and drew blood. Rotto smiled and recoiled to ready a fatal blow when the harvesting tool abruptly stilled in his hands.

The fugitive dropped his chin and witnessed the wet end of a saber emerge through his sternum. Rotto wondered at the taste of blood and his inability to breathe. Time slowed and he felt a hand thrust against his back and the force of the blade below twisting in a lethal direction. This was pain and death but not pain as he'd ever felt it before. This was misery's echo—the sum of all pain he'd ever caused another.

Rotto felt extreme thirst and his eyes rolled left and right; about him all was dry and brown, tinder for unquenchable fire.

It was done and Bino sprinted to Isabella. He found her bruised and lifeless. He released her, lifted her from the tree and wrapped her in his overshirt. She spoke words too weak for Bino to hear.

Giovanni approached, grasping his wounded hand. He knelt aside the pair, recognized Isabella and began to cry. "How can this be? Her sister, Mattia, are they all right?"

"Yes," Bino responded before fully appreciating the miracle of the stranger's presence in the grove. The artist faced him and asked, "You are acquainted with Signora Isabella?"

"Yes, of course, she may be all that remains of my wife's family. Stay with her while I fetch some water."

Bino delicately lifted Isabella's head and whispered in her ear, "Sweet sister, Giovanni has returned."

Isabella struggled to open her eyes before seeing Bino's hopeful expression. "Have you saved me, Bino, or be this heaven?"

He cradled her head and shoulders and said, "God saw fit to send another. He sent an angel. He sent Giovanni."

Isabella closed her eyes and fell silent.

Bino heard hooves upon the earth. He turned and noticed two mounted horses at the edge of the grove, their occupants not yet spotting him in the twilight. The artist released Isabella, stood and directed them forward.

Sitting awkwardly upon one of the animals was Padre Castani, his face etched with concern. Atop the other, standing tall in his stirrups was a member of the Serono guard. The uniformed servant dismounted and made his way to Rotto. He gave voice to what was obvious to everyone but the worried priest. "This man is dead."

Bino explained the horrible truth of Isabella's torture and rescue at Giovanni's hands. "If you doubt me, see the crest upon his sword; it belongs to Rome."

Full of questions, Padre Castani dismounted and relieved Bino of Isabella's care. He made a sign of the cross upon her forehead and chest and reassured himself of her survival—body and soul.

Giovanni returned and limped towards them from the clearing; he bore a leather flask overflowing with water. He wasn't more than five meters distant when Padre Castani rose from Isabella's resting place, turned and stared.

"Lord of ghosts! Giovanni, can it be you?"

The priest rushed to the exhausted soldier, nearly knocking him off thin legs. Questions and concern filled the air. There was immense relief at Isabella's rescue and joy at Giovanni's unexpected return, until the Serono guard spoiled the homecoming.

Absent Isabella's testimony, he explained, Giovanni would be held for Rotto's murder. Giovanni wasn't surprised by the charge and surrendered to the guard. He was far too weak to argue and remarked to the priest,

"What be another week in jail when French prisons have held me for nearly a year?"

Padre Castani protested loudly until the artist interrupted the priest and drew their attention. Bino declared the dead man a proven fugitive from justice in Monza. "Many witnessed him kill an innocent man, Feder of Casa Rabbia. A courier could confirm this with his mother and father within two turns of the sun."

"This man speaks the truth," said Padre Castani. Challenged by the Serono guard about how he could verify such a claim, the priest looked heavenward; *I violate my vow, Lord, to exonerate your servant.*

Padre Castani pointed to Bino and said, "I know this because he told me so in confession."

The guard appeared sympathetic and uncertain. Before him was an odd collection of humanity—a tortured woman, a wounded soldier, a witness to a distant crime, his priest and a dead man. Bino understood the guard's dilemma and requested a word in private. They spoke at length at the edge of the grove before returning and seeing Giovanni and the priest restore Isabella to consciousness.

The guard remained quiet and used the opportunity to revisit Rotto's corpse. The hilt of Giovanni's sword appeared to levitate above its victim's back. The officer placed his right boot against the fugitive's shoulder and pulled the saber from its resting place. The blood upon it appeared black and he held the hilt towards the moon, searching for an inscription. Satisfied, he returned to Giovanni and excused him from detention.

Giovanni's relief caused him to stumble and the priest was quick to support him. He spoke the only words his strength allowed. "Take me to Caterina, Padre."

The Serono guard turned to Bino and continued, "If what you say be true, and the priest attests to it, then ill fortune would seem to follow you. Take the second horse and do what you promised me a moment ago, mentioning none of it to anyone. The priest and I will use the other mount to restore *la signora* and her savior to Serono."

Padre Castani began an expression of gratitude when the dismissive guard raised a hand to silence him.

"Priest, 'twould be best the artist conclude his work and be gone. Pilgrims invite enough trouble; we don't need his."

The moon was high above when the group concluded its preparations. Bino and Padre Castani could scarcely imagine Caterina's current worry and pending joy.

The Serono guard collected Isabella's things and draped these across the neck of his mare. He placed his foot in her stirrup, lifted himself atop and received Isabella's limp form from below. He positioned her sideways while holding the artist's shirt and the remains of her housedress about her. Padre Castani wrapped an arm below Giovanni's uninjured side, lending support as both limped parallel to the guard and Isabella. The Serono guard tapped the mare's rib cage with his heels and the group began its journey home.

Bino waited until the four disappeared between the trees. He was alone, suddenly cold and not distant from Rotto's corpse. What could be found of the fugitive's purse and possessions was piled at his feet.

The artist went to the collection of things and kicked the bags, seeking the loudest. When he connected, the remaining horse was startled and backed away. Amid the fugitive's hardware he hoped to find a flint stone, some water and food. He discovered all but the latter so satisfied his need for warmth and nourishment with a fire, sips of water and a handful of apricots. He shared the water and fruit with the horse whose company made his present isolation more bearable.

Bino thought of using gathered wood to start a second larger fire upon which to throw Rotto's body. He rejected the idea, worried it might not honor the guard's command: *Make all evidence of the body disappear.*

The artist returned to the body of Feder's killer. Rotto's eyes were open and dark. Bino recalled the day of their first meeting. It sickened him to think how vulnerable Laura had been to this unholy excuse for a man. She was free of him now, indeed of all of her suitors—her non-response belying past expressions of devotion.

The artist returned to the fire and sifted through the remainder of Rotto's possessions. The coins would be restored to Isabella and the fruit bushels retrieved and carried to market. The rest, save the hardware, was thrown into the blaze.

Bino was poised to snuff out the flames and remove Rotto from the grove before noticing a third leather bag. He sat upon a stump and released its drawstring. He removed the contents, unfurling each in turn. Bino held what were illustrations up to the firelight. The first two were worn and unappreciable; he threw these into the fire. One remained and he opened it. *By what magic is this?*

The drawing was in his hand—a provocative rendering of Nica, drawn at the insistence of Signor Argento years before. Nica's figure, mystery and dark eyes beckoned him and called to mind the tenderness of their coupling. She had been a generous lover and asked little in return.

Bino remembered her kindness and patient tutelage, the way her flesh rose under his touch, the scent of her perfumed hair and the bliss she unabashedly expressed. She attached no shame to his desire and he reasoned himself a better artist for it.

But how can she be here? How can Nica be attached to Rotto? Is it possible? There can be no other explanation.

Rotto had been Argento's patron. Rotto was Nica's tormentor. He had stolen her from him. The longer Bino's eyes remained on Nica's image the stronger his regret grew. *Can you ever forgive me?*

Satisfied the villain had met his end, Bino brought his lips to Nica's portrait before touching it to the flame. He wished her peace and imagined her smile amid the blue and orange dance of the firelight consuming it.

His thoughts drifted to better men—Piero, Renato and Padre Castani. The sometimes poet was not bound to them by blood but by character and purpose. To a man they would argue in favor of the just path over a vengeful one. *Besides, how can a dead man be made more miserable than by God's hand?*

Bino understood what needed to be done. He threw earth on glowing embers before lifting the villain atop the horse and wrapping its lead rope about the palm of his hand. They stepped forward together, the artist and the damned, beneath the light of the moon.

The journey seemed longer but it was only an hour before he and Rotto's body arrived at the pond; it was here his crew sought and prepared the ingredients that each day made ready the chapel's thirsty walls. Bino marveled at the still, black water and the sway of the trees around it. The sky was cloudless and the moon high enough for the artist to observe both it and his tired reflection on the pond's surface.

The artist found a shovel amidst his crew's tools. He chose a spot twenty strides distant from the water's edge and dug a shallow grave. He led the horse to it and pushed Rotto's corpse from the opposite side. It fell to the earth with a slap and Bino half thought the jolt would restore life to the fugitive. He had his shovel at the ready.

With death confirmed, Bino made multiple trips with the horse to the shoreline, each time filling a mixing basin with earth, water and the mineral critical to plaster preparation—lime. The artist yoked the horse to the heavy basin and pulled each refill to Rotto's grave. Bino shoveled the sloppy mixture atop the body, drowning it in mud. With each of four spadefuls the artist whispered, *This be for Nica, this be for Feder, this be for Isabella and this be for God.*

When complete, Bino rested and stared at the mound. He appreciated the irony. The mixture that made permanent his chapel frescos would now dissolve all but Rotto's unrepentant soul. *Purgatory may have that.*

Bino looked toward the moon and made a sign of the cross. He united his stained hands and whispered a prayer of contrition. It wasn't enough to bury Rotto; he would need God's grace to settle him and find Laura.

The artist restored his tools away from the grave and abandoned the area on horseback. It was time to find the light again.

Caterina

When Bino had fled the inn earlier that evening, Caterina wrapped Mattia in a shawl and made her way with haste to the priest's home. Finding him there, she relayed Bino's urgent message. Padre Castani responded with disbelief, made an appeal to God and bid a seminarian to retrieve the local guard. When the guard came, he and the priest departed for the grove, leaving the innkeeper alone to wonder and worry.

Papa, Mamma, Giovanni, and now my sister, are we doomed to live life alone? Too frightened to return home, Caterina entered the church with Mattia. Here she could see and touch the familiar, recall countless lunches with her father and wedding vows spoken before the community of faithful. *Faith, I've needed more than my share, Maria.*

Twilight from the altar windows invited them forward and they found refuge there amidst a large sacristy candle. Caterina lit several smaller ones before returning to the nave and kneeling with her son to pray.

She made her appeal to Mary, invoking the name of *il giovane*— Pedretto, the terminally ill boy who'd been healed in the same spot two generations before. *I beg your intervention once more, Blessed Mother.*

I pray you rescue our Isabella; return her to us, Maria. And then thinking again of her father—*If you're listening Papa, speak for us.*

Caterina rose and repositioned a bench so that she might sit and lean against one of her father's stone columns. She reclined against it and nursed Mattia until he slipped into sleep. She followed when she could pray no more.

Long minutes came and went until the innkeeper was roused by the call of one of Bino's crew.

"Signora Caterina? Signora? Be you here, return home, Isabella is coming."

Laura

Laura and fellow novitiates leapt with a hearty knock upon their dormitory door. It was the call to prayer and meditation, the former a command, the latter her refuge from the unyielding schedule forced upon them by elder sisters in the faith.

She didn't mind rising before the sun, something to which she had grown accustomed. She did miss the comforts of Casa Pelucca—a bed of her own, warmed by a maid's well-placed stone, clothes with color, garden-fresh food and a looking glass to observe changes in her face and figure. The convent was inhospitable to vanity.

Better the mirror is gone; what abomination would I see absent my long hair?

Laura also missed the bond she shared with her mother and younger siblings. Those new to the convent were told neither to encourage nor expect communication from their families during the first year. Still, she expected something. Anything. It hurt that her father hadn't been moved to change course by her mother and Valentina. They had protested vigorously the morning she was cast away.

She had been heartened by one dear to them, the optimist, Renato. He had told her to remain faithful and see her way home again. He was sure of Bino's loyalty and apologized for discouraging Bino from making public his affection. What had Renato told her? *Bino didn't approach your father because I convinced him it would make quick and certain his expulsion. How correct you were, old friend.*

Where are you, Bino? When Laura was unable to sleep at night, she recalled the many instances she had challenged the artist in spirit-centered or philosophical duels. He never dismissed her questions and offered reasoned responses and, ultimately, his arms. *Those arms!* She missed his strength, passion, reassurance and art. He was her equal in all but mischief. *And now I find myself in a convent where to misbehave is a treble sin against sister, church and God.*

Sin—was there ever a more useless word? Forbidden thoughts and her separation from Bino made Laura mad with desire. She imagined him unclothed and smiling, pressing his flesh against her chest and legs while her fingers roamed his hair and shoulders. When her need grew too distracting, Laura would roll away from her bedmate and use her hands as she would wish the artist to.

Though not a prisoner, Laura thought of escaping. Others had and their names were no longer mentioned, not even in prayer. She knew she would leave some day and today, she reasoned, was one day closer. The dilemma for Laura was her adopted city. While she couldn't long abide the imposition of superiors, Monza was no longer an option; the village below the convent had won her heart.

Laura hadn't counted on falling in love with Lugano, its climate and the view from each window. Summers in Monza could be stiflingly hot; here there were fresh alpine winds and cool breezes off the lake. She imagined detailing it all to Bino in a letter.

I'm holding your hand and am content. I'm pleased because you're with me, sharing my appreciation for the beauty others take for granted. I'm smiling because you're the only person reacting the way I do to water so blue, autumn trees as brilliant and mountains as tall as your imagination. You would wish to recreate it and return it to angels in fresco.

"Anna, wake up!"

Laura had been given this name upon arrival and was stirred from her reverie by a rebellious partner, Clara.

"Very well," Anna responded, "I'll dress."

Dressing was the simplest activity of the day since no choice was ever necessary. Above their undergarments and stockings each newcomer wore a gray, one-piece smock; it differed modestly in color and texture from their superiors' clothing since final vows were not yet taken. Clara placed a matching cap atop Anna's closely cropped hair. The latter had been the first casualty of convent life.

Wondering at Clara's unusual haste, Laura asked, "Why so responsible this morning, sister?"

Clara smiled and whispered, "The 'queen' is bringing us to the lakefront. We don't wish to be left behind, do we?"

"True enough," whispered Laura in return.

When outfitted, the pair shook the cold from one another by embracing and rubbing down each other's arms. Their peers laughed and teased but Sisters Clara and Anna cared little and fled the dormitory in favor of the chapel and warmer stove. They found it quiet save for the voice of a cantor and the harmonious responses from all present. The Latin lyrics were lost on Laura but the mood and its message were not—*together we lift our voices for those unable to do so themselves.*

The women retreated to the dining room. Here they sat in long rows and gave thanks before receiving a hot bowl of porridge and warm cider. Laura cherished both on cold mornings and delighted in wrapping her hands about the ceramic cup. The cups were made and sold by their community to help support itself.

After breakfast, the sisters donned wool capes and gathered in the courtyard. Attendance was taken and when the convent Mother's "lieutenants" were satisfied, the gate was opened and the young women paraded to the lake front. Sister Clara took Anna's arm in hers and whispered barbs at the others. No criticism was spared and Laura couldn't help but be humored by the sting of it.

The morning sun warmed their faces and the mountain air refreshed. Laura inhaled deeply and set aside the burden of resentment. Whenever the lake came into view, she tugged on Clara's arm, stopped and stared. It was the bluest water Laura had ever seen and its luster made her jealous of the fishermen she spied returning to shore.

Laura wasn't sure of their destination but shifted her attention from the lake when pulled by Clara. Merchant wagons were populating the shoreline and both thought how wonderful it would be to sample their wares. It wasn't to be. Once upon them, the sisters were urged to look the other way *lest you be seduced by the devil's treasures.* Clara and Anna welcomed the diversion and smiled at the jewelers and dressmakers teasing them with their handiwork.

"The Lord would want you to have this, sister," taunted a young man, pacing alongside them with a necklace spread across the palms of both hands. The pair could only bow. He persisted, "You're much too pretty to take vows, 'twould be a shame; leave and marry me. This cart will be mine one day."

Laura greeted his boldness with a smile. It was the type of thing she would have said in a world apart from this one. Instead, she twisted her head, lifted her cap and winked at the boy. Clara coughed and pinched Laura's side to caution her.

A hundred steps farther the group arrived at an earthen courtyard; at its mouth stood two mature trees. Budding branches extended in all directions and softened the harsh light reflected off the lake's surface. Behind them, facing the water was a small stone church. Laura studied it and judged it to be no more than fifteen meters high. Above and equally distant from the center entryway were two rectangular windows. Centered above these, directly below the triangular peak of the church, was a third window, round and leaded.

The sisters stopped just as the chapel door yawned open. In its place a young priest welcomed the women inside. Sister Anna was reluctant to follow; she so wanted to remain outdoors. Until she had met Bino, she didn't even think it possible for a closed space to inspire prayer or the magic of transfiguration. Now the choice wasn't hers to make and she followed her sympathetic friend. "Come Anna, dreamers must sometimes wake."

The interior did nothing to change Laura's point of view. The light from the lake-fronting windows illuminated empty uninspiring walls. *Why?* She wondered. The convent Mother later explained. Lugano and many other northern outposts lacked the wealthy patrons necessary to attract gifted artisans from their schools in Florence, Venice and Rome.

Laura's feet betrayed her will and took their place alongside Clara. They were offered several wooden benches, selected one and for the second time that morning, sat in silence. Laura pretended to pray but grew restless and opened her eyes. She looked forward and marveled as a beam of sunlight traced a diagonal line across three archways supporting a tall and broad expanse above. Laura poked Clara and pointed to it.

"You'll get us in trouble. What is it, Anna?" whispered Clara.

"The wall, can't you see? It's a blank canvas—an immense and perfect one."

"What are you saying? Be quiet."

Laura smiled and thought of her mother's small chapel in Monza. *Bino rescued it from the greatest sin of all—being dull.*

Laura again poked Clara. "This could be beautiful— a place where people would actually wish to sit and pray."

"Sisters Clara and Anna, *silenzio!*"

The convent Mother stared with icy intensity in their direction. Laura thought she saw the priest adjacent to her smile.

Clara pinched Anna and she was forced to stifle a scream. It proved the justification necessary for the convent Mother to order the pair outside.

"What was that about?" complained Clara, once they were seated beyond the door under the shade tree. Laura was poised to explain when she spied the hosting priest walking toward them. The sisters stood and prepared for further condemnation.

The priest was young, blond-haired and disarmed them with a smile. "Please sit, sisters. Did something trouble you inside?"

Laura pushed Clara back onto the bench and remained standing. "*Si'*, Padre. The fault is mine alone. Your church is fine and I'm sure a good home."

Sensing Laura had more to say, the priest remained silent and mirrored her posture. Uncomfortable with the silence, Laura continued. She swept an arm across the vista of the lake and wooded hills and said, "God inspires here, Padre. How can your empty walls compete?"

Clara couldn't fathom her friend's candor and color filled her cheeks. Neither sister was aware of the priest's appetite for entertainment and honesty. "Forgive her, Padre. Sister Anna doesn't mean to offend."

The priest smiled and reassured Clara. "No offense taken; in fact, I admire Sister's candor. Your names?"

Laura spoke up, "I'm Sister Anna; this is Sister Clara and we agree on most things."

The priest laughed and extended both his hands to the women. "I am Padre Verdi; for now this is my home and I agree with you, Sister Anna, God's work is unfinished here."

The priest sat with them and continued, "I'm pleased to tell you something. While we have little to offer, the bishop received a letter from an artist willing to come and make beautiful our *chiesa sul lago*."

Laura's mood shifted and she felt warmth from the center of her chest through to her core. She did not know where to find Bino though believed him better suited for the task. She was poised to say so when the convent Mother interrupted.

Padre Verdi intervened. "Mother, do not blame Anna and Clara for a disturbance I myself caused. I waved to them in chapel and was just now explaining myself."

Though doubtful of his explanation, the older woman accepted it and whisked the girls away. Anna and Clara were ushered inside and prohibited from speaking another word.

Caterina

Caterina woke to an empty bed and Mattia's gentle purring in his crib. She delighted in her son's voice and wordless banter. She closed her eyes and listened before whispering a grateful prayer. The glow of Isabella's rescue and Giovanni's return had yet to fade and she made the short walk across the alley each day to express as much to the Blessed Mother.

The innkeeper recalled racing out of the church that evening, hoping against hope Isabella would be safely restored to her. Her mother and father were gone and Giovanni presumed dead by everyone save her. It was unspoken but undeniable that her faith in his return was fading too. Once she witnessed her sister swaddled in Bino's shirt atop a horse she believed mountains could be moved.

So focused was Caterina on Isabella's well-being that she paid no attention to the priest and the person huddled at his side. Bino's crew carried her beloved sister into the inn where Caterina dressed her wounds and comforted with blankets warmed by hearth fire. Care and attention restored Isabella to consciousness while Padre Castani begged her to pause. When he could stand her inattention no longer, the priest shouted, "*Piacere*, Caterina!"

Surprised at his impatience, she turned on him from across the dimly lit room and said, "What is it? Can't it wait?"

Padre Castani lifted and supported Giovanni and said, "It cannot; Maria restores Serono's son to you."

Giovanni raised his head and spoke the words he knew she longed to hear, "I'm home at last, Caterina."

The innkeeper's stomach leapt. She looked through the dim candlelit room at the worn and bearded visitor with her husband's voice. She stepped forward and wondered at the priest's curious smile. All within and without the inn heard Caterina's scream when she drew close enough to recognize her soldier's eyes. She leapt forward and she and Giovanni tumbled to the floor. The innkeeper cradled his head in her hands and wet him with her lips and tears. "Maria be my witness, we'll ne'r part again!"

Giovanni was helpless under her assault. All he could do was repeat the words, "I'm so sorry."

Healing began and several weeks passed before Caterina allowed Isabella to return to her parents' cottage. The apricot harvest was rescued and sufficient money earned to reduce indebtedness and restore the inn to solid footing. Caterina invited few details about events in the grove that awful night; she knew a life had been taken by her husband and she prayed for the soul whose madness made it necessary.

When he'd returned to them the day after, Bino relinquished his bedroom to husband and wife. Both thanked him for the truths shared to prevent Giovanni's arrest.

The artist sped towards the completion of his work and used what little time remained to get acquainted with Giovanni. He wasn't bothered by the soldier's polite curiosity. So inspired was Bino by Giovanni's courage in the grove that he invited him to pose as a character in Mary's marriage fresco. "You'll be forever present, staff in hand, protecting them and the unborn Christ child from harm."

Giovanni was struck dumb by Bino's generosity and talent. In little more than the duration of the soldier's absence, the artist completed several portraits and three, well-detailed frescos. The *Marriage* fresco was all that remained.

Not long after its completion, the bishop and representatives from Milan and Rome came to Serono for the chapel's rededication. On the appointed day, interested citizens and miracle-seeking pilgrims clamored for entry but were delayed by those with treasure and influence. A mass honoring Mary was said and communion distributed before the curtains fell, revealing Bino's four frescos.

Stunned silence greeted the artist and Padre Castani as the assembly of religious, moneyed families and local leaders looked from one wall to the other and back again. Those who'd been there before delighted in the change and the splendor of Bino's creations. Those making their first visit regretted not coming sooner and refused to believe the effort had been less than twelve months in the making.

The bishop hadn't intended to stay longer than was necessary. When he witnessed the influence of Bino's frescos and portraits of the saints, he elected to stay and accept credit for the inspired visions. Bino and Padre Castani were content to let it be.

Soon a commotion adjacent to the wedding fresco distracted everyone. A dozen pilgrims collapsed to their knees when an observant one identified Caterina as the Blessed Mother, "She stands here, Santa Maria, here, Maria!"

Caterina was embarrassed by the misjudgment and rushed out of the church. Bino fled to retrieve her, leaving Padre Castani to interrupt the bishop and explain the innkeeper's pivotal role in the artist's work. When he caught up with her beyond the courtyard, Bino was out of breath and the innkeeper in tears.

"I am sorry for this, Caterina. I should have prepared you."

She nodded before responding, "You must think me ungrateful."

"Not at all. It's only natural they would see you and believe you to be the Virgin herself."

Caterina laughed between her tears. "If they only knew how unlike Maria I am, Bino. I was so full of doubt, often faithless and fearful for my son."

Bino silenced her while gripping her shoulders. "And you don't believe the Blessed Mother was ever doubtful, faithless or worried for her Son?"

Caterina knew he was right but persisted. "I cannot help but try to honor the ideals and image you've created for Her. But what am I to say each time someone mistakes me for a miracle and falls to her knees?"

"You might smile and simply say, *Bless you child.*"

Caterina laughed and felt better for it. She changed the subject.

"You're leaving us, aren't you, Bino?"

"I must. I've gotten a letter from an old friend. He invites me to return with him to Lugano."

"It's Laura, isn't it? He's found her."

"Yes, but he wasn't permitted to see her. I don't know if she'll welcome a visit or find it in her heart to forgive me."

Caterina studied him. She recalled their first meeting, his polite stare, his subsequent confessions and invitation to pose. She reasoned him a lover of all beauty—someone both simple and substantial.

Caterina understood him to be proud while contemptuous of notoriety, wealth and power. This artist would forever find favor with anonymity. Art and the company of friends satisfied. She loved him, not as she loved Giovanni, but a love borne of admiration and friendship.

The innkeeper lifted a hand and removed a curl from the poet's eye. "Go to her, Bino. Be she worthy of your affection, embrace her and n'er part."

"And if she turns me away, what then?"

"That won't happen. Women find men most attractive when they seek us where we are, as we are and as we're meant to be."

"And what of my sins?"

Caterina smiled and responded, "Love is nothing if not merciful."

The artist embraced her. "I will miss you, friend."

Caterina separated and brought a sleeve to her eyes.

"Long after we're gone, Bino, our Lady's church will carry your signature. Sometime before then, return to Her; return to me."

The artist brought his lips to her forehead and each cheek. "You may rely upon it."

Caterina urged him to return to the bishop's dedication and accept the gratitude of the faithful. She understood Bino neither wanted nor needed their approval; art was his prayer and reward.

The innkeeper felt wealthy beyond measure and vowed not to be discouraged by Bino's absence. Giovanni's strength was much improved and he could again perform the chores once delegated to members of the artist's crew. Several planned to remain and assist notable artisans drawn to Serono by word of Bino's achievement.

The innkeeper had Isabella, Mattia, and her beloved soldier to buoy her spirits. And when these weren't enough, she escaped, sat in silence and appreciated Bino's frescos. They remained inspiring reminders of what faith and its inexplicability had wrought.

The evening before Bino's last meal in Serono, Giovanni and Isabella sampled the gift Caterina had prepared for the artist. Weeks in the making and begun after Isabella's rescue, the innkeeper had experimented with her father's recipe. She steeped apricot flesh, kernels and herbs within grain alcohol. The latter was secured from a healer with Padre Castani's help.

Caterina tasted and judged the concoction bitter. She refined the ingredients until she considered the serum smooth and delicately sweet. The innkeeper set the dinner table for the following evening, strained and poured the amber fluid into a flask at its center—the elixir's color mirroring that of the gypsy's illustration.

When Isabella and Giovanni sampled the brew, they winked at one another and said nothing. Their silence drove Caterina mad.

"You don't like it?" she queried.

Sister and soldier were quiet in their appreciation of the potion's strength and sweetness and asked for a second taste. They sipped again before breaking into broad smiles.

"It's delicious," admitted Isabella. "How did you manage such a flavor?"

The innkeeper answered, "I wasn't loyal to Papa's ingredients but can recreate the brew if you think guests would appreciate it."

"Appreciate it they shall," agreed Giovanni. Pilgrims are sure to return if only to enjoy another cup."

While his hosts busied themselves, Bino sat quietly at his drafting table in the church. He recalled the night years earlier when he had visited his work at San Giorgio's. At that time he'd been guided by candlelight and the threat of Brother Tomas's prosecution. He was free of those burdens now and appreciated his rebirth in Serono. It was here he found Padre Castani and had, in both the priest and innkeeper, faith-affirming friends. The artist was moved to an expression of gratitude, lifted his pencil and began his verse.

> *Serono, we honor Maria—your patroness and guide.*
> *As one you welcomed me; no longer need I hide.*
> *May these saints and scenes inspire during difficult*
>   *days ahead.*
> *Fear and greed consume; trust Our Mother's*
>   *love instead.*
> *I wasn't a believer in miracles. How could so much*
>   *sadness be?*

But the truth of faith is simple; you must first believe
to see.
Faith be one companion, though hardly enough in
the end.
My hand reveals another—a teacher, my mentor
and friend.

Bino lifted his eyes to his fresco of the Christ-child in the temple; he focused on the rabbi engaged with the viewer before resuming his verse.

The learned man who studies you with impassioned
eyes and beard of white,
Is better known as father to Leonardo than the prism
to my light.
Wisdom was his gift; the innkeeper, my muse
and guide.
Satisfied, I leave to seek another; loneliness I no
longer abide.
Maria, bless Serono and all souls dwelling here.
May they leave as I do, restored and absent fear.

The poet rolled his verse, tied it with a string and left it on the altar for Padre Castani. He surveyed his frescos one last time before leaving the church and his "children" behind. He made a sign of the cross, whispered the words, *I'm coming, Laura*, and stepped through the side entrance without notice or fanfare.

Twilight had come and the artist looked above and saw the first star in the sky. He smiled to himself and recalled the constellation Laura had brought to his attention the night of their introduction. He blew a kiss in its direction.

The next evening Bino sat with Caterina, Giovanni, Isabella and Padre Castani to enjoy a final meal. The fare was generous-roasted pig with apricot marmalade, fired vegetables and sweet wine. The food and drink satisfied and replaced the melancholy mood associated with Bino's departure. Stories and laughter were shared and when all settled, Padre Castani offered a post-meal blessing. The innkeeper then stood to speak. With a nod to the priest, Caterina began.

"When Padre Castani told me an artist was to come and make our church beautiful, I didn't imagine the artisan would share our home and cast me as Maria."

She attempted to continue without tears but these came and Giovanni stood to support her.

"Bino, you found our purses light, absent husband and father and with little hope of keeping the inn. Isabella and I had only each other and prayer and there were days when those weren't enough. You came without expectation, shared your time and treasure and transformed our church into one of which Serono can forever be proud. *Ti ringraziamo*. We humbly thank you."

Bino accepted her kindness, rose and embraced her. He detailed with good humor the futility in finding a woman suitable to sit as Mary.

"The whole while one perfect in form and spirit was before me. Dear innkeeper, you are the woman I imagined saying 'yes' to Gabriel."

Caterina silenced him while all nodded in agreement. She playfully thrust her hands against his chest and told him to sit for his gift. "While we cannot hope to equal your generosity, Bino, I've made something to warm your travels and share with special friends."

Bino was invited to close his eyes while the innkeeper poured a generous portion of her amber brew in his cup. When Caterina declared herself ready, Bino opened his eyes and lifted the cup to his nose. "A special drink? You wouldn't be trying to trick me to sleep and keep me here?"

The aroma delighted; it hinted of fruit and nuts and he let the sensation linger. "It's the scent of kindness and healing— one which will forever remind me of you, dear lady."

"Don't keep me waiting," she implored. "Taste it."

The brew didn't disappoint. It bathed the poet's tongue and throat with warmth while possessing a delicately sweet aftertaste—a gift from the innkeeper's heart and hands. The artist thought a moment and imagined.

"If flavors belonged to seasons, Caterina, your elixir would be that of brilliant autumn leaves."

Bino raised his cup. "Drink, everyone. Drink to our Lady's church, the gentle hands that crafted this treat, and to love restored."

Bino relished the brew that evening and upon the few occasions he returned to Serono. Caterina always had some at the ready. And Bino wasn't alone in his enjoyment. The amber mixture became a favorite among visiting clergy and guests to the inn.

Despite inquiries, Caterina kept the brew's formulation to herself. When she believed Mattia mature enough to appreciate its meaning, the innkeeper instructed him in its preparation. She spoke affectionately of Bino and the redemption tale behind its inspiration; Mattia pledged neither would be forgotten.

Bino

Lugano, several weeks later

Bino leaned across the gap towards his coach-mate. He placed the palms of his out-sized hands on Renato's arthritic knees and massaged warmth into them. Renato appreciated the gesture and said so.

Their reunion in Milan had been an emotional one. Bino had returned there from Serono the morning after Caterina's celebratory dinner. The friends agreed to meet at Santa Marie delle Grazie—the same church he'd accompanied Piero to following his confrontation years earlier with Signor Argento.

On the appointed day, Bino identified Renato sitting forward in the cathedral. Simply being in the same church with a person he held in high esteem was for the artist akin to receiving holy communion. He smiled somewhere deep inside and felt at ease. As he approached, Renato appeared to be sleeping and looked impossibly small amidst the cathedral's grand features. The artist walked to the altar, whispered a prayer and returned to his napping friend. When only a few meters separated them, Bino gently called Renato's name.

The old servant's eyes opened; he looked towards the voice and believed himself in a dream.

"Can it be you, son? In the flesh?"

Bino stepped forward and pulled Renato up from the bench, embracing him with vigor. Since the passing of his mother years earlier, Renato was the person he first thought of when asked if any family members had survived Lombardia's dark fever.

As they held one another, the artist recalled their proximity to the room hosting Leonardo's mural of Christ's last supper. His first visit stirred memories both happy and sad. He had once had the benefit of Piero's company and counsel here. His mentor was lost but not the echo of the seminarians chanting Saint Anselm's prayer.

Let me find you by loving you; let me love you when I find you.

Intended to mean the Christ, the words paralleled the artist's pursuit of reunion—reunion with his past, his dark, his light, mercy and Laura.

Bino's silent intention was interrupted by Renato's coughing attack and they released one another. His friend looked tired and unwell and the artist vowed to care for him.

The old servant argued otherwise and insisted Bino proceed to Lugano without him. "I will only slow your progress."

Bino wouldn't hear it. Renato was short on resources and Bino's purse sufficient for the pair to room in Milan until the servant was well enough to travel. Renato was given no choice but to agree.

Over the succeeding fortnight, the artist pushed a proposal through Padre Castani to Rome. In exchange for bringing his talent to Lugano, he inquired, would the bishop arrange a coach for him and a guest to travel there. Bino understood it would be otherwise improbable for Renato to survive the journey.

Credited with the transformation of the Serono church, the bishop was charitable and conditionally approved transport to the lake region. Bino accepted the bishop's terms and committed to what had already been agreed upon—a subsequent trip to Serono for finish work.

Their journey north to Lugano commenced and with their first day behind them, the pair and their travel mates enjoyed a fire amidst grazing horses. The sky was clear and cold and all were mesmerized by the moon's path above and between white alpine peaks.

"'Tis a good omen, Bino," offered Renato. "The moon lights our way and suggests a positive outcome."

Bino smiled and responded, "Were the words anyone's but yours, I'd place little faith in them. Do you believe she'll welcome me, Renato?"

"Signorina Laura? Only God knows. But if I were a betting man, not even the convent guard could prevent her from seeing you."

The following morning their journey to Lugano and its lakefront church continued. It was slow going because of poor road conditions and the attention paid by their coachmen to bandits. Warnings of the latter couldn't help but remind Bino of Rotto's inexplicable cruelty. The fugitive's corpse had been dispatched by his own hands and yet the artist still experienced nightmares of Rotto emerging phantom-like from the grave.

They experienced neither bandits nor phantoms and the carriage emerged unmolested from cloud-shrouded hills. It was a relief to the coachmen and all were able to relax and appreciate the view. The landscape was marked by expanses of green, interrupted by steep, snow-capped hills and the crystal blue lakes they fed. The artist could no longer doubt Renato's enthusiastic description of the village and its beauty. It mattered not to Bino. Lugano would be *beautiful because Laura dwelled there.*

They were delivered to the rectory and made the acquaintance of Padre Verdi, the young priest charged with responding to the needs of local congregants. He welcomed the artist and Renato, offered a room for them to share and expressed his enthusiasm for the work Bino was engaged to provide.

Privately, the priest did think it odd an artist of Bino's reputation had agreed to accept his bishop's ambitious proposal and modest wage. Padre Verdi intended to confirm both with his guest after the next day's tour.

The priest woke Bino and Renato the following morning and invited the pair to accompany him for a lakefront stroll. The old servant declined. A coat was offered to Bino and accepted; he and his host stepped into the cool morning air. Its freshness mirrored Bino's spirit.

The artist listened with care as the young priest spoke of Lugano, the church and its role in the conversion of souls so distant from Rome. Though not more than a two-day carriage ride from Milan, Bino confessed to Padre Verdi the sensation of feeling a world away.

Bino made no mention of Laura. Instead he described the evolution of his work within and without Lombardia. He concluded by expressing his desire to try something bold and his delight at the Bishop's invitation and approval. The nervous priest reached for the artist's arm and spoke the truth. He knew an engagement in Lugano was sure to have been rejected by any of the comparably skilled, though better-known, artisans from Milan and Florence.

"You must know something, Signor Bino. Neither our purse nor audience compares well with those of the south. I pray you understand and accept this. It comes with the gratitude of Lugano's community of faithful."

Bino considered the young priest's words and the sincere intention expressed through his eyes.

The sometimes poet began, "I have confessed my sins, Padre, and stand before you the most fortunate of men. I come to Lugano motivated by two things and the first I share with you now. These hands—my craft—are not my own. They are my prayer and petition. And what you'll soon see is God's response. What right have I to demand in treasure what God gives freely?"

The priest was humbled by Bino's words. He smiled, gripped the artist's right arm above the elbow and whispered a blessing with the wave of his dominant hand. They continued their walk in silence until reaching the entrance to the church. Padre Verdi pulled the lake-facing doors open and motioned for his guest to enter.

Bino stepped over the threshold and recognized *home*. Beyond the comfortable dimensions of the space, the artist was seduced by an abundance of light. He'd known and toiled in the darkest corners of grand cathedrals. Here, reflected off mountains white and a crystal lake, was the brilliant tool he so far lacked.

And magnifying the light was the canvas itself. Before him, supported by three arches, was a broad expanse of wall—one large enough to tell an important and detailed story. Bino had depicted Christ's *Passion and Resurrection* many times, but never with the proper scale and power they deserved.

Padre Verdi sensed the artist's excitement and followed Bino as he roamed from one interior vantage point to another. The artist appeared untethered and aloft. Bino's smile was broad and the priest overheard him whispering to an invisible ally.

It was true. With a nod to Piero's spirit, Bino recognized why his journey happened as it had. It was all clear—love and loss at Casa Pelucca, despair and redemption under the innkeeper's influence in Serono. It all happened because he and he alone had to come to this place to channel that suffering and joy into a permanent and powerful tribute to hope.

The artist spun about to locate his host, begged forgiveness and asked where he might put ideas to paper. Padre Verdi led him to a prepared space behind the altar. The priest pointed to a table equipped with parchment paper, tools and ink.

"You may work here undisturbed, excluding, of course, the Lord's day."

The parish priest had no experience with artists and was amused and a little worried about what might follow. He thought to question Bino before changing his mind and walking away. He was ten steps from the door when Bino interrupted him.

"Padre Verdi?"

"*Si'*, Signor Bino?"

"I said earlier two things motivated me to come to Lugano. The first is unselfish; I come to inspire. The second reason be…"

Bino suspended his explanation, stepped towards the priest and measured his words. His mind drifted to Caterina.

"I had, Padre, a kind and faithful innkeeper during my year in Serono. She and her priest heard my story and offered their own brands of absolution. I owe the truth and my second purpose to them. And for the first time in my life, I believe myself worthy of it."

"Yes, brother, continue."

"I have known the affection of a woman I wish to make my wife. Laura was the sometimes reckless daughter of a noble Monza family and remains in my heart." Bino paused and waited for a reaction from the priest. When none came, he continued.

"As a consequence of tragedy and her father's misunderstanding, Laura and I were separated. She was exiled here and is today among the novitiates within the convent atop the hill. I'm told she was assigned the name Anna and remains unaware of my presence and purpose."

Padre Verdi saw the discomfort in Bino's eyes and raised a hand to still him. "Anna? Though curious, Signor Bino, I believe Sister Anna and I are recent acquaintances. Be it a reunion you desire, you may count on my assistance and discretion."

Bino didn't doubt the priest's sincerity and embraced him. "*Ti ringrazio*, Padre. Forgive me if I appear too eager."

The priest steadied him with a smile and idea. "You will need models for your work, no, Signor Bino? The convent Mother is sure to delight in making an example of a particularly restless one."

EPILOGUE

The Artist and the Innkeeper is the story of the prolific, though underappreciated, Renaissance artist and poet Bernardino Luini. It is the remarkable tale of his journey and the redemption he finds through faith, his craft, the kindness of mentors and the women who loved him. My story reveals what I've learned and inferred from legend, biographer research and the artist's work. I was fortunate to have Bernardino's paintings and frescos to observe; none of his poetry survives.

It isn't known whether the artisan I affectionately call Bino met and had been acquainted with Leonardo da Vinci. It is clear he was influenced by the genius' work and observers have even made the mistake of crediting Leonardo with several of Bernardino's paintings. Others believe the bearded figure reappearing throughout Bino's frescos is Leonardo himself. Given the differences in their appetites and temperaments, I've instead identified the recurring image as Leonardo's father, Piero da Vinci. Their respective timelines and circles of influence suggest that this would have been possible.

Where documentation allows, *The Artist and the Innkeeper* follows Benardino's recorded history – his apprenticeship in Milan with Scotto, his engagements in Milanese churches, Casa Pelucca, Saronno and, ultimately, Lugano. The artist is sure to have crossed paths with many persons within and outside the church; representing them are characters of my own construction - Padre Castani, Signor Argento, Nica, Renato and Lady Rabbia.

The Pelucca and Rabbia families were important patrons of the artist; Laura, Federigo Rabbia (Feder) and Amarotto de'Gavanti (Rotto) are names taken from my research. The much credited innkeeper described in the legend of Amaretto di Saronno is not identified; Caterina and the names of her family members are my own invention.

In an effort to explain Bernardino's obscurity, biographer George Williamson and others recount anonymous tales associated with the artist. Among these are the untimely death of a priest and a Monza duel within area of the town that then became known as *tournament square*. Though impossible to corroborate the truth of these stories, any hint of truth may have diminished the artist's reputation among his peers. Together they inspired my creation and account of Tomas' death and that of Federigo Rabbia at the hands of Amarotto de'Gavanti – both named as contemporaries of the artist in my research.

The preface called attention to the mystery of Bernardino. Specifically, why did Renaissance biographer Giorgio Vasari make little mention of his prolific contemporary? Was Bernardino overlooked because of his disdain for power and treasure? Or could it have been rumors of accidental death, duels and moral failing? It's unlikely we will ever know.

I favor the romantic explanation. The artist and poet was neglected because wealth and notoriety mattered little to him. It was enough for Bernardino to paint, live simply and love the women we connect with in his frescos.

I have visited the artist's paintings in museums as near as Boston and as distant as Milan. I made my own pilgrimage to Mary's Church of Miracles in Saronno, a city better known today as the birthplace of Amaretto than site of Pedretto's miraculous healing by the Virgin Mother. I smile at the realization and word play; there would have been no Amaretto di Saronno without there first having been a Pedretto di Serono?

On the occasion of my fiftieth birthday in 2011, I went to see Bernardino's four frescos within the Saronno church. I delighted in the artist's images of Mary's life and left full of wonder at the magic that insisted I tell the artist's story. Outside the church that summer day, above the adjacent piazza, was a banner punctuating the moment. It was a wink from God to me which read, *fate questo in memoria di me* – do this in memory of me. I would. I did.

The artist's Saronno frescos continue to attract and inspire visitors. It would seem they had the same impact nine years after their completion when Bernardino's peer, Gaudenzio Ferrari, painted the domed ceiling above the sanctuary. He depicts the Assumption of the Blessed Mother through a brilliant fresco named *Concerto di Angeli* – a small and detailed rendering of heaven worthy of Michelangelo.

Two years later I travelled to Lugano, Switzerland. I went to resolve the second riddle plaguing art historians. What became of the sometime poet last seen here ~1530 and for whom no death is recorded? I arrived at Lugano's Piazza Bernardino Luini on a beautiful October morning. I imagined the lake facing church housing the artist's signature crucifixion fresco would be grand. Instead, like the artist's reputation, it was humble in size and modest by design. Nothing about it shouted, *look at me.*

I entered the small space, walked out of the shadow of the entryway and looked forward into the light. The image I saw there was glorious. And I understood how the artist lost himself in its creation. The boy from Luino, apprentice to visionaries, brother to monks and servant to clerics and noblemen, came to Lugano searching. Before me was the certainty of his discovery. In this city, where snowcapped peaks rise from the shore of an iridescent alpine lake, within a humble church, a Renaissance man left his mark. The artist came to Lugano, fell in love again and remained.

Bernardino's tribute to Christ's Passion and Resurrection within the Lugano church defies explanation. It unfolds in color on a vast expanse of wall supported above three arches. Within it are more than one hundred fifty actors in stories that command attention and convince me of Christ's suffering and humanity. The cross bears His blood and a mounted soldier weeps in recognition of his crime. Roman guards tear at Jesus' cloak while a dog wails and Mary succumbs to grief. Nearby, Mary Magdalene looks hopefully, expectantly above. I half expect her faith to rescue Christ from his suffering and will Him into her sheltering arms.

Bernardino reimagines Jesus' Passion; it unfolds from left to right and bottom to top, from its cruel beginning through Easter glory. In its company you are a living witness to Christ's interrogation, torture, entombment and resurrection. Little more than a decade shy of its five-hundredth birthday, Bernardino's Lugano masterpiece appears as vital and fresh as when the fortunate faithful attended its 1530 unveiling. To have been alive and witness the collective gasp, surely must have been something to experience and behold.

And what of the object of the artist's affection? Accounts hint at scandal and suggest that Laura, a Pelucca family daughter, may have been exiled to a life with women religious. I imagine the artist discovers her whereabouts and makes possible her rescue. A desire to avoid public scrutiny would have contributed to Bernardino's decision to remain in Lugano and live a non-public, family centered life. Bernardino was survived by children and more than one contributed to the region's artistic legacy.

Did Bernardino leave any clue to his discovery of Laura within his Lugano fresco? Stop reading here if you wish to visit and resolve the puzzle for yourself. It took me several days of patient observation to uncover such a clue. A guide was discussing Bino's brilliant *Passion* fresco when I overheard him say the heroic figure seated upon a white stallion is credited with being the artist. Handsome and confident, the mounted figure moves my eye to the foreground of the fresco. All about him, scores of characters react to Christ's murder.

There is much competing for attention before I make my discovery. There, behind the mounted artist seated upon a second horse, is the familiar white bearded countenance of his friend and mentor. I thought it unusual that this figure, with right arm outstretched, was pointing in a direction other than the Christ figure. What does the artist want me to see?

I follow his mentor's finger and there, partially obstructed, is the face I imagine as Laura's. My eye meets hers and I smile as if to shake a fellow romantic's hand across a five-century divide. Bernardino Luini came to Lugano, found his lover and painted his masterpiece. His journey was long, purposeful and redemptive. His art and legend are forever a part of my story.

POSTSCRIPT

Five hundred years ago a mysterious and romantic legend became a part of my story. Through its telling, the inspiration of its characters and our Creator's grace, I am no longer doubtful about the immortality of our souls.

We are each players in a wonder-filled love story and experience its rich texture. In this tapestry that is our history and lives are found a multitude of joy, sadness, passion, loneliness, laughter, fear, intimacy and isolation. We write the next chapter each day. The happy ending is up to us.

For those courageous enough to move towards their divine purpose, the *secret* is this; those who come before us, even long before us, conspire with our Creator to make easier our path. Their efforts are neither bound by time nor place.

In our hearts we know this to be true. When we're inspired, whether in the listening to a beautiful piece of music or moving speech, in the witnessing of childbirth or the sun setting over the ocean, in the feeling of a lover's embrace or the final words of an ailing parent, we glimpse beyond our own mortal selves. We can be moved to tears, *holy water,* differing in its chemistry because it is rain from a boundless place.

What connects us to the past, to prior generations of our family, is more than DNA or the blood coursing through our veins. What connect us are an appreciation for the women and men, their sacrifices and struggles, the hundreds of decisions made and the peace finding those who understood they did the best they could.

A passion for our history amidst the growing clouds of our culture move me to share this story. It is an account of a long-forgotten renaissance artist and his inventive muse who walked upon my family's native Italian soil five centuries ago. What they together accomplished blessed and altered the course of many lives, indeed my own.

Great grandparents, grandparents, my father and much-loved aunts and uncles, are gone now. The last to leave is the person I most credit with my faith, my mother Catherine. Her children and those fortunate to have crossed her humble path witnessed her goodness, even when repeated loss and hardship befell her. Because of her stories and daily example of gratitude and prayer, I acknowledge and am attentive to the divinity within all of us.

With my pen I honor my mother and father, my wife and children and extended family, the wonderful spirit of the Renaissance artist Bernardino Luini and the woman whose sweet invention, today known simply as *DiSarrono*, unites our stories. I walk in their shoes and hope to inspire those thirsty enough to follow.

ACKNOWLEDGMENTS

Writing has been a wonderful complement to my vocation as an investment adviser and financial planner. This creative journey, nearly ten years' worth of Thursday mornings, began as an outlet for stress following last decade's economic crisis. I was fortunate at that time to meet and benefit from the wisdom of a coach and fellow writer, Irene Tomkinson. Irene's encouragement, wisdom and candor made the telling and retelling of this story much better.

The list of others helpful to me is long. I must first credit my wife Catherine and children, Mike, Anya and Anthony; your love and support sustain me.

My now deceased parents Catherine and Carlo and godmother, Josephine DiMarco; your faith in something grander than ourselves and many sacrifices inspire reflection and creativity.

My siblings Glen, Carlo, Andria and Liana, in-laws Elaine and Laurie, their spouses and children, and my DiMarco family aunts, uncles and cousins; I appreciate the bond, good will and memories we share as family.

My Italian cousins Rosa Ioffredo, Lucia and Silvana Saggiomo, their children and husbands, especially Epimaco Ferrara and Gino Coppola. Your generosity and spirit remind me of the importance of remaining close to my heritage.

To my editors, Jason Buchholz and Nikki Van De Car at kn literary, and author, Josh Bernoff. And to my critical readers, Erin Hoffer, Beth Fantozzi, Emily Nagle Green and Caitlin McCarthy, if the *The Artist and the Innkeeper* reads well, it's because of your valued contributions, known and unknown.

To my artistic team, cover designer Anya Ioffredo, photographer Katie Jameson and illustrator, Nora L'Heureux. Together we've made our book beautiful.

To those assisting with my research, Frederick Ilchman at the Museum of Fine Arts, Boston and art historian Deborah Hartry Stein, I am grateful for your insights and introductions to Bernardino's paintings in local museum collections.

To sources of assistance in Saronno, Italy, the Reina family – owners and operators of ILLVA, maker of DiSaronno, and staff person, Claudia Grillo, who generously guided us through the production facility and the church housing Bernardino's frescos honoring Mary.

To my professional family at ALENA Wealth, Marioleni Mandelis, Joseph Victor and Kathryn Dunlop, your conscientious support and service to our clients made my Thursday writing time possible. And to the many professional colleagues who encouraged this project including Jim Weiss, Christine Moriarty, Robin Young, Michael Orentlich, Raymond DeVasto, Regina Ballinger, Michele Amoroso, Michelle Morris, Katharine Manning, Robert Holzbach, Sean Moynihan, Steve Bruce, Peter Isberg, Justin Rohn, Mark Whitehouse, Jason McKinney, Christopher Morse and my LPL family including Rebecca Power, Steve Van Houten, Dorothy Bickling and Robert and Rachel Clausen.

To the families ALENA Wealth serves, I honor your privacy and hold a special place for all of you in my heart.

We all have two types of friends and mentors who contribute to our perspective and wisdom – those we follow and admire, though haven't met, and those we are blessed to have present in our day to day lives. Among those I haven't met while learning much from are spiritualists Dr.

Wayne Dyer and Fr. Richard Rohr, and moral capitalists, Warren Buffett, Charles Munger, Ron Baron and Jamie Dimon.

Those whose presence, friendship and guidance I'm grateful for include David Freeman, Ed DePasqual, Terry Davis, Ron Mucci, Ira Guttentag, Nora and Scott L'Heureux, Jack Green, Bruce Herrmann, John Kibbee, Kurt Geitz, David Immel, Ralph Palmer, Chris and Virginia Andry, Andy and Patti Peterson, Jose and Lisa Tormo, Mike Eisenberg and Carol Holmes, Kelly Anne O'Connor and CJ Volpone, Larry Tennis and Jackie Sherry.

And finally, to the many past and present members of my three faith communities - St. Mary of the Annunciation Parish, Melrose, Massachusetts, Boston College High School, South Boston, Massachusetts and St. Margaret Mary Parish, Winter Park, Florida, I hold you in my heart and prayers.

RESOURCES

Texts:

Bernardino Luini, The Great Masters in Painting and Sculpture, George Charles Williamson, Chiswick Press, London, 1899.

Cyclopedia of Painters and Paintings, Edited by John Denison Champlin, Jr.; critical editor, Charles C. Perkins, New York, C. Scribner's Sons, 1913 (c. 1887).

Bernardino Luini, Masterpieces in Colour, James Mason, London, T. C. & E. C. Jack.

The Story of an Original Liqueur, Amaretto di Saronno, (product marketing booklet, c. 1970).

Churches and Highlighted frescos:

San Maurizio, or the Monastero Maggiore, Milan, Italy.

San Giorgio al Palazzo, Milan, Italy.

Santuario Della Vergine, Saronno, Italy.

> *Marriage of Joseph and Mary*
> *Christ Disputing with the Doctors*
> *Presentation in the Temple*

Adoration of the Magi
Saint Catharine

Santa Maria Degli Angeli, Lugano, Switzerland.

Passion of Christ

Museums and Highlighted paintings:

Pinacoteca di Brera, Milan, Italy.

Burial of St Catherine (fresco)
Girls Bathing (fresco)
Game of the Golden Cushion (fresco on canvas)
Madonna in the Rose Garden (oil on panel)

Museum of Fine Arts, Boston, Massachusetts.

Salome

National Gallery of Art, Washington, D.C.

Portrait of a Lady

Fogg Museum, Harvard University

Other Notable pieces:

Susannah and the Elders (a celebration of female virtue and justice, Liechtenstein)